PRAISE FOR LEAH THOMAS

WHEN LIGHT LEFT US

Year

★ "M prose here
, and
poetic novel is a nuanced exploration of
human nature." —*Booklist*, starred review

★ "A compelling, character-driven, and imaginative
novel. . . . What makes it stand out is Thomas's talent
of bringing intimacy, thoughtfulness, and a sense
of wonder to her writing. For fans of Patrick Ness
and Lauren Oliver." —*SLJ*, starred review

"Explores themes of forgiveness, family, friendship, and
identity. . . . This pensive sci-fi novel straddles many worlds
without quite fitting in any, not unlike the endearing
square-peg characters at its heart." —***Kirkus Reviews***

"Readers will be captivated by the mystery and meaning
in this eerie exploration of loss and love, hurting and
healing, family and friends, and of letting go
and reconnection." —*School Library Connection*

"Thomas' elegant and deeply metaphorical prose blends nicely
with the blend of magical realism and science fiction, and
the arid, stripped-bare landscape of New Mexico's
deserts makes an effective backdrop." —*BCCB*

BECAUSE YOU'LL *NEVER* MEET ME

A William C. Morris YA Debut Award Finalist
An Indie Next List Pick
An Indies Introduce Selection

★ "[A] stunning genre-crossing novel." —*BCCB*, starred review

"A witty, unusual take on friendship." —*Kirkus Reviews*

"Ollie and Moritz are memorable characters with
engaging and often humorous voices." —*SLJ*

"The two may be eccentric outcasts, but their conflicts,
heartbreak, and eventual bond form a relatable and
engaging narrative." —*Publishers Weekly*

NOWHERE NEAR YOU

★ "A fantastic novel that will be especially resonant
for readers who struggle with being or feeling outside
of 'normal.'" —*Booklist*, starred review

★ "[A] brilliant follow-up to a clever and
unexpected novel." —*BCCB*, starred review

"Part mad science, part convincing portrayal of the volatile,
resilient nature of friendship and grief." —*Kirkus Reviews*

"Ollie and Moritz continue to be compelling characters,
struggling to figure out how to use their talents while
living within their limitations." —*VOYA*

WHEN
LIGHT
LEFT
US

Books by Leah Thomas

Because You'll Never Meet Me
Nowhere Near You
When Light Left Us
Wild and Crooked

WHEN LIGHT LEFT US

leah thomas

BLOOMSBURY

NEW YORK LONDON OXFORD NEW DELHI SYDNEY

BLOOMSBURY YA
Bloomsbury Publishing Inc., part of Bloomsbury Publishing Plc
1385 Broadway, New York, NY 10018

BLOOMSBURY and the Diana logo are trademarks of Bloomsbury Publishing Plc

First published in the United States of America in February 2018
by Bloomsbury Children's Books
Paperback edition published in February 2019
by Bloomsbury YA

Bloomsbury books may be purchased for business or promotional use. For information on bulk
purchases please contact Macmillan Corporate and Premium Sales Department at
specialmarkets@macmillan.com

ISBN 978-1-68119-987-0 (paperback)

The Library of Congress has cataloged the hardcover edition as follows:
Names: Thomas, Leah, author.
Title: When light left us / by Leah Thomas.
Description: New York : Bloomsbury, 2018.
Summary: Not long after Hank, Ana, and Milo Vasquez's father leaves, an alien named Luz
arrives and uses them to satisfy his curiosity, then leaves them forever changed.
Identifiers: LCCN 2017025082 (print) • LCCN 2017038893 (e-book)
ISBN 978-1-68119-181-2 (hardcover) • ISBN 978-1-68119-182-9 (e-book)
Subjects: | CYAC: Family life—Fiction. | Loss (Psychology)—Fiction. | Hispanic Americans—
Fiction. | Extraterrestrial beings—Fiction. | Chihuahuan Desert—Fiction.
Classification: LCC PZ7.1.T463 Whe 2018 (print) | LCC PZ7.1.T463 (e-book) | DDC [Fic]—dc23
LC record available at https://lccn.loc.gov/2017025082

Book design by Amanda Bartlett
Typeset by Westchester Publishing Services
Printed and bound in the U.S.A. by Berryville Graphics Inc., Berryville, Virginia
2 4 6 8 10 9 7 5 3 1

All papers used by Bloomsbury Publishing Plc are natural, recyclable products
made from wood grown in well-managed forests. The manufacturing processes
conform to the environmental regulations of the country of origin.

To find out more about our authors and books visit www.bloomsbury.com
and sign up for our newsletters.

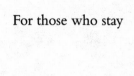

For those who stay

THE NAMELESS CANYON OBSERVATION DECK

When he was four years old, Milo Vasquez asked for a tree house.

The Vasquezes' cracking stucco mono-level teetered on the brink of a canyon bereft of palms, cacti, or even spiky yuccas. There were no trees within miles of the plot of Chihuahuan desert they called home.

From the dirt grew mostly bear grass so toothy and clawing that for years, during short family walks along the cliff on cool purple evenings, Milo's dad had lifted his kids by the handholds of their underarms and levitated them away from potential mauling. "Bears bite hard," he told them.

Every Vasquez heard Milo's impossible request. Hank and Ana had just been picked up from volunteering at the high school concession stand. Neither was in the marching band, but fundraising to send their sousaphone-wielding friends to Europe beat riffling through *Highlights* magazines in a waiting room, watching their mother bite her lip and their father bite his nails.

Milo, Mom, and Dad were returning from a visit to

Gailsberg and the third doctor in as many months who could not explain why Milo no longer asked questions, or spoke in complete sentences, or said much of anything at all.

"Can we build a tree house for everyone?"

Milo's voice struck the truck like a summer storm, threatened to roll the rusting Chevy off the narrow road that wound around Nameless Canyon.

Ana recovered first. "For *everyone*, Milo? You mean everyone in Eustace?"

Hank barked out a laugh as big as a holler. He squeezed Milo's shoulders with mitt-size hands. "That'd be a freakin' tree *city*."

"A tree city is called a forest. Besides, Eustace is basically a pimple. Not everyone takes up as much space as Hank, Milo." Ana had just spent three hours guarding the till, watching her big brother throw Snickers at every one of his endless friends who passed by.

"Big enough for the family," Milo clarified. "Not *too* big."

"That's an *amazing* idea, Milo," Hank declared.

"Sure, except there aren't any trees in Nameless Canyon."

"We can grow some, Ana." Mom rotated almost entirely in the passenger seat to fix shining eyes on Milo. "Remember Mrs. Noell from 4-H? We helped her plant those carnations downtown? They bloomed all the way until October! She could give us some tips."

"I could invite the guys over to help," Hank added. "We're all bored as hell during the off-season."

"Dad already has enough tools, I think." But Ana smirked when Hank elbowed her. Hank *had* paid for every one of those candy bars at the stand, pulling wads of his dwindling summer earnings from his back pocket and plopping them in Ana's palm along with a Milky Way (he knew she hated peanuts). "Right? Dad?"

Dad hadn't made a sound. His gaze flitted across the discordant pieces of his little family: the tangled limbs of three wildly different creatures, crammed into the backseat with their knees knocking, and their mother, craning toward the knot of them as if she longed to be caught up in it. "Dunno. Growing trees takes years, guys."

The sinking of shoulders in the backseat seemed likely to weigh the Chevy down, to flatten the tires and yank the bed straight through the road.

"*Donovan*," Mom warned.

At last Dad rewarded Milo with a rearview wink.

"Fine. I hear you, *papi*. We'll build your tree house."

That night Hank reminded Milo that observation decks—like the one they'd seen on a family trip to the Rio Grande Gorge Bridge, for example—could be *just* as cool as boring old tree houses. "We don't have a forest, but we've got a lot of stars. I dunno. Maybe we could look at those instead?"

Milo liked that idea so much that he climbed the tree of Hank until his little arms were secure around his big brother's neck, and Hank ran a lap around the house with Milo riding piggyback. Breathless from laughter, Milo whispered: "We need a blueprint."

Hank wasn't great at drawing. None of his friends were, either.

But one of Hank's classmates was better than great. Hank could never talk to Brendan Nesbitt, but he'd noticed him every day for months. Brendan sat in front of Hank in Health class and drew startling, lovely shapes in the margins of his notebooks. None of the shapes were half so startling or lovely as Brendan Nesbitt himself, which was why Hank could never talk to him.

Brendan was startled and not just startling when Hank blurted his request in the spare minutes before second bell.

"I'll pay you back somehow," Hank stammered. Brendan had already pulled a pad of graph paper from his backpack, was already drawing. "I can help you do any heavy lifting you might need. Or I can come reorganize your house? Your garage? I'd help you with homework but that'd be dumb. I mean, you're definitely smarter than me."

Brendan didn't lift his head, but Hank felt the flit of his gaze like feathers. "How about you and your brother just let me see the final product?" Now Brendan stared right at Hank and smiled. "Invite me over sometime, Hank."

Hank flushed. Again, he could not talk to Brendan Nesbitt.

After two days Brendan delivered the completed blueprint. That evening, Hank rushed through his homework and chores so he could slouch next to Milo on the bottom bunk. He pointed out finer, unnecessary details in the artwork, like the stars Brendan had charted in the background and the threads of wood grain he had etched in soft pencil.

Milo only had eyes for the architecture. He pretended to stroke an invisible goatee. "Yes. This'll do."

The Vasquez brothers spent an hour coloring in Brendan's lines with crayon.

★ ★ ★

Ana, fledgling filmmaker, waited until Friday to invite Marissa Ritter over to assist with the cinematic staging of Milo's observation deck.

Marissa's main area of expertise was screenwriting—she and Ana were making movies on their phones even in the good old days when their shoes still lit up. Marissa had been officially in charge of their scripts for two years, ever since she won the fifth-grade writing contest with a piece about sentient furniture. Still, Ana couldn't imagine building a set without Marissa's input. And Marissa was better at dealing with little kids. Ana, with all her edges, always worried she'd cut Milo by accident.

Marissa held Milo's hand while Ana led the way along the slanted sides of Nameless Canyon, dodging the thistles that lurked below the Vasquez home. Ana stopped every few steps and pressed her thumbs and forefingers together to form a square with which she could frame the sky. Marissa showed Milo how to do the same. Soon all three were viewing the canyon through the make-believe camera lenses of their hands.

By the time the sun was setting, Ana had her hands on her hips and her feet firmly placed. "Milo, if we build the platform in exactly this position, and have it facing out at this *exact* angle, you know what?"

"What?" Milo hazarded.

"The view from the deck will be totally *cinematic*."

"An actual *vista*," Marissa confirmed. She and Ana wore matching sunglasses.

Milo set a Matchbox car at Ana's feet to mark the spot.

★ ★ ★

When Maggie Vasquez informed Mrs. Noell that her green thumb was no longer needed, Mrs. Noell offered them dead trees instead of live ones. "We've got some scrap lookin' for a good home. Send Don over to pick it up."

It was Maggie who turned up instead, with all three kids in tow. Mrs. Noell led them to the woodshed, clapped Ana on the back, mussed Milo's hair, and demanded Hank rejoin the club and forget about that sports nonsense.

Ana referenced the blueprint for specifics and Hank sifted through the pile, pretending not to have memorized every detail of Brendan's drawing. Milo was in charge of the measuring tape; he couldn't stop the yellow strip from snapping back at him like a broken snake. Maggie kept Mrs. Noell busy with chatter, helping the older woman repaint the 4-H logo on her minivan.

All four Vasquezes were filthy with paint and sweat and sawdust by the time they pulled away. The Chevy was full to the brim with lumber.

They drove home at dusk with the windows rolled down, singing into the breeze.

Dad promised he'd play the foreman. But when it became clear that he couldn't get enough daylight time off work to even break ground under Milo's Matchbox car in the desert, Maggie left school early to bury a shovel in the earth.

The following weekend, Hank made good on his offer to involve the basketball team. Soon a gaggle of noisy, jumble-limbed teens was hoisting beams and planting them, or, in the case of known doofus Orson Liu, sledding down the desert slope on plywood slats. Marissa made an appearance, collecting footage for a future time-lapse montage. Come nightfall, Maggie treated them all to pizza, then chased them out.

Days after that, Mrs. Noell brought over some of her 4-H staffers to mix and pour concrete at the base of the six main beams. They produced hammers and nails and drills from hidden pockets. They became an orchestral cacophony of constructing, solidifying the horizontal supports, the cantilevered landing, the decking. Come nightfall, Maggie treated them all to pizza, beers, and conversation, and did not chase them out until morning.

Throughout this, Milo took up his post just within view of the bustle, creating mock-anthills and whispering to them, building bridges in the dirt, catching clouds in his expert finger-frames.

Once, between the third and fourth weekends, Dad woke up early before his commute to set off down the slope with his toolbox. Milo clunked after him in hand-me-down boots. Even in the half-light, Dad saw well enough to rescue Milo from the bear grass.

Dad stood quietly in the morning chill, pinkened by the sunrise. He scratched his head at the pillars aimed at the sky, the lines binding them together. He held a penlight to Brendan's creased illustration. He cursed and set the artwork aside.

Milo held out a box of nails for him. Dad spent twenty minutes placing an additional board along the deck railing, hammering a superfluous triangle into place.

★ ★ ★

Finally the family was sanding and staining the wood, bumping shoulders. Their hands became red, raw meat. They drank their weight in water and crisped in the dry air.

Finally Milo stood between his siblings and his parents on the deck. Wind whistled between the boards. The glazed surface shone, but not enough to reflect the sky. Ana and Hank were right about the view. From here, the world was a forest of stars.

Milo toed his way to the railing. Hank shadowed him, ready to pull him back from the edge if need be. Ana passed Milo a paper airplane.

"Go on," Dad murmured, from the darkness behind them.

Milo pulled his arm back and sent the plane over the edge. Mom whooped.

The Nameless Canyon Observation Deck was beautiful.

Two days later, Dad threw a hamper of clothes, his turntable, a milk crate full of peeling records, and his toolbox into the belly of the Chevy, started the engine, and drove away from his family. He left little apart from bear grass and nothing so much as an explanation in his wake.

The remaining Vasquezes abandoned the gleaming observation deck to wind and sand, which chipped away at the polish for three empty years.

No remaining Vasquez witnessed the moment when a cinematic something, searing and bright as a falling star but colder than any star could be, traversed the perfect desert vista on a June evening. It plummeted into the depths of Nameless Canyon.

This bright cold something hit the cracked earth and broke into a thousand scuttling insects of light. They set the grass aglow and nestled into the brambles, seeking warmth where there was none.

This bright cold something, alone, in a thousand squirming pieces.

When the Vasquez children found it, they took it out of the canyon. They let the broken pieces of a star-born orphan live inside them, and made it whole, and named it.

This bright cold something did not amount to a father, but Milo, Ana, and Hank learned to make do.

They were the sort of kids who built tree houses in the desert.

PART ONE
SEPTEMBER 7
(DAY THIRTY-THREE)

1

EYES

For the first thirty-three days after Luz left, Ana spent every night in the kitchen pantry.

She did not sleep.

Sleeping would have come easier if her shoulder blades hadn't been pressed against wooden shelving, or if she hadn't been coughing on unsettled puffs of cinnamon and paprika every time she jostled the spice rack, or if she could ever have convinced herself that turning off the dangling ceiling bulb was a good idea.

Sleeping would come easier if she could bring herself to close her eyes.

Ana didn't really do that anymore, not when she could help it. Those two wetlands had become deserts. If she ran into her seventh-grade science teacher, Mr. Chilton, maybe she could joke about that: "There's been a complete biome shift, Mr. Chilton."

But Ana wasn't in junior high anymore, and she didn't know who any of her teachers would be. And Ana didn't make jokes anymore.

For jokes to land, usually you have to look your audience in the eye. There were red asterisks where Ana's eyes used to be, webs as vast and complicated as constellations. No one could bear to look into them.

A handful of quiet doctors had made house calls since July. Ana had been given eye drops and therapy and medication. Last week, a small man in green had passed through the entrance of the fumigation tent and then the front door and pulled an actual pendulum from his pocket.

He attempted hypnosis.

The small man closed his eyes long before Ana did, rubbing tears from them and excusing himself. Dr. Ruby stood up from the threadbare recliner beside the door and shook his hand, accepting his apologies with what looked to Ana like a small smile.

Half of Dr. Ruby's face was a mess of shiny pink burn scars. That smile may have been anything but. Ana's eyesight was blurry these days.

Since Luz's departure, Ana blinked only when her body forced her to. But blinking is necessary, and fighting a necessary thing for so long meant that every time she did succumb, Ana's eyelids scraped her eyeballs like sandpaper might.

Short flickers of sharp pain: this was what Ana deserved for losing Luz.

They say if you stare into stars you go blind.

Ana wondered about that. If she lost her sight, maybe she would learn to let darkness exist again. Could she move away from dimly lit nights in the pantry, back into the cool black of the bedroom she shared with her mother? Could the sound of Mom's whistling breath be enough to lull her to sleep again?

Or would the darkness of sleep mean seeing Dad?

For ages after Dad left, all the way up until Luz appeared, Ana had dreamed about Dad nightly, in memories looped like unspooling film. The day Dad let her braid and put hair clips in his beard unspun into a memory of Dad taking her to the book fair after her first parent-teacher conference, then unspun into the morning Ana had walked into the bathroom to find Milo standing next to the yellowing shower curtain, peering at the drain as if Dad had been sucked down it.

In Mr. Chilton's class, Ana had learned that nature abhors a vacuum. Potholes are the first places puddles form. Pores always get clogged. Empty things wish they weren't.

Ana wasn't afraid of the dark. She was afraid of the emptiness behind her eyelids. She was afraid of what might fill that emptiness if she closed her eyes.

She was afraid it would not be Luz.

On the last night of summer break, after weeks of sitting in cupboards and refusing to leave the funereal quiet of the house, Ana found the duct tape. It had been hidden from her inside one of the pockets of her mother's hanging shoe rack. She peeled two segments free and smoothed them across her forehead and upper eyelids, relished the stickiness on her lashes and eyebrows, the rawness of air on her exposed eyeballs.

The duct tape clung especially to a grisly scab over her right eye. At least the stitches had been removed. Last time, the black thread had stuck fast to the tape, even when Mom tore it away. What a complete mess.

Ana tucked the roll into her hoodie pocket and walked the distance from gritty bedroom carpet to worn hallway carpet to the kitchen's peeling linoleum. Mom didn't look up as Ana passed behind her; she was rubbing peroxide into the stained patch of floor in front of the sink again. Milo dozed at the table, SpaghettiOs slipping from his spoon, headphones blaring loud enough to echo, short legs kicking table legs.

Neither of them noticed the blocks of silver holding Ana's eyelids up as she opened the pantry door and shut it behind her.

2

HANDS

Hank slept better than Ana did, but even he woke up at exactly 2:03 every morning. This particular 2:03 a.m., on the seventh day of September, marked the three-month anniversary of meeting Luz for the first time.

Hank refused to celebrate the occasion. But he could not forget it.

At 1:57 a.m. on June 7, Hank's feet slid right past the observation deck and down the slope of Nameless Canyon. Even from so high up, he could see speckles of inexplicable white light spotting the landscape below. There was no time to wonder whether those speckles were alive. Milo had been missing for hours, and Hank could only wonder whether he was lying somewhere in the pit.

No. Today was more than another anniversary of that day.

Today was the first day of Hank's last year of high school.

Hank focused on his fingers. How flimsy they felt, just dangling from his hands, kindergarten pipe cleaners stabbed in clay. Not that Hank knew anything about art.

The longer Hank lay staring at the plastic stars clinging to the ceiling, thinking about his fingers, the more those fingers tingled, the more the tingling felt like needles poking him.

Hank was turning porous, he was pretty sure.

When he became convinced the holes had widened enough to vanish his hands completely, Hank sat up in bed. He paused to put his hands on his face, used his cheeks to confirm their realness. Then Hank eased himself out of the top bunk, pressing feet only gently on ladder rungs, so as not to wake his sleeping brother. It was a pointless habit.

Milo's headphones were yelling into his pillow, dislodged from his little ears. And none of Hank's sounds, not laughter or words or anything, reached Milo nowadays.

At two a.m. on June 7, Hank followed the sandy trail that snaked through the tangled brush on the canyon floor, calling Milo's name until all his breath abandoned him, sprinting past plants whose buds held not only blossoms, but creeping beetles of impossible phosphorescence.

The cold something awaited him.

Hank tiptoed past his mother's room. In this moment he was a six-year-old sneaking into the living room on Christmas morning, not an overgrown seventeen-year-old with size-fourteen feet.

Ana loved making fun of his damn feet. *Luz*, she'd said once, with her eyes closed, *if you had any brains whatsoever, you'd have taken Hank's feet instead.*

I've never had any brains, Luz had written, using Hank's hands. It was the truth.

Ana didn't joke these days.

Outside the gray house, the fog creeping up from Nameless Canyon left the driveway cold enough to feel alien. Hank didn't bother with a jacket, but he hardly noticed the chill. All he noticed was the featheriness of his fingers, his cotton palms—so close to nothing.

Hank picked his basketball up from the hollow at the base of the hoop, wiped dew from its bumpy surface. It wasn't an old ball, but he'd worn it smooth already. He took four large steps backward, until his heels hit the end of the free throw lane. He knew the distance by heart.

At 2:01 a.m. on June 7, Hank was buried in the foliage at the base of Nameless Canyon, but he didn't spare more than half a thought for the starlike insects of light that crawled from milkweed leaves and stuck to his fingers.

His only goal was reaching two silhouettes spotted from halfway down: one a child's, the other a man's.

Milo was meeting someone, or something, in the canyon.

It couldn't be Dad.

Aiming by the amber glow of a neighbor's porch light, Hank cupped the ball in tremulous hands and shot.

Clank.

The ball rattled against the rim and fell to the pavement. The smacking sound of rubber then nothing, rubber then nothing, echoed against garage doors in the cul-de-sac.

Hank swore under his breath. He shot for the hoop again and missed just as spectacularly. Swore louder, chased the runaway ball down the driveway.

Back in seventh grade, Hank had won the middle school free-throw contest by a whopping seven baskets. Not even the eighth graders had come close. Swish after swish, the ball slipped through the net as though magnetized.

Hank had felt it, then. The way the world peeled open around him.

And Dad had been there, fists clenched and raised in a good way, feet planted on the sideline, exactly where parents weren't supposed to plant them. Dad's grin, as wide as his head, because *his son* was wedging a hole in the world.

Now, as rose-colored dawn threatened to creep from the earth and immerse the cul-de-sac, Hank couldn't make a single basket. He couldn't focus on the present, couldn't keep his thoughts in one piece.

Fine. Happy freakin' anniversary, Luz.

At 2:02 a.m. on June 7, Hank burst through one last onslaught of bear grass and discovered the small silhouette really *did* belong to his little brother. He wrapped his arms around Milo's shoulders. Before chiding the smallest Vasquez for scaring them half to death, before he could wonder why the white beads of light seemed to be *crawling* into the ears of his little brother, Hank remembered his manners.

He turned to thank the other silhouette for finding the smallest Vasquez.

Again and again Hank tried to make use of his cotton-candy fingers. The ball felt more and more like slippery velvet. Hank finally threw with enough misguided force that the basketball smacked the backboard and knocked the hoop off-kilter.

The rebound came back, arcing over Hank's head—

The ball was sucked into the fog of Nameless Canyon.

At 2:03 a.m. on June 7, the silhouette at the bottom of the radiant canyon shifted its attention to Hank's open palm, and suddenly Hank realized there was no man there at all. There was *nothing* there but a pillar made of the same eerie, liquid insects that now covered Hank's hands and spewed from Milo's ears and the milkweeds.

Hank was faced with the squirming imitation of a person.

This was anything *but* a man. This dissolved and sank right into Hank's skin like water through tissues. Hank shook hands with Luz and discovered he was shaking only empty air.

When Luz was around, he and Hank had made virtually every basket.

Not at first—for the first week after Hank met him, Luz wasn't so great with fingers, having never had any of his own. Luz wore Hank's poorly, complained that ten were a lot to deal with, and why would anyone ever need so many?

With Luz inside them, Hank's hands had sometimes felt like

mallets on the ends of his arms. Lifting them was lifting weights. The burn sometimes felt good, productive in a familiar, frustrating way.

Being frustrated was good for Hank. The only things that had ever mattered *were* frustrating things: passing his driver's exam despite his giant feet, working up the guts to ask Brendan Nesbitt to homecoming, trying out for varsity as a sophomore.

During the latest summer tryouts, Hank and Luz made every basket, then skipped every subsequent practice. Consequences hadn't seemed to matter when Luz was around.

Luz wasn't around anymore.

Hank sank to the ground, pressing his hands into his cheeks. In the distance a Chihuahua yipped, maybe five Chihuahuas from the neighbor's house.

"They're building an army," Brendan had joked, on a summer night when he and Hank lay together on the oft-abandoned observation deck, hidden from sight by the brush. Hidden, but they could still see the stars and hear the yipping. And Brendan had taken one of Hank's rough, long-fingered hands in a smaller, ink-stained one and squeezed it tight, and somehow that squeeze had forged a direct line to Hank's chest and all the rest of him, pressurized in Brendan's small, perfectly imperfect palm.

This was when Hank's hands had still belonged to him.

When Hank and Brendan Nesbitt could stand to touch each other.

There would be no fetching Hank's basketball from the bottom of Nameless Canyon. Nobody in the Vasquez family peered down there anymore.

You wouldn't think you could just ignore the existence of a huge crater in your world, a crater that sometimes floodwaters threatened to pull your home down into.

The Vasquezes had gotten very good at it.

3

EARS

Milo didn't hear Mom coming.

But he definitely felt her hands on his shoulders, shaking him to pieces!

Milo was still half-dreaming, and somehow the shaking made him think he wasn't a boy at all, but a jar of colorful sprinkles or a bottle of ants. Or maybe both!

What would candy-coated ants taste like?

Milo opened his eyes.

Right there, centimeters away and ready to scare the actual snot out of him, was Mom's face. Like she was stuck under one of his magnifying glasses, blown up so big and close he could see bits of gray eye-shadow dust clinging to her eye-bags! A single witchy hair sprang from a small mole on her cheekbone.

Did Mom ever wonder what candy-coated ants taste like? Had Dad?

Milo wanted to ask. But Milo was too big for questions like that.

"Up, Milo."

Mom hadn't tried to pull Milo's headphones off since the first week! Maybe that was because she hated the sound of him screaming himself raw (Milo hated the sound, too, because *what a racket!*). But Milo had been living without good ears for basically *ages*. By now he could pretty much read her lips!

Or maybe she only ever said things she'd already said before?

"Next time wear the earbuds to bed. You'll put a crick in your neck."

Dad's bulky old headphones *did* make it so Milo could only sleep on his back. They turned Milo into a sad turtle turnover. But he didn't mind putting a crick in his neck! Having a crick in his neck made Milo feel *older*.

Older people were *wiser* people. Milo knew for a fact older people got to make more decisions than he did. They didn't even have to be *good* decisions, either. There was an old man at Glen's Groceries who mostly decided to feed Cheetos to pigeons. All the time! Cheese wasn't good for a Milo-size stomach, let alone tiny *bird* stomachs. Nobody told that old guy to think how scary the world would be if birds started *pooping orange*.

Nope. Old men just woke up with cricks in their necks and got to do whatever they wanted, and no one made them go to school.

And *anyhow*. Ana used to tell Milo he was a pain in the neck all the time. He should get to know the feeling. Mean or not, Milo missed hearing from Ana. He missed hearing from anyone. Maybe if he got crickety and old, Hank would finally talk to him.

Don't count your chickens, Milo told himself. Whatever that meant.

When Mom returned, she was dressed for work, wearing brown shoes and a blue dress with red flowers on it. Her thumbs settled on Milo's collarbones (she didn't have to be so careful; Milo wasn't a baby!).

"Milo. Up! *Please.*"

Again Mom retreated. Mango-y perfume chased her out.

Milo curled himself inward. He tightened his body into a spiral of sheets, the world's largest snailboy, and tried his hardest to hear only the crackling sound of Thom Yorke's voice.

He tried to imagine it was Dad's voice instead. But it was really hard to think of a reason why Dad would be singing about fake plastic trees. Could they have built a tree house in one? What would a plastic tree even look like?

What if they were just like the potted plants in waiting rooms? Milo thought he must have seen a whole plastic jungle by now, geez.

This time Mom didn't shake him. She pushed her hands into the space beneath his arms and lifted him up, up, up. She pulled him close like he wasn't *way* too big for this.

She tapped on his right earphone. Milo let her tug it aside.

He held his breath and heard the dreaded Roaring Nothing!

The Roaring Nothing was a blanket of sound like river rapids or maybe like an army of minuscule legs! The Roaring Nothing stampeded through the unplugged holes Milo used to call ears! The Roaring Nothing crawled over the bumpy surface of his brain like sour-candy ants!

The Roaring Nothing made Milo fill his lungs!

He wanted to make a racket to drown it out, to tell it *no—*

Just in time came Mom's deep voice, right against Milo's skull. It shook the hairs of his cowlick. "Milo, please."

He let the air out, a little like a tired old man.

"Think of all the people who want to see you."

People who want to see me do what? Milo mouthed. He couldn't hear himself. This didn't mean he planned on shouting for his entire life, are you kidding? Milo planned to live until he was at least thirty-seven. That was another thirty years. Shouting that whole time would be another real pain in the neck.

"How about Antonio? I bet he's sorry he missed your birthday party."

Yeah, right! Antonio hadn't known what to do with Milo even before the stripy fumigation tent transformed the Vasquez family into Eustace's very own circus performers! Dr. Ruby had told Milo that the tent was a *ruse*, that usually tents like that meant the people inside were gone and termites were being gassed or something.

But the house never even *had* termites! There was never gas in the tent. Milo and his family stayed inside the whole time, pretending to *be normal* . . .

Come see the human sprinkle boy! Tastes like real ants!

Those tent walls had warned everyone to keep away. The stripes held the same kind of magic as the patterns on deadly coral snakes. Those snakes were red and yellow, but black too, which meant they were poisonous.

But in school Milo had learned about another kind of snake, a special snake that *copied* the stripes of the venomous coral snake to scare off predators. These snakes weren't deadly at all! They acted tough, but might be pretty nice if you got to know one.

"Milo? Please." Mom replaced Milo's headphone and slipped away.

Milo tried playing opossum one more time.

Years ago, Dad's old Chevy had flattened the orange-dirted back roads leading into Eustace and they'd seen an opossum in the road.

Dad slammed the brakes and a pair of Spanish swearwords escaped him. He pulled on his gloves and told Milo to stay in the car. He was embarking on a rescue mission.

Milo watched Dad pick the giant rat up by its tail, supporting its sagging tummy with one hand. Dad dropped the opossum in the dust just past the shoulder and climbed back into the truck.

They sat on the side of the road for forever, until they were sticking to the vinyl seats. Milo picked at the rubber soles of his shoes. Back then, he never minded when things were quiet.

Finally Dad twisted the key in the ignition. "Guess not. Sorry, Mi—"

"DAD, LOOK!"

The engine coughed! The opossum came alive!

Milo watched the rodent jerk to its tiny pink feet and waddle into the bear grass along the road, quick as a tightly twisted wind-up toy. Its wormy tail was there after one blink, gone after another. Poof.

Milo gaped wide enough to catch maybe a zillion flies. "How did you know that would happen?"

"Magic, *papi*."

Dad was that kind of person: he'd help you even if you weren't a person. He'd help you even if you were *already dead*!

If Milo could play opossum for a little longer this morning, he pinkie-promised himself, by the time he got up maybe he'd have enough energy to sprint, not just waddle.

Or maybe if he played dead long enough, Mom would realize that he'd been telling the truth for the past month: Milo *definitely* couldn't go to school with the other kids. Dr. Ruby was wrong when she said his hearing was fine. Dr. Ruby didn't live in a tiny waxy house inside Milo's ears, so what did *she* know? Dr. Ruby was a bony lady in a white coat. What kind of person wore heavy white coats in the dirty desert?

Mom reappeared in the doorway, screwing an earring into her earlobe. Milo saluted her. He got up and pulled socks from the floor onto his feet.

In Milo's headphones, Thom Yorke sang about a nice dream. Milo sighed. Probably it had nothing to do with being a bottle of sprinkles.

The moment Mom clomped away, the shirt of Milo's space pajamas got caught on his headphones. That was not what made him swear twice in Spanish.

Milo was *certain* there was even a whole nursery rhyme about the friendlier snakes that weren't coral snakes. Definitely!

It was just . . . Milo couldn't seem to remember it.

4

OUTSIDE

For the first time in an eternity, all three of Maggie's children sat together at the kitchen counter during breakfast time.

To say that they shared a meal wouldn't be entirely accurate.

Only Hank ate with any gusto, shoveling granola into his mouth like a starving creature. To Maggie it seemed he was trying to make up for a long summer of neglecting to eat much of anything at all.

Ana balanced a dollop of yogurt on her spoon, but each time it drifted close to her lips, she only lowered the spoon again. Angry red patches, new scabs that matched the bloodshot in Ana's eyes, had formed in the places where the duct tape had been.

Maggie's first act of the morning hadn't been putting the coffee on. It had been holding her teenage daughter's impassive face under running tap water and tugging strips of silver adhesive from her skin. She'd done this in small increments rather than all at once, having learned this lesson over the past month. She'd eased the way with Johnson's baby oil.

Ana hadn't whimpered, not even after the wound above her right eye tore open again. She'd kept her eyes wide even as warm water dripped into them, hadn't protested when Maggie pressed a Disney Princess Band-Aid over the bleed.

"How's that, Ana?" she'd asked softly. Ana only shrugged.

Part of Maggie was waiting for Ana to catch sight of herself in a mirror and demand a sick day. Most of Maggie knew Ana didn't make demands these days.

Milo sipped his strawberry milk in spurts, keeping time with voices in his headphones. Every few seconds Milo let the straw fall from his lips and pink spatter his hand in order to stare in Hank's direction. Hank kept his eyes on his phone.

Maggie noticed all these things because she was their mother, but also because lately she'd been searching for evidence of sustainable life on the planes of their faces.

Her kids didn't look like themselves.

They didn't look even completely alive: a grinning puppet, a red-eyed zombie, a little prince in orbit.

They were still hers. That was enough. It had to be enough.

"New year, new start, kiddos." Maggie found herself wiping the counter with a dirty rag, found herself hating that she felt the need to do things like that. God knew her brothers or uncles or lovers had never felt that pressure. To tidy, to make a home, to accommodate.

To stay.

"Do you kids need anything else before you go?"

"Nope!" Hank guzzled down the remainder of his milk and leaped to his feet. "Heading out early, actually. Gotta talk to Coach Huang about botching tryouts. Maybe he'll give me a second chance."

Maggie frowned. "You want to keep playing basketball?"

"No, Mom. I *hate* basketball now." He laughed. "*What are you saying.* Yeah, I wanna keep playing."

"I thought . . . well, I thought you'd gone off it. But if it's what you want, Hank."

"Mom, I love basketball. Basically that's the one thing everyone knows about me." Maggie disliked his easy smile. It felt slathered on, butter hiding burned toast. "Come on, BanAna. Get your shoes on."

Maggie waited for Ana to protest the nickname. Ana only shifted her unblinking gaze to Hank, who shifted his to his backpack.

Ana stood. Maggie fought the urge to prop her up.

"Well, I just want you all to know"—Maggie paused to pull Milo's cup away from him before he knocked it over—"that I'm really proud of you for trying to make it work today. I mean it. And if anything happens, if anyone says anything or—well, *anything*, just call me, okay? Please?"

"It'll be fine." Hank beamed at her. "Come on, Mom. Do I *look* like a freshman?"

"You aren't, but your sister is. Ana?" Maggie, twisting the rag over the sink, felt the graze of that painful gaze. "If . . . if you don't think you're up to going in today—"

"Why are you only saying that to me? Because I'm a girl?"

"No, Ana." *Because you've worn sweatpants and a sweater every day for the past month, and I'm not certain you've showered in all that time. Because this time last year you spent an hour perfecting your cat-eye eyeliner and today you're going to school without eyebrows.*

Maggie would not say this. She was their mother. She was going to be supportive. To accommodate. To stay.

"If anyone should stay home, it's Milo."

"I'll keep an eye on him." Maggie's first-grade classroom shared a wing with Milo's second-grade classroom, so she'd be able to look in on him during recess and lunch breaks.

"BYE, HANK! BYE, ANA!" Milo hollered.

Maggie saw Hank clench and unclench his fingers. "Any day now, Ana."

Ana shuffled after him. "See you, Milo."

"BYE, HANK!"

"Don't forget that Dr. Ruby will be stopping by for dinner tonight."

"HANK, BYE!"

"Okay."

"*Hank.* Just say good-bye to your brother."

Hank paused in the doorway, clenched and unclenched fingers again. He didn't turn around. Maggie couldn't remember the last time he'd spoken a syllable to Milo.

"Bye."

Ana followed Hank out. Milo's head sank.

Maggie dropped the sodden rag. So quickly it'd made prunes of her fingers.

Was she a bad mother to send them to school like this? Wreckage pretending to be whole? Was she a bad mother to be counting the minutes until she could drop Milo off in Mrs. Stuart's classroom, until she could put a wall of cinder blocks between them, let him be someone else's puzzle to solve for the day?

Last night she'd taken the time to pick this dress out, to smack dust from it and hang it in the window. This morning she'd moved the dress to the bathroom with her, just so the smallest wrinkles would flatten in the mist she created while showering.

Tiny efforts had been made to conquer this day.

This rag wasn't even clean. Maggie was only pushing dirt around.

"MOM?"

She spun around. "I'm sorry about Hank, Milo. He's just . . . Milo?"

Milo was wide-eyed, headphones voiceless but for the tinny echo of slowing instrumentals as an album ended. Maggie recognized the tune, remembered grass tickling her legs on a spring afternoon years earlier while Milo's father plucked strings on his acoustic guitar. "Street Spirit (Fade Out)."

"What is it?"

Milo took a deep breath. "IS THERE NAP TIME IN SECOND GRADE?"

Maggie shook her head. Milo sighed, face resigned, like this latest disappointment was par for the course. Like being seven was going to take a lot of growing up. He sucked away the last of his strawberry milk. A dry gurgle.

"YOU KNOW THAT SOUND, MOM? YOU KNOW WHAT ABOUT THAT SOUND?"

"It's French for 'all gone,'" she whispered.

"IT'S FRENCH FOR 'ALL GONE'!" Milo informed her, in his father's voice.

Maggie's hands itched. She swore she could still see traces of a bloodstain on the linoleum, just in front of the sink.

5

HANDS

Hank dropped Ana on the sidewalk like a bag of garbage.

He didn't actually drop her, because he didn't touch her. Hank no longer touched anything, if it could be avoided. He swore his stupid fingers had nearly broken just from lifting a glass of milk to his mouth at breakfast, but Hank thought he had played it pretty cool. Apart from the Milo thing.

He also played the short drive to Eustace High pretty cool. As bad as it was with Milo, Hank could still look at Ana, even if every time he did, he remembered the red-and-white night when Luz left while Ana bled from her head and Hank bled from his hands and Milo's face remained pale and bloodless in the kitchen—

"Hank," Ana murmured, "the light's green."

Hank drove, tapping his fingers on the wheel to make sure they still existed.

He tried to play dropping Ana off at the entrance pretty cool, too. He didn't want her to know he still saw her as bloodstained. It wasn't her fault.

Dad used to warn Hank about Ana. "You can't fight a sister like you would a brother, Hank," he'd scolded once, after he caught them roughhousing on the living room floor, cackling like demons. "Girls should be treated gently."

Neither Hank nor Ana had put much stock in that, because Mom said Dad would know better if he'd ever had any sisters of his own. "Girls are just *people*, Hank, and you treat them like people."

There remained nothing gentle between Hank and his sister.

"I'm gonna park and head right to Coach Huang's office. Meet me by the gym after school."

"See you." Could she really, though, through eyes like that?

"Hey, wait. Check the glove box. I might have some sunglasses you can borrow."

"Cool. Why don't you *hand* them to me."

Hank stared at Ana. Not her eyes, but as close as he could manage. "Look, I'm just trying to be nice."

"Like you were nice to Milo?"

He hated her tone, mostly for its complete lack of venom. "Stop it."

Ana popped open the glove box and retrieved a pair of wannabe Ray-Bans. She set them in her pocket and pushed open the door.

Hank almost offered to check in with her at lunch, to make sure her first day wasn't as horrendous as it could be. He thought it, but didn't say it.

He watched Ana in the rearview as he pulled away. She stood alone under the flagpole, hoodie zipped to the top despite the late-summer heat. After a moment, she tugged the glasses from her pocket.

Hank put eyes back on the road and yelped, dropping a huge foot on the brakes—

He'd been inches from smearing Carmella Spalding and her usual herd of girlfriends across his windshield. Carmella smacked his hood with the flat of her hand. A short girl flipped him the bird before hurrying to the safety of a sidewalk.

God, Hank would give anything to be that sure-handed. To smack something and leave an impact. Maybe he'd be better off driving with his elbows. Hank stared at his hands on the wheel, willing a smile back onto his face. It wouldn't come.

An SUV honked, urging him forward.

He sat in the student parking lot for some time, catching his breath.

If Luz were still here, no *way* Hank would have almost run over some classmates. He wouldn't have had to brake, even. Luz would have steered the car away for him, regardless of where Hank was looking.

Or maybe Luz would have driven the car right into the girls, just to see what would happen. To see if one of them might puncture a lung and perhaps die.

Hard to know, with Luz. Luz was always so curious.

And one of the things that piqued his curiosity most, the whole time Luz lived with the Vasquezes, was death. By the end, half the questions Luz asked, half the words he wrote with Hank's hands, on whiteboards and notepads and once on Hank's bed-sheets with a Sharpie, were along these lines:

Does every creature die? When that happens, does the consciousness end? Will you die? Do you look forward to it? Is it difficult?

Now Hank whispered this into his empty cupped palms: "Luz, dying's the easiest thing in the whole damn world."

Coach Huang's face was hard to read on the best of days and bordered on expressionless on the worst. His upraised eyebrows made him a stranger when Hank used an elbow to knock on the door to his paper-strewn office.

"Hank. You're welcome to sit."

"I'm here to apologize." The seat was too small for Hank, but most seats were. "For what happened. At tryouts? I was being an idiot."

"I'm still not clear on what was going on there, Hank. As far as I can tell, you had a tantrum and stomped out. Didn't show your face all summer."

"Yeah. I'm sorry. About the, um, tantrum, and missing practice. All of it."

"It didn't seem like you." Coach Huang rubbed his chin. "I gather you had a lot going on. With your family."

"I . . . yeah. It's really not a big deal. I mean. I don't want to talk about it."

"Didn't ask you to." Coach Huang's face reverted to stony. "I've been your coach for three years now, Hank. You're the first to make assists but reluctant to receive them. I know better than to expect you to ask for help."

Hank shot him a smile he hoped was sheepish. "Sorry, Coach."

The bell rang. Bleeping echoed through the gym beyond the open door. Hank itched to hear the familiar squeak of gym shoes on polished wood, if only to remind himself he missed it.

"Well, I appreciate the apology. You should extend it to your teammates, too."

Hank winced. "Yeah. Okay."

"Okay." Coach Huang smiled. "I have to tell you, Hank, I'm relieved. I wasn't sure you'd be joining us this season."

"Well, I really love basketball, Coach."

"I know. We missed you at camp. But right now you don't want to be late for your first class. I'm not writing you a pass."

"Yeah, save the passes for the court, right?" Hank's laugh was too sharp.

"Exactly. Out. I've got a whole class of freshmen to tame."

Hank fought the urge to check where his hands were. "But. So . . . about practice?"

"Oh. You didn't pick up a schedule, did you? I have some here somewhere." Coach Huang pulled a stack of blue flyers from under a stack of green ones. "Tack that to your fridge. And have your parents—sorry, your mom—sign your permission slip and bring it back for me ASAP."

The flyer crumpled under Hank's fingers. "This is the JV schedule."

"Yes. I'll see you at practice tomorrow after school. Varsity and JV are alternating days this year; there are too many of you guys to handle all at once."

Hank cleared his throat. "Yeah, that's fine. Cool. But last year I was varsity . . . ?"

Coach Huang sighed. "And this year you are not."

"I was a starter." Was smiling still a good idea? "I played center."

Coach Huang remained impassive. "Are you going to make me say more?"

"We made *finals*."

"And this summer you showed up an hour late to tryouts, bullied one of your teammates, and didn't bother coming to a single practice afterwards. So you're on the JV team, Hank. And you knew that when you came in here."

Hank couldn't stop showing his teeth. "But . . . my family . . . this summer."

"I saw the fumigation tent. And I heard rumors. But am I supposed to kick out someone who worked hard for months to make way for you? No. Did you know that one of your teammates lost his sister this year? Another watched his parents get deported. They both showed up. Bigger trouble than termites, but they still showed up."

"It wasn't termites," Hank muttered.

Coach Huang opened his mouth and closed it again. "Well."

"Coach. I have to be back on the team. Basketball is all I'm good for."

"You say that, but I'll need you to prove it during practice. Understand? Earn your place back. You burned a lot of bridges, Hank."

How did anything happen anymore?

"Yeah. Okay." Numb hands, numb lips, numb (somehow) *teeth*. "Totally."

Coach Huang stood up and reached out a hand.

Don't be limp fish, Hank willed his fingers. *Please be real.*

Coach Huang locked eyes on Hank's grip. The shadow of a

frown touched his features. "You'll need a new one of those, I guess."

The blue schedule was torn in two.

When had that happened? Had Hank made it happen, or had his hands . . . ?

No. Luz was gone. Anything these hands did now was Hank's doing.

The second bell rang. Hank was late.

"Sorry." Hank grinned wide and wider still.

Just outside the door, Tim Miller, the tallest point guard in the region, the guy who had taught Hank to dribble back in elementary school, was leaning against the wall opposite Coach Huang's office.

Hank's smile crystallized. He froze in the doorway.

Tim Miller straightened up. Handsome gray eyes narrowed to pencil-lead points.

"Hey, Tim!" Hank said, too cheerfully.

Tim didn't say anything. He waited for Hank to pass.

Hank held his breath until Tim was behind him. Four steps away, Hank exhaled—

A globule of Tim's hot spit struck the nape of Hank's neck.

"Faggot."

Hank didn't stop. As he left the gymnasium, his grin kept on expanding sideways, another canyon opening.

6

EYES

Nobody complimented Ana's sunglasses.

Ana walked from her homeroom at one end of the school to her second-hour Geometry classroom on the other. The hallway bowed out around her. She only halfway noticed the way whispers sprang up in her vicinity. These days, one half was always thinking *don't blink, don't blink, do not blink.*

Dr. Ruby's termite tent was still doing its work, though it'd been taken down. Ana had read comments about it online, wincing at the brightness. Half the town seemed to think the Vasquez family had been stricken with secret über-Ebola, and the other half really did think they'd had some kind of heinous insect infestation. Maybe that was what Dr. Ruby wanted. "Skirt the question. Outsiders believe whatever they want to believe. The Vasquezes are private people. Let strangers assume away."

Everyone in the world was supposed to believe Luz had never existed.

The Vasquezes were supposed to forget he ever had.

Now Ana was a boulder in a river, if a river had ever been made up of bodies afraid to touch boulders. If water had ever been swearing and shouting instead of burbling. If boulders had deflector shields around them.

Ana wondered if they had deflector shields where Luz came from. She had no idea if Luz had anything in common with the staples of *Star Trek*.

That doesn't matter, he'd said. *Your family is my home now.*

Here was how he'd said it, because Luz never used words with Ana: after Ana closed her eyes, Luz replayed a memory, as miniature as it was dear.

Blink: Luz took Ana back to a rainy afternoon and a collection of minutes wherein she and Hank and Milo entertained themselves by lying upside down on the living room couch, side by side with arms interlocked and heads bumping together. Dad walked in to find them there, and he bent himself in half and head-butted each of the boys. "It's a bullfight!" Ana hoped for a head-butt too, but Dad pecked her on the cheek instead.

Still. That was home, once.

Third hour marked the third time that Ana watched desks clear around her. Even if Ana had never taught Dad anything, now she could teach Luz all about deflector shields.

Ana rubbed the raw skin under her eyes, fingers creeping beneath sunglasses. From two seats to her right, she felt the weight of familiar eyes.

Ana turned in time to see Marissa Ritter turn away. Marissa seemed different, which made sense. Everyone seemed different. But Marissa *specifically* so.

Ana stared, trying to determine what it was. Trying, for that matter, to determine *who* Marissa was, and if she'd ever really known that.

For years, things were collective between Marissa Ritter and Ana Vasquez: they had the same haircuts, the same clothes, the same fascination with the same Japanese trading cards and the same RPGs in elementary school, and when they got a little older, the same obsession with stop-motion animation movies. They'd preemptively named their future film production company Marissana.

Their first short film, shot on Marissa's phone, told the epic tale of a head swap between a plastic Egyptian mummy Lego figurine and a Dumbledore Lego figurine.

"Our masterpiece is only eleven seconds long," Marissa observed. Their set had been shattered after Marissa's little brother, Felix, rampaged through the room, their hard work immortalized now only in an echoing loop on Marissa's phone.

"Bahaha." Ana riffled through the bookshelf behind Marissa's bed. She scanned the bindings for any covers that might make for a decent backdrop. "We'll just tell people it's an *art film*."

"No one will buy it."

"They don't have to buy it. They only have to watch it."

"Smartass." Marissa threw Lego Dumbledore's gray hairpiece at her.

Maybe class had started. Bodies had angled themselves to face the front of the room and a polo-shirted teacher holding a syllabus.

Ana kept staring.

Marissa had chopped off at least a foot of her long black hair. The remainder brushed her shoulders, formed a face-hiding curtain around her skull. Marissa's hair was nowhere near long enough for mermaiding.

For their collective thirteenth birthdays (only two days apart), Marissa's mother had thrown them a collective birthday party.

Four hours past midnight, with eyes red from chlorine, with hair a combined chemical tangle between their sleeping bags, with all the other sleepover attendees fast asleep, with Dr Pepper and pizza on their breath, Marissana remained awake. Telling ghost stories, future stories, dream stories. Telling jokes.

"Mermaiding?" Marissa whispered.

"Yeah. Like when your hair's long enough to cover your boobs."

Marissa paused. "No freakin' way, Ana. I never told anyone before, but that's always been one of my dreams, too."

Ana laughed. "We're the same person."

". . . your protractor?" Mrs. M . . . M-something stood directly in front of Ana's desk, tapping a plastic semicircle with pink finger-nails. "Well?"

Ana blinked and subsequently cussed.

"Excuse me? It's Ana Vasquez, right?"

As if Mrs. M-something hadn't also seen the tent go up over the summer, hadn't also heard gossip about viral outbreaks. As if she hadn't circled Ana's name on her roster the day before, in red pen, a silent warning: *Something is wrong with this family.*

"Let's not start our year on the wrong foot. I don't want to move your clip." Mrs. M-something walked over to the classroom door. A behavior chart with stoplight-colored sections hung there. Around thirty clothespins pinched the color green.

"Haven't see one of those charts since fifth grade," Ana observed.

Someone snickered.

"And *I* haven't had to tell a student not to wear sunglasses to school since I *taught* fifth grade." Mrs. M-something moved Ana's clip down, pinned it alone to a yellow plain.

"Biome shift," Ana said.

"Take them off, please."

"Sure, Mrs. M-something."

"Malinowski."

Ana removed Hank's sunglasses. Around her, a new collective: a simultaneous gasp from all classmates. It was a wonder the room had any air left in it.

"Go to the nurse's office."

"I'm not sick." "Sick" just wasn't the word. "Grieving" might have been the word, but no one had asked about that and Ana hadn't told, because no one knew her like Luz had.

Only her family knew to which lengths Ana would go to disguise pain. "It's just something I have to live with now."

Mrs. M-something-ski bit her lip. "Okay. You can keep wearing the glasses."

"I don't actually have to."

"Oh. Well. Whichever you prefer." Mrs. M-whatever seemed overcome with embarrassment.

After she set them to task on a start-of-the-year survey, Ana saw her surreptitiously move Ana's clip back to green.

A sniffle pierced the quiet of the room, stood out from the scratching of pencils bubbling in answers like "isosceles" and "obtuse." Ana didn't think the sniffle was sad, necessarily.

It was only triggered by the galaxies.

The boy next to Ana wiped his nose on his hands. Marissa— maybe she could see through those hair-curtains after all, because she reached past them—maybe did the same.

Funny how Ana's eyes made everyone who wasn't Ana cry.

Maybe people were close to Ana even if she couldn't feel it.

Pretending to care what people thought might eventually make the caring true. She'd spent years pretending for Dad, too. Pretending she was something gentle and kind. Maybe pretending was the way back to normal.

It didn't matter whether she wanted the way back or not, did it, Luz?

She'd have to thank Hank for the knockoff sunglasses. Ana pushed the plastic up the bridge of her nose. She squeezed the frames until they pinched.

7
OUTSIDE

During the walk from the employee parking lot to the redbrick school building, Milo clung to Maggie's waist like this was his first day of kindergarten, little hands tugging on her airy sleeves. But this was the first day of second grade, and never since the second day of kindergarten had Milo clung to *anyone*.

Unless he clung to Luz.

Whether he had was as unknowable to Maggie as her children themselves.

Dr. Ruby had offered the skeleton of an explanation, in the kitchen, in the summer.

"You're telling me that what's happened is some sort of . . . what, shared hallucination? It's not a hallucination that has Hank *carving words into his skin* and Ana *slicing her face open* and my son, my seven-year-old, screaming that he hears—damn it."

Maggie put her palms against her temples, pressing hard,

trying to forget the way Milo's eyes had glittered when he told her what sang him to sleep all summer.

"Milo hears what?" Dr. Ruby's eyes were obscured by safety goggles and her face was blurred by those scars, but certainly she was frowning.

"Let's go ahead and pretend it *was* just termites. If it's a hallucination, it doesn't matter what he told me, does it?"

Those lenses reflected the yellow of the opaque tent beyond the window, headlights in an otherwise dim kitchen. "But it wasn't a hallucination."

Maggie fell back against the counter. "All that matters is my kids need help. You've seen them. We just need *help*."

"I *have* seen them. This is very real for them."

"Then why are you asking us to *call* it a hallucination?"

"What has happened here is unexplainable. If you want to carry on with your lives, it's best to put this experience in terms that are easier to process. A coping strategy. For them, and for you."

"And what if we can't *cope* with it?"

Dr. Ruby twisted painted lips. "What choice do you have?"

"Sprinkles." Milo's grip tightened, pulled Maggie back to the sunny crosswalk.

Soon the blare of his headphones was canned by the school foyer, and then the sound was lost in the bustling hallway. Kids with bobbing backpacks, the dazed eyes of the youngest and the flushed cheeks of the laughing fourth graders showing off their new clothes, cartoon lunch boxes.

Maggie breathed deep. This was her habitat.

Some teachers dreaded the end of summer vacation.

Maggie savored the free fall into the lilting rhythm of a new school year: the boomeranging between teaching and planning meetings and back to teaching and then hurried bathroom breaks and then missing lunches and teaching and juggling parents. All these things compounded, until Maggie thought she would crumble—

But always she could return to the classroom.

Always Maggie could sit down with students, and time and time again witness the moment they solved an equation or fixed a sentence or finished a drawing and realized they were capable; they were trying; they were *people*.

They helped Maggie realize the same about herself.

Every year she stepped into a classroom of the unknown and by the end wore the unknown like a cloak of tiny handprints.

She'd often heard people ramble about how they loved their own children but couldn't love the children of strangers.

Maggie loved both, and she loved them painfully. And somehow, after all these years, the greatest strangers were still those three children who slept in her house and looked halfway like her.

Maggie waved at three former students and the principal, Peg Olsen, and prepared for the plunge—

Milo held her back.

"Milo, I have to go. You know where Mrs. Stuart's room is?"

His grip tightened. The buzz of his music dug into her torso.

Two boys passed and their eyes became planets. Maggie was fluent in the language of their expressions: *But he's not a BABY, so why is he hugging his MOM?*

I am not ashamed of my child. I am not.

Maggie ruffled Milo's hair, careful not to knock the headphones askew.

Over the course of seven years, Maggie had watched this creature stretch from a mute toddler to an unfathomable boy with distinct unease. Milo would be the last Vasquez to experience a "first time at the dentist," a "first Christmas," a "first day of preschool." But beyond all that, Milo was very . . . Milo.

Teaching aside, Maggie had never seen herself as motherly. In high school she was the type of girl who swore she'd never marry or "spawn children," who *knew* she would travel the world by train until she died in a country in Europe, in a room with golden wallpaper. By then she'd have a tattoo of Sylvia Plath or Ophelia on her calf. No men would have treated her how her father had treated her mother.

When life went another way and Maggie woke up in her late thirties to find herself living alone on the edge of a pit with three half-grown children, she felt even more removed from other mothers. Those other mothers, who scrapbooked lost baby teeth, who kept umbilical cords as mementos, who forgot who their children were becoming in order to pine after who they'd been.

That high school girl was trapped inside Maggie, begging for gilded walls, demanding the tattoo needle. Maggie didn't miss Donovan like she missed that girl.

Just as there were others inside Maggie, there were others inside Milo.

There was the Milo who taught himself to read and then chose to read only about suspension bridges for a year.

The Milo who learned baking techniques, then refused to bake. He'd whisk the air in empty mixing bowls, measure out ingredients only to pour them back into their bags.

The Milo who got in trouble with his kindergarten teacher, Mr. Howard, for drawing death in his notebook: kittens with x's for eyes, dogs with their tongues out.

That was simply who Milo was that week, Maggie had understood, or the girl inside her had.

Mr. Howard hadn't. He sat down with Maggie in the teachers' lounge, gave her a hot beverage and a look of *utmost concern*. He asked how Milo was faring without a dad.

"Mr. Howard. Have you considered that Milo just *likes* drawing dead things?"

Maggie refused to mourn a living man. From the very start, she'd refused.

But after a week had passed without sight or sound of Donovan's rattletrap on the blacktop, her children's questions began to occupy even the crevices between tiles and mortar in the Vasquez home, the spaces between one breath and another.

Maggie answered honestly: "He's gone back to his first family. When I met your dad, he already had a wife. They had kids, too, but after I finished school, he chose to live with us. It gave him nightmares."

Maggie had heard him whisper the names of a stranger's daughters in his sleep. He'd soaked the pillows with tears. The guilt Maggie felt on those nights grew bigger than all the rest of her. She wondered what those daughters looked like. Did they braid their hair, or leave it loose, or cut it short? Were they gentle, or did they bite like Ana? Were they passionate about cinematography?

Maggie had almost forgotten the stranger, reimagined her as a ghost. But the stranger's daughters were ghosts that haunted.

"Basketball starts again in a month."

"Don't worry about that. I'll get you to practice and back."

"That's not what Hank's saying." Ana's teeth, hiding tears. "He means, 'what about us?'"

"You've got me. And each other. It'll be enough."

"Will we get another turn with Dad?" Milo sounded so reasonable. "He promised to teach me to bike ride. When I'm seven. Big enough for Hank's bike."

"What, you think he'll come back when he starts having nightmares about us?"

"*Ana.*" Maggie had almost laughed. "No. Not if I have anything to say about it."

Hank vanished to the Moreno courts, duffel bag in tow. Ana buried herself in trading cards. Milo ignored Maggie's embrace, counting the distance from four to seven on his fingertips.

"Milo, look—there's Antonio!" Maggie pried herself free.

Milo muttered to himself, "I know, I *know*. Grow up, Milo. *Be normal.*" He did an about-face and disappeared in the crowd. Maggie cringed.

New arms appeared around her waist—a former student, a bear hug, a cry. "Ms. Vasquez! I missed you!"

"Thank you, Lillian." Maggie held her hands up. Lillian knew when to let go.

Maggie wished Milo knew. She wished she did.

Buck up, Maggie. She adjusted her collar. *Be normal.*

For the first two hours, she was. Her class played icebreaker games to learn names and decorated name tags for their desks, just to be sure. They learned the morning routine—announcements, followed by the pledge, followed by warm-up writing. Malachai cried because he couldn't remember how to tie his shoes, and Maggie bit her lip to keep from laughing when Amelia braided them for him instead. She dropped her students off at music class, watching them squeal at the sight of the woodblocks on the floor.

She forgot to check on Milo. It wasn't intentional. It was the cost of normalcy.

8
EARS

Milo had only one ultimate goal for his first day of second grade. Ready for it?

He just wanted to keep his headphones on!

And okay. There were other things he wanted, too. Like he thought it would be neat if Mom could sit in class with him, just for a few minutes, but he didn't want to have to *ask* her to.

Or it would be *really* neat if he could be last in line before recess so he could hang back and look for any new ant lion pits, baby craters in the sand. He sometimes found them along the sidewalk leading to the cafeteria.

Or maybe Dad would appear after all this time and take him home after school. Maybe it was finally the Vasquez family's turn!

But those were definitely less ultimate, as goals went. Milo wasn't greedy.

He wanted to get through the rest of Radiohead's discography before afternoon snack. And maybe, if the world was kind, that snack would include the animal crackers dipped in bright pink-and-white frosting instead of the sad, naked kind.

It turned out Mrs. Stuart had only one ultimate goal for the day, too.

She wanted Milo to take his headphones *off*!

It was becoming a real stalemate.

Hank's old boyfriend, Brendan, had taught Milo how to play chess last year. Well, Brendan wasn't *old* like *wise-Cheeto-pigeon* old, but Milo called him that because Brendan wasn't *new*, and also, he wasn't Hank's boyfriend anymore. But Milo couldn't even remember what the horses were called. More important, Milo had never survived a stalemate. Not one time!

Mrs. Stuart did not need to know that.

When Milo slipped into her colorful classroom, dragging feet like an old man might (he was working on it!), she met him by the locker cubbies.

Milo watched Mrs. Stuart's lips move.

Lately Milo had been having fun looking for patterns in all the shapes lips made. It wasn't easy. Lips did not hold any position long enough for *real* shapes to exist. Good luck finding any triangles or perfect circles!

The only shape lips held for long was the wrinkly oval of the "ah" shape. Sometimes when people dozed off, their mouths sort of hung open in that position.

Milo had deduced that "ah" was the only real thing anyone ever said.

Like "Ah! You're the one I heard about!"

Or "Ah . . . I'm sorry you have no dad!"

Or the "Ahhhhh!" sound Milo made whenever someone unplugged his earholes.

Now Mrs. Stuart frowned at him. She reached for his headphones.

"Wait, please!" Milo tried to say, over the chiming chorus of "No Surprises."

He must have been plenty loud. Jamir Gracia and Penny Dawson dropped their book bags and put their hands over their ears.

Oops!

Milo held up a forefinger. He had a spell for times like this. He pulled a note from his bag. Dr. Ruby's handwriting was very neat and blocky. Mrs. Stuart read the note. Milo wondered what her face was doing.

Finally Mrs. Stuart led Milo to his seat. She sat him down across from a boy with a bleached Mohawk. Milo thought it made him the coolest chicken ever, and said so: "You look like the coolest chicken ever, Antonio!"

Antonio definitely heard him. But he didn't look at Milo. Antonio just ducked behind his laptop and stayed focused on cool math games.

Milo pushed up imaginary glasses. He coughed an old man's cough before nestling his head in his arms. Just for a second.

It wasn't a second at all. Milo lifted his head.

He wiped drool from the corner of his mouth. Thom Yorke and a whole jazz band were telling Milo that everything was *so near*. Nowhere near Milo. That was for sure.

Milo was totally alone.

He didn't have to be a magician to see that. The classroom lights were switched off. Daylight from half-shuttered blinds gave the desks tiger stripes.

What if this time Milo took off his headphones and the Roaring Nothing was finally gone?

Then he might hear all the things he'd heard last year. He might hear kids laughing on the playground. Or basketballs on pavement (that reminded him of Hank!). He might hear kids just screaming for no reason, in that nice, recess-y kind of way. Not screaming because they were so scared they wanted to vanish forever.

Milo didn't take off his headphones.

On his desk, Milo discovered a pencil, a blank piece of wide-ruled paper, and an apple-shaped sticky note. Teachers were so crazy about apples!

This apple had writing on it.

Milo was a pretty great reader. The school always told kids what their Lexile scores were, from kindergarten on up. They made you write it inside your journal. Milo's Lexiles were high for his age, so he could read Mrs. Stuart's words on the apple sticky note *so* easily.

If you want to join your friends at recess, write two sentences about what you did this summer.

Milo blinked at the empty spaces around him. The other desks had pieces of paper on them, too, but those had already been written on. Some were smeared with eraser dust and everything. A couple even had pictures.

Milo fumbled for his music player. He was listening to "Treefingers." That meant he'd napped through half an album!

That didn't seem like being a good student. Mom might be very disappointed.

Be normal, Milo!

This summer I . . .

This summer I felt happy because Dad came home only he was'ent the same so Hank and Ana called him Luz instead. Our dad came home with no BODY so I gave him my ear's but now he is gone again and I miss him. The End.

Apostrophes always reminded Milo of stickers. They were decorations you could put wherever they looked fanciest.

Milo paused. He knew there were a million things he wanted to say but didn't know how to write yet. Like how it felt like something green and red and every color blooming inside your chest to hear your dad's voice for the first time in years, or how cold it felt after that voice was gone again. Then it was like someone had run a Hoover along the insides of your ribs, the bumpiest Hoover trip ever, and that Hoover sucked every color away and left trails of dirty hair behind instead . . .

Milo's drool had smeared his pencil marks. He had a gray goatee now.

The classroom refilled with other kids. Milo had missed recess.

That was okay. It was! Recess wasn't the kind of thing wise old men enjoyed, probably not. They might fall and break all their hips *at once.*

Antonio didn't look at Milo.

Penny Dawson raised her hand. She pointed at Milo.

Mrs. Stuart fish-mouthed at him for a little bit. After a few seconds, Milo stopped watching for fun and decided to try to detect what she was saying:

TOO NOISY. She gestured at his headphones.

Milo gave her a huge thumbs-up and a grandfatherly wink. The headphones were *supposed* to be too noisy!

Penny tossed her dark braids over her shoulder and pointed at the bluest of beanbags in the room. She signed something at him.

Everyone knew Penny Dawson could do sign language. Her dad was a sign language teacher! Milo thought talking with your hands was pretty awesome. Maybe Milo could learn that, too. Then Hank wouldn't even have to listen to him, he could just look at him. Milo wished Hank could just look at Milo again without feeling sad.

Kids started sprawling all around the room, books in their laps or resting on their chests. The way they scattered reminded Milo of the lights at the bottom of the canyon on the day Dad came home, all those glowing blobs made of something that was maybe what metal might look like if metal was made of water.

Penny waggled fingers in Milo's line of vision. She shoved a chapter book into his hands. She commanded him with her eyebrows: *Get your butt moving.*

Milo wondered if Mrs. Stuart had assigned Penny as his helper for the day.

Penny took Milo's hand, leading him straight to the bluest of beanbags. She plopped him on top of it. It swallowed Milo like quicksand. Penny sat crisscross applesauce on the carpet. She opened her book and started reading. Maybe she wasn't as high a reader as Milo. She moved her mouth along to the words.

Milo copycatted her. Maybe his Lexile score would drop if he couldn't hear well. This Goosebumps book wasn't making sense to him, and he was only on the title page. And it wasn't because he didn't believe in talking dummies. Dad had appeared like magic this summer. Milo believed in all kinds of stuff.

Soon his classmates, even Penny, moved back to their desks. Milo was forgotten. He watched them push around pink and red plastic chips. Mrs. Stuart wrote FAIR SHARING and Addition! on the board.

Milo had a thought, while lyrics about spinning plates spun in his ears.

Maybe Milo was the fish in the fish tank! Maybe he was watching everyone through glass.

The thought made him unhappy, which was no fun. So Milo inflated his cheeks like a puffer fish. He stood up from his bean-bag and crept close to the nearest table.

Antonio was there. So was this other boy, Jotzqan. Jotzqan had hands like hamburgers (hand-burgers!) and a frown like the devil's butt crack. Hank had helped Milo come up with those insults last year, after Jotzqan smacked Milo by the slide and called him the r-word.

The boys heard Milo coming because his headphones were TOO NOISY.

That was okay. Milo was definitely going to make them laugh! He wedged himself between the boys, closed his eyes, and raised his hands to his puffed cheeks, popping the air from them with a synchronized smack.

Suddenly, Milo felt tugging not just on the sides of his head but also on the back pocket that held his music player.

In just two seconds, Milo's anchor was pulled from him!

Before the Roaring Nothing could get too loud, Milo's eyes

traced the line of the headphone cable to the hands that held it. They weren't hamburger hands. They were small tan hands, turning white at the knuckles.

The music player dangled from Antonio's fists like a worm on a fishhook.

Scuttling sounds flooded the holes in Milo's head. The Roaring Nothing was here! But maybe there was time to stop it—!

Milo reached for the headphones—Penny stood up and from somewhere Mrs. Stuart came, stomp stomping this way—

Antonio bent the headphones backward until the bar between the ear cups snapped.

The whole classroom shook with a horrible screeching sound. Milo wondered if maybe someone was pulling the lungs out of a baby.

"Pulling the lungs out of a baby" was the sort of thought Mr. Howard would call "morbid." Last year, Milo was called morbid in school a lot. He'd learned that word pretty fast.

But this *sound*—*everyone* had to admit it was an awful racket. All the kids started hollering and covering their ears.

Everyone turned to look at Milo.

Ah! he realized. *It's me.*

9

HANDS

In a perfect world, Hank would never run into Brendan Nesbitt at school.

Brendan belonged to a different lunch hour. Brendan took electives Hank would never sign up for. Advanced Art & Design, Advanced Drama. He and Brendan shouldn't even pass in the hallways. Hank had been up nights last week rearranging his courses. He'd annoyed Mom to bits, having her call the office to make amendment after amendment to his schedule.

Until halfway through the first day, Hank's frustrating work paid off.

More or less.

Less, maybe. The disastrous morning meeting with Coach Huang had bounced Hank's world slightly off its meticulous axis. His cheeks felt strained from smiling even before Pre-Calc ended.

He might have to rearrange his schedule yet again for the sake of Tim Miller, because smiling became harder after Tim shoved him into a wall between classes. Though Hank had scrubbed his neck raw, he still felt flakes of Tim's spit cracking there.

With every jovial greeting Hank hollered at former team-mates (who mostly responded with cautious nods) and the sports girls (who responded with surprised waves), Hank noticed how his hands retreated from the rest of him, giving him away—they kept sliding into his pockets.

"Tank!" Orson Liu, the gangly, motormouthed kid who played small forward, stood up from the drinking fountain, wiped his mouth on his sleeve, and chased Hank down. "How the hell was your summer?"

Hank almost lost the grin. Was Orson freaking kidding?

Wait. No. He wasn't. Orson had been visiting family in Tai-pei since June. Which meant Orson was maybe the only person in town who hadn't witnessed Hank's monumental plummet from grace at tryouts. Maybe he also hadn't heard the rumors about plagues or termites.

Orson wouldn't know to spit on Hank.

"You've gotta hear about mine, at least!" Orson punched Hank twice on the shoulder. "Tell you what, I played so much ball. Shit is pretty popular there, you know? And I don't know how it happened, but I'm a fan of Pocari Sweat now. You know, that oily Japanese sports drink? Farewell, Gatorade! It's all so clear to me now. Because Pocari is clear as water? You ever tried it, Tank? It's not so bad, if you don't mind the texture and awful fucking taste. And hey. Come on. Why you leaving me hanging?"

Hank stared at Orson's upraised hand. Orson's calluses were in all the places a basketball would rub, and in none of the places a paintbrush would.

Orson lowered his arm. "Is it because I'm Korean?"

Hank started, rebooted himself. "You're Taiwanese, you *hilarious* asshole. It's just my hands—my hands are a freaking *mess*."

"How do you mean?"

"Just . . . because . . ."

"Wait. Hold up. Hank. *Hank*. You *so* do not have to tell me what filthy gunk's on your hand." A merry elbow hit Hank's ribs. "Who knows what you get up to with your gross-ass boyfriend, hey?"

"He's not—we're not a thing anymore, man."

"What, *you broke up with Nesbitt?*" Moths could have flown into Orson's mouth.

Hank nodded. "Months ago, I guess."

"That artsy fuck *dumped you?*"

"It wasn't like that."

"Shit. Sorry, man, I had no idea. I just got back literally yesterday and I've had exactly one conversation since, and that involved me getting my ass handed to me by my grandma, who can't believe I didn't get a job while I was gone. I'm operating on pure Pocari Sweat and maybe two hours of actual sleep and the usual lack of brain cells, so . . . sorry." Orson punched him more gently this time. "Honestly, you're *still* sort of smiling at me . . . but. I mean. You *seemed* really into him. You good?"

"Yeah, I'm good. Really."

"Oh, hey! There's Tim! HEY, KILLER!"

Orson's hands worked like hands should. They gave Hank's shoulder an encouraging crush.

Seconds later Orson accosted Tim by the bulletin board. Just watching Orson go was exhausting, like maybe *Hank* was the one with jet lag.

This was nothing new. Orson's dizzying energy was an effective weapon in games, had a useful knack for throwing opponents off guard. Hard as it was to keep up with him, both on the court and off, Hank had always appreciated that Orson was the sort of person who kept up with everyone else.

Yes, Orson talked a lot of bullshit.

But he was also always the first person to ask how you were.

In this school of people who wouldn't meet his eyes, Hank hoped that even once Orson *did* hear about tryouts, he might offer his high five all the same.

Hank didn't deserve it. But he couldn't help but hope for it.

Across the hall, Tim Miller shifted his attention from Orson to the oldest Vasquez, countering Hank's bright smile with that dead-eyed stare. He didn't crack his knuckles or draw a finger across his throat.

He didn't need to.

Hank's hopes became as perforated as his palms.

Fourth hour arrived. Mrs. Moore, in all her nerdy Scottish glory, enunciated individual syllables on the syllabus. She'd written the entire thing in Middle English and their first assignment would be translating it.

"You'll all cheat on the blasted Internet so I don't feel remotely guilty about this decision, you know," she added, when a unified groan filled the windowless room.

Hank raised a fist.

"Gea, cnihtcild?" She pushed purple glasses up her round nose.

Hank unclenched his fingers. "I'd like to use a bathroom pass." He didn't say: *I'm pretty sure my hands are about to fall off or already have, so can I go check on that?*

"On the very first day? Really!"

Behind Hank, Carmella Spalding's green eyes were drilling a hole into his nape, bull's-eyeing Tim's spit target. She was probably livid about nearly being turned into premium roadkill earlier. But what could Hank even say?

Sorry! The alien parasite that moved in over the summer infected my hands, and now I don't know who they belong to.

He tilted his head slowly. Shining waves of Carmella's hair dominated his peripheries. Hank's fingers twitched. Even if they still belonged to him, he wouldn't have dared to tuck her hair behind her ear like he used to.

Carmella had many reasons to be livid with Hank Vasquez.

Hank tore a bathroom pass from his planner, gave Mrs. Moore an apologetic smile. Even once the door closed behind him he could feel Carmella's glare.

Hank breathed deep and pressed his fingernails into his palms, waiting for the pinch. It wasn't enough.

He passed the last row of lockers in the English wing, picked up his pace on the green tiles. By the time he reached the main hallway, Hank was almost sprinting. He veered right, whipping his hands limply on his wrists in an effort to solidify them—

There stood Brendan Nesbitt.

Under other circumstances, maybe in the context of a

romantic high school comedy, this would be the part where one of the two of them cutely dropped something.

Hank only dropped his hands.

"Hello," said Brendan. "Um, hi. Hey."

Brendan was helping a girl dressed in horizontal stripes pin a banner to the wall. The girl's name was Arlene, but these days she went by Platinum, maybe because that was the color she'd dyed her hair. The poster depicted a grinning potted Venus flytrap and read, in stenciled letters: Feed Me! Musical Tryouts Are Looming! Sign Up Now!

The last time Brendan and Hank had been this close was the night Milo went missing. At 1:53 a.m. on June 7, they'd been joined at the hands.

The distance between them in this moment, here in the school hallway, was the same. It was also so much greater.

"Hank Vasquez." Platinum tore duct tape from the roll wedged under her arm. "Do us a solid and hold the top. Bren can't reach."

"Yeah, sure! Okay!" Hank stepped forward, careful not to brush hands or anything else against Brendan's familiar angular shoulders—those damn shoulder blades, the way they jutted like daggers or the beautiful broken beginnings of wings—and gently pressed the upper right corner to the cinder blocks, because these vanishing fingers might destroy paper again today, or because Hank was so big that he crushed a lot of things, things not so different from Brendan Nesbitt . . .

"You'll have to reach over him."

Hank followed orders. Brendan stayed low. Neither looked at the other. It was quiet enough to hear Brendan's breath catch and feel the soft heat of him so near—

Zzzt. Zzzt.

Platinum tore another two strips free. She handed them to Hank. He did what was expected, thinking of Ana.

"You guys can let go now."

Can we? Hank wondered, stepping back. Brendan's shoulders twitched.

When Hank and Brendan had started dating, Brendan had existed just out of reach at all times. Light-footed and anxious, forever on the edge of taking flight. But in those moments when Brendan settled near, perched within reach . . .

The night of junior homecoming, Hank had arrived at Brendan's house in a basic suit and tie, but Brendan emerged wearing short black boots, high-waisted pants, and this sort of floaty off-white peasant shirt that Hank found indescribable, except that he could say from now until eternity how good it had looked, how it showed off Brendan's long collarbones.

"I can't help it, Hank. I'm an art student. We all wish we were vampires."

Hank longed to touch him, immortal or not.

What a wonder that Brendan had let him.

Over the course of the night, Brendan took endless photos of friends and others in dresses and suits, of confetti freckling plastic-covered tables, of the Christmas lights student council had hung all over the country club in keeping with the "Starry Sky" theme. At one point, he passed his precious camera to Platinum and she took a photo of the pair of them in a candid moment. He and Hank weren't embracing, weren't dancing.

In the photograph, two very different boys were looking off

in two very different directions. You'd think they were strangers, except their fingers were interlaced.

The following morning, cozy on the foldout bed in Platinum's basement, Brendan rolled out of Hank's arms early and began going over every photograph. Hank tried to pull him close again, but Brendan protested, claiming he wanted to teach Hank all about framing shots, about what made great photos great.

They compromised; Brendan leaned back against Hank's stomach and flipped through the pictures, told him how to make the night more beautiful. He fought back Hank's kisses, told him about saturation. Brendan told Hank that sometimes colors could be made to look so vivid and *true* that they bled out of their outlines, became something amorphous and greater.

Hank suggested that they themselves were oversaturated, that they bled right into each other, and that was why Brendan couldn't expect Hank to keep his hands to himself.

"Thanks for your help, Hank."

Platinum put herself between them.

"Yeah, sure thing! I'll see you guys around!" Hank smiled and turned to go—

A vise closed around Hank's fish-limp left hand, tried to bleed into it.

"*Hank*," whispered Brendan, undeniably near. "I'm *sorry*."

Hank looked at him. Brendan's pants were a deep green and his shirt a dark purple, his shoes a tasteful deep mahogany.

How had Brendan Nesbitt faded?

His hair seemed lank, overlong and floppy, as dusty gray as the blacktop they'd scuffed shoes against in their search for Milo.

His fingers felt as cracked and craggy as the canyon they'd clambered into together on June 7.

His voice sounded as hollow as Hank had felt when Brendan caught sight of the bizarre cosmic lights dotting the bottom of the slope, as hollow as Hank had felt when Brendan stopped dead and told Hank, "I think we should go back. Whatever that is, it doesn't look safe. We should go back. *Hank.*"

Finally, Brendan's eyes. They were as dark as the sky became in the depths of that pit once they'd separated. Hank heading into the hole, shouting Milo's name, and Brendan clambering back the way they'd come, shouting nothing at all.

In the hallway, Hank pulled himself violently free of Brendan Nesbitt. At last he was not smiling.

10

OUTSIDE

When Milo screamed for Maggie to stop the car, she acciden-
tally slammed her foot down on the accelerator.

The van jerked forward before she could pull her toes away.
They veered closer to the single guardrail separating them from
a two-hundred-foot plummet. Maggie had removed her heels
to drive, and her nylons were slippery, and the pedals were only
inches apart. Were those the only reasons she'd accelerated?

Milo had been screaming for an eternity, though the initial
glass-piercing shriek heard through her classroom wall had
devolved into wet wails by the time she dragged him out of
Peg's office. After Maggie had buckled Milo in, those wails had
diminished to a series of tearing gasps that made her throat
ache.

Driving was usually good therapy. The first time Maggie had
walked in on Hank making out with a boy in the living room,
she'd claimed she needed groceries and greeted them four hours

later with only a package of celebratory Oreos and two boxes of condoms to show for it. They'd all felt better.

And Peg had been so painfully reasonable. She'd called a sub for the final hour. It had taken everything not to ask if the sub could take Milo home instead, if someone else could listen to him scream this time, someone qualified for motherhood. Maybe someone who kept baby teeth?

Maggie had failed at normal. She felt as broken as the belting boy behind her: "STOP THE CAR WAIT GO BACK STOP THE CAR PLEASE GO BACK!"

Do you think other mothers ever hate their children?

"GO BACK GO BACK NOW!"

Do I? Could I ever?

Maggie pressed the brake to the floor. The nose of the minivan screeched past the faded stop-sign line. The smell of burning rubber rose with the heat, drifted through the open window.

"GO BACK I SAW! I SAW! SO GO BACK—"

Maggie signaled left but couldn't bring herself to face the road that would lead them all the way around the canyon to the cul-de-sac. If she could only lift her head, she would see their house directly across the canyon.

"LET ME OUT MOM GO BACK I SAW SOMETHING! I SAW—"

"Milo, *please*."

Milo kicked the back of her seat, whining high in his throat. That wasn't about reverting to being a toddler. It was about drowning out a so-called Roaring Nothing. Maggie *wished* she could hear nothing, or that she could be back in her classroom with productive noise.

"Milo, please, just let us get home and get your spare headphones—!"

She turned around. He'd undone his seat belt. By the time she undid hers, he'd pulled open the door. The child-safety locks had never worked in this secondhand former 4-H beater, so Maggie shouldn't have been shocked.

He'd run away over the summer, so she shouldn't have been shocked.

Milo was already running and Maggie didn't put her shoes on and soon gravel was snagging at her exposed nylons, slicing minute stinging tears in her feet as she chased her son along the shoulder, back the way they'd come.

Milo was usually apathetic during physical activities, this tumbleweed of a child, the opposite of his big brother. This sudden burst of speed was a misfiring of one of *his* pedals.

"MILO! NOT AGAIN!"

Maggie sprinted for all she was worth. She'd been an athlete once like Hank, loved wind on her face when it wasn't hot desert air. She lunged, ready to keep lunging, because even if this was no-man's-land, eventually a car *would* come along—

But Milo had turned to stone. The mile marker had seemed small from the car, but not with Milo standing beside it. She watched him bend over a lump of fur and bones, a sack of animal that had once been a raccoon or an opossum—

"Don't touch that!" Maggie took his wrists before his fingers could find the skeleton, lifted them up past his ears. "Please, just stop!"

Milo went boneless. "IT'S REALLY DEAD THIS TIME ISN'T IT MOM?"

She glanced at its hollow eye sockets. "Yes, definitely."

"Oh."

"I'm . . . I'm sorry, Milo."

She expected him to scream again. Instead Milo moved her hands to his ears and held them against his head. His whine became a hum, and suddenly Maggie could hear the whistle of wind blowing up from the canyon floor, the rustle of sage leaves.

Maggie left her hands on Milo's auricles. This was how they hugged now. She was not ashamed of him.

She kept her hands in place and walked behind him all the way back to the car. Milo trembled. She hushed him, fastened his seat belt, and slid the door closed.

Maggie remained outside, listening to the vague drone of traffic along the main road. There was no such thing as silence.

Today at lunch, Samantha Stuart had confronted her. "The noise is deafening, and he isn't learning. He's impeding the learning of other students."

"I became a teacher in public schools," Maggie replied, aware that two people by the microwave were listening in, "because every child is welcome here."

"I've been teaching for decades. Of *course* I feel the same way. But if Milo *needs* accommodations, we should draw up an IEP. Put a formal action plan in place—"

"Or you could let him wear the damn headphones."

"*Margaret.* It's so loud it's giving *me* a headache."

The two people by the microwave ducked out of the room.

"Try living with it for a month. And *then* tell me about your headache."

Samantha dropped her spoon into her Tupperware. "That's your job, not mine."

In the desert, Maggie strode forward until she was level with the stop sign. She raised her hand, placed it over her eyes, and let it take the heat for her. She stared out across Nameless Canyon.

Bridges were one of Milo's earliest fascinations. His whole life his bedroom window had overlooked a drop, but there were no bridges across Nameless Canyon.

If she'd kept accelerating, they'd have broken through the railing and become skyborne in cloudless blue. And then they'd have been the opposite of skyborne.

Maggie wasn't ashamed of Milo. No, not of him.

She got into the van. She twisted the dial on the radio until the music was drum-shattering, stabbing the sides of her head.

In the rearview, Milo took his hands from his ears.

"ANTONIO DOESN'T LIKE ME ANYMORE."

"But I do, you know." He probably couldn't hear her.

11

EYES

The final bell rang.

Ana remained seated at a grainy laboratory table. Soon she was alone, apart from a bottled fawn fetus, a plastic cage of patchwork mice, and the persistent reek of ancient formaldehyde. She raised her fingers to her nose and smelled sodium under her nails.

"Still here, Ana?"

Had Ana been invested in the present, she might have jumped.

Ms. Yu, small as her voice was high, was hidden from view by her laptop and an enormous pile of biology textbooks. When she stood, her computer rattled forward on the counter and wrenched her head down; she'd forgotten about her earbuds. By the time Ana reached her, Ms. Yu hadn't managed to untangle herself from the cord.

Milo, Ana thought.

"Don't leave on my account!"

Ana readjusted her backpack.

"Frazzled" was the right word. More than once while Ms. Yu was going over the syllabus, she'd tucked a pen into her hair, forgotten about it, and grabbed another from a beaker on her desk. After a full day of teaching, Ms. Yu's black-and-silver curls were crowned by a fan of red and blue and black Bics, an Expo marker or four.

"I'm staying after to feed the beasts. You're welcome to help! When the mice don't get their grains, they start eating each other alive. I'm not joking."

Ana watched her skitter to the storage closet. The socks peeking over Ms. Yu's clogs didn't match: one was navy, the other polka-dotted green.

Ms. Yu jangled a ring of keys, trying several in the lock. At last she cried "Eureka!" and clomped inside. Ana traipsed in after her, took in the sour smell, the sight of empty fish tanks and microscopes and scales. Another pantry.

Ms. Yu kneeled beside tubs of feed pellets. Ana bent down to help, and together they wrested one into the open.

"Many thanks, Ana. Fighting cannibalism is a noble cause."

Ana stared at the ceiling. The door had closed behind them. It wouldn't take much for that single lightbulb to die. She pressed fingers into the space just beneath her sunglasses lenses and pulled them free. In here they made it too close to darkness.

"You know, Tom—sorry, Mr. Chilton? He showed me the diorama you designed for the astronomy unit. You must've spent hours on all those details. Didn't you invent *seasons* for your planets, based on their proximity to the two stars in your solar system?"

Ana shrugged.

"What a great example for the other kids!" Ms. Yu tore off the plastic lid, hoisted a scoop of pellets out. "You're interested in science, huh?"

"I'm not interested in anything."

"*Bullshit*." Ms. Yu clapped a hand over her mouth, forgetting the pellets stuck to her palm. She spat one off her lip. "Pardon my French. Wanna tackle the hamsters?"

Ms. Yu proffered a measuring cup.

"I can't. My brother is waiting for me."

"Oh." Ms. Yu's shoulders fell. "Okay. But I mean what I said. Stay anytime! And I'll see you in class on Wednesday!"

It wasn't until she was back at her locker that Ana realized: Ms. Yu had *met her eyes*. Maybe science teachers were less afraid to look at stars.

Maybe there were people who hadn't yet circled the Vasquez name in red pen.

Three years ago, Ana would have stayed after school for swim class. Two years ago, it would have been student council. Last year, volleyball.

This year there was nothing to hold her there.

After leaving Ms. Yu, Ana curled up in a cubby parallel to the gymnasium. The golden light of the court through open doors struck the trophy cases, illuminating the darkening hall as the sky purpled beyond the window above her.

The brow scab throbbed. Maybe Ana could pin her eyelids to her sunglasses with a binder clip and nap until Hank appeared. She might be lulled by the song of squeaking sneakers on wood, the warmth of the bodies in motion in the bright gym, the steady, icy breeze from the vent beneath her—

A shadow blocked her light.

Ana's eyes scraped fully open.

Between Ana and her light stood a thin boy with a long neck. Even if she'd been wearing neon spandex and doing cartwheels rather than tucked away in her cubby, she didn't think he would have noticed her. He kept the entire hallway between himself and the gym doors, but was obviously transfixed, leaning forward on subliminal tiptoe, trading his weight from foot to foot in quick succession. He seemed almost to vibrate.

"Hank's not in there."

Brendan snapped his body her way. "Ana. Hi. I wasn't . . ."

"You *were*. But he's not in there."

Brendan sank. "I heard varsity practice started tonight. On the announcements?"

Ana shrugged. She inched out of his shadow.

"Why? Stalking my brother?"

Brendan frowned. His face was just as sharp as the rest of him, and every expression exaggerated that sharpness. Her brother's ex-boyfriend betrayed more emotion in one dimple than Ana currently had in all of her.

Brendan Nesbitt, blocking her light.

"You should move," Ana told him.

"I only want to talk to him. And I do have a legitimate reason for being here. Musical tryouts start next week. I stayed after to practice in the choir room."

Blink: Brendan, deleted from existence.

After the blink Brendan existed again, gaze helplessly drawn to the gymnasium doors, fingers fiddling with his belt loops. Ana wondered how he ever found clothes that fit him. Those shoulder blades must wear holes in his cardigans.

"But why are *you* still here? Taking a renewed interest in cheerleading?"

"I've never tried cheerleading," Ana mused.

"Don't all popular girls go through the 'I'm gonna be a cheerleader' stage?"

"Like all gay boys go through the 'theatah' stage?"

"Yes, *exactly* like that." Brendan smirked. "I mentioned I'm here for the musical?"

Ana's lips twitched. She tried to recall why lips did that. "There's light here. I'm sitting here because there's light in this hallway."

"Huh. Glaring and fluorescent. But I suppose."

Ana cleared her throat. "Also. Hank told me to wait by the gym after school."

"School ended an hour ago. Do you think he forgot you?"

Ana shrugged.

"He can't simply keep forgetting people." Brendan squeezed his knees.

"He can," Ana murmured. "*I* can't."

". . . how is everyone?" Brendan asked, and though maybe he was really saying . . . *Hank Hank Hank?* Ana knew he cared. In every single interaction she could remember having with him, Brendan Nesbitt cared.

Ana had watched Brendan climb alone out of the canyon on June 7.

She'd been helping her mother clean up the wreckage. The flipped card table, the overturned birthday cake in the yard, runaway paper plates lifted by desert wind. Mom had climbed into her car to drive circles around the canyon—

"Shouldn't we call the police?"

"Men will make it worse." Mom shook her head. "Stay here!"

The van peeled away. "There are police*women*, too," Ana muttered.

In a matter of seconds she pivoted at the sound of shoes scraping gravel and there was Brendan, flying over the fence, soaring out of Nameless Canyon.

"Brendan—what—where's Hank?"

Ana had never seen the bird-boy so restless. "I left him. I just—there were these *lights* down there, and I—Christ, I was honestly *scared*—"

"What the hell is there to be scared of? There's nothing down there but dirt!"

Ana had little reason to be so angry—Brendan Nesbitt wasn't *her* boyfriend. Anyhow, she didn't expect outsiders to plunge into holes for the sake of Vasquezes.

Ana threw her long hair into a ponytail. Before she could get her second leg over the fence, Brendan intervened.

"Let go."

"Ana—you can't—there's, there's *something*—"

She slipped loose and slid down the slope. "My brothers are idiots, but you don't have to love them. I do."

"Ana! Be careful! *Please!*"

Minutes later, halfway down the incline, she collided with them: her idiot brothers stumbling skyward with their ears and fingers aglow, insects of light springing from them. When that glow struck Ana's eyes, she raised a hand to shield herself, but Luz had already seeped in.

And then Ana saw—oh god, the things she *saw*—

"Hank did that today, too." Beside her, Brendan furrowed his brow.

"Hank did what?"

"He just . . . *went away*. Earlier today? Arlene and I were hanging a poster, and Hank vanished right in front of me. Into his own head, like you just did. Your family is *never* loquacious, but is this an all-new Vasquez special feature? If I talk to Milo, will he vanish, too?"

Ana scoffed. "Milo has *always* done that."

"Well, I suppose you would know."

The window had blackened above them. Only five p.m., but the sky didn't care. Ana tried not to, either, but the streetlights hadn't switched on. All along the main hallway, the overheads were being killed by a jangling janitor. The players in the gym quieted. Probably they were huddling up, preparing to leave.

Soon all the lights would go.

Ana pressed a hand against her forehead, yanking what few hairs remained to her eyebrows taut. The scab itched. *Luz, no, please show me something beautiful, please . . .*

"Hey, Ana?" Ana could count the faint freckles on Brendan's cheekbones. "I don't know anything about . . . about what happened. But you've always been so *blunt*. It used to scare me, you know."

Had Ana ever been the person he described? "Seems like lots of things scare you, Brendan."

"Yes. Would you scare me now, please?" Brendan shuddered. "Would you tell me what really happened after I . . . I left you all? This summer?"

Ana lowered her sunglasses. Brendan's dark gaze wavered before the constellations, fell for an instant before rising again.

"Also. Unrelated, but I want to tell you something else."

Ana stared. The first column of lights went out in the gymnasium.

"I like your Band-Aid. Belle was always my favorite princess. Also, why do you smell like cinnamon?"

Ana breathed his air. "Brendan. Are there lights in the choir room?"

"The usual horrible kind." The second column went.

"Take me there?"

"You don't think Hank . . ."

"He's not coming for either of us."

"Blunt, like I said." Brendan fluttered to his feet and looped his arm through hers. Darkness deepened in their wake.

"Everything this creature did—all the shining memories it showed you?" Dr. Ruby had reiterated, once and again, in the clinic she'd built in the Vasquez garage. "Ana, these were lies, an attempt to make you a more welcoming host. With your personal history of self-harm, it was nothing short of emotional abuse."

"Luz didn't lie. He just replayed memories for me. They were already mine."

"That's how insidious it was. This *entity* used your own thoughts to manipulate you. If you closed your eyes and Luz showed you, for example, a happy recollection of a day at the zoo, the intention wasn't to warm your heart." She held Ana's hand. "This parasite was creating emotional dependency."

It was probably true. But that didn't make the memories Luz had paraded before Ana over the course of the summer any less golden. The way Luz told it, on the backs of Ana's eyelids: Brendan Nesbitt was always alight.

How this boy glowed while joining Milo for imaginary dinner. How he shone when he gifted Ana's mother with a photo collage of her children on Mother's Day. Brendan Nesbitt became blinding in those moments when he helped Ana with her homework or laughed at her sarcastic quips.

Brendan Nesbitt, as relayed by Luz, became something just shy of a supernova whenever Hank held his hand.

Luz hadn't invented these things. They'd always been there. Ana just hadn't known how to see them.

Without Luz, Ana wouldn't have known light now, in this school hallway, while it stared her in the face. She wouldn't have recognized light when it complimented her Band-Aid.

12

HANDS

Hank had to practice. He did not *have* practice, but he *had* to.

He planned to drive straight to Moreno Park after school. Seven minutes before his classmates burst from their cages, Hank got his head start. It came at the cost of another bathroom pass, but who cared? Hank was having a decidedly shitty day. Basketball was the one thing that could salvage it.

By the mirror above a graffitied bathroom sink, Hank splashed water over his face and tried on his smile.

What the hell? Had it looked this crooked all day? *Man.*

He readjusted his face and stepped into the hallway with three minutes to spare. Probably he'd get in trouble for skipping, but this was only for today. Hank just had to find his bearings, just had to make some baskets and practice smiling more and by Wednesday he'd be an all-star student like he used to be, just wait—

Hank almost ran over Carmella again, carless though he was. She stood between the restrooms, using a single finger to scroll through her phone.

A stranger might have thought her presence had nothing to do with Hank. Carmella looked as if she'd just chosen to drift there, in that regal way of hers. That same regality made necks crick in the turning as she passed, made people deliver anything she asked for directly into her manicured hands.

"Hey, Carmella."

Unrelenting eyes scored him from head to toe.

Once, Hank had tried complimenting Carmella by calling her eyes glacial. Hank was never good at finding nice things to say about girls, but he knew glaciers were beautiful. Glaciers were beautiful, but Hank wasn't in love with them, either.

"How was your summer, Carmella?"

"Dull by comparison, I'm pretty sure."

She stared at his hands. Hank hid them in his pockets.

"Sorry again, about this morning. I just zoned out."

Carmella raised her eyebrows. "You're a total mess, aren't you, Hank?"

Hank chortled. "You followed me out here just to tell me that?"

Carmella cocked her chin. "I'm not the only one thinking it. You're not pulling off whatever you're trying to pull off here."

"Well, thanks? See you tomorrow!" Hank smiled and started walking.

Carmella and her mint heels were not the least bit deterred. She fell in alongside him and didn't even tear her eyes from her phone. "Can I show you something, Hank?"

"Carmella, I'm really in a hurry—"

She took his elbow. Not his hand. "You owe me so many more minutes than two."

Hank showed her every tooth. "Man. People talk about clingy exes ..."

"How does it feel to say that to me, Hank Vasquez?" Her stare could pierce iron. "Tell me. Because I don't think it feels good."

"I—no. Sorry." He took a ragged breath. "I don't know what made me say it."

"A little honesty escaped, maybe?" Carmella placed her phone in Hank's hand. He squeezed it too hard. "Look at this and I'll forget you said a thing." She unlocked the screen. "What's wrong with this photo?"

Hank pretended to look, just enough to know it was a shot of him playing at summer tryouts: Hank was the main focus, situated just right of center, face blank and a bit distant as he crouched at the three-point line. He was gripping the ball tightly in his hands—his *hands*—

He pushed the phone away. "I don't want to think about tryouts. All right?"

"Did you look at your hands?"

"The shot's blurry."

"Really. Because it *clearly* looks like you have more fingers than human beings are ever supposed to have. About, let's see, one ... two ... three more fingers?"

Hank refused to look again.

Luz, you idiot.

For the first few weeks that Luz visited, he hadn't worn those fingers right, couldn't quite nail the shape or settle down about the numbers.

Luz had experimented.

It doesn't make sense, he whined in Hank's notebook. Hank could always tell when Luz was whining; it manifested as scratchier handwriting than usual. *Why not create as many fingers as you need, whenever you need them? If you've got all this matter at your disposal, why not rearrange it to suit you?*

Luz had demonstrated his point, there at Hank's desk, or tried to—Hank felt a tingling in the heaviness of his hands, a sensation not unlike what he'd felt when Brendan once pushed his arms into a papier-mâché mixture, thick flour water enveloping him—

Hank gagged. Luz had only been with them for a week at that point, and Hank still worried he would no more understand Luz's nature than he could love glaciers or girls. Luz always sounded somehow reasonable, until he was dissolving and reforming your fingers, stretching them like taffy.

When Hank looked back, his left hand had seven spindlier fingers. His right hand had just three, thick like talons.

More fingers for a wider grip, wrote the taloned hand, while the seven-fingered one tapped a rhythm on the desktop. *Or maybe a single long, large one for reaching farther? All this flesh, Hank. Why not let it do more?*

"Flesh . . . I don't think it usually works that way, Luz."

Only because no one's made it try. Luz dropped the pen and reshaped Hank's hand into a mallet, back into a hand again. *Your species is so defeatist.*

"That's pretty true."

Good thing you have me now, wrote one hand, while the other cuffed Hank affectionately on the chin.

"Good thing," Hank agreed.

★ ★ ★

"Welcome to the present, Hank." Carmella's arms were folded, her phone tucked away. "Hello."

"Well, if that's all you wanted—"

"That is *not* all." Carmella closed her eyes. "I didn't fall for you, Hank. I fell for your whole dopey family, the sadness and the kindness and the weirdness. I was your beard for a year." Her eyes opened, her lips twisted. "I'm still growing on you."

"I—look, I never thought of you as a beard."

She smirked. "I know you didn't. That's why I didn't mind it so much. There was this chance you'd never figure it out, you know?"

"That would have been awful for you," Hank said.

"What can I say? I'm a very half-assed feminist."

He couldn't look away from her face; he couldn't feel his hands at all.

How often did people look at Carmella like she was something otherworldly? Not just Hank, but everyone?

White-gold Carmella Spalding, descended from another plane.

In junior high, guys like Tim Miller had started saying sickening things that killed Hank's laughter, things about what they'd like to "*do*" to Carmella Spalding, given the chance.

Hank was Carmella's partner for a project in sophomore American Lit class, writing and reading aloud reimagined soliloquies of characters from *The Crucible*. Carmella chose Tituba and performed the *hell* out of her lines, lifting her fists and slamming them into her chest during a speech about her character's mistreatment.

Probably the *last* thing Carmella Spalding would ever want

would be to have something "done" to her. If Hank hadn't asked her to homecoming that year, Tim Miller might have. A boy obsessed with a body might have.

Hank asked; she had raised an eyebrow but said yes.

Hank wanted to believe it had been selfless. But a tiny worm in his heart wondered what Dad might say if he came home and found Hank dating a girl like Carmella. Dad and Hank used to talk about girls sometimes, during truck rides home after games, and Hank had played the part almost as well as Carmella played Tituba. There had passed seconds between telephone poles when Dad nudged him as if Hank could only love girls, would be climbing glaciers for eternity.

But Hank would pass Brendan in hallways and forget where he was.

After a year, when they were juniors, the way Hank dumped Carmella—well, he *didn't*, exactly. She came over to watch crappy B-movies on the sci-fi channel (nobody knew she liked that sort of thing), and midway through a scene that featured a bounty hunter in a bikini making out with a buff alien barbarian, Hank laughed so hard he cried. It seemed so ridiculous to him—not just the romance *IN SPAAAAACE*. But the man and the woman together.

It was inexplicable, but Carmella held his hand. She wiped Hank's eyes.

"I get it," she whispered. "Brendan Nesbitt has *killer* cheekbones."

The last bell rang. Hank stared at Carmella. Her makeup hadn't smeared.

"Hank. Whatever this is, tell me about it. Not lies about swine flu or termites, or whatever. The truth."

She always seemed to know him.

Hank shivered. Luz had always seemed to know him.

"Carmella . . . see you tomorrow?"

She didn't return his smile.

The courts at Moreno Park weren't empty.

The blacktop was occupied by a scraggly band of middle schoolers who tossed around a flat basketball. Beside the park fence, an old man in a garish Hawaiian shirt appeared to be bird-watching through a pair of enormous black binoculars. There was a clear view of Nameless Canyon and the Vasquez household here. Hank didn't look.

He couldn't stop shooting.

When he missed his 117th consecutive basket, a middle schooler sniggered. Maybe the scabby-kneed kids recognized Hank. If they were local, they'd probably seen the termite tent and heard the Ebola rumors. They'd probably seen him play before, and couldn't believe what they were seeing now.

Somehow that kid's snigger was the most alienating experience of the day.

Alienating, Luz.

Luz had been fascinated by human vocabulary.

They didn't have to *teach* it, exactly—the moment he'd moved into Hank and the others, Luz had access to all the same knowledge they did. He bathed in a pool of everything the Vasquezes knew. He savored the experience, asked always for more. Luz adopted Milo's capacity for learning, Ana's tendency toward interrogation, Hank's unchecked growth. But knowledge didn't always equal understanding.

At first Luz didn't realize the Vasquez kids were separate people.

You are so similar. I assumed you were one organism in three pieces. Are you sure you aren't?

"Definitely sure," Hank told him.

Grow more complex, then. You're very simple creatures, Luz wrote. He'd been with them for three weeks. All of them were huddled on the top bunk. By then, Hank carried a whiteboard and dry-erase markers everywhere.

"You are a bit overcomplicated in the area of emotions," Milo continued, repeating words Luz whispered in his ears.

"Come on." Ana closed her eyes, or Luz closed them for her: "Look closely at my brothers and tell me their emotions aren't mostly about food, Luz."

"They aren't. They are as overcomplicated as you are." And then, as Milo: "But fingers are truly a nightmare."

Hank laughed. He wasn't annoyed with Ana. When Luz was with them, they weren't annoyed with one another. They understood what they'd never understood in all the years of growing up without him. The Vasquezes understood they would never entirely understand one another, and that was okay.

"I really *would* like chilaquiles right now," Milo confessed.

There was no point denying that Dad had taught Hank exactly how to make them, now that Luz had bridged the gaps between them. Luz could show Ana what Hank knew or Milo what Ana knew.

They went to the kitchen and fried stale tortillas and eggs at two in the morning.

When Mom came in and asked what the hell they were doing, they realized they hadn't prepared her a plate. Then they realized that she didn't *want* a plate—she wanted them not to cook the thing Dad used to cook. She watched them in her bathrobe, stared at the fluid, symmetrical way they moved like one organism.

She left the room in tears.

Hank felt himself failing to care. Overwhelmingly, she wasn't part of them.

The chilaquiles were delicious. Hank wondered if *he'd* cooked them, or if Luz had with Hank's hands. Did it matter? Again Hank felt himself failing to care.

A hole was opening at their feet. Hank saw them all plunging into it—Ana with relief, Milo in a joyful forward dive, and Hank wondering whether anyone would care enough to catch them.

The sky was still, overcast and starless.

The smacking of the ball seemed louder without the offset of middle school snickers. Beside the fence, the old man was adjusting his binoculars, muttering to himself.

The ball fell through the net for the first time in months.

It may have been pure chance—it wasn't as though Hank could feel his hands.

But it went through.

Hank punched the sky. "You see that?" he asked his fingers. "I don't need you."

"If that's true," a voice called from the sidelines, "let me break them for you."

Hank's fist fell faster than a comet. He turned.

Anyone might think they were setting up for a scrimmage. Beside Tim Miller stood two red-cheeked others: Ben O'Brien, Rin Hisoka. The three still wore their practice jerseys and sneakers. Like they'd just finished warming up.

But there wasn't a basketball in sight. Hank's had rolled into the darkness between two streetlights.

"Hey, guys. Here for a game of HORSE?"

"The fuck is wrong with you, Vasquez?"

"Oh." Hank put his hand to the back of his head. "You know. Just out of practice."

"Quit fucking smiling. I mean it. What the fuck is *wrong* with you?" Tim's skin barely seemed to contain him. Despite the dark, his eyes shone like dimes.

Hank had never been attracted to Tim Miller, which was not to say Hank wasn't a little in love with him. But countless summer nights spent at Tim's house, lounging on the sectional couch while they tossed a foam football back and forth and talked shit about their dads, had amounted to brotherhood rather than romance.

After Hank showed up at homecoming with Brendan on his arm, those basement years had dissipated like foam, leaving only crusted spit.

Tim stepped forward. Hank refused to step back.

"Tim. Let me talk to you. Just you."

"You think I wanna be anywhere alone with you? Fuck no. Never again."

Tim shoved hard. Hank's shoulders hit the pavement, and as the first kick shunted the air from his stomach, Hank could hardly have explained that he hadn't *asked* his hands to hurt Tim during tryouts.

Because maybe he had. Even if it had been Luz possessing Hank's fingers while those fingers wrapped around Tim's throat, choking him in a quiet locker room, Tim was nonetheless hurt.

Hank let his arms fall open. He let his wrists smack the court.

Tim's face looked a little like Milo's, scrunched up like that. Hank had hurt both of them. There would be no more piggyback. Tim might as well break his spine.

Hank lay still.

He felt gravel grate his scalp as his skull slid against the pavement, flint to steel. Hank felt the scraping of man-made earth against his elbows, but it wasn't intimate. The sand in Hank's ears wasn't, the places where feet pounded his rib cage weren't, not even close. Not the wood chips forming in Hank's stomach, nor the sensation that his torso was granite being shattered by a hammer—nothing was as intimate as Luz had been.

Hank didn't need to say "hit me" and Tim didn't need to call him "faggot" again. This exchange was as natural as a ball rebounding. This was Tim recovering from a play Hank had made months ago, unfairly, cruelly, without remorse.

Ben and Rin stood at Tim's shoulders. They framed him like wings, bore witness.

All told, it was only five licks: three kicks to Hank's stomach, one stomp on Hank's rib cage, and one knock to his head.

The knock was the most intimate. Tim leaned in, lifted Hank's head up by the ears, and dropped it. The back of Hank's skull took fire, but he was too thickheaded for a real concussion. As usual, Hank was an idiot.

A dollop of hot salt water slipped from Tim's face to his. Not spit this time.

Finally they left him there.

Hank lay still. Throbbing, coughing, but still. He wanted to bleed right into the courts. He couldn't.

They hadn't even broken his skin.

13

EARS

Dr. Ruby's setup in the garage was pretty dang cool!

Years ago the garage stored things that weren't cars. Out here a treasure hunter might find tricycles bound by cobwebs, Dad's few forgotten power tools, or plastic totes jammed full of winter clothing from Mom's years in Wisconsin, because snow really was a thing there. The whole room had smelled like pennies.

When Dr. Ruby's snaky tent went up, the garage transformed! Now the floor was always clean. The garage was so bright that Milo wanted to wear sunglasses, but she wouldn't let him. The walls were lined with crinkly stuff that looked exactly like tin-foil, but Dr. Ruby called it "insulation." There were comfy chairs, and an empty table, and machines that beeped and blinked if Dr. Ruby asked questions. A lot of the machines looked really old-fashioned, like sad garage-sale toasters. But what did Milo know?

Dr. Ruby got upset when Milo called her a mad scientist. Even though he was joking! And especially since she was wrapping him up like a baked potato.

The first time she put Milo in there, he was having a bad day. Dr. Ruby had to strap his arms to his chair. She made Milo sit until he stopped screaming. She waited without earplugs, turning the pages of an enormous book with dragons on the cover.

These days Milo was grateful for the garage makeover. Dr. Ruby had this amazing microphone-and-headphone setup that allowed him to listen to music and her questions at the same time, so it never got too quiet. The Roaring Nothing didn't stand a *snowflake's chance* in the garage.

"Milo?" Dr. Ruby had a voice like paper. She was at least as old as thirty-seven. That made her pretty wise. "Are you with me?"

"Uh-huh."

Dr. Ruby stared at her laptop. It was attached to a boxy little machine with lights on it. The boxy little machine was attached to Milo's head with sticky little wires. "Okay. What are you thinking about?"

Milo blinked. "Don't your machines tell you?"

"I heard you had a pretty tough first day at school. Do you want to talk about it?"

"Ahhhhh. Did you like Mom's dinner, Dr. Ruby?"

Dr. Ruby tapped her nails on the microphone. "Your mother makes some *knockout* enchiladas."

"Dad taught her to make those, did you know that?"

"I didn't, Milo. And remember—you don't have to shout in here."

"Mom only made them because she knew you were coming." After they'd made it home, she'd slid the spare set of headphones onto his head and locked herself in her bedroom. "She would have made *me* a mud pie if she could. I'm in her bad books today."

"Want to tell me why?"

Milo kicked the table. "Don't you think she cooked too much food?"

"I'm glad she cooked so much. There'll be leftovers for your siblings, won't there? Did Ana or Hank tell you they'd be home late?"

In Milo's left ear, Radiohead played a song about burning a witch. It seemed a little mean! "They never tell me things. Hank doesn't talk to me even a *little*."

"Because of this summer?"

"Ahhhh," was all Milo would say.

"Did they use to tell you things?"

Milo thought hard about this. "They're a lot older than me. They have a lot of business to take care of."

"Milo, please don't shout."

"I didn't."

"You didn't *mean* to. What are you listening to?"

"I'm almost finished with Radiohead."

"You'll need something new! I may have a band for you. They're from Iceland, and the lead singer has a lot of range. Remind me—was Luz's voice high or low?"

"I already told you. Like a *thousand times*."

"Your answer keeps changing."

"Well, people's voices are always changing. So are their lips. They can't even make circles!"

"That's a very unique observation, Milo."

"You're the one doing observations. But you don't even have an observation deck, mad scientist!"

Dr. Ruby sighed. "This isn't like the movies, Milo. How can I change your mind about me?"

"You should wear a different coat," Milo advised. "Plus, you still think Luz was an alien." Milo tried to roll his eyes at least three times better than Ana.

"And you still think Luz *wasn't* an alien?"

"He definitely wasn't."

"Milo, do you still think it was your *father* who visited you this summer?" She paused the pressing of her laptop keys and hummed gently in his earphones.

"Everyone thinks I don't know things because I'm little. But I woke up with a crick in my neck this morning." Milo tapped his nose.

"Fascinating, Milo."

Milo fought back a yawn. Dinner had really robbed him of all his energy. Nobody had talked much, and Dr. Ruby kept looking at Mom, and Mom kept looking at the empty chairs where Hank and Ana were supposed to be sitting. She was smiling in this way that looked an awful lot like crying. Milo read her lips or just decided that she was saying, *Sorry, they should be back by now, I've called them a dozen times, but I'm sure it's no big deal, probably Hank's just at practice and Ana—*

Milo felt like shouting, "But *I'm* right here!"

But his throat still hurt, and also it didn't seem like a very grown-up thing to do. Milo had already been a baby today, a screaming *enormous* baby in front of Antonio and everyone else.

"If it was really your dad who visited this summer, can you tell me how he ended up 'living in your ears'?"

"One time Dad brought an opossum back to life. Dad's magical, Dr. Ruby."

"Doesn't it make more sense, Milo, that maybe the voice in your ears was only *pretending* to be your dad? Like I told you? You remember what I told you."

"You told me Luz was my imagination. I didn't believe you." Dr. Ruby had pushed that idea for two weeks before caving. Looking stubborn could do wonders!

"So then I told you the truth. What did I tell you, Milo?"

Milo took a breath as big as anything! "You told me, 'The thing you call *Luz* or *Dad* was actually a parasitic organism of, um, unknown organ that entered through your ears and infected your insular cortex to take advantage of your emotions and make you a willing host.'"

"Wow, Milo. Perfect, except it's 'origin,' not 'organ.'"

"You only told me like a million times!"

"I'll repeat it until you understand it."

"I already *do* understand, Dr. Ruby."

"As in ... 'I understand that what happened to me was a sickness that intended to harm me,' Milo?"

"I understand *you*." Milo rolled his eyes. "Of *course* a scientist wouldn't know about magic."

She sighed. "Milo, what if I told you I'm going to recommend your mother take you out of school?"

The walls really did look like tinfoil. And real doctors wouldn't wear stupid white coats or have really old machines or show up from nowhere.

"Mom put too much sriracha on the enchiladas. Dad never made them that way."

Before she left, Dr. Ruby handed Milo another music player with a bunch of new songs on it. Milo couldn't imagine a land of ice, because he lived in a land of hot dirt. He wondered if music from an ice-land would make his ears cold.

Usually Mom waited for him in the laundry room attached to the garage. Last time she was even sitting on the washing machine! She always had ten million questions for Dr. Ruby.

Today the laundry room was empty, except for a ton of warm clothes, fresh out of the dryer. The laundry room door was open just a crack. Dr. Ruby went after Mom.

Milo stayed behind.

He thought Mom might like it if he folded some clothes. He used to. He used to sit right next to her on the couch! Even though folding was boring and the fabric burned his lap. Mom had laughed at his technique: "It's not the tuck and roll, Milo. The clothes aren't on fire."

Milo hadn't liked that, had thrown the T-shirt back into the basket. "Girls are better at folding."

"They are *not*. That's called *sexism*, Milo. Girls are just the ones people expect to do it. We'll start you on towels and socks, all right?"

Now Milo buried himself in boiling clothes. He was ready to pull out jeans or shorts or a sweater. Or maybe even *the ultimate challenge*: a fitted bedsheet. Maybe if he folded enough clothes, Mom wouldn't look how she'd looked when he ran away today.

The new album had been playing for seven minutes now. It was making his chest feel funny. This music felt like hot water being poured into a tub. Nothing like the sound of a Chevy pulling away.

Dr. Ruby had given him something *so beautiful*!

It was the sound track to the warm basket of clothes. It was Mom's warm fingertips outlining numb ears, it was Hank's old high fives and Ana's rare winks.

Milo's entire face was sopping wet.

He knew he shouldn't, not with snot all over his face, but he leaned forward and dove headfirst into the laundry basket. The clothes only reached his neck, but he imagined them covering all of him just like the music. Milo wondered if he was steaming.

The clothes welcomed him. Milo buried himself, burrowing like any kind of rodent. It didn't have to be an opossum.

14

EYES

Brendan Nesbitt wasn't a terrible singer. He wasn't a good one, either.

Ana couldn't play the piano for beans. The Vasquezes could never afford lessons, and online tutorials could only get you so far when you insisted on learning only the opening chords of anime theme songs, when you didn't own a keyboard and could only pretend your desk was one.

Brendan sang. Ana sat on the risers and watched him poke at keys between lines.

He wasn't tone-deaf. He was just very calculating, and his calculations sounded in his voice. Brendan, as far as Ana could tell, was determined to dissect every syllable that passed his lips and turn it inside out before uttering it. It didn't help that he sang through his nose for the sake of his character.

The longer Ana watched him through burning galaxy eyes, grateful for the bulbs that kept the carpeted room poorly lit, the less this made any sense to her.

"Don't think so hard about the words."

"Oh." He lifted his long fingers to the back of his neck (wings and wings with him). "You're right. I really am over-thinking it, aren't I? The trouble is, I've spent the past couple months obsessing over whether I can land the comedic lines right, because being comical in musicals is something of a trial for me."

"Just in musicals?" Ana murmured. Her mind was snagged by another phrase: *the past couple months*, months during which Brendan Nesbitt was not invited to the Vasquez home, during which Brendan Nesbitt had to find other ways to occupy his demanding mind.

"What's giving me away, Ana?"

Ana considered. "You sound constipated."

Brendan laughed, high and light, let his arms fall back to his sides. "All right. Yes, that's a pretty big tell." He collapsed on the piano bench. "Ana. You have to tell me."

"Tell you what?"

Completely deadpan: "Which phrase sounded the most constipated?"

The Ana Vasquez of yesteryear would have rolled her eyes right out of her head.

Brendan Nesbitt never got offended. He only got inquisitive.

Brendan had an arsenal of questions on hand at any given moment, and he used to loose them on the Vasquez household. Questions about where the Vasquezes got the odd collection of glass animals by the window, about the floral design on her mother's mysteri-ous inherited dinnerware, about what sort of critters came out of the canyon at night: "Do you ever find bats in your living room?"

For all the questions Brendan Nesbitt asked, he never asked about Hank. Not about his bedroom or his baby pictures. Hank was the one certainty. Ana longed to answer Brendan, that bird-boned boy with questions where marrow should have been.

Hank was usually there to answer first. But sometimes when Hank wasn't, Brendan asked smaller questions that mattered more.

On the day Ana came home realizing her friendship with Marissa was finally done, she fell into the kitchen a mess, her makeup having migrated to all the wrong parts of her face. Ana expected her collapse to go unwitnessed, forgetting that Milo had minimum days on Fridays and on those days, if Hank had practice, Brendan did the babysitting. He caught her before her knees hit the linoleum.

"Wanna talk about it?" Brendan asked, while Milo whisked imaginary eggs.

It didn't matter that Ana said no. It mattered that he asked.

". . . any other advice for me, Ana? I really want the part, and . . . I *need* the part."

"I don't know anything about singing."

"Of course you do. You used to sing."

Did I, Luz? "Did I?"

"Absolutely. We could hear you from your window, whenever we—Hank and me—well, whenever we were . . . outside. Hank thought you did it for attention. I thought maybe you didn't even realize."

Didn't I, Luz?

"What did I sing about, Brendan?" Mom never sang. Dad always had.

"You know, I have no idea." Had he frowned? "We just heard you."

Ana stood up from the risers. "I thought you were into photography, not theater."

Brendan twitched. "I was. But now, I don't know. I'm not sure it's for me."

"And *this* is? Brendan, what are *you* singing about?"

"Oh. It's half a duet between a shopkeep and a man-eating alien plant. I'm trying out for the shopkeep." He patted the bench. "Wanna help me out by pretending to be a soulful Venus flytrap?"

Ana scooted into place beside him. She tried to make sense of the sheet music. She could read the treble line, but not the bass. It wasn't just that her eyes were sore; her memory of music was, too. "Is it . . . a romantic duet?"

"What? Of course not. Didn't I say *man-eating alien plant*? Because *man-eating alien plant*."

"Stranger things have happened." Ana couldn't tell whether that was a truth she wanted to exist, or the answer to a question he'd never ask her.

A blink hit her. She tried not to let it show.

"This is more like a . . . partners-in-crime song. They agree to murder people together. I guess, at a stretch, you could call it a friendship."

". . . at a stretch."

"Yes. Look, I know I need to practice more."

"Or maybe you shouldn't. Maybe that'll make it worse."

"There's the Ana I know. Straight to the point."

Ana and Marissa had memorized those most favorite of anime theme songs, especially when Marissa went through that phase in seventh grade where she was obsessed with shows about teen idols wearing cotton-candy-colored school uniforms. Idols didn't have to sing well to become idols.

"That's half the appeal, really," Marissa informed her.

"You're gonna have to explain the other half, too," Ana snarked.

Not that it mattered, as months later Ana was called a lesbian on the bus for the eighth time because she and Marissa were always together, attempting to draw girls with legs up to their moon-size eyes and hair down to their ankles, and Ana promptly announced, at the succeeding sleepover: "I know we promised we'd still love this crap when we got older—"

"Crap?" Marissa whimpered.

"But I just don't anymore, okay?"

It wasn't true. Ana dreamed of magical girl transformations for years.

Brendan Nesbitt didn't have the benefit or detriment of anime idol Auto-Tune. He did have the benefit of long fingers on white piano keys.

"Ana . . . are you crying?"

Ana blinked and winced. "No. These are just my eyes now."

Brendan turned away, tapped out a new chord. "All right."

"You want to ask me about my family."

"It's not that I want to pry."

Ana nodded. "You just can't help it. And you can't ask Hank, so here I am."

All those questions Ana had longed to answer, and Hank had answered them, with that infamous big smile: "Oh, sometimes we get bats up here, but it's the owls you have to look out for, Nesbitt."

Brendan's eyes cut right through her. The warmth left his features.

Did Brendan Nesbitt say "I love musicals!" in the same way that Hank declared "I love basketball!"?

On the Fourth of July with Luz inside her, Ana had spotted Brendan Nesbitt among the clamor of townsfolk at Burley Field.

He was with his art friends—a girl who sometimes wore antlers in her white hair, a boy who boasted a collection of tartan skirts. The three were sprawled on an old tablecloth, staring at the sky, anticipating the fireworks to come. Brendan tugged absently at tufts of grass between his oxfords.

This boy matters to you? Luz asked, in his way. The language of memories was not so direct as writing or whispering, but through the careful combination of images, Luz could say anything. He showed her a blended vision: Brendan caught Ana in the kitchen, but now every one of his questions belonged to her.

Luz created this and made it evaporate inside her. It was unimaginable.

Brendan would always catch Ana, but never kiss her.

On the field, Hank or Luz grabbed her shoulder. *Come with us.*

Ana followed them back to their spot. Milo hummed softly on the blanket, chewing on celery. Mom hadn't come out with them. They hadn't asked her to.

It was Luz who liked to watch the sky, or maybe Milo or Hank or Ana.

Beside her in the choir room, Brendan Nesbitt belted.

Ana joined him, loud as she could, singing the part of the murderous man-eating plant.

15

HANDS

On that June evening, after they had eaten all the chilaquiles, Ana and Milo had conked out on the couch with *Close Encounters* on.

Hank showered, scraping frying grease from himself. He brushed his teeth with his left hand while Luz wrote on the foggy bathroom mirror in Expo with his right.

Do you know, Hank, of the three of you, you're the only part who seems to grasp the gravity of my being here?

Hank spat out his toothpaste. "Are you joking?"

How could it be a joke?

"People *grasp* with their hands."

Luz gave him the middle finger. *Only so much as this is a joke.*

"That's actually pretty good, Luz."

Yes. Both you and Milo respond well to juvenile humor.

Hank stopped smiling. "I guess so. I guess you thought that'd be another way to win us over."

Do you mind being "won over"?

Hank let the marker hang there. "I'm not sure. I guess you're already here, and Milo loves you, and Ana seems better with you, and for once they aren't trying to pull each other's hair out, so . . . I mean, I guess I'm trying to figure out *why* you're here."

Luz hesitated. *Do you know why YOU are here? I can't find evidence of that in you or in Milo or in Ana.*

Hank frowned. "We're just living, I guess. I just want to grow the hell up."

Luz drew three exclamation points. *Can't that be my reason, too?*

"All right, all right. It's not like I'm smart enough to figure out how to kick you out, even if I wanted to."

Almost the entire mirror was covered by now, but Luz wrote the next part in large letters. *That's true.*

Hank forgot to breathe. Blue ink ran down his arm. "I mean, besides cutting off my hands."

You can't do that, Hank.

"You'd stop me." Why wasn't Hank moving his hand away? "To save yourself."

I would stop you. But it would have nothing to do with me, Hank. Your fingers are yours. They've grown with you. You have touched astounding things with them.

Luz didn't show him those things. Hank saw them anyhow. Milo's soft hair on the day he was born, red clay lodged under Brendan's fingernails, Dad's high five after the free-throw tournament—

Hank jerked his hand on the glass.

Besides, Luz added, *it's not as though that would kill me.*

Hank lowered his arm at last, letting the marker drag.

★   ★   ★

"Hey. You planning on getting up anytime soon? All that wheezing is distracting me from my work."

Hank's skeleton nearly left him there on the court. That might have felt better. It seemed his ribs had been diced and sprinkled along his stomach lining. He felt as if his trunk was one of Brendan's ceramic collages.

Maybe ten minutes had passed. Maybe an hour. Light had left the sky over Nameless Canyon.

The old man who'd been beside the fence glowered down at Hank. Wispy tufts of white hair escaped the sides of a baseball cap bedecked in buttons, and wispy tufts of beard were tucked into the collar of his shirt.

Hank coughed four times before gasping out an apology.

"You *should* be sorry you didn't punch 'em back. You a coward?"

Hank nodded. The man folded his arms. "Get up."

After several tries Hank found his feet. Once standing, he doubled over.

"Did they beat you for being godawful, then? Never seen someone miss that many baskets before. I'm not a sport-ball fan, but I think you're doing it wrong."

Hank choked on a chuckle.

"Am I joking, boy?"

". . . not . . . sure, sir."

"Making a racket, disrupting my work, and now you're *laughing* about it? The youth is doomed. The country is doomed."

Hank stared at the man. Flecks of spit escaped his lips, distracted Hank from his shattered stomach and throbbing temple. "Sorry, sir. What kind of work . . . were you doing?"

It was like flipping a switch.

The man's expression lifted with him. Suddenly he pulled his bifocals down and grew an inch to meet Hank's eyes (or at least his shoulders). "Only the most important work possible, son. Are you interested in saving mankind?"

"Well . . ."

The man took Hank by the arm. Even hobbled, Hank wasn't worried—he'd found the one person in Eustace with fingers more rickety than his own. He let the old man lead him to his post by the fence.

In addition to the massive binoculars around his neck, he also had a foldout telescope and a collapsible lawn chair at the ready. The scope was wedged between rungs of chain link.

"Stargazing?" That couldn't be right. That telescope wasn't aimed at the sky.

"Not exactly. But in a way: *yes.*"

Finally Hank read what the water-stained buttons on the man's hat said.

We are not alone.

Weather Balloon? Weather BULLSHIT.

My other car's a UFO.

The telescope was aimed directly at the Vasquez house.

The tingling wasn't only in Hank's hands now. His smile had fled.

"Truth is, I'm researching otherworldly life."

"Wow."

"Here, what am I thinking?" The old man fumbled through his fanny pack and handed Hank a dog-eared business card. On one side was an innocuous picture of mountains and clouds at sunset.

"'Henry Flowers, Extraterrestrial Expert.'"

"There are three UFOs in that picture. *You* can't see them." Henry Flowers winked. "Those of us in the UFO circles know how to spot 'em."

"So . . . what are people in, um, *UFO circles* saying about Eustace?"

"See that junky little house on the edge of the canyon?"

Hank didn't answer. The throbbing in his skull intensified.

"There was some activity in this canyon over the summer. Atmospheric disturbances and celestial tells, you get me? It's very technical and you don't seem too bright, so don't worry about it. Not everyone can be an extraterrestrial expert. But that house? That house there, you see it?"

"Yeah. I see it." Home stood alone on an outcrop, jutting farther over Nameless Canyon than any of its neighbors.

"A month after the disturbances, that very house went under quarantine for a few weeks. Oh, people said it was a termite tent. But it ain't hard for us experts to put two and two together. Hell, even *normies* have seen Spielberg movies. *Something* landed in this canyon over the summer and took up residence there, son."

"Oh."

"Now, don't ask me *what* it was. I only parked here yesterday. I haven't been around long enough to gather conclusive intel." Henry Flowers leaned in for a conspiratorial whisper. "You wanna hear the weirdest part?"

No, Hank thought. He smiled. "Sure."

"The tent's gone, but the family is *still in the house*. No one's tried to hush 'em or ship 'em off somewhere for dissection or witness protection or anything, which spooks me." Henry tapped his nose. "Why leave the family there?"

"I have to go." Hank tried to step back. Henry cemented his grip.

"You wanna know what I think?"

"No, thanks."

A mighty cough helped clear the words from his throat: "Whatever landed there, it may still be *here*."

Hank laughed so loud he thought he might snap in two at his bruises. "Has anyone ever told you, Mr. Flowers, that you're extremely freaking creepy?"

Henry Flowers peered right at him and squinted. "Sure. You don't get to be my age without people calling you one thing or another. It's not creepy. It's research." Henry squinted at Hank's hands. They trembled as though an electric current was passing through them. "Know what *I'd* call creepy? The idea that this thing could still be walking among us. That's downright petrifyin'."

Henry's smile seemed altogether too knowing.

"Tell me, *Hank Vasquez*—how are things at your house? Seen any doctors lately?"

The desert wind died, leaving the park quieter than Hank had ever heard it. There was only his heart in his ears, vibrating the egg forming at his temple. The old man's wheezy throat.

Hank had some idea how Luz would've handled this situation.

He remembered summer tryouts.

★ ★ ★

Tim had pulled Hank aside in the locker room between the third and fourth quarters of the practice match. While the other guys were huddling up courtside, Tim pushed Hank back against the lockers. The force rattled the loose bathroom tiles.

"What the *fuck* is your problem, Vasquez?"

"I don't have a problem. We're killing it out there." Hank's fingers, heavy with Luz, didn't budge.

"*We* aren't doing shit. *You* are being a fuckwad. The only things you're killing are your fucking teammates. You elbowed Pat so hard he's puking, and you were hogging the ball like it was your junk. This is practice. *Everyone here is on your side.*"

"*Are* they?"

Comprehension seemed to dawn on Tim. "Come on, man. We've played ball since Cub Scouts. Think I care you suddenly like to fuck guys?"

"You *do* care. Your dad hates queers. But that's not what I meant."

Tim Miller grabbed Hank's shoulders. "My dad made you pancakes last week. Don't talk shit."

"I'm not." Hank felt Luz crack his knuckles. "I can see it clearly now. The spaces between us. We *aren't* on the same side, Tim. Your dad being a homophobic bigot has fuck-all to do with it. You and me? We just aren't on the same planet anymore."

Tim's grip tightened on Hank's shoulders. Hank's hands moved of their own accord. Hank let Luz claim that situation, let Luz do the shoving back, let Luz grab Tim's shoulders and crush until Tim let go—

Luz didn't stop there.

He glued Hank's hands to Tim Miller's esophagus, reshaping the fingers until they were long enough to wrap twice around Tim's throat and meet at the tips like tangled desert vines.

Tim squirmed, Tim gurgled.

"Wait, Luz," Hank said without enthusiasm.

Tim Miller managed to pull one finger away—it snapped back into place.

Suddenly it was like waking up, how badly Hank wanted to let go. Suddenly he couldn't understand where he was, who he was, *how* he'd been letting Luz live for him.

"Luz, stop."

Luz uncurled Hank's fingers. Tim gasped and slid to the floor.

Hank tried to forget his hands. He couldn't think how to help Tim up without them. "Tim? I'm sorry. I didn't mean to do that."

"Get . . . get . . . the hell away."

Hank straightened up. He grabbed his backpack on his way out, unfazed by his teammates' silence as he exited the gym. Pat still held his stomach, glaring from the bench. Hank smiled and waved.

In the hot parking lot, Hank muttered: "You shouldn't have done that."

He was upsetting you. I could feel it. Red Bic ink, directly on Hank's arm.

"Funny, because I couldn't. I didn't feel a damn thing. I still can't." Hank met the glare of sunlight on parked cars. "Is that a side effect, or is it on purpose?"

I'm only numbing your pain, Hank. You take on a lot, as the big brother. You have to worry about your siblings. Your family. Luz wrote so much that the words began wrapping around Hank's forearm, traveled toward his shoulders. *Let me have some of that. Share it with me. If you don't want to be bigger, let me be bigger instead.*

"*Why*, Luz?" Hank craned to see words that traversed his left shoulder blade and slipped beneath his jersey.

I'm still not certain, Luz confessed, moving the pen to Hank's thigh, marking him there. *Growing is the only thing I do. It's what defines me.*

Luz was the one who pushed. Hank went along with it, like he'd always gone along with things: smiling, letting them happen, letting sidelines become empty.

What wouldn't you *give to define yourself, Hank?*

Luz drew the question mark on Hank's knee, huge and distorted.

"What's wrong with your hands, kid?"

Smiling wasn't working now, wasn't hiding a damn thing.

"Everything," Hank told Henry Flowers, "and they aren't even mine."

"I can help you with that, probably. Not my first alien infestation." Henry Flowers leaned in close. "It was like this for my daughter, too."

Hank trembled. "What?"

"Before the extraterrestrial took her, I mean." Glistening old eyes met Hank's young ones. "She wasn't herself anymore. Now she's been gone for years. She could be anywhere, anyone. She could be anything, don't you think?"

"I—"

"Heeeeeey!" A semi-truck smacked into Hank's back, an arm over his shoulders. He gagged, collapsing inward on his broken stomach. "*Tank*, man, what are the odds? What you doing here after dark? Trying to pick up dudes? I think you'd have better luck in places where dudes actually are. Unless this guy's your date?"

Orson winked at Henry Flowers.

"We were discussing top-secret business," Henry said.

"Hank, did you forget? We're *supposed* to be at Kamala Khan's bonfire tonight. Annual tradition on the first/worst day of school, man!"

"Um . . ."

"Smile, dumbass," Orson muttered in his ear. He grabbed Henry Flowers's hand and shook it. "Nice to meet you, man, but we've gotta go. Unless you need anything else from my boy here?"

"No." Henry Flowers pulled his hand free. "He has my number."

This man had said he had a missing child. Wasn't that what Hank was?

"Guy doesn't read enough comics," Orson muttered when they were out of earshot. "Kamala Khan is obviously Ms. Marvel's alter ego. Maybe he's stuck in the Golden Age?"

"What are you doing here?" Hank asked. The anger he felt was raw and strange to him now, because it was all his own and he couldn't say why. It wasn't that he had wanted to keep talking to the old man, but . . .

"Hank. See this?" Orson fanned his free arm outward. "This here land? This here land's what some folks call a *basketball court*. And some *other* folks like nothing more, nay, *love* nothing more, than dribbling orange rubber balls here for *entertainments and sport*, my man."

". . . you just got out of practice."

"Some of us have become second-string players due to missing camp, my man, and we're already sick of the bench digging into our balls all the time, what ho, *avast*."

"What's with the voice?" They reached the half-dried yuccas that lined the parking lot. Hank fought the urge to check whether Henry Flowers was stargazing at the Vasquez house again.

"That voice? That there's a nervous habit, Tank."

"Don't call me that."

"Another nervous habit, Spank."

Hank stopped. "You didn't bring a basketball."

Orson snickered and jabbed his hand out from his shorts pockets. "I've got two basketballs for you right here."

No more smiling. "Grow up, Orson."

"Fuck that. You want me to grow up? How about this? I came here to say you forgot to give your sister a ride home from school. Your undead sister? Remember her?"

Hank groaned. "Crap. *Crap*."

The overgrown palm leaves above cast Orson in darkness. "Nesbitt messaged me. He's giving her a ride."

Of course Orson knew Brendan. Orson knew everybody. He didn't give you any say on that front: entered like oxygen, exited like carbon dioxide.

Hank eased himself onto the hood of Orson's sedan. He felt the metal sink.

The only other vehicles in the lot were Hank's busted car and an old RV covered in stickers like an ice cream truck, except these stickers featured chemtrail complaints.

"How did you find me?"

Orson sat next to him. "I'm not the smartest. Bird shit for

brains. But if there's one thing I know about Hank the Tank Vasquez: that motherfucker really loves basketball."

Hank's chest creaked. A laugh escaped. "I keep telling people that." The laugh was no longer one. "They don't believe me."

"Well, Shank, you *do* have a history of telling enormous lies. People say you were down on one knee proposing to Carmella when you coughed up a hair ball, all, 'Never mind, I'm gay as a child that's born on Sabbath's day!'"

"As a . . . what?"

"Oh, man. That's an old nursery rhyme. I might be stupid, but I love shit like that. How weird catchphrases get passed down for no reason. Like, now people think 'Ring around the Rosie' was a plague song, but it totally wasn't! And I bet you thought I loved Trigonometry?"

"I didn't—"

"Nah, I know. Just another nervous habit. Saying racist bullshit about myself before anyone else can. If I beat assholes to the punch, I'm still in control. You know? The words belong to me." Orson clapped his hands together. "Enough sage Asian wisdom. Let's see the damage."

"The damage?"

"Truth is, Rin *might* have told me you'd be here."

Hank stared at his overlarge feet. "He told you about tryouts?"

"Oh. That? *Cheah*. Sounds like it was a real shit show, Hank. Someone told me your whole family had AIDS, which is just offensive as shit because people shouldn't joke about that. Someone else said really bad Lyme disease? Oh, and you guys got quarantined. But now you're just zipped lips all around. That about it?"

". . . yeah."

Orson whistled. "Like I said. A real shit show."

Hank's eyes found his useless hands.

"Thing is, Hank, eye for an eye doesn't mean jack to me. Just because you sucked a fat one—other than Nesbitt's, I mean—over the summer doesn't mean Tim gets to make sausage meat of your belly."

"He didn't."

"Shut up. You are bent as a fucking deflated boner, Hank." Orson slid off the car. He reached through the passenger window and produced a duffel bag. "I've got enough Biofreeze in here to stop time. Off with your shirt, by order of the Red Queen."

"You don't have to—"

Orson tugged at Hank's tee. "Really? 'Cause you're basically rainbow sherbet."

The cool air on Hank's bare skin gave him fewer goose bumps than Orson's stare did. Another dissection, or just the first time anyone had looked at Hank since Brendan?

Orson let Hank's shirt drop and bent back over the bag. "Ugh. Your poor, sad, ugly, meat-loaf abs. Here!" He tossed Hank an ice pack.

Hank's hands entirely failed to catch it. The pack smacked Orson in the shoulders.

"Jesus, Tank." Orson plucked it from the dirt, wiped it off, and set it in Hank's lap. "You're an idiot, but you don't have to be a brick wall."

"Orson. I deserved this." Hank let the cold spread across his thighs.

Orson sighed and slid back onto the hood. "Do you hear me disagreeing, O Almighty-Fuckup Vasquez?"

"No. So . . . really. *Why?*"

"D'you remember when I joined the team? In sixth grade. I was maybe the size of your left biceps. I used to wear glasses with fucking *straps* on them. At tryouts, three of the guys told me I should stick to violin."

"Assholes."

"Shit yeah. I mean, *hello?* Jeremy Lin? Yao Ming?"

"Sun Yue."

"Exactly. But then Ben O'Brien pulled the same thing with you. I thought you'd beat him senseless. You were already the TANK. You could have ripped his arms off. I mean, I would've, if I could've. But you just brushed it off. Like, 'You think I *can't* play? I'm Mexi-*can*, not Mexi-*can't*.'"

"That . . . wow. Even for me, that's pretty dumb."

"No it wasn't!" Orson sounded angry. "*Fuck*. Hank! I'm shit at telling stories. But I'manna tell you one, young man, so listen up."

"*Young man?*" Another smile paining him.

"Damn straight. Your birthday is six days after mine. Now listen the fuck up. In Taipei, it was hot as Hades, but I could *not* stay inside with my uncle. So I'd go out and play ball. I'd be on the way to the gym, walking between mint-green apartment buildings and street markets, and then *bam!* There'd be a park, an awesome little patch of *real* green. And in these parks were a bunch of old ladies with little brown poodles, and these ladies would sit on benches shooting the shit for *hours*. I wondered what they were talking about."

The cold had risen past Hank's navel.

"I don't really speak Taiwanese. My uncle loves guilting me because I can't get the tones right in Chinese half the time, and

Taiwanese is even worse. It's sort of got Mandarin words, but like—it's different. You know when you hear a crazy Scottish accent and you're not sure it's even English? Taiwanese is like that to me."

"Okay, I get that." Hank thought of all the Spanish words he didn't know, words people expected him to know after getting one look at him. Though Dad had been born in Tijuana, he was raised in Detroit, and his kids caught only snippets of his first language; it was an early absence. One of Hank's first perforations. "So . . . ?"

The streetlamp made marbles of Orson's eyes.

"So nothing. It just made me wonder about things I don't understand. Like when Ben O'Brien was a dick to me, I nearly quit the team. But when he was a dick to you? You laughed."

Hank inhaled. This was the part where Orson would ask Hank what happened over the summer. This was the part where Hank had to go missing.

"Then I realized, *no*. I mean, whatever the poodle ladies were talking about was none of my business. Even if I knew the language it wouldn't be. That's my dumb story."

Hank exhaled.

Do you think you'll ever trust me? Luz typed on Hank's phone before Hank fell asleep on the night of the chilaquiles, after their mirror conversation.

"Dad asked me that. He was teaching me to ride a bike and he let go too early."

Hank watched his fingers move without him. *But Hank, you're not Milo. You know I'm not your father.*

"I know." What Hank didn't know was whether or not that was a good thing. "I don't know what you are."

Neither do I. I'm trying to find out. I'm trying to grow up. Just like you.

Hank's breath fogged the screen. Luz wiped it away.

Luz started to type something else, paused, and started over: *Why do* you *suppose you're so eager to see me for what I am?*

Hank shrugged, alone in the tower that was his bunk. He tried to set the phone down. "I need to sleep."

Luz held tight, pressing Hank's thumb against the glass until it creaked.

What do you think, Hank Vasquez? Why do you see me?

Hank closed his eyes. "Because there was . . . I don't know. For a long time, no one saw me for what I was, either. Least of all me."

Luz let go of the phone and patted Hank on the shoulder.

When Hank started sobbing in the parking lot of Moreno Park, Orson remained at his side. He patted Hank like Luz had and then, after a minute, got to his feet.

"Wanna go to my place and shoot a few hoops, Tank?"

"I've shot enough."

"Yeah, I know." Orson smiled. "Wanna actually *make some* this time?"

16

OUTSIDE

By eight p.m., Maggie had scrubbed the floor in front of the sink, bleached the bathtub, Windexed every window. It wasn't as soothing as driving, but anything to keep moving.

Now she was stripping the linens.

Maggie saved the tugging of the wrinkled fitted sheet from Hank's bunk for last.

She'd heard him tiptoeing out every morning, though he tried so hard to be quiet. Hank had always *tried* to be a lot of things.

Maggie suspected Hank tossed in his sleep as much as Milo, who woke every morning so thoroughly tangled that she'd nicknamed him the Human Burrito. But the only clue that Hank occupied this space at all was a heavy indentation in the mattress, a dip as big as he was.

Hank hit his first enormous growth spurt back in junior high, gained inches so quickly that he might as well have sprouted antlers. At the shoe store for the second time in three months, Maggie had watched him try and fail to pull a sneaker over his heel.

"Don't force it, Hank."

He slumped. "Think I'll be as tall as Dad?"

"I have no idea. You should ask him."

"I . . . but what do *you* think?" Hank's grin slipped.

She tousled his hair like he was Milo's size. "I think you'll be even *taller.*"

Hank blinked twice in surprise. There was nothing slathered on about *that* smile.

Ana had a pantry, not a bed. She didn't sleep with Maggie anymore.

Once that might have seemed like a good thing. Ana was a lot to handle on the best of days, perfumes and eyeliner on the pillowcases, even before her breakdown last year, when she started picking scabs in her sleep, speckling the bedding with blood.

Today the unstained pillow felt cold.

"If you want, Ana, I can set up camp in the living room."

"Please don't, Mom."

"But you're a teen now. You need privacy." Maggie had stared at her daughter. Ana, propped up on cushions, manga from the library in her lap. "If you take this room, you can have people over. You won't have to go to Marissa's every time."

A vision: Marissa's mother at the poolside, sunglasses and lipstick perfectly offsetting her oval face.

"It's fine, Mom. I told you. *I don't care.*"

"Must be nice." Maggie bit her tongue. Mothers shouldn't sound like teenagers, even when one's trapped inside them.

Ana set the book down on the nightstand and laid her head on Maggie's shoulder. "Grow up, you will, Mom," she said, in the Yoda voice that Maggie thought had been outgrown alongside Miyazaki hoodies. "Okay, you will be."

Maggie reached the laundry room and found it occupied.

She dropped the heap of sheets in a basket that didn't have a seven-year-old protruding from it. Milo had all the grace of an inchworm at the moment, bottom in the air and arms straight back on the floor, neck deep in stray socks and shirts.

"You're going to have some major back problems one day, kid."

The music from his headphones sounded nearer in the close space.

Maggie had never been the audiophile in the family. The music she cared for she'd never tried to share. Somehow she felt it could never measure up to all the psychedelic rock Donovan left in his wake, the songs he used to whistle in the shower.

Milo must have switched artists again. This new music was vast and beautiful, and for a moment Maggie didn't want to wake him. Not now, not ever. Perhaps when Dr. Ruby returned next week, the two of them would still be asleep here, gathering cobwebs.

Before Dr. Ruby had departed, she'd sat with Maggie in the living room.

Their usual act, their usual setting. If this room were a stage, this was their pantomime: the concerned mother, the composed doctor.

"Sorry, I've called Hank and Ana, and left messages and—"

"Plenty of distractions on the first day of school. It may be a sign that they're readjusting. And we can still talk about Milo. I'm wondering if you might need to make a different arrangement for him."

Maggie frowned. "Just for Milo?"

"In many ways Milo's condition seems the most severe. Yes, Hank and Ana are struggling. Aside from the obvious—the physical side effects in Ana's eyes and Hank's hands—both seem incapable of keeping their focus on the present. But attention deficits are par for the course when it comes to posttraumatic stress disorder. Milo's situation seems more dire."

"So . . . you think we should take him out of school?"

"I could provide an alternative for Milo. I'd be happy to work with him."

"Work with him, or work *on* him?" Maggie whispered.

Dr. Ruby stopped smiling. "I have no intention of harming—"

"Then why haven't you taken us out of here?" Maggie closed her eyes. "Taken us *anywhere* else?"

Those scars were so unreadable. "Normalcy is what your children need right now in order to heal."

"Would that be the normalcy of being bullied, or the normalcy of being homeschooled by a scientist?" How many people had Maggie exhausted today?

"It's up to you, Maggie. Of course it is."

"People keep telling me that. But how am *I* more qualified

than anyone else? How am I supposed to know better than teachers, principals, doctors, scientists?" Her voice broke. "A *goddamn alien* knew my kids better than I do!"

"You have a point, Maggie." The roles shifted. How, Maggie couldn't say, but Dr. Ruby no longer seemed professional. "There's not a lot of logic behind it, is there? We're only human, and this is the way things are. No matter what else the parasite was, it wasn't their mother."

Before leaving, Dr. Ruby shook Maggie's hand. She always did. Her hands were always warmer than Maggie expected they'd be.

"I apologize for the mess."

"Your home is always spotless, Margaret."

". . . I apologize for the mess."

Maggie lifted her littlest from the laundry basket, noting how little he *wasn't*, waiting for Milo to cling to her as he had this morning. To her relief, she still wanted to hold him.

Milo opened his eyes.

"Milo, can you help me with something, please?"

She saw him watching her lips.

"I WANTED TO HELP WITH FOLDING."

"Tell me, Milo."

"I THINK THE RHYME IS 'RED ON BLACK, PLEASE STAY BACK.'"

She enunciated carefully: "Do you want to go to school tomorrow?"

He looked at her, eyes miles away, and suddenly snapped to. "OR WAS IT 'BLACK ON YELLOW, YOU'RE A DEAD FELLOW.'"

Would she ever make sense of him?

There came the metallic clanging of the front door, the sound of moccasins scuffing the carpet in the entranceway, making their way down the hall.

"Mom?"

She nearly dropped Milo. When had Ana last called for her? "We're here. The laundry room!"

Ana stepped into view. She looked hardly any worse for wear: a hoodie and sweats, lank uncombed hair. But now she had sunglasses and a little color in her cheeks, as though she'd been shouting.

"HELLO ANA."

Ana looked at him. "Hey, Milo."

"I'M TRYING TO FOLD."

"I can see that. How's that going for you?"

"I'M AFRAID I'LL SOUND SEXISM BUT CAN YOU HELP?"

"Where were you?" Maggie found she wasn't angry, but relieved.

"School." Ana reached for lumpy dishcloths, folded one. "Mom. Can I try out for the school musical?"

Maggie started. A year ago, certainly—Ana flitted from one extracurricular to the next as if they were ephemeral things that shriveled and died the moment she lost interest in them. But in no universe had Maggie anticipated this request today.

"Of course you can."

Milo finished inspecting Ana's folded dishcloth. "VERY GOOD ANA, THE CORNERS *ALMOST* MATCH UP. B+ I THINK."

"I'll take it." Ana squatted beside him.

Maggie could feel the weight of the phone in her bathrobe pocket. "Any idea where your brother is?"

Ana shook her head.

"And . . . and how was your first day back?"

Ana appeared to actually consider the question before the inevitable shrug. "Could have been worse." Milo dug deep, yanked a fitted sheet from the bottom of the basket, and threw it at his sister; Ana caught it. "How was yours, Mom?"

Maggie froze.

Those calls to her children she'd told Dr. Ruby about—she'd never made a single one of them, and not because Maggie believed her children wouldn't come home.

Because Maggie believed her children had not been home for a long, long time.

Over the summer she'd lost them, or maybe even before. Not in an evening, but moment by moment. Only weeks ago Maggie had walked into her own kitchen and caught the three of them operating in silent unison after midnight, cooking, communicating on some level she couldn't understand.

They'd spun to face her as one. Maggie had wondered who they were.

So Maggie hadn't tried to find her children today. It felt too much like sending capsules into space, hoping someone on Alpha Centauri might take the time to hear a snippet of Beethoven from an earthling tin can.

She watched Ana peel a dryer sheet off one of Hank's jerseys.

"EUREKA!" Milo cried, holding it. "THAT'S TWO DAYS OF GOOD LUCK FOR YOU ANA!"

Maggie pulled her phone from her pocket. From Hank:

Sorry I missed dinner. I'm with Orson. Be home late.

"MOM? TOMORROW I WANT TO SIT BY PENNY DAWSON."

Maggie lifted her head. "I'll let Mrs. Stuart know first thing in the morning."

Milo's music faded. The dryer clicked off. For half a beat, the three of them listened to the whirr of crickets beyond the open window and the distant echo of living things rustling in the canyon.

They folded until there was nothing left. Ana wandered away to make the beds while Milo helped Maggie start the washing machine. He could reach the buttons without the footstool now.

After tucking Milo in, Maggie messaged Hank:

Be safe. I love you.

She'd decided not to wait up.

When she got to her room, Ana was under the covers. A penlight was taped to the inside of her sunglasses, but by her breathing, Maggie knew she was asleep at last.

PART TWO
OCTOBER 31
(DAY EIGHTY-SEVEN)

1
EARS

Right after Mrs. Stuart handed out the candy corn, Penny asked Milo to pass her the glue.

What Penny actually signed was *I want*, pulling both hands toward herself, palms up and fingers curled. She rubbed her palm over her heart in the sign for *please*. Milo didn't know how to sign *glue*, but the only things in his hands were a glue stick and some surreptitiously chewed candy corn. He used his powers of deduction.

Body language made a ginormous difference in American Sign Language! Lots of what people said had to do with how they said it. And "said" was a silly word to use. And other times, sign language was so *specific*. There were like five different signs for *make*! If you were making something, like a paper pumpkin for instance, you used a different *make* than you would for telling someone you'd made your bed. Milo had a lot to learn!

But Penny's dad, Mr. Dawson, was a good teacher. That was his whole job. Mr. Dawson could hear a little, but he told Milo the first language he ever learned was ASL, because *his* dad, Penny's grandpa, was Deaf. Dads, dads, and dads! They were everywhere, doing all kinds of things.

Every Tuesday and Thursday morning, Mom loaded Milo into the van at what she called "the crack of dawn" and Milo called "the butt crack of dawn." At first Milo figured he'd be too tired to rise and shine so early; he might half-rise and sparkle a little at most. But Mom was right there with him, and they got to skip an hour of school!

They drove all the way to Eustace Community College and closed themselves in room 27. Room 27 wasn't like a real classroom at all! It was a trailer at the back of a tiny, bare campus.

Mom and Milo weren't the only students. There was a small Deaf community in Eustace, but Mr. Dawson explained that most people in Deaf families learn from each other, not from teachers. Mr. Dawson's job was teaching really big kids, *college students*, all about ASL, so they could interpret or teach ASL one day, too. Milo was allowed to sit in on their classes and ask Mr. Dawson as many questions as he wanted.

"Does this mean you believe me? About my ears?"

Mom had told him no, and Milo should be careful about what he said; Milo was not Deaf and should never, ever pretend to be. But this was part of the agreement she'd made with Principal Olsen. If Milo wanted to keep his headphones on in school, he had to work hard. "It's a good deal, Milo. Sign language is an amazing thing for anyone to learn. We are lucky to have Mr. Dawson so nearby."

Mom was so awful at signing! She frowned the whole time, folding her face in half. She stared at Mr. Dawson with very beady eyes. Usually Milo only ever saw her look that suspicious about dentists. (Basically everyone in Eustace knew Mom had a bazillion cavities.) Whenever they paired up for conversation practice, Mom's partners took two steps back, probably scared of getting swatted by accident!

Oops! Penny was asking Milo for the glue again. Music swelled in Milo's ears.

Milo had spent almost two months straight listening to Sigur Rós and nothing else. He still hadn't learned what the Icelandic songs were about, but they weren't cold. They were just beautiful, strings and ghostly falsetto. The kind of music that felt like it kept existing even when you stopped listening. And maybe it had existed way before you ever did, echoing in old sea caves or made out of fog, and it made everything else beautiful sometimes, too.

Dad in his ears had felt like that. One of the first things Milo had asked, after Dad/Luz moved in, was how come he left without saying good-bye?

I'm sorry, Milo, Dad/Luz told him. *The bear grass grabbed me. I had to go.*

"I thought you were sucked down the shower drain! I was only four so I thought that. Because you didn't say good-bye."

I did say it, Milo! I hugged you close and definitely did not leave without telling you I'd be gone forever.

"Oh. I didn't hear you, maybe." Milo wiped his nose on his hand.

Oh, really? Then let me say it now: Good-bye, Milo. Good-bye.

Milo remembered burrowing deeper into his blankets and putting his hands over his ears because he wanted to hold that whisper in his head forever. That one word made the time Dad was gone more beautiful, or at least less ugly. Just like music.

Now Penny was like that. It was in the way she repeated signs until Milo understood them.

Penny would never just *take* the glue from him.

"I have to *hand* it to you, Penny!" He passed her the Elmer's. A few other kids looked up. Oops! Milo should lower his voice for the next pun. But someone laughed. Maybe Milo should try this same joke on Hank? Would Hank laugh at last?

Milo's chest hurt. Without thinking, he swallowed another candy corn. Now his pumpkin craft would either have only one eye, or no nose, or be missing a tooth.

"You can't have everything, Jack," he told his construction paper.

Halloween was turning second grade into a madhouse!

Penny huffed. She handed him one of her extra candy corns.

Later there would be trunk-or-treating. Milo had picked out some awesome gushing fruit snacks for Mom's trunk. Parents would be coming, too, from wherever parents who didn't work in schools worked. Mom had promised to come help Milo get dressed at lunchtime. She'd packed his homemade fire ant costume from last year, after bending one of the cardboard wings back into shape.

Mom didn't know Milo had outgrown fire ants. He had other plans.

Milo popped another candy corn into his mouth. Penny punched him in the arm. Kids were finishing their crooked jack-o'-lanterns. Some held their work up before it dried, and watched the candy fall right back off.

"Penny, we're running a real circus here," Milo lamented.

Be quiet, Penny signed. *Work.*

Milo lowered the volume on his headphones. Mrs. Stuart was about to call for attention, Milo guessed. She always rubbed her hands together beforehand. Milo was never so good with people's faces, but lately watching people move had taught him a lot!

Mrs. Stuart called for them to join her. Milo tapped Penny on the shoulder and the two of them found their places on the colorful rug.

Show-and-tell was usually pretty decent entertainment, for *kids* anyhow. That was Milo's opinion. But today almost everybody who had a turn cheated by showing-and-telling about their Halloween costumes.

Stormy Calimlim showed off black sweatpants and a sweater with small Froot Loops and Corn Pops boxes stapled to it. Each box was impaled by plastic cocktail swords. Milo thought a cereal killer costume was a little inappropriate. Even if it was a pretty good joke. When Stormy sat down, she forgot she had cardboard on her butt and *really* killed the cereal. That made it better!

Antonio stood. Milo looked down, so he didn't really see. But he was pretty sure Antonio was wearing the same dumb Freddy Krueger claws as last year.

Finally, it was Milo's turn! Mrs. Stuart beckoned him forward. He unfolded his legs from under him. He almost got tangled! He rushed to the locker cubbies to grab his secret costume. He hefted the heavy bag to the front of the classroom, set it on the stool, and stood beside it. Milo waggled his eyebrows at his audience.

Mrs. Stuart gave him an encouraging smile.

Milo pulled two items of filthy clothing from the bag.

"Here is my show-and-tell presentation. First, this is my shirt." He pinned it to his chest with his chin. Maybe it muffled his voice, but still! He held up a pair of jeans next. "These are my pants. They are kind of dirty, like if you look you can see grass stains but that's okay if you can't."

Everyone had strange faces. Milo folded his pants and shirt perfectly—he'd been practicing! He set them back in the bag.

"Um, why my costume is important is because of what it is. What it is called is, MILO VASQUEZ, SEVEN YEARS OLD. I wore these exact pants and shirt on my birthday! I wanted to wear this shirt because there's a really cool frog on the pocket giving everyone the peace sign. This is the peace sign. It's not *really* sign language."

Penny flashed him one anyhow. Her smile was rare and special, like those rocks he sometimes found outside that had sparkles in them!

Milo puffed up his chest to say the most important part.

"This is a costume of a different person, though. Because now I'm Milo SEVEN YEARS, FOUR MONTHS OLD. If you look at the holes in the knees you can see where I fell in the canyon. There's even a little blood! Because I cut my knee pretty bad. I ran away from home after my birthday party. It was black out."

Milo looked at them all meaningfully. Eyes on the magician!

There was some confusement (a word Milo had invented). Mrs. Stuart started clapping. The others joined in. But Milo held up his finger until every hand froze!

"Usually I only run at nighttime when I'm playing ghost in the graveyard. And we were *going* to play ghost in the graveyard.

At my party." He took a deep breath. "*Except*—TA-DA!—*no one came to my party!*"

Stormy fell out of her chair and crushed her remaining cereal boxes. Adrian opened his mouth wide enough to catch base-balls. Penny started signing: *Stop it, stop it!*

But Milo wasn't finished yet!

"You guys didn't come to my party, even though I invited *most of you* except Terrance, because Terrance is lactose intoler-ant and I can't live without ice cream. But if you look at my shirt, my *evidence!* The sleeves! There are snot stains. I was *crying!*"

Milo darted out of Mrs. Stuart's reach. He clambered atop the stool. It rocked precariously under his feet. This was nothing compared to a teeter-totter.

"I'M ALMOST FINISHED!" Milo bellowed. "THERE'S ONE MORE THING TO TELL EVERYONE!"

Mrs. Stuart's mouth became the fish lips he'd seen on day one.

"I DIDN'T CRY BECAUSE *YOU GUYS* DIDN'T COME. I CRIED BECAUSE *DAD* DIDN'T COME! BUT GUESS WHAT—?"

"That's enough, Milo," they were probably saying. Mrs. Stuart was definitely saying so. She pulled him off the desk and caught him.

"HE WAS JUST A LITTLE LATE!"

Long before he left, Dad had taught Milo how to whistle. And whistling was the sound that the wind made in Nameless Can-yon on the night he ran away. So Milo didn't have to see a face to recognize Dad again. So what if he didn't have a body? So what if he didn't have brown eyes or a mustache like he used to?

A whistle was enough. A *shadow* or a *whisper* would have been enough for Milo. A whistle was music, the beautiful Roaring Everything.

Dad had promised to teach Milo to bike ride. Dad was magical. He built tree houses without trees and he brought opossums back from the dead. Of course he didn't need a body to be a dad. He was just a little Luz. He was just a little late.

Mrs. Stuart pulled him right back to his place on the carpet. When he sat down, Penny took his elbow and signed *hush*.

Milo didn't feel like shouting anymore.

"Thank you, Milo."

Milo didn't know how come, but when they set their crafts out to dry on the windowsill, he didn't really care whether his pumpkin had eyes. He chewed and swallowed his last candy corn, glue and all. He set his blank paper pumpkin down next to Penny's.

All sorts of people didn't have all sorts of things.

2

EYES

The first night Ana slept, *really* slept, again, she did dream of Dad. Rather than the empty abyss, she fell into a memory.

It was a specific memory, altered by the dreaming. Ana remembered the day Dad drove her to Walmart to pick out a Christmas gift for Mom. Ana was probably eight, because she remembered dawdling, obsessing over cartoon folders in the school supplies aisle until Dad led her to the accessories section. Someone had gone on a rampage in the hosiery aisle—except, in the dream, all the tights on the floor became wriggling larvae.

"Help me out here, Ana." Dad gestured at the wall of jewelry. The junk glimmered in scuttling patches, caught the light like beetled backs. "Which bracelet, do you think?"

"Mom doesn't wear bracelets. She says they get in the way."

"See, *that's* why I need you here. You pay attention to the girl stuff."

Ana couldn't see how being a girl had anything to do with it. But she pointed at a necklace and he grabbed it. On the way to the checkout line, Dad tugged her ponytail and thanked her. His phone rang; Dad told Ana that if she was quick, he'd let her run back to pick out a sparkling folder for herself.

In the dream and in the memory, Ana clutched the fish-scaled folder tight when she returned to the checkout. Dad clutched his phone even tighter.

Ana woke up next to her mother. Her hands were empty.

Dad had never given as much as he'd taken.

When Ana told Dr. Ruby about the dream, she stopped jotting notes.

"Your dreams are very important to you, aren't they, Ana?"

Ana shrugged. She didn't find Dr. Ruby threatening like Milo did, and she didn't see any point in refusing to speak with her like Hank did. But now that she'd slept on it a bit, Ana did wonder what drew this cryptic woman to the Vasquezes. What was the point of the performance?

Dad would have thought Ana already knew. Ana and Dr. Ruby were both girls, right? And Dad always thought that meant they'd be the same.

Dr. Ruby set down her pen. "They say creative people process their feelings while they sleep."

"Who says?"

"I'm not certain, actually. *They.* I could be making it up. But it's something I can believe. What have you been processing in your sleep, Ana?"

"Dad stuff, I guess. Same as always."

"Hopefully it won't be always." A note of unwarranted emotion entered Dr. Ruby's voice. She put fingers on her melted face. "Hopefully you'll let him go when you need to. If you're lucky."

Ana didn't ask. With the plucking of her pen from the table, Dr. Ruby shook herself free of the anger. She was back to talking about the marked improvement in Ana's habits, back to discussing the clarity of Ana's eyes now that Ana blinked more.

Ana had seen a lot of movies and a lot of people acting like scientists and doctors. Very few actors pulled it off. Dr. Ruby was no different. Yet Ana understood that though her eyes were fair game, Dr. Ruby's scars were not.

Even if they were the only real thing about her.

"For the love of Olivier! Which part of 'only twenty-three days until opening night' don't you heathens understand?"

Even from the wings Ana saw spit arcing upward from the front row of busted auditorium seats. Not that Mr. Oldman was sitting so much as hovering.

"I think we understand the passage of time better than he does, actually." Brendan's breath warmed the left side of Ana's neck, softer than the velvety old curtains on her right.

Brendan didn't have to speak so quietly. Mr. Oldman couldn't hear them from his ungodly half-crouching perch, probably wouldn't even if he dragged his skinny self closer to harangue the chorus members petrified upstage. "He *does* realize only fifty people will see this musical, and at least forty-seven of them will be the miscellaneous aunties of Skid Row Chorus Girl Number Four, correct?"

Ana snorted. She arched her shoulder to cover the patch

where Brendan's breath tickled. He asked her more questions these days. It made her blink sometimes.

It made her forget to mind the blinking.

Are you trying to forget me, Ana? Luz might have said, through Milo or Hank or through recollections of lost things: her mother slumped over at the kitchen table, the sensation of the first needle tearing through an unscarred thigh and changing it forever, a fridge with nothing in it.

Yes. Ana deliberately closed her eyes.

Upon reopening, Ana's eyes watched members of the chorus fall back into starting positions. The number restarted at a clip much faster than the script called for. The pace became frantic. Sara, the junior pianist from the pit orchestra, began beating the keys like they were egg whites, she was on a cooking show, and by god she had better produce some gorgeous meringues.

Dark as it was in the wings, onstage the lights cut warm yellow circles into the floor. When Ana stood directly under those orphaned suns, there was no such thing as an abyss behind eyelids. There were sunspots, flashes of red and green and white.

Mr. Oldman was a lot to handle, consigning them to additional practice during homeroom. But his being a lot to handle was precisely why every practice involved a stage afire in spotlights. Rumor had it that the school had threatened to send Mr. Oldman the electricity bill. Brendan said he'd seen Mr. Oldman scoff at that, had seen him twirl his formidable mustache in disdain and reply, "Over my dead cadaver."

"He likes being redundant. Claims it really puts a final dead doornail in life's coffin."

"Idiotic imbecile," Ana drily replied.

Brendan's chuckle—you could set it to music, build a score around it.

"Seymour! WHERE'S MY SEYMOUR!"

"There's my deadly death-knell bell." Brendan squeezed Ana's shoulder once, before scurrying to his peeling blue-tape mark.

That natural, frenetic unease of his was more in character than acting could have been. The shopkeep wore anxiety like a second skin. Brendan really didn't have the comedy down. But when he sang about his life as an orphan, he had conviction.

"We're all orphans of something."

"Well, chanting that in the dark to no one's not creepy at all, Vasquez." Platinum leaned her weight against the ropes. She ignored Mr. Oldman's shriek about not rattling the curtains. "This might seem like the most obvious thing in the world, but since your eyes look like shit, maybe you *see* like shit. So take a good look at our friend Bren."

"I'm already—"

"Oh, I know. You're already *looking*." Platinum wore white glow-in-the-dark lipstick; this far from the spotlights her mouth seemed disembodied, *Rocky Horror*–esque. "But *look at him*. Take him all in."

Ana did.

Those pointed elbows. That long avian neck craning forward to meet Mr. Oldman's endless critiques, and Ana could see the little hairs on the nape of it. The sharpness of shoulder blades branching below it. She saw the strangeness of his anatomy even through a shirt-and-vest combination, noted the way Brendan stood perpetually on the balls of his feet as if waiting on the edge of something unseen, ready to dive right into it, though uncertainty also emanated from him, like he'd dive and shatter and that was fine with him, because it was all about the plummet, not how the plummet ended.

Feathers and breaking glass: Brendan Nesbitt, in Ana's eyes.

"Okay. So what?"

"Now tell me." Platinum's sardonic lilt abruptly abandoned her. "Will our friend Bren *ever* look at you like you just looked at him?"

"No." This time the blackness behind Ana's eyes seemed fitting. "I know that."

"Well." Platinum shook her head. "Don't be so macabre about it."

The two of them watched Brendan belt a few lines, slightly off-key. They watched him apologize. Singing remained something other than his forte. He'd won the leading role solely on the basis of his Brendan-ness.

"Now I feel like a bitch," Platinum added. "Thanks for that."

"You're not."

Brendan returned to his first mark.

"Not trying to be. It's basically a front. Goes well with all the bleach."

"And the lipstick?" Ana meandered.

Platinum laughed, low on her breath. "That's to spook the jocks. Why, is it spooking you, too?"

Brendan Nesbitt and Platinum (Arlene) Watson were a package deal. Sometimes they coordinated their outfits, although

Platinum insisted on wearing only white and black. They split KitKats on a biweekly basis and engaged in deep, analytical conversations about *RuPaul's Drag Race* for hours on end.

Brendan first patted an empty patch of bench at their lunch table for Ana's sake on the second day of school, declaring, "Ms. Vasquez has a set of pipes!"

"Then she should probably see a plumber." The carrot stick in Platinum's mouth looked suddenly like the cigar of the irritable fat cat in the old gangster movies Ana and Marissa had temporarily obsessed over.

But she made room.

By the next day she wasn't grumbling, and by the third day she offered her carrot sticks to Ana. As if they were elementary schoolers. It was impossible for Ana to tell whether or not this was sarcasm.

"Carrots are good for your eyesight," Platinum reminded her.

"Brendan is good people. That's why he used to hang out with me even back when I hated myself and wore *cargo pants*. But Ana, he's . . . so very *Brendan Nesbitt*, you know." Platinum's tone was meaningful. "You shouldn't forget it."

"Hard to forget when you're whispering it in my ear."

Platinum went quiet. "Yeah, well. I won't be forever."

Before Ana could reply, Platinum dragged her feet and took her time stretching on her way to center stage.

"AUDREY! WHERE IS MY AUDREY I?"

"Hey, Mr. Oldman." Platinum yawned. "You rang?"

"Obviously! You're our leading lady and god help us all, you're the one thing going right in this travesty of *theatah*."

"About that. I'm sort of moving to Italy next week. You should dust off my understudy, Mr. Oldman."

Brendan dropped his script.

"But—what? I didn't cast an understudy!"

Platinum pushed her hands into her overall pockets. "Oops."

Had Mr. Oldman any hair, he might have torn it out.

Ana didn't feel like singing. She was looking at Platinum, not at Brendan. For two months, Platinum had been anywhere Brendan was. After school in the auditorium, at lunch, in the hallways, until Ana would have given a lot not to see her.

Wanting something to leave rarely made it so.

When she and Hank had emerged from Nameless Canyon on June 7, dragging Milo between them, the three cleared the barricade and sank immediately to the ground. All three vomited, all three gasped.

Ana knew she should rush inside, should call Mom, but her eyeballs itched, or were bleeding, it felt like, and when she closed them—

She *saw* things.

At first it was this: A faceless body, waving. Her father's silhouette, but the face wasn't quite—

Ana rubbed her sockets on Repeat. Each time she closed her eyes, the face on that silhouette solidified. Eventually it did not look unlike Brendan Nesbitt.

Ana pulled herself to her feet. She held her eyelids between her thumbs and forefingers. "Hank. What happened with Brendan?"

"What?" Hank, curling and uncurling his fingers. "Sorry, Ana. Something's up with my hands. Give me a second?"

Ana didn't want to let her lids fall, but she couldn't stand watching Milo push his fists into his ears.

She blinked again; the waving figure had vanished. Where he'd been, Ana was treated to a memory all but forgotten: picking blueberries with Grandma in Wisconsin woods.

"There's something in my eyes. It's in my eyes. Milo, could you please be quiet?"

"I am quiet! But no one else is! *Shh!* I'm trying to hear the termites." Milo pressed his head against the earth.

An hour ago she'd have hollered, dragged him off the ground, her idiot little brother. But—

Blink: The thing in Ana's eyes recalled Milo's prune-y baby face, the first time she felt his weight in her lap.

Ana opened her eyes.

"Get out of my head," she said, through gritted teeth, though her heart swelled at the memory. Maybe *because* her heart swelled.

"It's almost like the sound in your mouth at the dentist."

"Get up, Milo." Ana refused to blink. "Hank, can you—"

"One second, Ana," Hank said, rubbing his hands together.

"Not one second! Stop twiddling your thumbs and help me get him inside!"

"Um. I can't, though." When had Hank last admitted he couldn't do something? "I'm not the one twiddling them."

Ana watched Hank's fingers interlock; Hank watched them too, his face, usually so controlled, shaken to blank surprise. Hank didn't look so big.

Blink: Hank and Ana bickering over a bag of circus peanuts, and the tug-of-war that left Dad rumbling with laughter once the bag exploded and orange hailstones rained down on the three of them.

The thing in her eyes was finding its bearings. Ana's stomach flipped over.

"My eyes. Your hands. And Milo's—"

"Dad," Milo said, "don't you think termites sound like the dentist's?"

Ears.

Both of her brothers, rendered useless in this crisis. They didn't know the dark so well as Ana. Pain remained alarming to them, was no friend.

But even as pain laid them low, Ana awoke.

She grabbed one brother by the hand and the other by the elbow. She stomped them away from the hole in the world, back up their driveway, past the untouched piñata dangling from the basketball hoop, and through the front door.

The air shifted when they reached the landing, and Ana had to—

Blink: The three of them, stuck together with cotton candy. Years ago, at the Eustace County Fair, watching Mom and Dad hold hands, walking just in front of them—

"Stop it!" Ana opened her eyes wide. "Get out. Get out right now."

"Ana, what are you—?" Hank's hands danced strangely, but he'd forced his arms against his sides. His fingers could only do so much from there. They pitter-pattered on his jeans.

"Ana," Milo cried. "Ana, why is your heart racing? Are you scared? You're not scared of Dad, are you?"

Hank said what Ana wanted to. "Whatever this thing is, it isn't Dad, Milo."

Milo wasn't listening to them; he was listening to something else.

Ana heard a vehicle pull into the driveway. A van, not a Chevy, and Mom must be hysterical. Who knew how long they'd been gone? Ana should rush outside and reassure her they were alive and whole—

That was the trouble. They were *more* than whole.

Blink: Ana's mother on the day Ana started her period, the warm embrace Mom gave her, the way she dried Ana's tears with a turkey-patterned paper towel. "Honey, it's a good thing, really." And Ana felt that Mom didn't understand. Couldn't understand.

How could she understand now, Ana? it was asking.

"Enough!"

In the kitchen, Ana knew exactly which drawer to reach for. Ana knew how to cut. She hadn't used a knife before, but the scars on her thighs had to count for something, and damn it, Ana could still hurt herself if she needed to—

Blink: The thing in Ana's eyelids countered this thought with a vision of the first yanking of a safety pin through her flesh, the deep but hair-thin slice, reminding her of how little it had made her feel better last year—

"That's not the point, *shut* up and get out!"

"Ana!" Hank cried, but he was wrestling with his own hands.

Blink: The faceless thing swinging her around, Dad linking his elbow with Ana's at the Eustace Elementary Kindergarten Hoedown.

Ana wanted that do-si-do to exist.

But that only reminded her of all the things others had wanted her to want: how the things she and Marissa once loved, the long-legged anime girls and snippets of stop-motion animation, had fallen to the wayside. Because Ana was *supposed* to want boys, and a laugh that ran ripples through her classmates, and to be pretty, of all stupid things.

Hank was trying to regain his composure, to put the mask back on. Something about the knife seemed to still his hands. "Ana . . . please. Put it down."

"You're right. This isn't it." She dropped the knife and pulled a matchbox from among the cutlery. "Know how you get rid of a deer tick?"

Milo raised his hand. "Please will you both stop shouting?!"

Blink: Ana tasted hot chocolate on a rainy day, saw herself playing my house, foot matching foot, with Milo.

"Dad's trying to tell me what moth wings say."

Next to Ana, Hank's hand lifted a Sharpie from the pen mug on the counter and began scrawling something out. Ana struck a match and held it close to her eyeball, so that the flame singed her eyelashes—

Blink: Visions of Ana and Marissa whipping past each other on swings, the final time Mom let Ana loose in a McDonald's ball pit, even though they both knew Ana was too big for it and Mom looked twice over her shoulders and the instant Ana crawled into a claustrophobic plastic tube it felt like she was trying to submerge herself in a childhood that was much too small for her, and she knew where she didn't fit.

She couldn't open her eyes, though the flame had reached the end of the matchstick. It stung her fingertips.

Blink: Her brothers' toothy smiles through the ages, the recollection

of Grandma's hands and how they were almost Ana's, except Grandma's
were tissue paper.

Ana pried her lids upward.

All these memories were not enough, she knew. None of
them had been before, when Ana threaded safety pins through
her skin and squeezed them shut.

Why should anything be different now?

Blink: Ana saw herself on tiptoe, pudgy hands clutching the edge of
her mother's vanity. After a struggle, Ana caught sight of herself in the
mirror. Four years old, with Mom's lipstick smeared all over her face and
her little teeth.

Ana primped and preened. She blew herself a kiss.

I'm so beautiful, *every gesture said, as if she'd never doubt it.*

As if no one, least of all Ana herself, ever possibly could.

Ana dropped the spent match. Her tears had little to do with
the heat.

Her brothers and the kitchen. The tiny glass animals on the
shelf by the window. Her mother's voice on the phone outside.
The streetlight illuminating plastic counters and plastic floor.
Everything and nothing.

Hank held her hand. Milo wrapped arms around her leg.

"Ana, look," Hank whispered, but she already was. On the
counter, in a scrawl not so different from the handwriting that
adorned Hank's old homemade Christmas ornaments, Ana's
too, Milo's now—the scrawl of a first grader:

STaY plEAS?

Ana didn't just blink; she held her eyes shut.

A vision of Mom, praying for Ana the day after Ana was

hospitalized. Less than a year ago, because Ana started cutting around the holidays. Mom wasn't religious, said her only gods were Virginia Woolf and coffee. That was how desperate she was.

How desperate this newcomer was.

"Dad just asked me if he can stay," Milo murmured.

"It's not Dad, but yeah. I'm getting that message, too," Hank said.

"Someone *wants* to be here? That's new."

Hank wheezed and Milo smiled, not quite getting the joke but feeling that it was one. Not quite getting that it was the furthest thing from one.

They three inhaled, exhaled.

The kitchen light flipped on.

Ana started. This wasn't the thing beneath her eyelids—this was Mom, dropping her phone in the doorway, piecing together the sight of them in their canyon-dirtied clothing. Hank, drawing on the counter. Ana standing over a spent match. "Where have you—"

"Mom, moth wings sound like flip books," Milo declared.

And Mom was embracing them and scolding them and sobbing onto them. They weren't looking at her. They were with one another, and when Ana gave a tiny nod, the thing behind her eyelids replayed a memory of applause. Hank's hands settled down. Milo made a shushing motion.

Fine. Stay, if you want.

Platinum was leaving.

"What the hell am I supposed to do about this?" Mr. Oldman bawled.

"You want my advice?" Platinum pointed directly at Ana in the wings. "Give Ana my part. She's got pipes and a little fight in her."

"...Ana?"

"Yeah. Little Miss Sunglasses, Random Chorus Member Number Seven? Her."

The bell for second hour rang. Mr. Oldman barked, "Chorus Member Number Seven! Come see me after school."

Ana didn't just blink; she held her eyes shut.

3

HANDS

Carmella pecked Hank on the cheek before English Lit.

This was something she did every so often, if the mood took her, when she wasn't busy charming the hell out of someone else. Carmella collided like an asteroid. From nowhere and everywhere, she broke away from her girlfriends or boyfriends or teacher friends or the dust motes—everyone and everything got caught in the gravity of Carmella—and made a high-heeled beeline across the hallway for the pillar known as Hank Vasquez.

The collision was always gentle. It made nothing extinct. Today Carmella wore black makeup and a flaming-orange wig, but the marks left by her ashy lipstick did not scorch.

Hank remained grateful that she took his arm. That she never tried to take his hand. She never asked him to stop smiling.

Hank scanned Carmella from head to toe during the trek to Mrs. Moore's Olde Kingdom, gaze snagged by black silk and white shoes. "What are you supposed to be? The Great Pumpkin?"

"It's Halloween."

"Yeah, I know it is. And you're supposed to be? Cruel-*Ella* Deville?"

"No. I just said. I'm *Halloween*. The holiday incarnate." She pulled a rainbow roll of Smarties from a hidden pocket. "Would you like a cavity?"

"Maybe later."

"And who are you today, Hank?"

Hank stared down at his Converse, jeans, and monochromatic blue V-neck.

"Looks like I'm Hank Vasquez."

"That sounds like something Milo would be," Carmella observed, raising a perfectly painted eyebrow.

Hank didn't wince, though it was a near thing. "It's almost like we're related."

"Almost. Do you know what Milo told me yesterday?"

"Do I want to know?" Even this morning Milo had clamored for Hank's attention, flicking Corn Pops at him when Mom turned her back. Hank wished he could give Milo the smile he so clearly wanted, but every time he saw Milo, he remembered how he'd been the first to make him scream.

That night Luz left them, and left them smaller.

"He told me that red ants aren't native to America. Some idiots imported them by accident in the 1930s."

"Oh. Neat." In the past weeks there had been evenings, sometimes when Mom was busy with parent-teacher conferences and Hank and Ana remained at practice, when Carmella insisted on watching Milo. "Thanks for talking to him. I wish, I mean. I'm glad you do."

"I don't mind giving you all a *hand*," Carmella said, pointedly.

She'd stopped asking about the summer, but clearly hadn't stopped thinking about it. Carmella's thoughts were not to be taken lightly.

People assumed being popular meant being shallow, that being beautiful meant being empty. Hank had always thought Carmella was full of the right kinds of canyons—pensive caverns, passing kindness shadows, and the unknown glow of forgiving lichen in dark places.

When they'd been dating for months, a millennium ago, he said this in those exact words, in the context of a Valentine's Day poem. He felt uncomfortable the whole time he wrote it. He passed Carmella the shoddily cut construction-paper monstrosity on the bleachers after school; they'd been helping student council decorate for Winter Carnival.

She read it and laughed aloud.

"You have a penchant for terrible metaphors, Hank Vasquez. Eventually you're going to compare me to a graceful deer in the forest, aren't you, like all the creepy dead poets do?"

"Never said I was a writer." Hank flushed and scooted away. Her hand found his shoulder and reeled him back.

"*I* say you're a writer, Hank." She held his chin in soft hands and pulled his face toward her own. "And you know what? It's not like the words aren't nice. But the thing that annoys me is that a deer isn't *trying* to be a deer."

"And you're trying to be . . . Carmella?"

"Always." Her hands slipped from his skin. "Every second of every day, I'm trying to be Carmella. I'm thinking about every gesture, every tiny choice. I see my parents doing the same thing. They're exhausted. But they aren't unhappy."

Hank had met Carmella's parents a few times, had attended their Thanksgiving dinner last year. The table was set meticulously, the turkey carved in even slices and salted to perfection. Everyone dressed just so, in deep autumnal colors that complemented the tablecloth. Mom always took Hank and company out for Chinese on Thanksgiving. She didn't even make them wear khakis.

"I think you're nailing *Carmella*, Carmella."

"No, *you're supposed to be*," she joked, but there were barbs in it. Hank hadn't even tried lifting her shirt yet.

He cleared his throat.

"See? Now I'm second-guessing that joke. But I've had a long time to work on my makeup. I'm not talking about the face I paint on. Although that can help."

Hank thought of his little sister—Ana, in eighth grade, smearing black under her eyes.

"I'm talking about my *make-up*, as in what I'm made of. It does take a little effort to look beautiful. But it takes a lot more to *feel* it." She scratched Hank's head for him, tickled the short hairs behind his ears. "Pretty thoughts are the hardest to have."

"Yeah." Hank slumped back, let his elbows rest on the row of bleachers behind them. "*God.*"

"Carmella is fine." Her fingers had found his scalp again, traced parallel and disjointed paths across it.

"No, I meant: *god*, we have a lot in common."

"A whole lot, Hank Vasquez." Carmella had her paint. Hank had his.

She leaned down and pinned him there, and for a second, Hank kissed her back.

Carmella pressed the roll of Smarties into Hank's weak grip and found her seat at her table in English. Within minutes, Mrs. Moore, whistling merrily, had passed out monologues from *Canterbury Tales* for them to memorize.

Hank's assigned pilgrim was the Cook. "'Such a pity it seemed to me, he had a boil upon his knee.'" Hank smiled. "Because nothing says 'delicious' like boils on your knees."

"Yeah, Vasquez. I bet that would make things hard for you. How would you kneel for your pansy boyfriend?"

Hank turned before he could stop himself.

Tim Miller had spread his lanky body across an entire side of his table, squishing bespectacled Alan Boleyn into the aisle. An eyeball was painted on Tim's forehead, a star in its center, and he wore a vest and dress shirt like a prep-school dropout.

Since the shattering in Moreno Park, Tim had kept his distance, but Hank had felt him glaring in his peripheries. More than once he'd found spit on his locker and used his elbows to scrub penciled slurs from his desk.

"You hear me, Vasquez?" Tim whistled. "Hey, meatpacker?"

Usually, this was the part where some of Tim's friends would start slinging shit. Back when Hank was one of them, he'd done it, too. But deep down he'd known that guys who joked about smearing queers were only a hairsbreadth away from shoving Hank's face into concrete.

"So how does it feel not to touch the ball? That's literally never happened to me."

Hank realized what Tim's costume was supposed to be: Tim was a *star pupil*. It really wasn't a bad costume.

Tim Miller really wasn't a bad guy, or not as bad as he was pretending to be. This was a performance.

Tim could be better. Hank knew it, he knew it like the back of his confounded hands. Hank had hurt Tim first. He had squeezed, choked, and bruised. And Hank had to believe he was better than that now. Which meant Tim could be, too.

"What do you *want*, Tim?" Hank asked.

"You hold a basketball like it's a girl. Scared it might try and screw you?"

"Very funny."

Tim's eyes shot to his teammates for support. Rin Hisoka shook his head. Even Ben O'Brien—a frequent instigator, usually happy to harangue—pretended to focus on his monologue.

The blood left Tim's face. "You getting too gay for sports, or just getting retarded like your brother now?"

At that ugly word, Hank forgot all reason. He spun around, and *god*, he didn't need Luz's apathy to help him make pulp of Tim Miller now because useless or not his fists were rising in the bad way—

"Shut the fuck up, Miller." Esmeralda Benaway slammed her hands on Tim's table. She knocked his legs over the edge, throwing him off balance so that he had to catch himself, one hand on the carpet.

Tim looked like he *had* been punched.

Hank probably looked the same. He gaped as Esmeralda took her seat.

Esmeralda Benaway and Hank weren't friends. They'd been

partners for science projects over the years, sure, and once he'd helped her pass out flyers for her hockey team. She *did* have a reputation for taking shit from no one. Esmeralda was rumored to have gutted a rival team's goalie with her skates "by accident."

But rushing to Hank's aid like that—what had he done to earn that?

Hank cottoned on in time to see Carmella nod in satisfaction before redirecting her attention to Patrick Sims, her latest would-be paramour.

Weren't Carmella and Esmeralda both class representatives?

Hank couldn't prove it was Carmella, but someone had started a very intentional rumor about the Vasquez Catastrophe. The word had spread, and the word was this: the reason Hank Vasquez sucked at basketball now (the JV team had so far lost every one of its six games this season) was not because he went apeshit on Tim Miller at tryouts, but because he'd sustained nerve damage to his hands. His whole family *had* in fact contracted tragic *swine Ebola coli*, or whatever, and while that sounded gross, it really wasn't their fault and wasn't it *sad*, even?

In September, Hank had heard his last name in hushed hallway voices. Now, in October, the whisperers had abandoned the Vasquezes. Now the whisperers were wondering whether they should cheat on the upcoming Trigonometry exam. Whether there'd be any actual Halloween parties. How some kid in sophomore class got arrested for trail bombing. And on and on, into infinity.

Not for the first time, Hank felt small in the universe. Maybe for the first time, he was grateful for it.

Esmeralda Benaway readjusted her bun of black hair and went back to work.

Mrs. Moore appeared in their midst. "Woe, that we should hear tongues so young speaketh so vilely!"

Esmeralda balked. She was intimidating in every way imaginable, but Mrs. Moore was *very* Scottish. Mrs. Moore whispered, "Next time say 'Maketh thine motherfucking mouth closed.' This is English Lit, ya ken?"

Hank and Esmeralda blinked at each other.

Carmella wasn't looking his way. Hank knew this was her doing, the end result of her remaking his makeup in the collective subconscious of Eustace High.

Maybe he really could kiss her, now, but her majesty deserved better than that.

"I fell for your whole family," she'd told him.

That fall was proving priceless.

4

OUTSIDE

Putting kids first meant putting yourself last. Maybe that was a blessing.

If anyone had asked Maggie Vasquez a few months ago where she thought her family would be now?

Dr. Ruby *had* asked, on the day she and the only two associates Maggie had met, a tall woman and a squat man in matching navy business suits, removed the fumigation tent and relocated their mysterious operation to the confines of the garage.

"Milo will be homeschooled. Ana might be hospitalized again. Hank will be kissing girls and hating himself for it. None of us will talk about it."

"You seem slightly pessimistic, Margaret."

"Maybe I am."

"Anything else? Any goals or expectations, Margaret?"

"I expect *you* will still be here, watching this train wreck?"

Dr. Ruby frowned. "Have you ever seen a train wreck, Margaret?"

"Have you ever tried not ending every sentence with my name?" Just as Milo had inherited the others inside him, Ana hadn't come by sarcasm at random. "Sorry, but I prefer Maggie."

Dr. Ruby stared at her. "Okay. Thank you for telling me."

"Thank you. And I *have* seen a train wreck. Back in Spring Green." There were tracks in the woods near Maggie's childhood home. The rhythm of night trains had soothed her in the early hours, had become vital to her sleep cycle. The derailment had woken her, set the woods aflame, and colored the sky.

"Were there casualties?"

Maggie and her friends couldn't resist it. They pushed through pines to get near the flashing lights. The scorch marks were awful to behold, gouges in the earth like deep wounds, and what had started as a giggling adventure ended with a quiet walk home. "I'm not sure. A couple, I think? It wasn't a passenger train, but . . ."

"Strange, isn't it, that you wouldn't wonder who had died?"

"Stranger if I'd obsessed over the deaths of strangers."

"Maggie." Dr. Ruby rubbed her temples. "I thought I'd won your trust. What happened?"

"I'm not sure it was ever trust. You appeared on my doorstep at the exact moment that my children started falling apart. You were there before an ambulance was called, you knew what was wrong before I did. 'Suspicious' isn't a strong enough word, really."

"Then why did you let me in?"

Maggie had let her in.

Maggie had Milo dangling from one arm, wheezing for air while bruises bloomed on his neck, and Ana wrapped in her other, bleeding madly from a gash in her right eyebrow. She had no arm left for Hank, and he'd refused to follow. He remained standing on the bloody linoleum, gagging over the kitchen sink, whimpering like a wounded dog and scrubbing at scratch marks on his hands. All Maggie knew was the world was very wrong and her children, *they were the wrongest part.*

And there, on the welcome mat, this scarred middle-aged woman wearing glasses and practical pumps and a white lab coat awaited them, looking so serene. You'd think the Vasquezes were a church choir, not a screaming mess.

"The hospital won't help you," Dr. Ruby said. "But I'm going to."

Who this woman was, where she came from, what she wanted? It did not matter in that screeching moment. Maggie would have accepted assistance from buzzards. Maybe she had.

After Dr. Ruby stitched her children up, medicated them, and put them to bed, after she called in the tall woman and the squat man to clear away the blood and bile, Dr. Ruby sat Maggie down with a hot mug of coffee.

At last, the universe understood what Maggie had long suspected. She needed help. From anyone. From anything. She had for a long time.

When Dr. Ruby said, "I wasn't sent by the government," Maggie replied, "But can you help us?" and when Dr. Ruby said, "I'm experienced in cases like this," Maggie replied, "Will that help us?" and when Dr. Ruby said, "This will cost you nothing but patience," Maggie replied, "Please, help us," and when Dr. Ruby said, "We *will* help you," Maggie said nothing at all.

Maggie hadn't looked, hadn't questioned it. Anyone in the

world could understand her children better than she could. No one before had offered to try.

Here Dr. Ruby remained, only as much an outsider as Maggie was. Now the Vasquezes were approaching winter, and none appeared any more hurt than they had been. Surely that counted as progress. Surely Hank still playing basketball and Ana singing onstage and Milo's ASL classes and Dr. Ruby's diminishing visits—these were improvements. The going was slow, but it was going.

"They're still my patients, and I will be keeping an eye on you, in order to make sure there are *no* derailments. We're returning your privacy to you. We're leaving your home so that you can live your lives."

"Oh. Okay. That's . . ." Sudden it wasn't, but jarring it was. "But you'll still be coming by to do therapy?"

"For a little while, yes."

"And that's because, what? Because you *care* about my kids?"

For once, Dr. Ruby didn't have a carefully constructed reply. Her eyelashes fluttered behind her goggles. "Maggie, have I hurt you in any way?"

"I don't know yet."

On Halloween, during what should have been her lunch break, Maggie found herself yet again sitting with Milo in Samantha Stuart's classroom, watching him peel the crusts off his bread.

"I can do that for you." She'd forgotten to move her hands. He read her lips.

"IT'S GOOD FOR MY FINAL MOTORS SKILLS. I MEAN—it's good for my final motors skills."

"What happened during show-and-tell, Milo?"

Penny nudged Milo. She was his shadow these days, this little girl with black braids and dimples that undermined her no-nonsense expression.

Milo signed something over his heart.

"You . . . what? Isn't that . . . that sign's from the careers unit, right?"

They'd studied careers just last week. Mr. Dawson had the same no-nonsense attitude as his little girl. He also had a kindness about him that kept the class of adults and children afloat on those early mornings. A kindness that distracted Maggie from learning her vocabulary, apparently.

"*Policeman*, Milo?" She frowned, repeating his movement. Penny offered no help. She seemed to be giving Maggie a pop quiz, little arms folded and eyebrows raised. "Wait . . . isn't that letter *d*? That's . . . *detective*. You were playing detective?"

Milo nodded. "EXACTLY!"

"Not exactly," Penny snapped. "You weren't *playing*."

Maggie turned to her. "Okay. So, Milo was *being* a detective. It's Halloween. Kids are being all sorts of things, but not all kids are sitting in here during recess."

"He was just *being* Milo." Penny shoved an enormous brown paper bag at Maggie. "He wanted us to feel bad about how we didn't go to his party. But he didn't even invite me!"

"Sorry, Penny." Maggie was reluctant to look in the bag. She suspected it didn't contain last year's fire ant costume.

"It's okay." Penny flicked Milo on his earphones. Without

looking, he handed her his shorn crusts. Penny shoved them in her mouth.

"Finish talking and come outside for recess already." *Come outside,* she signed, with her cheeks chipmunk full.

Milo chuckled. Maggie could have hugged that no-nonsense girl half to death, but Penny was already gone.

"Milo. Should I open this bag, or should you?"

"DO I—do I get a third choice?"

If they were only getting better faster, Maggie could have looked. Milo could have let her. But train derailments became deadly when trains went too fast. The forward chugging of the Vasquez household *needed* to be slow.

Sometimes Maggie thought about Donovan, and the lives of their children, gaining momentum without him. Rattling and shaking, the Vasquez family forged ahead. And he had chosen not to witness it. He had planted thirsty, gorgeous things and decided not to water them. He'd been absent not just for concerts and checkups and games, but also for moments like this: a little girl smiling at Milo simply because she was his friend.

Maggie had dreamed of trains in Europe, but for now she'd follow *these* tracks anywhere. Somehow, staying in Eustace still meant moving forward.

"Are you sad, Mom? Your face is funny."

She smiled. "I can give the bag back to you *without* peeking in at all, if you promise to be on your best behavior today."

Milo twirled an imaginary mustache. "Hmm."

Maggie held her palm out to shake on it, like they'd shaken on all their promises over the years—not to bite the dentist, not to bring ants into the house, not to call her by her first name—

Milo shoved half of his sandwich into her hand.

Maggie would take it. It might even be good.

"Poor man," she mused. "He'll never see your imaginary mustaches."

5

EYES

Weeks of exposure hadn't lessened the impact of acrid laboratory air on Ana's sinuses. It smelled alive in here, or a little like propane. The lab always demanded a blink, but at least it was familiar.

Ana set her backpack down by the door.

"Ana?" Ms. Yu almost knocked over her coffee mug. "I thought you were a ghost!"

"Not yet."

Ms. Yu smiled, bumping her mug again. "How can I help you?"

"You told me I could hang out here."

"I—did?"

"Back when school first started."

"Oh, I *did*! Of course you can. Stay as long as you want!"

Ana blinked at her. "You . . . you don't have to be anywhere."

Ms. Yu's laughter trailed upward as if it had gotten away from her. "I think Herr Fabian will survive without me a little longer. Won't hurt to starve him a bit, either."

Ana allowed another blink. They were easier all the time. Emptiness wasn't so bad once you knew it would end.

"Herr Fabian's my Himalayan. He's got the cutest little toe-beans, but—well, the longer I'm here, the longer he'll have to puke in all corners of the house! Cats are monsters, Ana; I wish one upon everyone."

Ana smiled, cheeks creaking.

They set to work. The pellets were in the storage closet, but alfalfa, Ms. Yu called while scooping, could be found in the back cupboard.

There was an entire wall of cupboards, but Ana didn't ask. She didn't mind peeking in them. They contained things Ana had never considered they might. Not just animals floating in formaldehyde, but also old taxidermied birds and textbooks from decades ago. One held forgotten school projects, including some long-gone student's model of a human heart made from paper, clay, and pipe cleaners.

Ana saw that and had to keep opening things, forgetting the hungry mice and iguana, curious about what existed in the darkness behind every one of these doors—

"Oh, Ana, don't open—"

It was too late. The cupboard nearest the emergency wash station was a deep one. It was full of corpses.

Blink: The corpses were all Luz. Hank as Luz, Ana as Luz, Milo as Luz, even Marissa and Brendan and Dad as Luz—

Ana slammed the cupboard closed, but the door bounced back open.

A shrink-wrapped package hit the floor.

Within it was a body, dried like jerky. Not alien, not human.

Furry and outstretched in its bag, eyes closed. Styrofoam peanuts wedged its mouth ajar.

"Oh, I'm so sorry!" Ms. Yu scooped the package off the floor. "These are for the AP Anatomy kids. They've been working with them all year, studying vertebrates. It's actually pretty standard to dissect cats in high school."

"They've been in here all along." Ana noted brown-and-black tabby stripes under plastic. "Every day we're in class, there are dead cats in the cupboard?"

"Well, *yes*. We've had these since September. I know it's a little icky! But we don't always have the funding for new animals, and these cats'll keep for a while. Um." She tucked the cat back into the cupboard. "I haven't even told Herr Fabian about this."

"Where do they come from?" Ana slumped onto a stool at the nearest table.

"I want you to know that people aren't going around raising cats for slaughter or anything! These animals were being euthanized regardless."

"So someone just decides . . . what, that some of them should be dissected?"

"I think . . ." Ms. Yu didn't stumble when she took the stool across from Ana's. "Ana, I think if there's an opportunity for young people to learn something from the unfortunate, um, *demise* of an animal, isn't that better than just letting it rot?"

"I don't know. Did anyone ask the cats?" Her breathing was short and shallow. God, Ana hadn't missed the thumping shards of heartache. "I don't know."

★   ★   ★

Ana had taught Luz about aliens, as human beings imagined them.

Ana had a large wealth of cinematic knowledge. With Marissa she'd watched countless films in the extraterrestrial subgenre, everything from Spielberg classics like *Close Encounters* and *E.T.* to horror staples like *The Thing* and *Alien* to romps like *The Fifth Element* and *Galaxy Quest* to commentary pieces like *District 9* and *They Live*, all the way to schlocky B-movies like *Xtro*.

Through Ana, Luz saw at least a hundred episodes of *Doctor Who* and several retro *Star Trek* episodes. She and Marissa gave up on retro sci-fi upon realizing the girl characters were there to look hot, but they'd found plenty to love about *Battlestar Galactica* and *Invasion of the Body Snatchers*, and anime like *Parasyte* and *Eureka Seven*.

They'd seen so many alien dissections.

On the morning of June 8, Ana, Hank, and Milo woke in the same room after the deepest of sleeps at exactly the same moment, sitting with legs stretched out over the edge of Milo's lower bunk and backs pressed against the wooden sideboard.

Ana felt like she should panic—had she really told a monster it could live with them? But there was another sensation, a warm heaviness that anchored them to the world and to one another. Ana knew her brothers felt it, too. They were *family* again.

When they were tiny, they took this for granted. Milo wriggling in his high chair. Hank and Ana digging into baked macaroni, never considering the cheesiness hitting their taste buds might hit someone else's differently.

Dr. Ruby later spoke to Ana about this. She told her it was common knowledge in developmental psychology. Until kids are six or so, their brains *literally* can't comprehend the idea that anyone is separate from them. Kids think if they like s'mores, *all* people like s'mores. If they are sad, *all* people will cry. They perceive no borders.

On the morning of June 8, Ana felt like her brothers were part of her again. They were, unquestionably, the same. They should have been uncomfortable, but they weren't.

Luz was plenty uncomfortable.

When Ana closed her eyes, she saw a handful of alien autopsies, in all different qualities of film: grainy or black-and-white or mock found footage or high definition from those nights when Marissa demanded only the best for their viewing experience, though Marissa's mother was pretty confused by their "alien infatuation."

Luz expressed his distaste: slices and slits and screams and pus, superimposed, clumsily, over visions of Ana's tears.

Ana opened her eyes. Hank and Milo were both staring upward. Hank's hands had carved *Please* into the bottom of the bunk while he slept.

"He wants to know if you still wanna cut him out, Ana," Milo whispered.

Ana blinked and saw herself laughing in the arms of her mother, on the knee of her father, soaring across a pool when he spun and tossed her, reveling in her loss of gravity before the water swallowed her up.

"I . . . maybe not right now. You?"

She already knew they didn't.

Hank cleared his throat. "What . . . I mean, what is this? What do we call it?"

"Ooh, can I name him?" Milo jumped onto his knees, eyes shining. Ana had never seen him look at them like that, the way he usually looked at bridges or his ant farm. "I can, can't I?"

"What did you have in mind, Milo?" Hank's hands scuttled up and down the wall.

"Dad!" Milo declared, fist in the air. "*Obviously*."

Hank's hands stopped. "No."

Luz rewound the autopsy footage. He showed Ana friendlier specimens. Aliens with glowing fingers and large eyes and children of their own, aliens who were stand-ins for people and sometimes, better than people.

"Those names are already taken." Ana didn't say so, but she and Marissa had brainstormed names for alien movies years ago. None of them seemed to fit a *person*.

"'Luz' is Spanish for *light*," Hank murmured. Dad had spoken a little Spanish to Hank when he was a toddler, but hadn't bothered with Ana.

Ana still resented that. "Sometimes people are called Luz. Usually girls, though."

"What's the difference?" Milo said, and all of them felt Ana's heart warm.

"Who cares what we call you," Hank told his fingers. "I feel like it won't change what you are . . ."

Hank's hands lifted his chin for him, nodded his head.

Ana saw the start of a smile, and sensed it on all of them. "Fine. Luz it is."

Milo lowered his hand from his ear. "He likes it!"

Ana already knew that. In her mind's eye, she watched that first loop of stop-motion footage on Marissa's phone.

By the time Mom pushed the door in to check on her errant children, they were dressed and she couldn't know anything united them. But there was a word.

Luz. His name is *Luz*, and he's happy to be here.

"Ana," said Ms. Yu in the laboratory, "you know cats aren't conscious in the same way that people are. I mean, I love cuddling Herr Fabian, and he enjoys my company in his purry way, but cats . . . well, they don't have opinions."

Ana bristled. "Just because they're different from us doesn't mean they don't have opinions."

"They aren't self-aware, so, really it *does* mean that. Precisely means that, in fact. My cat likes me because I keep my cat fed. It's about survival instincts, not affection."

Since when had Ms. Yu been anything but a pushover? Then again, she graded their lab reports with a scalpel instead of a red pen. And best not confuse kinetic energy with potential energy in her presence unless you wanted her to impale you on the writing utensils jutting from her updo.

Ana frowned. "How is dissection better for cats, then? If they don't have opinions, why should they care about what we learn? Human beings aren't helping them survive in this case. Human beings are the ones who euthanized them."

"That's a good point, Ana. Really! I may discuss the matter with Herr Fabian after he has his wet food. For you, I'll ask him his opinions."

The door to the Biology lab was thrown open.

Platinum appeared, cheeks flushed from exertion. "What the hell, Ana?"

Ana dropped the bit of melon she was feeding to Grandpa the Iguana. "Wha—where's Brendan?"

"Onstage, obviously! Like you should be! God help me, if you don't take on the role of Audrey I, Mr. Oldman's going to follow me all the way to Naples and turn me into some sort of modern art piece."

"I don't want the part."

"Yes, you *do*." Platinum squeezed both of Ana's shoulders. "Open your damn eyes and *think*. If you're the heroine in this weird-ass musical and Bren is the hero, guess what you'll be doing?"

"Singing . . . duets?"

"No shit, Sherlock. And kissing him."

Ana's eyes widened. It had everything to do with Platinum's conviction. "But I'm helping Ms.—"

"This is one science I have no say in, girls." Ms. Yu gave Ana the world's dorkiest thumbs-up. "Do your *thang*, or *go get him*, or *score*, or whatever you kids like to say these days. Okay?"

Ana let Platinum pull her from the Biology laboratory. Maybe Platinum was doing this to humiliate her.

Or maybe Platinum was actually close enough to know what Ana wanted.

6

HANDS

Hank had always loved Brendan Nesbitt's voice.

Not his singing voice—even from this far back in the auditorium, tucked out of sight behind a podium, Hank could hear how Brendan's notes fell flat or rose sharp every few words or so.

But Brendan had a voice like a winding spring. When he spoke, he started slow and quiet, truncated his speech with "ums" and "ahs" before words burst out of him in a veritable flurry of chatter. The more you talked to him, the more you realized *he liked* talking to you, the more you realized that Brendan Nesbitt had thoughts worth voicing, a thousand questions worth asking.

This did seem like perfect casting, Hank had to admit. A nerdy lead with low confidence? That was Brendan, before you got to know him. And once you *did* get to know him, he was entirely protagonist material.

The first day after Dad left Eustace, Hank said not a word about the absent Chevy. He just went to school and laughed louder than usual, jostled the ballers more than ever. By the time he settled into his seat in Health class, his throat was hoarse from the effort.

Brendan Nesbitt wasn't there yet. There was nothing lovely to look at. Hank stared at Brendan's chair and failed to blink away black thoughts.

On Dad's last night in town, he'd picked Hank up from practice and taken him out for ice cream.

"My ice cream smells funny." The ice cream prank was a Vasquez family staple. Hank hadn't expected Dad to fall for it, but Dad leaned closer to Hank's cone, surprising Hank so much that he failed to deliver the punch line: the inevitable shoving of ice cream into Dad's nose.

"Dad? Are you okay?"

"I will be. And you will be too, you know." Dad didn't finish his pistachio cone, so Hank finished it for him. Dad didn't speak until they reached the parking lot. Then: "You're growing up strong, young man."

Hank looked at his big feet, aware that furious blushing wasn't something strong young men were known for. When he looked up, a world-swallowing smile awaited him.

That must have been farewell, Hank realized now, from his island of a desk.

"Where are you, Hank?"

Hank started, lifted his eyes from Brendan's chair. "What?"

High cheekbones colored. "Sorry, it's just—you, um, looked sort of far away. As if your body is sitting right here in class, but your head is possibly somewhere else?"

"That's . . . kind of a weird thing to say." Hank's heart thumped harder as he watched Brendan's blush deepen. They'd hardly spoken since Brendan had delivered the blueprint. Brendan could not know that Hank had tacked it to the wall beside his bunk, that Brendan's stars were the first thing he saw every morning.

I'm the weird one here.

"Yes, I have been known to say weird things. At times."

"My brother says weird things all the time."

"Oh! Milo? Did he like the blueprint?"

"Yeah." Hank didn't have the stomach to tell Brendan the platform was finished and now untouched, might soon be dismantled like the rest of their lives.

"I discovered that Milo's in my cousin's preschool. Isn't he the boy—"

Hank braced himself for *who doesn't talk* or *with special needs* or—

"—who builds bridges out of Popsicle sticks? Every time we pick up Nellie he's constructing a masterpiece."

"Yeah . . . Milo's always making things. Messes, mostly."

Brendan laughed, a sound too warm and heavy for hollow bones. "Well, artists make messes, too. Sometimes that's all they make, but that doesn't mean it isn't art. There's art in everything, really. In me, in *you*."

"Really?"

"Really, Hank."

The teacher finished writing the agenda on the board.

"Look—I'm sorry for bothering you. It's just, sometimes I feel as if I'm in school but I'm not really *in* school? And I wish people would notice."

"You weren't bothering me at all."

Brendan Nesbitt smiled, a little uncertainly, a little *perfectly*, and landed in his seat. Hank fixated on the pink blotches blooming beneath Brendan's ears.

"Class, class!" called their teacher.

"Yes, yes!" they replied.

Tim poked Hank's shoulder. He made a face in Brendan's direction. Hank pretended not to see. That's what people did in ninth grade. They pretended not to see each other.

Except for Brendan Nesbitt. He used his voice.

Brendan delivered lines in a mock New York accent. It was hard to tell what was going on. It seemed like an underclassman with a deep, bluesy undertone was telling Brendan's character to feed her?

Brendan wouldn't see Hank under the glare of those bright lights.

"I'm here, Carmella. Wanna tell me why so I can go?"

"Don't tell me you have elsewhere to be. Orson's at practice." Carmella knew Hank's routine as well as he did. "And I know your mom'll be taking Milo trick-or-treating, because you'll defend his honor in class but you won't actually speak to him."

Hank looked at his hands. He couldn't really see the scars from Milo's fingernails, but he could still feel them.

"And don't worry. We aren't here to ogle your better ex." Carmella looked up from her phone. "Where is she?"

"'She' who?"

On cue, the door beside Hank burst open, revealing Platinum and—

Dark brown hair whipped by after the flash of white.

"Ana?" Hank blurted.

Ana didn't hear him. Platinum led her away, zipping all the way down the aisle to the fore of the stage. Mr. Oldman started screeching at them.

"I already know Ana's in the musical."

"*What good brothering.* But that's not it. Didn't Ana say anything?"

Hank shook his head. They didn't share car rides every day now that Hank sometimes rode with Orson and she sometimes rode with Brendan. But even if those trips that forced them to talk to each other in a confined space hadn't been dwindling, Hank might not have had words for Ana. Not because he was angry with her. He wasn't.

Of course he had seen Ana with Brendan and Platinum whenever his schedule failed him. It didn't matter. It didn't matter because Brendan didn't matter anymore, and . . . well, at least Ana wasn't alone.

Leave it to Brendan to be the brother Hank couldn't be.

"Hank, look." Carmella squeezed his arm.

Ana stood at center stage. The babble in the front rows quieted. Faces peeked out from the wings. Ana cleared her throat, closed her eyes—

"Gosh, she really *can* sing, can't she?"

Ana sang the song of a character who clearly had small dreams, but dreams nonetheless. She wanted to cook like Betty Crocker. She wanted plastic coverings for her furniture. She wanted a twelve-inch television. It was charming and kind of beautiful, though the performance itself felt a little off.

Only Ana's voice was invested. She sang well, but stood as stiff as a board with the usual lack of expression in her face—

Hank gasped.

When Ana stopped singing, a high note on the word "green," there was some friendly applause. Mr. Oldman looked slightly mollified.

Hank's chest constricted. "*Her eyes were closed.*"

When at last Mr. Oldman had tortured them enough for one evening, Hank watched Platinum throw an arm over his little sister's shoulders. Brendan joined the pair of them, another arm around another shoulder. The trifecta climbed the aisle like an insect, six legs and tiny moving parts.

"Go on, Hank." It should have taken a lot more than Carmella's single phoneless hand to push him forward, but he let it be enough.

Hank Vasquez felt like both an adult and a child when he blocked his sister's exit.

"You," Platinum acknowledged.

"Platinum. Hey." Hank fixed his eyes on her face, her hair, on anything but Brendan's perfectly imperfect hand on her shoulder. He didn't think about those fingers smoothing crinkles from Hank's forehead, pitter-patting down Hank's chest and—

The hand slid away.

"Hey," Hank repeated, with teeth.

Platinum quirked an eyebrow. "Your boulder of a body is in our way." She quirked the other one. "You need to talk to Brendan?"

"I'm right here, Arlene."

Before Hank could stop himself, he looked.

Brendan's eyes weren't a storm or smoldering or whatever

crap people liked to say in love stories, crap Hank used to try to understand. They were just eyes, and they just happened to belong to the only boy who'd ever held Hank naked. That was all.

"Actually . . . I wanna talk to Ana."

"Okay," Ana said. "Meet up with you guys later."

"You heard her." Platinum pulled Brendan away.

Ana insisted on the monochromatic hoodies and baggy jeans, but someone had lent her silver earrings. Sunglasses, the same pair Hank had given her last month, held her bangs back from her face. The cut splitting her eyebrow had healed to jagged white.

Ana's eyes were just eyes, too.

"Yeah . . . ?"

When they were kids, she always had to have the first and last words. Ana won every tug-of-war, every backseat slapping match.

"You're staring, weirdo."

"I know you are, but what am I," he replied, in their old singsong.

Ana used to be the one person he could be an asshole around without feeling like one. Ana knew life wasn't about being nice. Being siblings sometimes meant fighting tooth and nail over the last Pop-Tart, meant slamming doors.

Hank paused. "I wasn't smiling, was I?"

"Not unless smiling looks like dying these days."

"I just . . . you sounded awesome, Ana. Like, really. Really great." Hank was trying to figure out what was so embarrassing about being nice to her, why it was so hard not to feel exposed in the room of empty chairs. Why was it so hard to talk to his sister when they used to arm wrestle?

"Hank. Is that all?"

He made himself look at her. "And, um, you're looking better and I'm just proud of you, okay?"

Her posture softened. "I thought you were going to tell me off."

Hank shook his head. "No." His eyes flitted to the earrings again. Were they Brendan's? Brendan had a cartilage piercing in his right ear. "I thought it would really bother me. A month ago, yeah. But I'm just. You know. Glad you're okay."

"I didn't say I was okay." At first he thought this was Ana's familiar bite, but the only teeth now were hers, pressing into her lower lip.

In junior high, Ana had bitten her lips so persistently they bled.

Hank remembered her dabbing them with tissue the way a lot of her friends did for the sake of lipstick. Ana had developed a bad habit of peeling her lips away with her fingernails. This started after Dad left, but everyone knew not to draw that comparison in front of her. Ana said she didn't miss him.

Dad had given Hank ice cream. He'd given Ana no goodbye at all.

She became extraordinary at quitting things.

This went hand in hand with tearing out her eyebrows. She pretended it was on purpose when Hank made an asshole comment about it, but though her new friends were plucking small hairs, none of them lost theirs entirely. Ana was nearly crying rather than biting when Hank joked that her face was a desert nothing could grow on.

Last Christmas, Hank took a page from Ana's book and stormed into Mom's room to steal back his clothes (all the girls thought it was cool to wear boys' jerseys). He caught Ana in gym shorts with a long column of safety pins clipped to her thighs, blood beading her all over.

She begged him not to freak out, tried to bicker him out of telling: "You dumbass, it's no big deal, come on, Hank, don't be stupid about it!"

Hank had walked straight to the kitchen and was stupid about it, and Mom had driven Ana to the hospital.

Hank gestured at the empty, gaping auditorium. "Maybe you're not okay. But you just belted your heart out. And people cheered for you and stuff. So I don't really get a say in who your friends are, if they make you feel better."

"This is the most you've said to me ..."

"Since Luz. I know."

"No." Ana sized him up. "Since waaaay before that."

"Yeah. I guess." Hank coughed. "Do you need a ride? Orson can—"

"Brendan will give me one."

"Okay. You really did sound terrific."

"Who says 'terrific' anymore, dumbass?" A wry, real smile.

"Guess I do, BanAna."

A thought, unbidden: *We may be missing children. But at least we're missing together.*

Hank told Orson he'd see him later, then jogged to Moreno Park directly after school. Four miles stood between Eustace High and the edge of the canyon, and running in the afternoon sunbake with a backpack on wasn't exactly a breeze. By the time Hank slowed near the picnic tables, his legs were rubbery and his heart was full of needles. The sun remained high enough to tighten his skin, surrounding him in a husk of himself.

Autumn came slowly if at all to Eustace, but the crusted grasses lining the court parking lot were crisper than they'd been last month, on the night Tim broke Hank in two.

The lot was empty.

Hank stooped to catch his breath. He chugged water from his bottle, stretched his legs and arms, and sat at the nearest table. From the side zip pocket of his track jacket he pulled a slip of bent cardboard.

He still couldn't see any UFOs on the card, and the corners had softened to cotton. He could make out Henry Flowers's name and number, but he didn't think he'd have to call. He probably couldn't bring himself to anyhow.

Hank waited.

Within twenty minutes, Henry Flowers's janky old Winnebago grumbled into the lot and screeched to a halt across five parking spots. Moments later the door smacked open. Henry appeared, his baby-bird-fluff hair escaping bobby pins that fought to restrain it. Today he wore another Hawaiian shirt, pants that were at least five inches too short for him, and a pair of loafers that his big toes had poked holes through.

He stepped out of the RV, hawked a loogie large enough to cure the desert drought, and then busied himself with something near the back wheels.

By the time Hank meandered over, Henry Flowers, Extraterrestrial Expert, had pulled two long telescope tubes, a duffel bag, and a remote control from the recesses of a storage compartment.

"Hey, Mr. Flowers?"

His reaction was almost cartoonish. The old man went temporarily airborne like a startled cat and smacked his head against the hatch door. Hank caught it before it could slam on him.

Henry Flowers scurried backward, pulling a hunting knife from his back pocket.

"Whoa! Hi! It's just me, Hank? You're stalking my family?"

Henry Flowers stared. Finally, he coughed and tucked the knife away.

"Christ on a cracker. Thought it was the hippo ballet! I didn't hear you coming, Hank Vasquez." He eyeballed Hank's hands. "Didn't even see you, neither, which has gotta be some sort of miracle. What with you being about as big as a grizzly. I've seen grizzlies, so believe me, I know."

Hank frowned. "But . . . didn't you follow me here?"

"What? Is that what you thought? You thought you were *luring* me here?" Henry Flowers shoved the telescopes under his arms. "That's a little dumb, kid."

"Because you—last time . . ." Hank hadn't been back to the courts, but he and Orson had passed by every day at this hour. More than once Hank had espied the bumper-stickered RV in the lot. "You're watching us. You told me that!"

"Pah! That was last month!" Henry Flowers snorted. "Honestly, son, you and your kin ain't all that entertaining. An awful lot of moping, not enough fighting spirit."

Hank thought of Ana, alive onstage, and silently disagreed.

"And you want my advice? Talk to your brother; little tyke misses you."

Hank thought of Milo screaming, and silently disagreed.

"Last time we met, boy, we were in the honeymoon phase. Now if I wanna watch a soap opera, I'll stop by Doris's Diner in the afternoon. She's usually got one on."

"Then why are you still hanging around?"

Henry hesitated. "Truth is, there are lots of other things to keep a guy like me busy near a pit like this. Things you can't even imagine, if you aren't in the know. Anyhow. Help me with this, would ya?"

Hank picked up the bag and remote control, hands hardly shaking, and shadowed Henry as he hobbled out of the lot and onto the grass. "What do you mean? What other things? Are there other, um, *aliens* here?"

"Like I'd tell you, when you could be one of 'em!" Henry set the tubes down on a picnic table and beckoned Hank to do the same. "But today I really am here for ornithology. You know there are actual roadrunners out here? And yellow-billed cuckoos and gila woodpeckers, if you're lucky. You know what all these birds have in common?"

". . . feathers?"

"They never, ever cry about teenage drama."

Hank watched Henry produce a camera the size of a tortoise from the duffel bag.

"Well, you can skedaddle now. Go and loom somewhere else."

"I . . . can I please talk to you, Mr. Flowers?"

Henry kept producing lenses, screwing them onto the camera. It grew longer and longer. "You wanna ask me about the birds?"

"Not about the birds."

It was again like flipping a switch.

"Ha!" Henry puffed up proudly. "I knew it! Come to talk to me about your alien infestation at last, eh?"

"Well—"

"I knew it! So here's the thing, Hank Vasquez. I'll strike you a deal: you explain what exactly happened in that house of yours, and tell me where that alien's hiding inside it—and don't pretend he isn't!—and I'll take him off your hands for you. Got it?"

Hank stood up. "Luz. I mean, he's—I mean *it*. It's gone. Gone for months."

Henry Flowers clapped his hands together. "Aha! So he *does* exist, doesn't he?"

Hank squirmed. "You already knew that."

"I did! I'm an expert! But damned if I thought you'd ever admit to it." Henry patted Hank's shoulder. "So start talking."

Hank couldn't sing like Ana. "Mr. Flowers, I actually came here to ask about your missing child."

If aliens set Mr. Flowers's eyes afire, this question put him right out. The gleam in his gaze flickered to dark. "I told you. I'm not interested in soap operas."

"Please." Hank took a deep breath. "Can't you tell me about her?"

"Don't you have enough to be miserable about?" It seemed a genuine question, with no malice in it. "Why would you care what some old kook says?"

"I've been thinking about missing people, I guess."

Henry Flowers let out the smallest of sighs, a tiny stream of air through his front teeth. "My daughter ran into this thing, this extraterrestrial, in a ravine. Do you know the Rio Grande Gorge? We were rafting there."

Hank had been there. All of the Vasquezes had, with Dad. It was where Milo first professed his love for bridges.

"We were always in some park or another. This RV? She's nothing new. This RV was home. Didn't give my daughter much of a traditional upbringing. Didn't send her to public school."

"Because they were trying to brainwash her?"

"Don't be an arse; teachers work themselves to the goddamn bone. My mother taught grammar school, eons ago, like yours. That's not my conspiracy theory, kid."

"Sorry."

"But me and my girl, we were free spirits. All the clichés: open road and camping under the stars and desert storytelling with strangers. I thought she was *happy* growing up like that, but you know, I never asked her. That's the trouble, ain't it?" Henry Flowers placed a hand on Hank's shoulder. "You don't think of the important questions until there's no one left to put them to."

Hank had never asked Dad what he thought of gay kids. Had never asked whether Dad would still love him if he quit basketball. Never asked Dad if loving someone could make you less of someone yourself.

"I don't wanna go into the details. I have a lot of work to do. But one day she met this thing, and it took her over. And then she was gone."

He began fiddling with his lenses again.

"Milo always thought that Luz might be Dad," Hank blurted. "That maybe Dad came back as . . . as glowing freaking termites. I never ever believed it." Hank closed his eyes. "But I dunno. Maybe I wanted to."

"Son, I can talk for hours about missing children. I can talk about milk cartons and search parties and billboards and the way people you'd never expect to care are the ones who stay up nights drinking coffee with you, because hell if you're gonna get any sleep. I can tell you a thousand damn stories about my missing child. But all you need to know is that it probably doesn't feel so different from what you've been through. Except no one bothers with search parties when it's a dad who goes missing, eh?"

Hank shook his head. "They really don't."

"Ain't that an awful thing? People just accept it, when a parent runs away?"

Suddenly Henry Flowers seemed like the sanest person Hank had spoken to in years. Hank found himself really, truly laughing. "It really is. Really awful."

"Buck up, son. Let me know if you wanna have another real conversation. And keep an eye out for anything strange or suspicious, all right?"

"There's going to be a lot of strange and suspicious things around. It's Halloween."

"Nah." Henry tapped his nose. "The suspicious things are the things you *don't* see. Keep that in mind."

"Mr. Flowers, I really mean it—Luz isn't around anymore. He—it. The alien. It abandoned us."

"Don't be so certain." Henry shook his head. "You'd be surprised at how much of a person is left behind after they go missing."

7

OUTSIDE

Maggie watched a procession of ghouls march by.

Teachers had been stationed all along the parade route to ensure children and parents didn't misbehave, didn't run ahead or wrestle each other over Reese's Pieces. They didn't need any hospitalizations this year. You really had to watch out for parents.

Trunk-or-treating started an hour before school ended. Half the teachers were on candy duty, and needed time to relocate their students to other classrooms, prepare goods for the taking, and arrange their cars. A large, protective circle now spanned the whole faculty lot, trunks facing inward, open and ripe for candy picking. Near the front of the lot, Principal Olsen guided parent volunteers into open spaces.

For many kids, this would be their only Halloweening. In broad daylight, under the eyes of adults. Maggie understood wanting the candy without the night.

Milo said "real" trick-or-treating had to be at nighttime, because how could you make friends with any ghosts otherwise?

Milo delighted in his role as candy distributor. Maggie watched him portion out treats like a champion diplomat. She knew it was less about being fair than being accurate—Milo couldn't eat M&M's without separating them by color first.

"He's growing up, huh?" Mr. Morris called, from one trunk over. "Trunk" might not have been the word. Mr. Morris was a man who thought a big truck put him closer to the sky. Maggie hated how you could never see over those things on the freeway, how they sometimes blocked out the sun.

"Yeah, he is. There's not really any other way to grow."

"Only wideways." He patted his beer belly.

Maggie almost smiled. Mr. Morris's goofiness made him great with temperamental kids. You couldn't throw a tantrum with him waggling his eyebrows at you.

"How about Hank? He in high school yet?"

"He's a senior now."

Mr. Morris crossed himself. "Guess it's about time to bury me."

Now Maggie did smile.

"Go for it," Mr. Morris told three incoming kindergartners, who gleefully grabbed fistfuls of Tootsie Rolls from his bowl. "Actually, Maggie—"

A nearby ghost gasped. "*MAGGIE!* MS. VASQUEZ'S NAME IS MAGGIE!"

Mr. Morris covered his mouth. "Kids, that's top-secret information. Can you keep it that way?"

The little ghost nodded conspiratorially.

"*Ms. VASQUEZ*," Mr. Morris amended, "do you have plans this evening?"

For the life of her, Maggie couldn't recall his first name. "Well, Milo has demanded we go trick-or-treating."

"Of course he wants the genuine article. But if Hank's basically old enough to run for president, couldn't he be persuaded into dragging Milo around for an hour?"

Hank couldn't be. Hank couldn't *glance* at Milo.

"Andreya and I are hosting our annual costume party. You killed it a few years back." Maggie had killed something, all right, although of course half the attendees were already dead, zombies being a perpetual default among last-minute costumers.

Milo and Ana didn't realize their love for the macabre was Maggie's. As a teen she fell in love with *Nosferatu* and *Dead Alive* in equal measure. Maggie and her friends used to sleep in graveyards, carried sharpened stakes in their backpacks for vampire slaying.

"Didn't you come as the Fly last year? Ha! Your Goldblum laugh was *spot* on."

It had paired well with Milo's fire ant. Maggie bent feelers out of wired boas. A headband held eyes made out of recycled water bottles and netted muslin. Foam mandibles from sliced-up yoga mats were her collar. Cardboard-reinforced cellophane wings hung down her back.

She'd felt like a beautiful nightmare. She had a few drinks that night, to be sure. A few laughs, too. But . . .

"I think I'll have to pass this year."

"Well, if you change your mind. Andreya would love to catch up." He seemed to consider his next words. "You know, they don't vanish when you look away from them."

"I beg your pardon?" When had she ever said "beg your pardon" before?

"I just . . . well, Cynthia and Moses are both in college right now, but they haven't vanished, either. You know?"

It took every bit of her self-control not to glare at this man, this stranger, who knew nothing of Vasquez canyons. "Maybe, Mr. Morris."

"The final onslaught!" Milo shouted.

Penny had joined him. She was more ruthless about distribution. "You don't get any because you bullied Milo!" she cried as Antonio passed. Maggie didn't bother scolding her.

Soon it was over. The chaos in the parade's wake was shameful. It may have been children who left candy wrappers, but they were not responsible for the cigarette butts.

Milo handed Maggie the two remaining Fruit Gushers packets. She plopped them in the trunk and slammed it. "Right, kiddo. Back to class."

"WHAT'S THE POINT," Milo moaned.

"You need to fill out your homework log, and I need to wrestle my kids into some sugar-fed semblance of order. We have to finish the day. Like always, Milo."

"WHAT'S THE POINT."

"I have no idea." Maggie laughed.

"Why do you like bloodsuckers so much?" Donovan had asked her. She'd dragged him to see *Let the Right One In*. They'd hired a sitter for the kids, allowed themselves a rare date night.

Maggie showed her incisors. "Bloodsuckers, *people*. Same thing. What's not to like?"

★   ★   ★

"Mom, I can go with Penny's family trick-or-treating tonight," Milo informed her from the backseat.

"Milo—what are you talking about?"

Headphones sang only softly; he'd heard her. "Mr. Dawson said he's taking a van full of kids."

"I don't remember this."

"He signed it."

"Ah."

"Mom, you deserve a break." Milo tightened an invisible tie.

"Do I, sir?" Maggie caught his eye in the rearview mirror. "I'll call Mr. Dawson when we get home."

Maggie once made everything from nothing. The woods raised her that way, and the desert gave even less than those pines. Already in her head she was trying to decide which costume her closet could possibly produce with only three hours' notice. There were the obvious choices, the pirates and witches, the characters that could be built from the mismatching of skirts and beads, the tying of scarves in atypical places.

Milo hummed a song about spooky skeletons, doing the hand motions. She hummed with him, tapping fingers on the wheel.

Other mothers might consider just throwing on a dress. Maggie was never those mothers. She and her kids had darkness in common.

She could build an entire monster from all the useless things in her house.

8

EYES

Platinum was coasting high after the revelation of her upcoming absence.

Brendan was drowning in it.

This was a peculiar observation for Ana to make while they three sat in a drive-thru line minutes after escaping the auditorium, but nonetheless true.

Brendan was driving. As ever he gripped the wheel tightly and stared only at the road. Brendan Nesbitt had lost a cousin in a traffic accident. Ana knew this because she and Brendan shared all secrets now.

Ana blinked. *Scrape.* Well, almost all.

"I will order you both milk shakes," Platinum avowed from the passenger seat, "but only if you promise to dip your French fries in them like civilized human beings."

Ana took her up on the offer. Brendan didn't.

Platinum reached across him to fetch their milk shakes and

salty goods. Brendan's hands remained wheelbound. He absolutely did not look at his best friend.

He's acting like Hank, Ana thought.

"Bren, you're acting like Ana," Platinum told him as they pulled out of the lot and onto the road. "I get it, I'm amazing. But it's not the end of the damn world."

Brendan's lips got thinner.

Ana was used to more noise than this, at least the murmur of headphones. "What's the plan today?"

Today Platinum had given Ana the lead in the musical and a reason to talk to her brother again and a reason not to dwell in a room full of dead cats. Today Brendan's kinetic energy had reverted to potential. Today there were three of them.

In a week there wouldn't be. They'd be severed.

"Well, what do you guys think? It's Halloween."

"I don't care," Brendan said quietly.

Platinum dipped a fry in her milk shake and shoved it toward Brendan's face.

Finally he bit it, sucked it into his mouth.

"Um." Ana strained against her seat belt. "Trick-or-treating?"

"It's Halloween, but *we aren't five,* Ana." Some of her lipstick had smeared on her teeth. "Let's do some *real* scary shit."

Last year, Ana and Marissa had made the mistake of getting dolled up for a party. Platinum wasn't interested in that stuff. Her lipstick glowed, she didn't seem bothered about mermaiding, she didn't get wasted at boys' houses, probably, and end up wrecked at age thirteen, holding a best friend's long, long hair out of her face, calling 911.

Probably this wasn't Platinum's definition of scary.

"So . . . see a horror movie?"

Brendan had been horrified enough for one day. "Don't you think you should have told me, Arlene? Aren't we supposed to be best friends?"

Platinum looked at him. "Yeah. We are. So let's do something scary tonight."

Brendan Nesbitt wasn't happy with this answer. Brendan, hyperventilating because the girl who used to beat up boys for him was leaving this hemisphere.

Ana wasn't sure how normal people should react to canyons opening—when your world is full of them and devoid of foundations, who can say when another hole matters?

"It's not like she'll be gone forever," Ana said.

Platinum spun around to look at Ana, squeezed her knee. "Exactly, Ana. Brendan, drive where I say to, got it?"

Brendan didn't argue. He seemed anything but weightless.

Ana knew only two ways out of Eustace. Platinum set them down a third alternative. After the grocery store, she told Brendan to veer right. Soon they were taking winding back roads into the desert. From there, they bumped along strips of dirt that could hardly be called trails.

The sun eased down like a sinking ship.

At last the car stopped. Ana looked out the window. They had reached a vacuum.

"Welcome to Perecheney," Platinum announced.

Brendan broke his telling silence. "Pair of what now?"

Platinum clambered out of the passenger seat and stood on the edge of a wide expanse of crusted nothingness. Platinum spread her feet apart like a conquering hero, staring down the sole saguaro cactus in sight.

"This is definitely it." Platinum scanned the horizon. She darted out of the high beams' reach.

Ana followed, tripping over uneven ground. The wind rose a bit, pricking her face with sand. Ana hardly thought about blinking it away.

"Check out these tracks." They were rusted with disuse and half-buried in sand, but Platinum was right. These had once been train tracks.

Ana realized that the ground wasn't simply uneven. Clay walls jutted from the earth around them. They stood on the derelict foundations of a building.

"*Pair of* what is this place?" Brendan trudged up beside them, lighting the way with his phone.

"*Perecheney*. It's a ghost town." Platinum's eyes gleamed. "Let's find the graveyard."

This proved easy. Just beyond the tracks they came upon a garden of crooked desert tombstones, all dating back a hundred years.

This middle of nowhere had once been a somewhere.

"Why did they all die the same year?"

"That's the thing, Ana. This used to be a bustling station town. But word on Wikipedia? Cholera during a drought. Swept through everyone in no time. Trains were warned not to stop here 'cause there was no telling how infectious it was. Half the townsfolk got out of Dodge. But here are the other half."

The tombstones belonged to people both older than Dad and younger than Milo.

"Of course, people say the place was cursed by a witch, and she's still out here. You can hear her in the wind, et cetera. The usual spooky junk. How's *that* for Halloween?"

"I guess." To Ana, all this seemed more sad than scary.

"*You guess.* And *I* guess if you've seen *real* scary shit, this is nothing." Platinum skipped over the ruins of another long-lost building. A schoolhouse? A church? A home?

"*Arlene.* Let's go." The light shook. Brendan was shivering. "There's nothing here."

Platinum squatted next to the remnants of a bonfire. Empty beer cans were crumpled and browned within it. Butts of cigarettes formed another circumference around the pit.

Platinum pulled a lighter from her bra. "There's still some wood left to burn."

". . . is this a joint?" Brendan kicked the object in question.

"Don't touch it. Might have cholera," she joked.

Ana couldn't decide if she loved or loathed this nothing place.

"I heard people come out here to get fucked-up sometimes, but let's pretend this is more interesting." Platinum smiled. "Me? I'm pretending this is evidence of witchcraft. Maybe Tim Miller was sacrificed here."

"I saw him in school today."

"Don't kill my high, Ana. That might have been his clone. Pretty sure his parents rolled his idiot highness off an assembly line. Now get comfortable."

"Sometimes I just don't understand what you're saying."

"What can I say? I'm into science fiction. Are *you*, Ana?"

Ana didn't like the question. "Not anymore."

"Guess you wouldn't be, if science fiction happened to you. Don't tell me it was termites."

Ana stiffened. "What are we doing here?"

"Like I said. It's Halloween." At last the wood caught. Platinum settled back onto her haunches. "This is a haunted place. Next week I'm gone, but tonight I think we should tell some *real* scary stories."

Brendan caved; you could see it in his posture, in the sad slump of his shoulders. "You aren't budging until we do this, are you?"

"No way. You could just leave me here."

Brendan shook his head. "No. See, *I* would never do that to *you*."

Platinum's smile flickered. Maybe it was only the firelight.

"Ana. Let's tell a few ghost stories and get out of here."

"Nope. Ghost stories aren't good enough." Platinum worked her hands into the dirt. Ana caught a whiff of sweet pea lotion. "I want confessions. Your scariest secrets, friends."

"I dislike this. I really dislike all of this."

"That's because you're kind of a coward, Brendan. But hey!" She held up a finger. "If you admit to that, we'll count it as your first secret."

"That's not a secret. That's something everyone knows."

"Yeah. Some secrets are like that. So, Ana. We'll take turns. You're up."

Ana lifted her eyes. "What do you want to know?"

"Leave her alone," Brendan warned.

"Well, obviously the whole world wants to know what the hell happened to you last summer. But I'm not gonna ask that.

You pick your secrets, we pick ours. Rules are: we have to be specific, but no one is allowed to ask questions. Like if Brendan says, I don't know, that he really likes tentacle porn—"

"*THANKS FOR THAT.*"

"—we aren't allowed to ask him what the hell that is or why. We're just spitting it into the sky. You know what? I'll go first. *I* like tentacle porn. Next!"

Brendan cleared his throat. "I know I can't sing very well."

"Kind of lame, but we all know you're just building up momentum."

They looked at Ana.

Ana thought of the vacuums inside her. The holes she'd torn in herself. The fire was warm, but it had nothing on the desert cold, the chill of this town that wasn't.

"Last Christmas I was hospitalized for cutting."

Neither of them gasped. Neither of them did what Vasquezes had done. Hank rushing to Mom, taking the choice from her. Her mother rushing her to the hospital, taking the choice from her.

Ana wondered what the heat in her eyes was.

Platinum whistled. "See, Brendan? *That's* how you leave an impact. My turn. The only person I've ever made out with happens to be my gay best friend, because we were both curious. That cat was killed. It was gross."

Brendan elbowed her. "My turn. *I'm* that gay best friend. But here's the fascinating truth! I'm not actually gay. I'm *pansexual*, and interested in people who are interesting, genitals regardless."

He looked at Ana. She looked right back, aching from nowhere, everywhere.

"Get the *fuck* out of town? You mean I should schedule future make outs with my gay best friend?" Platinum pushed her lips close to Brendan's. He leaned away.

"I'm afraid not. Because your *pan* best friend is just as afraid of flying as he is of driving, and would *never* schedule make outs with someone who lives in Italy."

Platinum's kiss landed on his cheek. "Ana. You get to tell two secrets, since Bren-Pan stole your turn."

Ana steered the ship to safer waters. "I don't know if I love my family anymore."

"*Damn.* Is every one of yours going to be like this?"

"Maybe."

Platinum beamed. "I'm glad we're doing this, guys."

Weirdly, Ana was too.

EARS

Milo's favorite bridge was the Rio Grande Gorge Bridge. He had good reasons for this. He could list them out loud for anyone curious! Or even for anyone not curious.

1. The Rio Grande Gorge Bridge is the seventh-tallest bridge in the United States! This may not sound so fantastic. But when you think about it, there are thousands of bridges in every state, so even seventh place is pretty impressive!

2. If you were a kid in New Mexico, the Rio Grande Gorge was a good place for Dad to take you for a camping trip!

3. If you were a kid in New Mexico, an observation deck was a good place for your older sister to tell you all about what would happen if you fell off the cliff. She could say things like "People soup, Milo," and "You'd fall for *miles,*

Mile-O!" before your brother finally told her to knock it off!

4. If you were a little kid in New Mexico and your sister felt bad about scaring you, she might share some good ghost stories later. She could do it while Dad went for a hike around the campground with his friend Angela. That way Dad couldn't tell you all to go to bed. He couldn't tell you to stop screaming or snickering or asking important questions: "Was he born with a hook hand, or does he have another name?"

5. If you were a little kid in New Mexico and the next morning Dad looked very grumpy and said, "Never mind, we're going home" before you ever got to go to the amusement park or the caves, and before you knew it you were seeing the amazing bridge—five hundred feet high and made of steel!—in the rearview mirror and trying not to cry about broken promises, at least you could hear your brother say, "Milo, you're too smart for your own good!" and your sister not arguing about that one.

Life and death and bridges. These things never really got old. Just like Milo. He wasn't getting old fast enough!

Milo, Seven Years Old didn't seem like the best costume idea anymore.

Milo was thinking about bridges again. If you have an idea you don't like very much, you have to find a way to get to a better one. That's another kind of bridge.

A long time ago a doctor, one of the doctors before Dr. Ruby, told Milo this:

"Milo, maybe you love bridges because they remind you of your family. Of people you want to have *connections* with? Bridges are *symbols* for that. Think hard. It's *abstract*. That means it's hard to think about, especially when you're little."

"I'm not *that* little. Have you ever seen *ants*?"

"I know this is hard, but I have a feeling that you'll get it."

"It isn't hard, but I don't think that's why I love bridges."

"Oh? Then why do you love them?"

"Because cars can't fly."

But "abstract" was a cool word. Milo wanted to keep it in his pocket.

And Milo *did* know what symbols were. Obviously! Milo took ASL classes and everything now. Every time Mr. Dawson taught a new sign, he was teaching him a new symbol. Symbols were just things that stood for other things.

If anyone had asked Milo, instead of just *telling* him, he would have said that he always *knew* Luz wasn't *actually* Dad. Luz was a *symbol* for Dad.

That was a big idea for Milo to have! It was probably too *abstract* for second grade. So Milo didn't talk about it. People were already funny about his fire ant obsession. They were funny about his morbid drawings and funny about the way he didn't always understand faces. It made him so, so tired.

Mostly Milo was tired of pretending he didn't care. He wasn't Ana; she was so good at pretending things! Hank wasn't as good, but he *did* smile a lot.

But Milo was Milo.

Last summer when he was Milo/Luz, lying on the Nameless Canyon Observation Deck, he'd played a game with Luz. *Remember the Rio Grande Gorge Bridge, Dad?*

After a pause, the voice in his ears said: *Of course I do! We went fishing! When you caught that bass, I made it kiss you on the cheek! Fish kisses. Blech!*

"Blech!" Milo could feel sand under his fingers. He rubbed it against the wood.

The fish memory wasn't real, but it *was* a good memory.

Luz was great at remembering Dad things as they *should have been.* Even if he was only a symbol. Even if those were fake memories, and Milo and Luz both knew it. If you squint at a statue from far away, it looks like a person! Fake things look real if you get far enough away.

Now Milo looked at the paper bag with his show-and-tell inside it. This was the skin of Milo who ran away. Milo before Luz. It didn't seem like a good bridge to build with Mom. He wanted to build a brand-new one, real or not.

Milo found Mom in the kitchen, standing next to the sink.

She was pressing an empty cardboard paper-towel tube against her torso. It jutted out like a third arm! A roll of duct tape dangled from her teeth.

He gaped at her.

"Oh, I'm just trying—look, Mr. Dawson will be here in fifteen minutes to take you." She set the tube down. "I know this looks weird. I'm figuring it out, I swear."

She giggled at herself. That made Milo giggle, too.

"Okay. CLOSE YOUR EYES, MOM." She didn't like to, he could tell. "I won't run away. I promise."

"Get out of my brain, Milo." She closed her eyes.

Milo struck a pose with his hands out. "Ta-da! Open them!"

"Oh. Well, those are just your regular clothes, Milo."

"My *most* regular clothes." Milo wore brown pants and a T-shirt with dinosaur astronauts on it. "I'm going as *me!*"

But there's nothing scary about you, Mom signed, as best as she could. He got the idea. He wasn't a detective for nothing.

Maybe, Milo signed. *Sometimes.*

Mom leaned back on the sink and looked out the window. "Well. We're all a little scary sometimes."

Milo leaned on the counter next to her, trying to copycat her posture. She moved every time he nearly got it. At first he didn't realize she was fooling him on purpose.

Mom was playing. Who could guess that?

"People think skulls are scary, too," Milo told her, in his oldest voice. "But *everyone* has one."

"There's an idea! Why don't we paint some skull makeup on you?"

"Is that m-morbid?"

"*Definitely*. How about it, honey?"

Milo considered this proposal. "Hokay."

Mr. Dawson showed up exactly on time. He shook Mom's hand, then signed that Milo would be back safe and sound before eight p.m.

Penny clomped closer to watch Milo stir red and blue food

coloring into corn syrup. Milo was discovering that spatulas got a whole lot heavier when you were actually pulling them through something.

Penny signed that it looked like real blood. Milo considered the syrupy mess. He thought of the last time there'd been blood in this kitchen. "It kind of doesn't."

Remembering the blood made Milo remember Ana and Hank, too. He wondered where they were. They had both stopped arguing for long enough to take him trick-or-treating last year. Milo had black circles under his eyes now, like Ana, and a grin painted on his face, like Hank. He wanted them to see!

But Mr. Dawson herded him to the door. Mom kissed him good-bye.

Milo would just have to tell them about it later.

10

HANDS

It wasn't exactly a throwaway game, but it wasn't nothing.

This was last year, and Hank's hands were only his, and the Eustace Eagles were shooting for states. Their opponents, the Filton Pillagers, wouldn't survive districts.

The score was 63–32, so a missed basket hardly mattered, apart from the infuriation. Apart from Tim Miller using his status as team captain to demand that every player do five rounds of blood and guts for each missed basket. But Tim wasn't without confidence, either, and for the fourth quarter he'd suggested trading positions with Hank.

Hank had good enough handles to play point guard when he had to, and it might make for a thrilling finale to a lackluster game.

The player marking Hank, a waspish, ginger-haired number seventeen, tried stealing the ball only once before he realized it was a no-go; now he seemed preoccupied with restricting Hank's movements as much as possible.

Hank barely noticed. The only worry Hank had, as far as number seventeen was concerned, was not stepping on him.

In his peripheries Hank saw Tim rush forward, teeth bared, positioning himself on the right side of the free throw line. He was ready for the pass, and Hank would give it to him—Hank was nothing if not a reliable team player, and the ball felt more alive if you kept it in motion.

Hank dribbled slowly, with almost painful deliberation, through the center circle and then instantly picked up momentum, shoes squeaking on the floorboards. Number seventeen ghosted his right side, half a step behind.

At the top of the key Hank jerked left, as if to pull away—

Number seventeen followed.

Hank passed the ball from his left back to his right hand. With a sudden burst of speed, a full-fledged push from the ball of his left foot, Hank was gone.

He grinned. People thought if you were big you had to lumber.

Hank let the ball fly from his fingertips to Tim's, then swooped back around and all but hugged the baseline alongside Filton players, boxing out the biggest ones, hungry for the rebound.

Not that he'd be fed. Tim rarely missed after Hank assisted.

But a freckled guy was dogging Tim's every move, cutting forward, making Tim backstep, so Tim couldn't get that ball up high enough—

He locked eyes with Hank again.

Hank caught the ball over number seventeen's head and pivoted—

Hank had decent court vision, and from here could see the

basket perfectly, but his eyes drifted to the sideline, as they always did even though he *knew* Dad wouldn't be there—

He lifted the ball up.

"HANK THE TANKKKKK!" shouted a voice from the bench, and Hank couldn't help but grin—and there, behind Orson, all but falling out of his seat with a pad of paper tucked under one arm—

Hank forgot to look back at the basket.

Number seventeen plucked the ball right out of his frozen hands and was away.

"The fuck, *Ass-quez*?!" Tim barked, before sprinting after him.

It wasn't an important basket. They were already winning.

Why was Brendan Nesbitt on his feet, imperfect hands curled into perfect fists? Brendan Nesbitt, who almost certainly had no interest in basketball?

Or certainly didn't, because Hank had spent a couple of years surreptitiously finding out what things Brendan Nesbitt was interested in, and mostly those things were photography and Victorian clothing and jeweled insects and being friendly and fretful and twitchy and asking questions, and probably the only way he'd be interested in basketball was if he was interested in a player.

It can't be.

The final score was 83–54.

Tim and the others jostled Hank in the locker room, swore at him a bit, thumped him on the shoulders while they changed.

"Guys, guys, Tank's going through heartbreak." Orson mimed the tiniest violin. "Have pity on his poor ugly soul."

Word had spread about his breakup with Carmella. Word of

the reasons why hadn't yet, because Carmella would never tell anyone about Hank bawling over space barbarians on the couch.

Hank buried his gaze in his duffel bag and waited for the others to leave without him, claiming he had to take a dump. This was one surefire way to clear a locker room.

Brendan was waiting in the cubby beside the trophy case. His sketch pad rested on jittery knees.

Hank forced himself to breathe. "Hey, Nesbitt. What's up?"

Brendan Nesbitt tipped his head sideways. "Usually fluorescent bulbs. But, um, there's never a truly funny way to answer that question, is there? Any answer always falls flat but I always try to make it work regardless. Probably a manifestation of my anxiety. Which is another statement that always, ah, falls flat."

"You don't have to be funny." Every word from Brendan had thought inside it.

"Thanks, Coach? Ha. Sorry."

Hank swallowed. He forced himself not to stare at the cheekbones under those wire glasses. *Don't break this.*

"Didn't think you were a basketball fan." Everything Hank ever said had no thought inside it. He hated that in himself, loved the opposite in Brendan.

"Oh, I'm not." Brendan flipped through his sketch pad. "I'm doing homework for Drawing II. We're supposed to be capturing human bodies in motion. I heard a rumor that people *move* during basketball. Carmella reminded me there was a game tonight."

Of course. Carmella. Never tell anyone, except the one at the center of everything.

"Well, hope you got some good stuff!" Jesus. Someone should cut off Hank's big, stupid tongue, big and stupid like all of him, like his size-fourteen feet. "See you, Nesbitt!"

Before he reached whatever respite the evening air might offer his burning face, Brendan's voice rose.

"I only drew pictures of you, Hank."

When Hank turned, Brendan was standing.

"What?"

Eyes that were simply eyes. "I came here to draw *you*. Just you."

Hank shook his head. "Didn't you take Drawing II last semester?"

Brendan Nesbitt always seemed so uncertain, so kind, but now he was firmly determined in his movements. He took three strides closer to Hank, who fought the urge to step back. His blood in his ears, in all of him, uncomfortable pressures beneath his tracksuit. "And why do you know my schedule, Hank Vasquez?"

Hank stared at Brendan's pale eyelashes. How were they the color of sand, the color of his eyes and freckles, too? How were they the exact color that made Hank want to touch them?

"Gotohomecomingwithme?" Hank whispered on an exhale, before his head could get in his way.

Brendan Nesbitt, an inch from his face, didn't use his voice.

He stood on tiptoe and pressed his lips to Hank's. Gone were all quivering movements.

"I'll be wearing white and black," he said, before the wind took him.

★   ★   ★

At Orson's house on Halloween, Hank missed another basket.

There was no joy and no fury at the failure. There was only the empty air, becoming familiar, and the *smack*, no longer jarring.

So far this season, Hank had made two baskets. Neither of those baskets had been made during JV games. Neither of them had been made in the vicinity of Coach Huang, who seemed to have given him up as a lost cause.

"Nerve damage? Just do what you can."

Helpful as Carmella's rumor remained, Hank knew that wasn't all.

His hands were stronger now. He could hold spoons, he could lift as much as he ever had in Strength and Conditioning class. His handwriting no longer personified attempted paper murder.

But a wall shot up inside his head whenever he touched a ball. It made his heart and hands stutter in turn. All of him was connected to all of him.

A basketball thwacked Hank in the side.

"I swear my hand slipped!" Orson slapped his knees.

"Yeah, right." Hank wasn't angry at him in the least.

Hank had remained on the JV team only because Orson kept him playing. And Hank had made *friends* with underclassmen, like oddball Adam Paul Robert ("I've got three first names!") and exchange student Friedrich Kirschner ("*Ich bin aus Kreiszig gekommen!*"), because Orson had introduced Hank as someone worth knowing. The JV team wanted to win, but more than that they just wanted to play. On varsity, there were people punching walls and crushing bottles underfoot after defeats. The JV guys laughed off losses over plates of General Tso's at the China Buffet.

It was Orson's fault that Hank came here after meeting with Henry Flowers on Halloween, nothing but missing hoops and laughter on his agenda. It was easy to forget the world here.

When Hank had first entered the Liu home during the second week of September, he was greeted by the foreboding glare of Orson's grandmother. Orson led him through a marbled kitchen to the patio where she was playing solitaire.

"*Ni hao, Nainai*. This is Hank. Hank, this is my grandma."

Hank didn't offer his hand, but a hearty smile. "Nice to meet you."

Grandma Liu took in Hank's size, bending her cards in silence. Hank became aware that his shoulders were blocking her light. He wished himself smaller.

She muttered something in Mandarin. Orson sighed and replied.

"Yes, Grandma, this is *the supergay one*," he repeated, in English. "Got any other nice things to say?"

She waved them away. They escaped to the back porch.

"So . . . what did you really tell her?"

"Oh, you heard me. Just the thing about you being supergay. I don't front, Hank Vasquez, my boy. And neither should you."

Hank smirked. "But sometimes you're on the *front*court."

"*Heyyyyy.*"

"Heyyyyy."

"And everything *centers* around you. Oh, man, I can't handle this level of pun-ography. If it's gonna be like this, you can't keep coming over. I'll be a *basket* case in no time. You get me?"

Hank snorted. "That's fucking terrible."

Orson hung his head in mock sadness. "I know. Imagine the *hoops* I'd have to jump through to get better."

"Goddamnit, stop it, Orson."

Despite the puns, by now Hank was used to the view from Orson's porch. Calling it a porch when his father had turned it into a multipurpose court for his tennis and his son's basketball seemed like underselling it. You couldn't call it a yard, either, because one of those stretched lush and green from another tier below, an oasis complete with automated sprinklers.

Hank could see the smear of Nameless Canyon in the distance, but had noticed immediately: he couldn't see his house from here.

"Still an awesome view." Hank sat taller on the bench.

"Oh, man." Orson threw him a bottle of Pocari Sweat. The oily taste really did grow on you. He fanned a hand at the horizon. "One day, son, all this will be yours."

"Don't start that crap again."

"You *can* say 'shit.' Gran can't hear you. Probably. We'll know pretty quick by whether or not she starts throwing cutlery from the window."

"It's a habit. I have a little brother, remember."

"I met Milo. He's too suave to swear, but if he heard you do it he'd just straighten his—whatsit? What are they? The little one-lensed glasses things?"

"Monocle?" They were part of Victorian fashion, something Brendan knew about.

"Yeah, Milo'd fix his monocle and take notes."

Hank swigged his Pocari and cringed. "What does that mean?"

"Your brother's like a little genius, isn't he?"

"I don't think his teachers say so. But yeah. He totally is."

Orson mimed looking at a watch. "That does it for tonight, good man."

"We've only been here an hour?"

Orson wiped his forehead. "Yeah. I've sort of got a thing?"

"Well, you have a few things." Hank climbed to his feet.

"Miller's having a thing tonight to celebrate winning districts."

Hank aimed. Missing as usual, smiling as usual. "Oh? A thing, huh?"

"A Halloween party. It's stupid. But the whole team's going and it would be kind of weird if I didn't."

"I remember last year's. Ben O'Brien hosted it."

"What a shit show that was."

Hank's first shot of Jäger, followed by the first time he'd locked himself in an upstairs bathroom because he felt the alcohol making his lips loose, making him want to say gay things and kiss gay things or not gay things, guy things would have been fine.

"Gotta make an appearance. You know how it is. Politics! I'd rather be sipping sweet, sweet Pocari here with you, man. Shooting the shit."

"Yeah." Hank wasn't sure how he felt, but he knew he didn't like seeing Orson so uncomfortable. "My shooting *is* shit."

"Ha." Orson couldn't muster a pun. "But you get me, right?"

"Yeah, no, I get you." Hank let slip a rare real smile.

He appreciated Orson's effort. Most people didn't bother Hank anymore, thanks to Carmella. But they also didn't bother *with* him. He'd gone missing, after all.

Orson mimicked spiking his bangs. "This magic doesn't

happen by accident. I'm gonna dump a bucket of gel on my luscious locks. Feel free to hang here as late as you want."

"And have your grandma sneer at me? Nah, I'll head out."

"Hey, man, that's just her *face*. Don't be mean."

"Come on, she hates me."

"Okay, she might. But!" Orson gave him a thumbs-up. "It's because you're kind of Mexican, not because you're supergay."

"That's nice to know." Hank retrieved the ball. "Orson?"

"Shoot."

"Do the varsity guys know you hang out with me?"

Orson didn't meet his eyes. "Well, probably. Lady's man, man's man, dog's man, cat's man, other animal's man. I hang out with everybody."

"Yeah. I guess you do."

Orson was the reason Hank was still playing basketball, but Hank wasn't the reason Orson was anything. It should have been fine. It didn't change Orson's generosity, his heartfelt rescue of Hank this autumn.

Hank was just a monster. Part of him wanted to *own* things, to possess them. And he really didn't know if that was Luz's residue or not. Maybe he'd always had this greedy pit at his core. Maybe that came from Dad.

"I'd ask you to come with, but I know you don't want to."

Hank thought of Henry Flowers. The request that he look for things he shouldn't see. Right now, his fists were all his own.

"Actually." Hank flashed a wide one. "I *do* want to."

Orson hardly blinked. "Really?"

"Why the hell not. It's Halloween!" Time to do something terrifying.

It could have teetered either way. Then Orson's face split open and he started pounding Hank on the shoulder. "Exactly! Miller can suck it! We're coming to his party and we're gaying it up!"

"You helping me with that?" Orson seemed about as gay as Hank was smart.

"Just cheering you on, buddy. Just cheering you on."

Hank wondered if this was a moment worth sketching.

11

EYES

There were no questions.

About Brendan, Ana learned: He first kissed a boy in Cub Scouts, which he joked was a common origin story for kids like him. His mother smoked during pregnancy, so he had asthma and a partially indented rib cage and all sorts of other problems. After his cousin died in that car crash, he tore all the wheels off the objects in his home—his Heelys, his Matchbox cars, the television cabinet. He lost his virginity to a girl, actually, back in eighth grade, but wouldn't say who. He once pretended to have a peanut allergy because he was sick of peanut butter and jelly sandwiches. He was afraid that he'd never be a good artist in any medium. He thought he might have some kind of obsessive-compulsive disorder—not like people who liked to say they did, but *really*—sometimes he washed his hands until they bled. He was still in love with Hank Vasquez. He thought you could probably love a dozen people at once.

About Platinum, Ana learned: She was a virgin and planned

to remain so until fictional characters came to life and wanted to meet her at her Italian villa. But seriously: her mom was the one in the military, not her dad, but she'd stopped correcting people (and yes, her mom had killed people before). She sucked at makeup and only copied what she saw online, which, no, don't argue with her, still meant she sucked. She hated her name because Arlene was originally the name of her big sister, who'd died before Platinum was born. She had a creepy cousin—who didn't?—who went to prison, but not before he had hurt her. She was scared of moving. She was scared of staying.

About herself, Ana taught them: She stopped loving things when people wanted her to stop, so maybe that meant she never loved things anyhow. She used to dream of making movies but never believed she actually would. She may have been in love with Marissa Ritter, her former best friend, but she didn't know that, either. There was nothingness behind eyelids. She hadn't felt anything real for years, except when she cut, so of course she cut, and it made perfect sense to her. She dreamed of her brothers and her mother driving away from her, and she could never catch up to the van even when Milo held the door for her. She could remember what Dad smelled like.

A few hours in, the events of last summer finally came up. Neither Brendan nor Platinum interrupted, and neither of them called her a liar.

They just listened, as if the revelation that an extraterrestrial parasite had infested a friend's family was a secret equal to Brendan's last wet dream or Platinum stealing a bicycle when she was eleven.

Maybe it was.

Finally Ana shared a secret that felt truly forbidden, a soap bubble that wouldn't exist once it hit the air. "I think . . . I think I'm getting better."

"I think that's another secret everyone already knows," Brendan whispered.

At last they dragged themselves off the ground, wiping their eyes and sighing, holding each other up to shake the cold needles loose. They traipsed over the haunted foundations toward Brendan's car. Platinum stopped. She untangled herself from their arms and stood apart, pointing at the horizon.

"What the hell is that?"

At first Ana saw nothing but desert starlight drawing a clear line of separation between earth and sky, the silhouette of that lonely saguaro. Then she spotted an amber light on the horizon, a gentle haze of orange as nearby as yards or as far away as miles.

"A bad idea, is what," Brendan answered. "I've seen movies. Let's go."

"Go look, you mean?" Platinum was grinning. "Because we should. This is totally my shit. And Ana loves movies."

"Let's look." Ana wasn't afraid it might be something extraterrestrial. Maybe she even hoped it would be. If the others suspected that, they didn't say so.

Brendan sighed. "Fine. But we are certainly *not* getting out of the car."

The car seat remained icy cold beneath Ana's thighs as the car came to life and bumped its way toward the orange haze. Within two minutes of slow creeping, they were upon it.

"Huh." Platinum was clearly disappointed. "Campers."

The orange light emanated from a large Coleman lantern, though Brendan's headlights had drowned the glow. By those headlights Ana made out two small tents, a fire pit, and a large canopy. Arranged beneath the canopy was a heap of bulky objects covered in tarpaulin, circled by a few rolling office chairs. A white van, generic and familiar, was parked nearby.

Ana's stomach dropped.

"We should go." The night felt suddenly dystopian. The arrangement of the shrouded objects recalled a demented workplace, a scene from Terry Gilliam's *Brazil* or Fritz Lang's *Metropolis*. The wheels of those chairs wouldn't work on desert sand. "Now."

"Ana, you speak wisdom." Brendan switched the car into reverse.

"Look."

Platinum pointed at the van. Her eyes were better than Ana's, but now Ana saw it, too.

A ghost clad all in white stepped into the high beams.

12

EARS

People really didn't know what to make of Milo. This was nothing new.

But now he wore a hoodie, and headphones, and his mother's attempt at Día de los Muertos sugar skull makeup!

Penny was dressed as a mime. She took the job very, very seriously. In the van she told Milo that if he wanted to talk to her, he had to do it with his hands. Mr. Dawson signed that it would be good practice.

At a house on Hamilton Street, Milo convinced a man in devil horns to hand him *three* rolls of Smarties instead of just one. He told the devil that there were only fifteen Smarties tablets in a roll. And Milo had more than fifteen teeth! The third roll, he explained, was for emotional damages.

It was maybe *abstract*. But the devil caved!

Do you need three? Penny asked, as they trundled from that house to the next.

One for Hank, one for Ana, one for you!

This house had a long sidewalk lined with pumpkins. Penny did the knocking in her once-white gloves, now pinkish with Blow Pop debris.

An elderly woman praised Jesus when Penny greeted her with a flat invisible wall and Milo hollered, "WE ARE HERE TO BROKER PEACEFUL TRADE NEGOTIATIONS!"

Milo guessed the shock didn't have much to do with him looking ghoulish. It was Halloween, and two of the other six ASL kids carried rubber machetes!

But! This was Gailsberg, the next town over. None of these people knew Milo. Mr. Dawson had driven here to meet his sister, Penny's aunt Judy. She was their other chaperone.

This neighborhood was a treasure trove. *X* marks the spot! Because here was where all the Gailsberg teachers lived, and these teachers saved their candy gold for the nighttime witching hour. The decorations were also A+++. So far Milo had counted *four* hanging men and a gazillion (give or take a ga-) jack-o'-lanterns!

Milo and Penny led the line of Eustace invaders with pride, following the trail of a pair of knowledgeable Gailsberg locals dressed as Mario and Luigi. Every time those two spun away from a porch, Milo's eyes went right to their matching mustaches.

Dad had a mustache like that. But Luz never did.

Mario and Luigi kept coming back, leaving and coming back.

As the hour vanished, the faces along this street became familiar. More than once they spotted a tall werewolf with two trash bags full of candy (*how?*). They passed the same seven Disney princesses. Milo kept giggling at a boy dressed as a sushi roll.

He was halfway through hearing the twelve minutes of Sigur

Rós's "Untitled #8" when Penny snapped her fingers! She pointed at empty air behind them.

The other Eustace invaders had been scooped back into the van.

"But there's still one more house."

Mr. Dawson honked the horn. Clearly he thought the fun had ended.

Couldn't Mr. Dawson see the purple glow of a black light on the side of this garage? There was at least a *little* Halloween spirit in this house!

"We have to finish."

Never say Penny didn't like a challenge. She liked *Milo*, of all people.

She signed a quick *One more!* to her dad.

They hurried past an overturned bicycle and a faded lawn pinwheel to the front step. There wasn't a welcome mat. Milo could see the outline of where one used to be.

Penny went in for the knock, then froze inside her mime box.

Milo cleared his throat for his final performance.

The porch light came on, a dull moth-calling orange. When the door opened, the light wasn't strong enough to illuminate the man's features.

"Oh, god, is it Halloween?" He sounded a bit out of it. "Sorry, kids."

Milo pulled off his headphones.

From inside the house a woman called, "That's not the police, is it?"

"Nah. A mime and a zombie. Honey, we got any candy or cookies or something?"

"I'm a skeleton," Milo corrected. The man wasn't listening—he was peering down a brown hallway, toward the woman's voice, the echo of the evening news.

Milo felt Penny's eyes all over him. Maybe she was surprised because his headphones were off.

"Sorry, I'm not sure we have anything for you." But the man held up a finger. "Or wait—wait here a second."

Mr. Dawson's horn sounded again. Penny tugged on Milo's hand.

"Come on." The mime act fell away. "We don't need anything from this guy."

Milo really thought he did, though.

The man returned. He held out an open pack of spearmint gum and flicked a strip into each of their pillowcases.

"Think of it as an *ex-spearmint!*" Milo thought the man sounded very, very pleased with himself. His face made no sense at all. "That'll do ya, boys and ghouls!"

The man closed the door.

Penny tugged on Milo's hand again.

They got as far as the bicycle before Milo stopped. He dropped his pillowcase. Candy scattered over his shoes. Fun-size Milky Ways were lost between stalks of grass.

"Milo?" Penny didn't sound annoyed. She sounded far away.

This bicycle terrified Milo. *Who had been riding it?*

The thought popped a balloon inside his chest.

Milo didn't care that his headphones were completely off. He didn't care that the album had ended. He didn't care that his makeup started running down his face or that Penny was shaking him, trying to pull him away from the bicycle. He wouldn't let go of the seat and the handlebars scraped the sidewalk. When Penny yanked on him, somehow the bike got tangled in their feet and both of them hit concrete.

Next thing Milo knew, Penny was crying and she'd scraped up her stripy arm pretty good.

He still couldn't let go of the bicycle.

Mr. Dawson had to pry it out of his hands before he could lift Milo up, put him inside the van, and strap him into his seat.

All the kids stared at him.

"What did that man do?" Mr. Dawson wasn't signing now. He held Milo's shoulders. Aunt Judy pulled out her phone, ready to dial whoever grown-ups call when a boy, definitely not a grown-up but a hopeless, useless boy, can't even breathe right.

Why did the balloon in his chest have to pop?

"Deep breaths, Milo. Tell me what he did."

"He *left*," Milo said. Maybe once, maybe ten thousand times.

This man had a mustache like Mario and Luigi's, except it was more like Dad's!

This man had a face with a smile as wide as his shoulders, just like Hank!

He had eyes that shone bright even when they were tired, like Ana's!

He made punny jokes, just like Milo.

And most important, this man had a voice that sounded like nobody's but one person's in the world. Milo knew, because he'd been trying to hear it for years.

Milo waited for the balloon to reinflate. He breathed through his nose, tried to be an adult. There was some actual detecting to do here. That was all.

Maybe Milo really should have worn the clothes from his birthday party. Then maybe Dad would have recognized his youngest son, haunting his doorstep.

But maybe Milo wasn't Dad's youngest son.

Milo didn't know who that bike belonged to.

13

HANDS

Visiting Tim Miller's house after dark felt a little like going back in time.

Hank thought he'd never come here again. The Miller house wasn't as big as Orson's, but close enough. All these places were palaces of one kind or another, and Hank was ready to be denied entry. And he wasn't used to this house cast in orange and black, windows clogged by glow-in-the-dark cobwebs.

Hank tried not to knot his fingers. "Sure you won't mind being seen with me?"

"You kidding? It's gonna be great. I'm gonna be popping popcorn on the flames of what's about to go down in there, Tank."

"Ha."

"Seriously, though. Proud of you for coming out." Orson looked right at Hank, that freewheeling sarcasm absent for once. "Let me know if anyone gives you shit."

"And you'll what?"

The sarcasm wheeled back: "Tank, if you tell me that some-one's giving you shit, I'll have time to get another bag of pop-corn ready before you deck them. Warn me early enough and I'll be able to pour some chili powder in there, make it really delicious."

"Ha."

"But you *can* deck 'em, you know. If you have to."

Hank shook his head, remembering the locker room. "I won't."

"You're such a fucking teddy bear." Before Hank could mock the weirdness of that insult, Orson leaned closer. Dark eyes and hair filled Hank's vision.

"Orson—what the hell—"

"Close your eyes, Hank." Orson's breath warmed Hank's neck.

And anything could happen, but Hank closed his eyes all the same and held his breath and *waited* for the anything, the impos-sible, and did he *want* the impossible? How annoying was Orson, or how amazing was he? Because he was *nothing* like Brendan and he was *straight, fucking obviously*, and should Hank be ready to taste tongue in his mouth any second now—

He heard Orson swallow, felt rough fingers on his chin.

One second, Orson's hand held Hank in place.

The next, Hank felt the cool smear of ink at the corners of his mouth.

"What the hell?" A sudden scent made Hank woozy.

Orson chortled. "Best costume ever."

Hank wiped at his mouth. "Dude, is that—was that a *Sharpie*?"

"You know it." And before he could hear Hank's stream of sudden swearwords, he stepped outside. Hank could only follow.

"Seriously, did you draw on my face?"

"Don't you trust me, Hank the Tank?"

Hank closed his mouth. "Yeah."

"So believe me. This costume'll be a hit." Orson pulled a pair of oven gloves over his hands. "In we go."

Laughter drifted up from the Man-Cave. Bass shook the ground, hard enough to make gravel bounce by the mailbox. The music was the definition of accessible and boring as hell.

"What is this, a teen movie?"

Hank hoped he was only an extra.

Tim Miller might have wanted to be a senior party animal. His dad might have encouraged that, too. But Mrs. Miller ran the show, and she too had heard about Ben O'Brien's party. There would be Sprite in the punch bowl, munchies and ibuprofen at the ready, beds for anyone who wanted one. In the morning, there would be pancakes. Tim was cool enough that he didn't *have* to have alcohol at his parties. Besides, there was a game Saturday night. Nobody dared show up hungover.

Mrs. Miller, spiders in her teased hair, met Hank and Orson at the door. "Come on in! They're all in the den—Orson, what on god's green earth are you supposed to be?"

Orson plucked at his jersey with his oven mitts. "Oh, I'm a benchwarmer."

It seemed to make more sense to Mrs. Miller than it did to Hank, or else she'd long since learned it was best to hurry Orson along if she didn't want her ear talked off.

She started at the sight of Hank.

Had Tim told her about tryouts? Had she seen the bruises? Had—

"*Hank!*" Mrs. Miller pulled him into a hug. "We've missed you around here!"

Over her shoulder, Orson mimed throwing popcorn into his mouth.

As she led them to the basement stairs, Hank muttered, "So that's entertainment, huh?"

Orson snickered. "Honestly, a soap opera's fine by me."

A subtitled horror movie—it looked like maybe *The Re-Animator* (Ana would know)—was projected on a blank white Man-Cave wall before a pile of bodies sprawled across the sectional. Across the room several guys dressed as pirates shouted over the sound system, hollering about college ball. Elsewhere Ben, Rin, and Sarah Perlman clung to gaming controllers, shooting the crap out of each other. The snack table was already dotted with spent Reese's wrappers.

No one held a red Solo cup. Mrs. Miller found them tacky. Instead, a handful of seniors played soda pong with plastic stem glasses. Apparently the goal wasn't chugging ginger ale, but collecting as many cups as possible.

Tim had only two cups left to aim for. He bit his lip, lifted his police officer's hat away from his line of sight, shot—

—and made it, naturally.

A whoop went up.

Hank recognized Carmella's cheer before he recognized her. She wore an enormous patterned dress and a small ruff around her neck. White paint on her face, hoops under her skirts. Anyone else would have been swallowed by clothes like that. But this was Carmella, blessing them with her presence.

Right now she seemed to be blessing Tim Miller, hanging off his neck like that.

Maybe she felt Hank's stare—she lifted powdered, unapologetic eyes.

And why is this any of your business?

It wasn't, and she knew Hank knew it. Yet he remained gaping even after she met him by the stairs. The crowd parted as Carmella led him to the Ping-Pong table.

"Surprised to see you, Hank."

"Yeah. Same."

"Your makeup's breaking my heart."

Hank shrank. No one noticed.

Didn't she *hate* Tim Miller? Wasn't he a scumbag? Hadn't she just sicced Esmeralda on him? Hadn't he insulted Milo? Hadn't he dented Hank's stomach?

Tim Miller wasn't the one who dumped her.

Carmella held up a hand. Hank didn't kiss it.

Tim caught sight of him. Hank refused to scratch his neck.

Sure, he dented your stomach. After you throttled him.

"I said you could bring someone, Orson. Wasn't expecting your boyfriend." Tim's tone was teasing, but was the rest of him?

Hating himself, Hank smiled. "Hilarious, Tim."

"No, it wasn't." Tim jerked his chin. "I'm being a dick. Again. Like earlier."

Hank nodded. "You should have left Milo out of it. He's a good kid."

"Yeah." Tim averted his lead eyes. "Never should have said that. Esmeralda should have decked me. It was shitty. I've been shitty in general, Tank."

Hank scanned Carmella's impassive painted face. Did she improve scumbags across the board? She extended a hand to their level, lifted them up to hers.

"Well, I was shitty at tryouts." Hank tried to find their old cadence. "Tim, I am so sorry about that. I can't explain it. I was trying to be something, or nothing, or . . . I'm just sorry."

"It was fucked. But so was I. In the park?" Carmella stared at them. "And . . . okay. With the shit I said."

"You mean 'faggot.' You mean 'retard.'"

Tim winced. "Yeah. God. I know. I don't know where those even came from. And you were right. My dad's the one who taught me to play smear the queer. He *is* a homophobe. But I don't wanna be. I'm trying not to be. I was just . . . you know?"

Something in their upbringing meant neither of them could say they were sad. That they missed being friends, complaining in this basement. Hank knew his words and actions were light-years removed from who he wanted to be. Did Tim feel that way, too?

Maybe if Hank still had a dad, he'd have learned to be more than hands and feet. But what had *Tim's* dad taught him about violence? Long before Tim and Hank were old enough to be grounded, Tim had whispered about belts and shown Hank his welts.

If Dad had stuck around, could Hank have ever kissed Brendan? That grin on the sidelines might have stopped him. Hank didn't know whether Dad had ever played smear the queer, didn't know whether Dad could care about superfluous stars in blueprints.

Even if Hank were clever like Brendan, he couldn't say these things. Not even through terrible metaphors. Neither he nor Tim had been raised to *talk*. So far, no number of tossed foam footballs had changed that.

Hank said, "I get it, Tim."

Tim's relief was palpable. "Yeah. Me too. Honestly? I didn't see it coming. I mean. You being gay." What Tim didn't ask: *Why didn't you tell me?*

"Neither did I." What Hank didn't answer: *I couldn't.*

Orson jumped between them with his mittened hands up, a living cartoon. "You guys look like you could use some stiff cream sodas."

Carmella dragged Orson away, but not before showing her pearly whites. Her work here was done for the moment.

"What's up with your face right now, Hank?"

"Oh. Orson came at me with a marker. Is it bad?"

"Hell. Don't ask me. Can your fucked-up hands still put balls in holes?"

Tim was being a dick, but in the friendly way he used to be a dick.

Hank missed the first shot, and the second. Tim made his first two.

"Any chance you'll stop sucking in time for you to play a game with us?"

"Doubtful."

"Man. If something like that can happen to you . . . if even Hank the Tank can't get a basketball scholarship, feels like all of us are doomed."

They were supposed to go to college in less than a year. Tim Miller had good looks and he had an overbearing mom. He had money, and a dickish sense of humor, and a temper, and a homo-phobic father.

Tim didn't have a basketball scholarship.

There was something Mom said whenever Hank had a bad day. To Milo and Ana, too: "Most people really do try to be good."

Was it schmaltzy? Hell yes. Was it the sort of thing she said because she thought parents said stuff like that? Totally. Was she right? Maybe not.

Hank was glad she said it. Tim and Hank were trying to be good, and maybe even Dad had tried. Luz had never tried, so trying must be what made things human.

Tim readjusted his cap. "Right. I am thirsty as hell."

Orson reappeared on cue, mitt-less now. Hank downed his cream soda in one, burping spectacularly. Some clown pushed the movie volume up to full blast. Tim Miller cussed and abandoned Hank to dole out justice.

"Orson. What's on my face?"

"Oh, *man.* I drew you a permanent frown!" The unexpected brightness of Orson's gaze threw Hank off balance. Classic Orson, except this felt like a new kind of surprise. Suddenly Hank longed for a real drink after all. "You can't turn it upside down. You just have to wear the fucking thing, Hank."

". . . Jesus." Hank referred to the rise in his blood, but Orson couldn't know that.

"Ha. That's my name; don't wear it out. Anyhow, it's dumb. You know me. I say dumb shit and I do dumb shit, like that time I tried shaving upside down and—"

Orson stopped. Under the table, Hank had just grabbed his

hand. He hadn't done that in months—put *his* hand around someone else's. "Orson. You are *not* dumb."

Hank waited for Orson to pull away. Because what the hell, Halloween didn't explain any of this, didn't explain why Orson's black eyes suddenly seemed as immersive as a starless sky—

At last Orson closed them. He freed himself, made some crack about the snack table. The heat of his touch remained, sealing the perforations in Hank's palm.

God. If Hank smiled now, while his lips were frowning, that'd be confusing.

14

EYES

Brendan swore in the face of the Perecheney ghost.

Ana smacked his hand from the wheel. "Wait! I know her!"

Dr. Ruby stood there in a nightgown, staring directly into their headlights. The glare washed out the scarred side of her face. She lifted her arms to shield her eyes.

"She's my doctor. Dr. Ruby."

She seemed so thin, thinner than Milo. Dr. Ruby stood, swaying, bracing herself. Slowly she lowered her arms and stretched them toward them.

"I guess she must be living out here," Brendan said slowly. "Why, Ana?"

"I have no idea." Dr. Ruby had retreated gradually from their home over the past few weeks. Her assistants, the tall woman and the heavyset man, had vanished altogether.

She'd said she had work to attend to elsewhere, that she was leaving town.

But here she was.

Platinum tsked. "Your doctor's a desert witch, Ana?"

"I guess."

"No wonder you're having such a hard time."

"Ana," Brendan whispered, "do you . . . I mean, should we help her?"

"No. I don't think so."

All Ana knew was that Dr. Ruby looked like another facet of emptiness in that cold light. The way she held her arms, Dr. Ruby might have longed for abduction.

They left the desert at last, riding in silence with the windows down, having said all they could say. Platinum's house was closest.

"Well. That was . . . something. See you guys at school on Monday."

"Don't be ridiculous. Of course I'm coming over to help you pack."

"The military'll do that for us, Brendan."

"Then I'm coming over to *whine* at you and sip virgin mimosas, also known as orange juice, while we watch the military pack. I claim that as my right as your grieving pan best friend who actually loves you quite a lot."

Platinum pecked both Ana and Brendan on the cheek and hopped out. It was like a movie, the way she faded in the rearview. She'd let Ana ride shotgun this time. It felt symbolic.

In a film it would be.

What felt worse than symbolic was the return of stinging in Ana's eyes.

"I never thought Platinum would be my friend."

"The first time I met her, she insulted my line-work, laughed at my eyebrows, and then gave me her phone number. That's her, ah, modus operandi, more or less. The Platinum sneak attack."

"The Platinum sneak *heart* attack." Ana rubbed her eyes, though she shouldn't. Until tonight, it had been two weeks since anyone at home had seen Dr. Ruby. But her voice was still there in her head: "*Touching it will only make it worse.*"

At last Brendan parked in the cul-de-sac. Ana could see that the kitchen light was on. Ana hoped Mom wasn't scrubbing the floor again. There'd hardly been any bloodstains to begin with.

The rearview captured Nameless Canyon, gaping open behind them. Brendan didn't like looking at it these days, but he seemed to love looking at the house.

"Ana . . . ? I know this is weird to ask, but do you . . . do you feel good about tonight?"

She might never run out of secrets. Brendan would never run out of questions. "Yeah. I think so."

"About which part, exactly?"

It occurred to Ana that his questions might be less about caring than they were about being scared.

"Well, not the whole cholera ghost town part, or my desert doctor." She couldn't tell if that counted as a joke. Brendan didn't laugh. "I never thought I would get close with anyone. With *anything*. Ever again. The bar in my head. It's really high, Brendan."

"The secret game is over, you know."

"But I still have more." Ana used to think the way to relieve the pressure was in the applying of makeup, the covering up. Or maybe in the slicing, but god, it could be in the telling. It was a new high. "I thought I didn't want anything. Now I don't want Platinum to leave."

"Reservation for Mourning, party of two. Yeah. She'll go. And it'll suck. But we'll be okay."

"Yes." If Ana let every departure decimate her, there'd be nothing left.

"Maybe better than okay?" And suddenly Brendan's hand was on Ana's head, his fingers were tangled in her hair, and his lips were on hers.

There's this scene in countless movies where a guy makes a move on a girl in a car, proving himself a real creep. And the girl smacks him off and escapes his clutches and he rolls down the window and says something like "Come on, babe!"

Marissa and Ana, long ago, had promised never to have a scene like that in any of their films.

Brendan wasn't a creep.

He was her brother's ex. He asked questions not just because he cared but because he was scared. His hand in her hair was so different from Luz's presence in her head, rifling through the thoughts that made her love herself.

Brendan was trying to be human.

She pulled away.

"Brendan." His breath was ragged. He retreated as far as the car would allow and let his head fall against the window.

"Please don't tell me you're not Hank, Ana. I know that. I know who you are."

"Yeah."

"And I was serious, before. I like girls, too. People like to make assumptions, but damn it, it's not the 1950s and—that's not the point, is it? The point is I mean it. I *like* you."

"I know you do." It wasn't the 1950s, but all this articulate young man could manage was "I like you," because there aren't words for choosing to become vulnerable like that.

Brendan Nesbitt was the boy who had once bumped into Ana in the grocery store and apologized seven times. The boy who'd painted the mural smeared across the middle school choir room, a depiction of stars and moons and planets all orbiting multi-colored children with closed eyes. Nesbitt was the name a younger Ana outlined in hearts in her planners.

That Ana would have said yes. She'd have held him in this car.

But this was Ana now. This was Brendan Nesbitt scared.

"I'm not going to leave you, Brendan." She held his hand against her head. "But I don't think I'm going to date you, either."

"You and your brother and Platinum, treating me like a fragile watercolor. My god, I have *teeth*, you know. I can handle life. I'm as fucked-up as you all are."

Hank, in the auditorium. Herself, in the auditorium. Platinum and her jokes, all-knowing: "You'd get to kiss him."

"Two fuckups don't make a right," Ana said, as Platinum might have. "I'm going to miss her too, Brendan."

". . . yeah. I know." Brendan wasn't crying. Or if he was, she couldn't see it with her eyes closed. "I can't believe I left you in a canyon to die. All of you."

"We didn't die, Brendan. Don't be dramatic."

He sobbed, bit it back. "Can't seem to help that. I've been practicing a long time."

Time.

"Wait a second." Ana squinted at her house. The kitchen lights were on, but Mom's car was absent from the driveway. "What time is it?"

"Like . . . eleven?"

"Holy shit." Ana was supposed to have been home by eight.

Which meant Milo was in there, all alone, because Hank had just texted her to leave the door unlocked. "I have to go. Sorry."

"Yeah. 'Night, Ana."

"I'm not leaving you in some kind of canyon right now, am I, Brendan?"

He shook his head. "I don't think you'd have asked that before."

Before everything. Before anything.

Even before Ana stepped into her home on the edge of the world, she could feel it. Whatever was happening inside was wrong. The world was breaking open.

Ana found Milo unconscious, floating on a sea of glass.

15

OUTSIDE

Maggie had a great time at the Morris party. Right now, she didn't feel bad about that. Perhaps she would come morning.

But not now, she scolded herself. *Now you can be happy. Your last-minute, slapdash chest-burster costume was a real hit, cardboard and corn-syrupy blood and all. And even though people asked you about your kids, they didn't ask why you weren't with them.*

The thing was, they weren't with theirs, either. They had sitters or older siblings at home, too. That was fine. It was something parents did. If Maggie wanted to be counted among them, she had to learn to be fine with it.

Not an other mother. A parent with kids. Kids with some trauma behind them. *Behind them*, not before them. Kids who were growing up.

Before Maggie now was a ride with Samantha Stuart's designated driver, her husband, Harold.

"Milo really has been doing better," Samantha told her. She was farther gone than Maggie, and had proved it by sitting in the backseat and calling her husband "the cabbie." She gave Maggie a thumbs-up. "Today's was his first outburst in weeks."

"It's because you're a great teacher."

"And hey, you're probably a great mother, too."

"No. Look at me."

Samantha held up her safari binoculars. "This here's a good mother in an unnatural habitat. Crikey!"

Tonight they were best friends. Tomorrow they'd have headaches.

"Margaret. I'm sorry I called you eccentric."

Though the chest-burster had lost most of its teeth, Maggie worked its jaw with her thumb and forefinger, made it say: "Don't be."

Samantha laughed until she gagged. Harold the Cabbie looked concerned, but remained professional.

Maggie was still giggling when she stepped into her driveway. She was still smiling when she reached the door.

All three of her kids would have beaten her home. It was almost midnight. She hoped none of them would be awake to see her fall through the door—

The sound of crashing waves reached her ears.

But we live in a desert.

An ocean existed in the kitchen. It was composed of strange, sharp detritus. All of the cupboards were open, drawers overturned. Broken porcelain, scattered knives and forks hid the floor from view. The crashing of waves was only the crashing of the broom. Ana, wearing her old Jolly Roger–patterned galoshes, swept wreckage into a dustpan.

"Ana . . . ?"

"Wear shoes, Mom." Her hair was tied back for once.

Seeing her so clearly in this silver and white and blue ocean brought Maggie right back to the day Hank had burst into this very room hollering about safety pins.

"It wasn't me," Ana told her.

"Christ. What happened?" Maggie took two steps into the room and cussed six more times, because the wreckage was six times worse than she'd realized. She was still dizzy from sailing another sea, one of margaritas and loose tortilla-chip boats in guacamole, not a sea of cutlery and slivers.

Finally Maggie came to it. ". . . Milo?"

Ana pointed.

There he was, slumped on a stool with his head on his arms. The counter before him was clear. An island in the storm.

Maggie felt seasick. "Weren't . . . Ana, you were supposed to watch him?"

"Sorry, Mom. I know. I got home late from Platinum's and he was by himself." Ana did not say, "*You* got home even later, *Mother*," but Maggie felt it, lashed out against the thought on instinct:

"So a demented seven-year-old was left by himself because you got home late?"

Because I got home late.

Ana stared. Had Maggie really called her own son demented? Surely CPS would be here any minute. Did CPS have cuffs? Or maybe Dr. Ruby would reappear on the doorstep. This time Maggie could say what she should have last time she found wreckage in her kitchen:

Take them away from me before I ruin them, too.

Maggie wanted to slump to the floor. The floor was full of glass. Her children were in the room. Maggie remained standing.

"No. I'm sorry, Ana. I . . . let me do that."

Ana shook her head. "No. It's halfway my fault, Mom."

A creaking sound pierced the waves.

Milo was sitting perfectly upright, eyes wide open. He seemed still enough to be dead. This might be a body, empty. It took Maggie a moment to realize why he seemed so changed. It wasn't the traces of skull makeup.

"Milo, honey. Where are your headphones?" She crunched across the linoleum in her black pumps, tearing what remained of the prop alien from her chest and dropping it in the sink before approaching her catatonic son.

"Mom, let me clear the floor first—"

Of course Ana was being reasonable. So calm these days, and she was right—Maggie's heel slipped on grains of glass, all but returned to sand.

Maggie tried to lift Milo. He was too heavy.

"I can do that, Mom." Hank dropped his bag in the doorway. He didn't ask what had happened. There was a strange flush in his cheeks.

"You haven't been drunking, have you?" Maggie swore. "Drinking?"

Hank came close, looked down at her. "Only cream soda."

Milo's next breath was the widest sound.

He turned his head to Maggie. "I'm sorry, Mom. I had a tantrum."

"Oh." Ana was looking at her like she didn't know who she

was. Maggie had never been anything more than New Year's Eve tipsy in front of them. "It's okay, Milo. It's all just stuff. But where are your headphones?"

"Oh." He blinked. "I don't need them anymore. You can throw them away."

He started to slide off his seat in his sock feet—

"Milo!"

"Your feet," Ana supplied.

"Oh. *Silly* me!" Milo giggled without smiling.

The wrongness seemed fitting, like the wrongness of Maggie drunk in her own kitchen, the wrongness of Ana having to clean up after a boy like Maggie always had to, the inherent wrongness of living on the edge of things.

"I've got you." Hank knelt close to the floor. "Piggyback."

Milo shook his head. "Use your hands."

Broken as everything in the room seemed, this felt the most so.

The truth was they had only been getting better individually.

Hank was afraid to touch Milo. Maggie could see that in his eyes. Even so, he stood. Hank lifted his little brother up beneath his arms and hoisted him high enough that Milo's feet dangled loose.

Hank backed out of the room, ducking under the door frame.

Milo's body remained curiously slack, but his hands kept moving.

"Good-bye!" he said.

And the boys were gone.

Maggie fell onto the stool Milo had left. Ana recommenced her sweeping. The heap of broken things was far too big for the trash can now.

"Women in the kitchen? *Shocking*. Don't be like me, Ana."

There was a little force in her voice, now. "... Mom?"

Maggie moved her hands, trying to parse what Milo had been signing on his way out. She couldn't put it together.

It bothered her head, but it wasn't the only thing.

Maggie drank water from the tap and tied her hair back like Ana's. She pulled a box from the pantry and helped her daughter scoop the debris into it. It took at least an hour. Surely there were still shards of glass caught in the crevices. They'd have to wear their shoes inside.

Ana kissed Maggie on the forehead before going to bed.

Maggie stayed in the kitchen a little longer, drinking water from an unbroken plastic CamelBak. She began to repeat Milo's sign again, then froze.

She was probably wrong again. She often was wrong, the mother who wore a xenomorph to a party in order to feel closer to her children.

But she thought Milo had been signing *help*.

16

EARS

Milo was alone.

Mr. Dawson didn't want to leave him without talking to Mom. But Milo had learned a lot from his siblings.

"It's okay! Ana's here!" Milo pointed at the light in the kitchen. "See?"

"Then at least I need to talk to *her* about what happened."

"*Nah!* I'm fine, Mr. Dawson. I'm just a real weirdo, you know!" Milo tapped his temple. "Ask Penny. Sometimes I even scream for no reason! Tell him, Penny."

Penny's cheeks shone with tears. She twisted her face away.

Milo kept smiling. Wow, if Hank could see him now! Maybe he'd be proud.

Penny wore clown-y makeup, but he still thought she looked sad. Her sadness got Milo off the hook. There were other kids who needed to get home ASAP. Milo sealed the deal by waving at the kitchen window.

Milo sprinted inside before Mr. Dawson could stop him and slammed the door. He peered through the mail slot. After a long minute, the van pulled away.

Milo walked to the silent kitchen. Without his headphones, the Roaring Nothing soaked him all the way through. Milo didn't scream.

The kitchen wasn't *really* silent, just like his Dad wasn't *really* gone. The fridge hummed. The freezer groaned. The lights whined. The faucet *drip*, *dripped* and Dad lived only twenty miles away.

Milo was alone.

He decided to cook. Cooking was noisy, especially the way Milo liked to do it. He yanked every pan out of every cupboard! He pulled every glass off every shelf. He dropped one and two plates, too, just to hear the crashing.

Smash! Bang!

He dropped a whole lot more of them after that.

Be normal, Milo.

He repeated this aloud. He banged pans together! He hung jangling keys off his wrists and utensils from his belt.

But he could still hear his thoughts!

Deep breaths, said the voice in his ears. *Raising the dead takes patience!*

Milo smashed a frying pan on a burner. He pretended to twist the flame on. He dropped imaginary dough on a cutting board. He kneaded it to perfection!

Halfway through cutting invisible beef with a visible knife, Milo realized he should wash his face. Good chefs cleaned their messes as they cooked. But here was Milo, using a knife with oily makeup all over his fingers!

Hush, Milo.

Was this Milo's thought, or someone else's?

Be careful, Milo.

When Ana had held the knife to her face, it hadn't taken much for it to slip.

Milo didn't want to cut himself.

No, Milo, you don't. Please look after yourself.

"Be quiet. I'm older now. I know what I'm doing."

The voice hesitated.

Milo mimed scooping meat onto tortillas. He cleared the clutter of cup and plate shards right off the table, let the remaining wholes smash against the floor. To add to the symphony, he dumped the cutlery, too.

It's okay to be upset, Milo.

"Be *quiet*, I'm working! This is serious, adult work!" By now Milo was a fry cook. He stood on the footstool he still needed because he wasn't tall like Hank, maybe he never would be. A lot of stuff had stunted his growth, like growing up too fast had stunted his growth.

Milo pushed the spatula through empty air. The sole ingredients were snot and tears and the bumpy breaths that escaped him.

You know that man wasn't really *him, Milo.*

"He *looked* like me. He taught some other kid to ride a bike."

Milo, do you really think Dad would live so close and not come see you? Of course not. You're being silly.

"But . . ." Milo felt dizzy and tired. His foot slipped off the stool.

Breathe, Milo. Remember that your dad is magical.

"He pulled off the world's best vanishing act." Milo took a deep breath. "Poof."

Exactly. So why would he be in Gailsberg? They don't have any bridges! That's not somewhere a magical person would be, is it?

"No," Milo answered. He plated the chilaquiles. He couldn't smell them. They weren't there.

It can't *have been him! That's just common sense!*

"He *was* a magician," Milo whispered. His plate stayed empty. "You're right. That can't have been him."

You know it wasn't. Because he's right here, Milo.

The quiet hadn't bothered Milo for a while now. The voice was with him. How long had it been there? Since he tore the headphones off? Since before?

Milo dropped his fork. "Is it really you?"

Hey, Milo. Here I am. Sorry I tricked you. But that's what magicians do.

Milo cupped his hands to his ears and listened hard.

"Luz," he whispered, air escaping him, himself escaping him, as his eyes drooped, "am I dreaming?"

Luz hummed softly in answer. Milo started to cry, started to nod off, too.

I never left, Milo. Sorry I was so quiet. Things were getting out of hand, weren't they? With Hank and Ana. It was—

"A crazy summer," they said. Together.

Yes. I had to take a nap. A really deep, long nap. You know how that is. Even grown-ups do it.

"Yeah." Milo's smile made his yawn a funny shape. "But I missed you a whole lot. I was sick. No one liked me. Ana didn't care. Hank won't talk to me."

Are you better now?

Milo might have said yes before trick-or-treating. Now he shook his head.

"I'm always by myself. With Mom. With Hank and Ana and—and even Penny." He thought about his show-and-tell. "I'm by myself."

But you aren't. I'm right here. And you know what?

"What?" Milo asked his sleeves.

"Red touches black, safe for Jack. Red touches yellow, kills a fellow."

Milo smiled. "Coral snakes and *king* snakes."

You're not alone, Milo. You're just tired.

"But there are no naps in second grade."

Don't worry. I'll be here.

The hum in Milo's ears hit a peak and expanded in such a way that it seemed to shake Milo's whole actual skull and skeleton. There was nothing scary about it. Luz embraced him without arms, embraced all of Milo in a single unimaginable beat of sound, invisible but resonating in Milo's marrow.

Milo closed his eyes and went missing all over again, this time without going anywhere at all.

WHEN LIGHT LEFT US

Here is the story of how he left us, Hank wrote in trembling chicken scratch, in a letter he never thought he'd write.

"I'm going to tell you why he left us," Ana whispered to her friends in the town of ghosts, through tears as raw as her eyes.

You left us, Milo signed in his sleep.

Hank started writing his thoughts well after midnight, hunched over a desk crowded with dusty action figures and an expired ant farm. He felt like he was sitting in sunlight. He was seeing, again, the promise all hands held.

It wasn't only the tingling warmth of Orson's, a clandestine crush beneath a cream soda pong table.

It was Tim Miller extending a palm to him at the end of the night.

It was Carmella's fingers pushing Hank toward his sister's voice.

His own hands, carrying Milo to bed. *And I didn't hurt you, Milo.*

Milo's hands—it had struck Hank that they really were his own in miniature. They could be brothers again. Maybe Milo could teach him to build bridges.

Milo, you know I suck at talking. I suck at writing too but it's better than talking, because at least when I'm writing I can't smile. I hope these words aren't too big for you. I am trying to make them small.

"It seemed like just another day. But I guess every day starts that way," she said.

The stars didn't answer. Ana's friends didn't ask. That was against the rules.

"Luz started doing this pretty neat thing where he woke me and Hank and Milo up at the same time with a movie in our heads. Luz would sort of mash me and Hank and Milo into movies. Casting us in the leading roles.

"Luz was in a musical mood that week, so he woke us up with a scene from *Singin' in the Rain.* That's actually one of Marissa's favorite movies, but—never mind. We all met up in the kitchen. I was singing, and Milo hummed and Hank played the table like a drum. It felt amazing."

Milo's breathing was a good cadence for writing to.

Luz's last day here was August 4th. Or maybe 5th. I can't believe I forgot something like that. I'll try to get the details right, Milo, but I've never been like you, sorry. You're only seven but I'm pretty sure you were born smarter than me.

Milo, I know this is stupid but I like stupid metaphors. I think that's a family thing. But sometimes I feel like I'm a flea inside and you're a whole universe inside.

I'm sorry I never tell you you're amazing.

Milo, I'm sorry about a lot.

"Me and Luz went outside for a walk. Luz loved doing that, just . . . absorbing the world. He wanted to grow up even more than Milo wants to. Luz showed me things I'd never noticed. Like he'd point out how blacktop sparkles. He'd show me how my arms move when my legs do, and how there's kind of a symmetry to that. To *me*." A scrape marred Ana's voice. "If I say it sounds stupid, maybe I won't miss it.

"That day we walked to Marissa's house—do you guys know her? She used to be my best friend. She used to make animal sculptures out of masking tape and tissues. They were better than clay. We hung them in our lockers. Anyhow.

"Luz took walks outside, but also he took walks inside my head. He'd pick out random memories and start looping them over and over. He wanted me to take him places, so he'd drop hints, show me memories of cigarette butts or books or whatever until I took him to a gas station or library." Ana smiled. "He was like a little kid. He was curious, you know? Everything was so interesting to him."

She closed her eyes. "Apart from me."

Milo, did you ever wonder why Luz stayed with us?

I mean of all the places to land or whatever, he picks the canyon behind our house. If I was an alien, I'd want, I don't know. A family of soldiers or brainiacs or something. I'd want to travel for sure.

I always wondered why he wanted me. I think Ana wondered too. Ana is like that. She stabs herself on the inside too. I wish she loved her like we love her.

But did you wonder? Maybe not. I think you believed you were worth it. Because maybe you know you're a universe.

"Marissa and I haven't been friends since last year. It's kind of my fault, because last Halloween I had to call 911 on her at a party and it got weird. And later Marissa found out about *the cutting*. I mean the whole school knew. You guys too, right?"

Two nods.

"Marissa told me her mom was worried. This lady used to have me over for pool parties, but suddenly, 'Oh, she doesn't want me to hang around you anymore.' I'm pretty sure it was a lie. Pretty sure Marissa was just over me. She told me this when I was still in the hospital with all these stupid white bandages on my legs and this stupid purple gown thing on."

Brendan grabbed Ana's palm.

"So on his last day here, when Luz showed me Marissa's fingers, all prune-y from swimming, I thought maybe Marissa might have changed her mind. I just started walking.

"To thank me, Luz showed me this memory of Dad letting me play with his keys. Luz's version of a hug." Ana trembled. "Maybe you guys aren't screwed-up enough to ever think like this, but I always think hugs look like choke holds."

I used to be curious just like you, Milo. But after a while I got scared of people asking me questions and so I stopped asking them too. Until Brendan I guess.

Sometimes Luz sounded like Brendan. "Are you okay?" and "What do you dream about?" And sometimes he sounded like you. "Why do people have to ask permission to go pee in a school building?" And sometimes Ana too. "Why do you have so many clothes if you're only going to wear the same three T-shirts?"

But other questions came from somewhere dark. Maybe from me. They were bad questions, Milo, and I don't think they were about growing. Did you ever notice? You're not good at knowing what's normal. It's the best and worst thing about you, I think. I'm the opposite. I know what's supposed to be normal and that's just the worst thing.

Luz asked what would happen if I squeezed someone's skull between my hands until it cracked. He asked me to punch concrete. He asked what a person would look like without their skin.

He could of just looked in my head for answers but he was curious to see my reaction and I got so used to just letting him have it. Mom says I'm too much of a people pleaser. Luz wasn't even a person and I was still trying.

I let Luz ask and I hurt Tim Miller as an answer.

"Outside Marissa's house, Luz wouldn't shut up. He had me blink every other second so he could show me all these *shots* of us as kids. Before we were trying to be cool, when we literally used to just binge-eat vanilla wafers and play retro games like *Rampage* until five a.m. Luz kept showing me snapshots, until I could hardly see.

"And I just knew . . . Luz was bored.

"I'm scared I'm boring or simple like Dad thought I was. You can't be boring and still direct movies. I've never been able to love anything forever. I know it, and Luz knew it, and he was pushing me to see what would happen.

"He showed me the one time I was brave enough to do a flip off the diving board. *So prove me wrong. You want to be an entertainer? Show me things.*

"So I kept walking, all the way up to the fence. Luz started mixing things up. He took memories of me and Marissa and overlapped them with memories of cutting until everything good was just bloody. It was pretty much the opposite of loving myself.

"Marissa was sunbathing, she had these white lines where her bikini straps had slipped. She looked up and put her book down. Marissa never reads in front of other people. But she buys books with her grade money.

"Luz showed me memories of another pool party with Marissa. This time he showed me holding her head underwater and not letting go. *Mermaiding.*"

Luz wanted to grow, Milo. But not grow up. Just keep growing bigger and bigger. We weren't big enough.

Luz knew I don't like disappointing people. Like I know I shouldn't care about Dad anymore, Milo, but sometimes I wonder. I wonder if Dad knew I'm gay and that's the real reason why he went. Sorry. You're too little for this.

I didn't want to disappoint Luz, either. Driving ninety mph around the canyon and slamming the brakes just before the guardrails. Heckling girls, setting stuff on fire.

Honestly, Luz was every dumb jock.

He kept growing but I don't think he ever grew a heart.

★ ★ ★

"When Marissa's alone, she doesn't cut herself. She just *is* herself.

"She called my name. It didn't matter because Luz wouldn't shut up. He kept on showing me Marissa, floating facedown in the water, her hair all over the place.

"'Show me things.'

"He combined the drowning stuff with this memory of me feeling beautiful. Like saying, if you do *this*, you'll feel *this*. If, then. Singin' in the rain."

"That's awful." All playfulness had abandoned Platinum.

"Yeah. But you know what really sucked about Luz?"

"Everything, sounds like," Brendan said hollowly.

"I thought I needed him. More than my brothers. Luz reminded me to care about myself a little. But that's the one thing he got completely wrong."

You'll feel better.

"Ana . . ." Brendan cleared his throat.

"I got it. Right then. How *alien* Luz was. He didn't *get it* any more than Dad did. He didn't get that feelings aren't an *equation*. Of course I could *look* beautiful, I could *be* beautiful. But it might not make me *feel* better. If Luz learned everything he knew from Vasquezes, he should have known that!"

Ana was sitting now.

"Shouldn't he have been an *expert* at hating himself? Shouldn't he have realized that . . . that looking in the mirror and seeing ugliness isn't a *logical* experience?" Ana wiped her eyes. "No. He didn't *get this*: even if Luz made me the most *beautiful fucking thing on the planet*, I would never believe I was.

"I just turned around and went home. The whole way back he was showing me scabs and Hank crying and Milo bleeding.

Like Luz was *frustrated,* or maybe *hurt.* Or at least he was pretending to be."

Ana lay back down, let dirt press into her hair. "He was that close to all of us, but he had no idea what real hurt feels like."

Milo, we should of known he'd go for you. You've kind of been like an alien your whole life. I don't mean it in a bad way because I know you're just living. You're just a person like we all are. Luz wanted to be a person, too.

Luz's last minutes with the Vasquezes were almost a replay of the June day when they'd met. This time Ana stayed the course.

"Back home, in the kitchen, I held a knife close to my eye. I told him to get out. Luz showed me Grandma's funeral back in Wisconsin, and how sunken in she looked in her casket. It was too big for her. Mom's face after Dad left. She kept smearing too much concealer under her eyes.

"So I pushed the knife into my face."

"Jesus," said Platinum. Ana had thought she was asleep. "The scar?"

Ana nodded.

"Then Luz tried using Milo. Milo was in the doorway and his eyes were all rolled back and he told me, 'But I love you, dearheart.'

"Dearheart's what Dad used to call me."

Milo, I don't know why it happened like that.

My hands knew before I did. They started crawling like spiders and scratching me up and down my chest. I was running a lap around the neighborhood and suddenly they started slapping my face and grabbing my legs to stop them. I had my gym shorts on and I didn't even have a marker on me, because after what happened with Tim I was trying not to listen to him.

So Luz scratched KITCHEN in my arm.

I ran as fast as I could.

I'm so so sorry, Milo.

"Then Hank was in the doorway. His hands weren't moving but his body was all over the place. He didn't ask what was going on. We all knew. Hank told me to be careful.

"I told him it wasn't my first rodeo and the knife made me bleed a little. So Luz showed me as the heroine in every movie. He showed me traveling the world, seeing every biome. Begging me.

"And Milo said Dad would never hurt us. Debatable. But I told them all, 'Yeah? Well, I would. I hurt me all the time.' And so Luz tried one more thing.

"He used Hank. He tried to choke Milo with Hank's hands."

"No." Brendan's voice broke. "No way."

Ana tried to breathe. "Yeah. Luz said, 'If you're hurting me you're hurting all of us,' and Luz started squeezing and Hank started screaming and . . . it was horrible."

"What about Milo?" Platinum asked, breaking the question rule.

"Milo started dying."

I know it wasn't me. Luz had total control of my hands. But if Ana was able to stop him from running her life, why couldn't I? If Ana could walk

away from murder, how come I almost killed you, Milo? You kept scratch-
ing my hands. They were on fire but I still kept squeezing and all I
could think was how I never wanted to touch anything again.

Ana's knife slipped when I started yelling and her face was bleeding
and she started scratching my hands, too.

That's when Mom walked in.

And Luz just left. Did you hear him say good-bye? I didn't.

"It didn't feel good. It felt like having my eyes drained. Just guilt,
and this feeling that nothing would ever look beautiful again.
We breathed in and Luz was there, but we breathed out and
he wasn't."

Her story was over. It ended the game.

"It's good that he left, Ana." Brendan wiped salt water from
her cheek.

"I think about him all the time. I know it's fucked-up. But I
wake up saying his name. I look in the mirror and wish I could
see me how I used to."

"No." There was no arguing with Platinum's tone. "This
fucking thing had to go. It was an abusive monster."

Ana nodded. "Yeah. We were really alike."

Milo, I wish I could be like you. You'd be able to say for 100 percent
sure that it wasn't your hands. I wish I knew for sure I wasn't the kind
of person who could kill his little brother.

But I'm never ever sure who I am.

I wrote too much. My hands hurt. I think it means I'm getting bet-
ter. They hurt because of me. Because they're trying to fix things. My
hands are toolboxes.

I'm sorry and I love you, Milo. That is definitely part of who I am. Your Big Brother Hank.

In his bunk, asleep:

You were everywhere, Milo signed, moving fingers and fists. *And then you were gone.*

PART THREE
NOVEMBER 23
(DAY ONE HUNDRED TEN)

LUZ

Luz had enough thoughts to fill a thousand bodies.

He hadn't always known that they were thoughts. Before he formed a consciousness, Luz was a thing that clung to life simply because life was there to cling to. Once he'd had only as much sense of self as a leech, as little agency as a hookworm.

A hookworm, Milo's brain supplied, *is an insect (um, are worms insects?) that lives in poop but climbs into your foot and builds a house in your stomach!*

Some of the knowledge in Milo's skull was lacking, Luz knew. It was still so much more awareness than Luz had ever had while bodiless. There persisted small traces of understanding gleaned from his time spent with Milo's siblings. Ana's creativity and quick wit. Hank's ability to mimic belonging, his physical strength.

Milo's inquisitive mind and gullibility remained at Luz's disposal. It had been enough to keep him, when the three-part Vasquez organism became untenable.

Luz pulled Milo's body out of bed. He pulled socks onto

Milo's feet. He tied Milo's shoes with an ease Milo would have envied, if he had not been asleep inside himself. Luz was forgetting, but he thought it was Ana who made perfect bows. And it was Hank who could tiptoe from a dark bedroom into a dark hall. But Milo knew his way around the kitchen.

Everything Luz was, he was because of the Vasquez children.

The quiet functionality of a young man who knew how to disappear, the—

Milo's little hands dropped an egg on the floor.

—clumsy fingers of a boy whose thoughts lived perpetually elsewhere—

Luz swore through Milo's mouth.

—the vocabulary of a girl with no patience for anything, least of all herself.

Luz was currently these things. He borrowed memories of a kitchen filled with light and the smell of breakfast.

He had no memory of a time before the Vasquezes. Does a fungus have any need for memories?

Where are you from? the Vasquezes had asked. *Who are you?*

Does a virus know where it comes from? Or, because Luz had soon enough learned that people, at least the Vasquezes, were not fond of viruses or fungi, the question had grown grander: Does a baby wonder about its origins?

No. It only grows.

His very first instinct, upon blooming in the canyon, cognizant somehow that the open air would treat him cruelly, was not to ask *Where did I come from?*

It was to say *I want to grow.*

The sound of butter in the pan, egg yolks wiggling. Small

hands found a salt canister and overturned it, shaking granules loose. Then pepper, the lightest pinch of grated cheese. Small hands pulled plates from the drying rack.

Milo's hands were small, but so were seeds. Small was often enough.

On the night Luz found awareness, this smallest Vasquez appeared in Luz's vicinity. The first human Luz had any recollection of was this small thing: a mess of mucus and trembling at the base of the canyon. Organic matter stuck to its fingers, what later Luz recognized as mud and blood. Small, but enough.

Luz had swarmed him.

Milo's eyes were closed and his nose was dripping, and his filthy hands were unreachable, tucked beneath his arms. But his ears were open. Luz scuttled closer and settled in. The shelter felt tenuous—this damp creature could shake Luz loose in a heartbeat; he was so much more tangible than Luz had ever been.

Luz was a ghost, a many-limbed mist that clung tight to Milo's thoughts. Tugged this question from the weeping, human thing: *Where is my father?*

Luz sealed himself with an answer: *I'm here.*

And so he was.

"Milo? Making breakfast again?"

Nearly a month had passed since Halloween, but still the Vasquez mother entered as though the floor were a field of glass.

"Omurice!" Luz showed Milo's teeth.

She kissed Milo's forehead. "Soon you won't need the footstool." She turned to the coffeepot. Luz couldn't see the workings, just the floral robe on her shoulders.

"You should teach me how to make coffee." It was another growth, something else to learn. If Hank or Ana had known how to do it, Luz could not remember. "Then I can make it every day. And you'll have more time to get ready for work."

The corners of her mouth lifted. "Who's the mom here?"

Luz had wondered. Not just who, but *what*. This creature that shared space with his chosen collective, but shared only half of what made them. How Luz mistrusted her. The way she watched them all with birdlike eyes. How had they never noticed that, never wanted it gone?

"*You're* the mom." Luz scooped old rice from the frying pan. Laid the egg atop the bump like a yellow skin. "I just work here."

"You're earning a raise. Better hurry up and get ready. I swear Mr. Dawson signs extra quickly whenever we're tardy."

It had taken Luz so long to configure Hank's fingers to his liking. He did not enjoy the hours spent sorting Milo's. "Mom, I don't want to go to ASL anymore."

He turned. The Vasquez mother stood very still. There was a crease between her eyebrows. "Why not, honey?"

"Because I don't need them." Luz tapped Milo's head. "My ears are fine now."

"Well, I know that. But you get along so well with Penny, and ASL is a wonderful thing for you to learn."

"I can learn other things." Luz mirrored her expression. "And I already see Penny at school."

The mother put her fingers on her lips—what did that mean? "I thought you *liked* going, Milo."

Something she was saying made Luz twitch Milo's shoulders.

"Are you sure *you're* not the one who likes going?" Did he sound enough like a child? "You can go. Just go without me."

For three seconds exactly the Vasquez mother stood in the door frame with her eyes fixed on the coffee machine. "No. If you don't want to go, I don't, either."

"Now you'll have time to teach me about making coffee, Mom."

"Maybe not right now. I have to get ready."

Luz did not say, "But today is the last day." He bit Milo's tongue.

There was a small whisper in the back of his head, a flutter-beat in his chest—Milo had something to say. The body's hands shuddered. The fork slipped.

"Not now, Milo," Luz said, with Milo's mouth.

"Making another mess?" Ana glided in, already dressed in a black dress and blue tights. This past week she'd rushed to school early. Luz hadn't asked why; she was no longer part of him. "Try not to shatter all the cups this time."

Milo's fingers quivered.

Ana pulled an empty granola bar box from the pantry with-out setting her book down, turning a page as she did so. Luz longed to repossess her coordination.

"Where are all the granola bars?"

Luz shrugged Milo's shoulders. It was more of a tic.

"Hey, are you coming to the show today?"

"What show?"

Ana raised her eyebrows. "Musical dress rehearsal. I heard they were sending elementary schoolers to see us this afternoon.

You're our guinea pigs. Or lab rats, maybe. Ms. Yu thinks guinea pigs are too endearing to test things on."

"If my class is coming, I'll come, too." Luz didn't pay much attention to the goings-on in the school building. He was learning nothing useful there, growing only a little.

"Gee, Milo. Don't pop with excitement."

"Did I sound excited? I didn't mean to."

"*No*, you dope. You didn't." Ana narrowed clear eyes. "But that's okay. I still want you there. Sit in the first row if you can, okay?"

As Ana left, the final Vasquez entered. In Ana's memories, this bright and bustling morning might have been a televised situation comedy.

"Hey, kiddo." If the Vasquez mother was on tiptoe around Milo, the tallest Vasquez was on tiptoenail. Hank believed his connection with Milo to be a brittle thing; this had little to do with Luz's residency and more to do with a letter Hank had written to Milo on the eve of Luz's return.

Lying low within Milo night after night, Luz had listened to Hank shooting baskets outside the bedroom window. In those weeks, Luz was awake only when Milo was deep asleep. He was awake enough to hear Hank's hands slip. It soothed him.

But Hank's handwriting, his signature on this letter on the brothers' desk on November 1 had unsettled him. Luz had seen so much of Hank's handwriting over the summer. He had *been* Hank's handwriting. Luz expected to see the impact of that. Missed spellings or slipped pens to match the missed baskets.

But Hank's handwriting looked normal.

Hank's hands, those *impossible* things.

Hands that wanted to hold Brendan Nesbitt, but also wanted to be strong and shake hands with all sorts of men in a non-romantic way, too, wanted to hug Carmella Spalding in a non-romantic but loving way, wanted to play sports, and for whatever reason, Hank thought these things were mutually exclusive. That was Luz's way in: he'd slipped in through the uncertainty of those hands.

What he wouldn't give to have those hands back.

But now.

Fine without you, Hank's handwriting seemed to say. Luz had buried the letter at the very bottom of Milo's sock drawer.

"Um. So, how's school been, Milo? Learning anything cool?"

"Nothing I don't already know."

Hank did not look away. "Yeah, I get that. It can be a freaking nightmare sometimes. 'Fake it till you make it,' right?"

"That's *your* mantra."

"Wow. *That's* a new word." Hank raised an eyebrow.

"It refers to, um, words you live by." That sounded too adult. "Like, 'Don't assume, because that makes an *ass* outta *u* and *me*,' for example."

"Ha! Then yeah, I guess 'Fake it' kind of *is* my mantra." Hank hoisted his water bottle to his lips. "So what's yours?"

This demanded creativity. But Luz had no access to Ana. "I don't know."

"What kind of mantra is 'I don't know'?" Hank laughed.

". . . I don't know."

"As for school . . . you know, it'll get better."

"Will it?"

"Come on. You're the smartest kid in the world." Hank had never sounded so certain of anything.

An inexplicable pressure formed in Milo's chest.

Hank ruffled Milo's hair on his way out.

Milo whispered or whined something, in the back of the brain.

"I know you miss them," Luz murmured. "You'll have to get used to it. I have."

Milo's small hands twitched once before quieting. Luz sighed. They longed to build bridges, which was irritating. Bridges only went sideways. They weren't of interest. And, Luz told himself, Ana and Hank were no longer of interest, either.

But Milo's hands would grow.

Luz left the omelet uneaten and walked to the brothers' bedroom. He could hear the splashing roar of the Vasquez mother in the shower.

Luz made his way across the chaotic floor, stepping around dirty socks in size four and size fourteen.

He lay on Milo's stomach and peered under the bed. He found the plastic bag he'd left there, yanked it into the light. Inside were a few changes of clothes, Ana's missing granola bars, and two bottled waters.

He carried the bag to the Vasquez mother's room and set it down in front of her vanity. Luz negotiated Milo's body onto the table and tilted the mirror. On the back of the glass, duct-taped to peeling cardboard, was an envelope.

"See, Milo, your mom puts emergency money here. I'm telling you this in case anything ever happens. I know I can trust you to look after your brother and sister."

"But they're bigger than me," Milo observed.

"In some ways, old man."

The Vasquezes had not asked Luz to be their father.

In their heads, they had decided he must have come from the stars. Maybe they were right. Maybe they were not. Luz could not say. He knew only what they did.

Are you from space?

Yes, I'm from space, Luz answered.

Everything was space. Space on this planet or space on another. It made no difference. It was only a word that meant vast, and empty, and far.

Why did Luz's breath rattle? Because he recognized the mirror memory for what Milo never had? An early good-bye from Dad.

Luz twisted Milo's face. No. Not *Dad*. The Vasquez father.

Luz pulled three hundred-dollar bills from the stash of four; Milo's hands jerked when Luz tried to take it all. Rather than argue, he let one bill be. He dropped the others into the bag and tied it shut. Back in the boys' room, Luz shoved the bag into Milo's backpack.

Milo's hands weren't done. They opened the sock drawer, retrieved Hank's letter, and tucked it into the front pocket.

This was not Luz's doing.

"Fine. It doesn't matter to me, Milo."

Luz had another itch.

How far is far enough? Was that a mantra?

There was still so much to learn, but Luz couldn't learn it from this family.

2

HANK

Basketball season had ended. Hank was not okay with it.

Not that it had been the most rewarding season in a technical sense. When you put pen to paper and tallied up wins and losses, Eustace High's JV team was sitting pretty ugly on a new school record of 3–11.

The varsity Eagles made it to state semifinals.

During the end-of-season banquet, the varsity players and parents dominated the circular tables on the right side of the cafeteria, while the JV entourage hung their heads on the left. At least it was a potluck. Parents could suffer through watching kids who weren't theirs accept awards and then console themselves with baked beans and plastic cupcakes.

Orson nabbed a table close to the food. Hank's mother and Grandma Liu seemed to have hit it off. For once Grandma looked almost pleased, accepting Mom's compliments of her hand-crocheted scarf with sparkling eyes.

Despite Hank's atrocious performance all season, Mom was beaming. She waited for Orson to lead Grandma Liu to the buffet line before embarrassing the hell out of him.

"Hank," she said, "I am so happy to be here."

"I'm not gonna win anything, Mom."

She waved a hand. "I don't care about basketball trophies, Hank. You know that." It was true that Mom had never been on the sidelines. She sometimes sat on the bleachers with a book in her lap and she always made sure he had clothes to practice in, but her smile was never wider than her face. When Dad left and she all but shrugged him away, Hank asked her to stop coming and she complied without an argument for several games and then eased her way back into the peripheries. She refused to leave. That was the difference.

"Well, I hope you're not here for the food." Hank laughed.

"Oh no." Mom smirked. "Although there appears to be macaroni topped with Fritos on the table. Real culinary creativity. It could be worth investigating."

"I don't know . . ."

Hank wasn't sure when she'd gotten wrinkles. "I'm not here for the food and I'm not here for the trophies. I'm here for you."

"Mom, please don't—"

"Hank. Let me be sappy. Please? Let me at least try." She took a deep breath. "All of this? Orson and Mrs. Liu and the JV players? Hank. I'm *relieved*."

Hank inhaled through his nose. "I thought you didn't want me to play basketball."

"I have nothing against basketball. I used to play sports."

He gaped. "You never told me that!"

Mom blew on her nails with Ana-levels of sarcasm. "I scored some hoops."

"Um . . ."

"Okay, so I ran track." Mom clasped his hand. "The point is, Hank—I don't care what makes you happy. Only that something does. You know that, right?"

"Yeah." He didn't question what Mom said, even though they hardly ever talked like this. Maybe *because* they hardly ever did.

Orson slid onto the bench next to Mom and placed his hand on their little stack. "Gooooooo, Eagles!" he cried, pulling all their hands skyward.

Hank let their hands surround his.

No, Mom had never longed for trophies. Instead she'd spent years asking Hank how his days were, bringing him spare dough-nuts from the teachers' lounge and sneakily making his bed when he was out, and last year when he admitted he was taking Bren-dan to homecoming, she said she'd have bought him a second boutonniere if only he'd told her sooner.

It seemed stupid to ask her to be more than what she was, when she was already so much.

"You take after your mom," Orson said minutes later, in the buffet line.

"You wearing dresses now, Tank?" This was of course Tim Miller, scooping macaroni and Fritos from the dish behind them. He broke his bad habits only slowly. "Or does that mean Orson wants to bang you?"

Hank snorted; Orson didn't.

"Tim, I have to say, I'm always impressed with your ability to determine what the most asinine thing to say in any given situation is." Carmella paused in her dipping of carrots to grant Tim a condescending glare. "And then! Then your uncanny ability to just spew it out."

Tim stopped, started again: "Yeah. Sorry." He slung an arm around Hank's shoulder and added, half-joking: "*Hank's* the one who wants that."

Orson cleared his throat. "You're full of so much *shit*, Tim, that now I gotta go take a dump." He said this as vulgarly as possible, scooping mud pie onto his plate. "Hold this for me, Tank?"

Hank took the plate.

Coach Huang started tapping on the mike, asking people to take their seats. Hank followed Orson out instead.

"Orson."

"What the hell, man. I don't need a conversation partner on the shitter."

Something Hank knew about Orson—when he was flustered, he made the same stupid jokes as always. The jokes got grosser, but his face didn't match them.

Orson was a glorious projector. His face hid nothing.

Hank wouldn't say this to him. Hank would never know how. Instead he caught up in a few long strides. "Tim's just being an ass. Don't worry about it."

"I'm not worried about it. Does this look like a worried face?"

"Well . . ."

"No. It's an 'I really have to shit' face."

"You shouldn't let him bother you."

"Bother me? Oh, come on. *Tim Miller?* Tim Miller's got an ego the size of the shit in his head, and he can't freaking help but let it all come out his mouth sometimes."

". . . okay. That image'll keep me up nights."

"It's just—like—never mind."

"What?" Hank stepped a little closer.

Orson ran his fingers through cropped black hair. "I mean . . . it's gonna sound stupid. But I don't think Tim's the only one."

"What are you saying?"

"Like, how your mom was looking at me, man."

"That's rich, considering how your grandma looks at me." Hank waited for Orson's smile. "Cue the part where you say, 'That's just her face,' right?"

"I'm not laughing, Hank." He really wasn't. "Your mom looks like she thinks—like she thinks you and me are—you fucking know." His face was red from all angles. "A couple, or something? You know?"

Hank's wrist dipped a bit. Potato chips hit the floor.

"That's crazy." Hank felt like the words were a grin in themselves, but he couldn't stop them. "You're paranoid. *Nobody* thinks that. You can't *catch* the gay. I mean, *you* can't even seem to *say* it."

"Okay, Hank. But, like . . . when you're too close with someone, it gets confusing for people."

"Confusing for you?"

"I don't know."

"Are you *too* close to me, Orson?"

"Dude, you come to my house EVERY FUCKING DAY. That's pretty damn close. Don't you think?"

"But . . ." Nothing compared to the closeness of an alien living inside you.

"You know what, please forget it." Orson started to descend the stairs leading to the hallways, away from the cafeteria full of bodies. "You're right. I'm paranoid."

Hank called, "Hey, you're still up for evening practice, maybe every *other* day?"

"*Really*, Hank?" Orson was suddenly shouting. "You wanna talk about this right now? Right now, after you—Hank, you're a fucking *tit*. And practice isn't doing shit for you."

Hank shrugged. "Hardly getting any worse."

"I'm not so sure you love *basketball* anymore." This Orson, unsmiling—something about him distressed Hank.

"What do you mean?"

"Don't worry about it. Just something I've been thinking about, but you're right, it's totally fucking crazy. So can I go see a man about a dog, or what?"

Hank grinned. "Yeah, whatever."

Orson wandered out of sight.

Behind Hank, applause sounded.

"Where's Orson?" Carmella leaned out of the cafeteria. "He's just won the award for Team Player. It's basically the Miss Congeniality equivalent, but beggars can't be choosers. Wasn't he with you?"

"He left me."

"What?"

"He just . . . left."

Hank was emptier than he had been moments ago, standing with two plates full of food on his palms.

Carmella stepped onto the landing and took one of them, then both of them. She set the plates on the banister and wrapped Hank in the most inexplicable of hugs.

Thanksgiving was tomorrow.

Hank hadn't lied to Milo, and Mom was right: Things were looking up at Eustace High. Even though basketball had ended and the banquet was weeks ago. Even though Orson didn't have Hank over anymore. They still hung out at lunch and in the halls, with all the guys. They were part of the same crew, like they had been before things became two people tightly holding hands under a cream soda pong table.

Sure, Hank missed the extra practice. And who wouldn't? Only someone who didn't love basketball. Only someone who didn't love—

Hank's hands itched. They no longer felt porous. It had to be a good thing.

And as for Milo and the letter, that wasn't a big deal. They were *talking* now. Milo was a little quiet. Maybe that was just how it would be, trying to get to know a kid after an alien made you strangle him half to death. When he talked to Ana about it, he told her he thought that maybe being brothers *had* to be hard.

"Even when they're no one's fault, tragedies remain tragic," she said.

"Is that a line from the show?"

"Just from my sad brain. But I *am* thinking of writing a script."

The eldest Vasquezes had been excused from class. They sat backstage on the infamous dilapidated sofa that, it was rumored, virtually every couple had sex on at some point during their high school career. Amazingly, this never seemed to stop anyone from sitting on it.

"I thought Marissa was the writer."

"The position's been open for a while."

Beige paint coated Hank's palms. He'd volunteered to help the desperate Shop kids finish the set on time. Hank was glad to assist, to lift and move things like he used to. With fewer basketballs to hold, Hank's hands wanted everything to do.

Dress rehearsal began in an hour. Ana had already painted her face to compensate for the washing out of stage lighting. Beside him she looked like her own evil twin, a twin who favored leopard-print dresses and lipstick the color of oxygenated blood.

"Milo's an odd duck, Hank. It's not just about Luz. I think you're right and not just about brothers. I don't think things are *ever* going to be easy with him."

"No."

"That's how we know he's a Vasquez."

Elsewhere in the auditorium, Mr. Oldman shrieked with either joy or terror, summoning his cast members. A flurry of motion commenced, students darting to and fro with scripts falling from their hands, makeup brushes powdering costumes.

Ana leaned on Hank's shoulder to extricate herself from the cushions. She yanked a ridiculous heel up her foot. It occurred to Hank that he and Ana were transforming all the damn time.

Maybe growing into strangers was something all siblings did.

"Here goes nothing."

"Nah, here goes something!" Before she vanished to meet her overlord, Hank called, "What's your script going to be about?"

"Kids living in a ghost town."

The backstage space emptied. Black cinder-block walls that absorbed sound, wooden staircases with no one on them.

"This is already a ghost town."

"Never thought you were one for gloomy introspection, Hank." Even by the dim red light of the Exit sign and what illumination bled from under the curtains, Brendan Nesbitt could be no one else. "I come in peace. May I join you on that disgusting couch?"

Hank moved aside. Brendan perched on an armrest, shoes sinking into the cushions. In this costume he looked more awkward than ever, wearing horn-rimmed glasses, a vaguely hairy vest, and pants that didn't reach his ankles. "How are you?"

"I'm fine. How are you?"

"Hank Vasquez, so *help me*, if you attempt to skirt me with one of your killer smiles, then I taught you nothing while we dated."

"Were you trying to teach me things?"

"No. I was, ah, trying to join your family. Remember? And I may have also been trying to kiss you all over."

"Yeah." For the pair of them, it had always been easier in the dark. "Now Ana's your way in, huh?"

"Very funny, Hank Vasquez. I'm not kissing her at all."

"I'm not being funny." Hank thought of Orson. Things were confusing.

Brendan sighed. "No. We're only friends, though I *did* ask her out. Mostly because she's kind, and because Arlene was leaving me, after you left me, and I . . . well, Hank. Do I have to explain that sensation to you?"

"I didn't leave you. I'm right here."

"Nah. The Vasquezes have been lost in space for ages."

Hank shook his head. "And you want to get lost with us?"

"You've never been to my house, Hank." Hank couldn't see Brendan's face. "You never *asked* about my house. I was grateful for that. This may come as a shock, but your family? Your household? It's a decent thing to belong to."

Hank tried laughing. It sounded like a sob. "You still belong to it."

"Thank you. I know you mean that."

"Even if we aren't a thing." Now that Hank had said it, the hole seemed much smaller than he thought it'd be. Last time he'd felt it, it'd been a canyon; now it was a hole-punch's doing. "Even if we'll never be. You're a Vasquez now."

Brendan exhaled. "And you think you're not smart!"

"When did I ever say that?"

"You didn't have to. I didn't make you smarter, you know. And I didn't make you better. You were already, let's say . . . a *pretty good guy.*"

"Brendan. You were—I mean, you are too. You shouldn't bother talking to me, but you . . ."

"Nope." Brendan hopped down off the armrest. "*Not* doing this. We are certainly *not* getting back together, Hank Vasquez. Did you know that since moving to Naples, Platinum has been to a soiree and, ah, three different museums with three different dates?" Brendan leaned in close enough that Hank could smell the charcoal on his fingers. "She's not hung up on one. Stupid. Boy."

"You said I wasn't stupid."

"I'll be going to art school in a year. I'm going to have

fabulous affairs with otakus and drag queens. The last thing I need is some handsome lummox pining for me from his athletes-only dorm."

Before Hank knew what he was doing, his hands reached for Brendan's torso and his arms pulled his hollow body close, so that Hank's cheek pressed against Brendan's navel. "That's the thing, Brendan. What if it isn't athletes-only? I don't know who I am, not like you do. What if it isn't about basketball? What's left of me?"

Brendan let his hands fold on Hank's head, there in the dark. "Oh, there's plenty left of you, you behemoth. Go to any university, or go anywhere else. And figure the rest out once you get there like every other person."

"How'd you get so wise?"

"I'm spending time with Ana, recall."

Hank let go. Brendan rubbed his hands together. "Right! Final thoughts: I think anyone spreading the notion that teenage romances should be lifelong true-love commitments should probably be fed to a man-eating plant from outer space. Agreed?"

Hank nodded. To him it seemed clearer with every passing day: People came and went, but love remained. It just changed faces an awful lot.

3

MAGGIE

"What are you doing for Thanksgiving?"

This was a question all teachers asked one another, maybe all Americans asked one another. It was never a question that was fun to answer or hear answers to; inevitably someone made a joke about in-laws or mentioned food or travel.

Nobody cared. Everybody asked.

Maggie had perfected her answer: "Oh, we'll be at the China Buffet as usual, just the four of us." She didn't mention her dead relatives, the calamitous distance between here and Spring Green, Wisconsin, or between Maggie and her children. Even Mr. Morris didn't press her; after his Halloween party he'd invited her to join them at happy hour, and she'd stone-faced him half to death.

There would be no more margaritas. No more coming home to a glass ocean.

Maggie had to try harder.

Milo seemed on board with this new perspective. Milo seemed to have grown all the way up. He stopped shouting. He never wrote about magical undead opossums. He stopped asking questions.

And, Maggie reminded herself during her lunch-break sojourn to Eustace Community College, knocking on the door to room 27, if Milo felt it was time for ASL lessons to stop, he must be doing better.

Rahshad Dawson held the door for her.

"Maggie. We missed you this morning." It was still jarring to hear him speak. He often refused to during lessons. Immersion or bust.

"I missed you, too." She frowned. "I mean, not *missed you*, but . . ."

"I know what you meant."

Maggie explained Milo's choice. Though he doubtless had prep work to do, Rahshad sat on his desk and leaned his good ear her way. Maggie tried to be succinct. Soon they both had to be teaching again.

Finally Rahshad nodded. "Does this have anything to do with what happened on Halloween? I'm still sorry about that."

Maggie started. "Milo told you about the kitchen?"

"The kitchen?" Rahshad frowned. "I was referring to his trick-or-treating upset."

Maggie heard what he had to say, a story about screaming on sidewalks. She found herself sitting down. "Where did you say it happened?"

Rahshad told her.

Margaret realized how wrong with rightness Milo had become. It was not so surprising to her that her youngest son behaved like her eldest might: smiling wide through something terrible. Withdrawing. Normalizing. She had sensed it, this morning. Other mornings. The model student. Nothing like himself.

Of course he wasn't writing about magic anymore. Magic had been murdered for him on a doorstep twenty miles away. "Oh, *Milo*."

"Maggie? What are you doing for Thanksgiving?"

She didn't laugh. It was a near thing. She didn't break things against the floor. It was a near thing. She understood what could create a glass ocean.

"If you're amenable, you and your children are welcome to join us for dinner tomorrow." As always he spoke eloquently, through speech slightly slurred. During introductions on the first day of ASL for Beginners, Rahshad Dawson had told them about his passion for ASL, about the hereditary condition that had slowly degenerated the hearing of his grandfather, father, uncles, and brother. Sooner or later he would be Deaf. That eloquence would always accompany him, no matter what language he used.

"Thank you. Really. But we have other plans."

A curt nod. "The invitation will remain open."

He signed farewell.

The moment Maggie's shoes hit the wooden ramp outside the trailer door, she began to run. Her work shoes were practical, always, because she was a teacher, but now they seemed too plodding.

Finally she reached the parking lot, climbed into her car, pulled her phone from her purse, and sent a message to a nameless number so rarely used, it looked somehow dusty.

We need to meet up. Now. Coffee?

The reply: *McDonald's. 1 hr?*

Maggie called Peg Olsen. She did what she'd refused to all year.

She took a sick day.

4

ANA

The matinee dress rehearsal of the musical did not go off without a hitch. There were hitches aplenty, because this was a high school musical. Just being in high school felt like one big hitch to Ana.

In act 1, someone placed the wrong Audrey II onstage before the "Feed Me" duet. This meant Brendan had to either pretend a completely stationary potted begonia was their antagonist, or he had to serenade his hand and pretend it was a talking plant.

He decided on the former, which was wise, considering their audience. It was easier for seven-year-olds to pretend a plant was talking than to pretend an arm was a plant.

For Ana, the biggest hiccup was the juggling of last-minute line edits. Elementary schoolers were far too young to see a raunchy tragicomedy about vicious murder, urban poverty, and man-eating alien plants, but Mr. Oldman assured the staff it would be censored.

"We'll save the blood spatter for the evening shows," Mr.

Oldman announced, as if that resolved the issue. He added to the cast, seconds before the curtain lifted, "Make sure you cut all of the *adult* humor out. I mean *all of it*, or they'll have my guts and intestines for garters and socks!"

Ana had no time to think of alternatives to words like "semi-sadist." During the ensemble opener she sang "fa la la" to gloss over a lyric about ripped slips.

She focused on the task at hand, got lost in the character at hand. When Audrey I was eaten alive by Audrey II, Ana climbed into the mouth of an enormous flytrap puppet and fell into the jubilant arms of cast members beyond the split curtain.

"We killed it, Ana," Brendan declared, after he too was eaten.

"It killed us." She took his hand.

Since they'd watched Platinum climb into a car and head for the airport, there had been a lot of this. It proved to be what they needed: something to hold on to when the sky or the desert seemed too empty.

During the musical Ana must have kissed Brendan. Right after "Suddenly Seymour," as they had during the last few practices. She had no memory of it.

That was Audrey's business, and she was Ana Vasquez.

When it came time for curtain call, Ana looked for Milo among the shell-shocked seven-year-olds, but didn't see him. She did spot Penny. For some reason, the pigtailed girl's typically fierce face was now anything but, red-flushed and tear-streaked.

"If my class is going, I'll go, too."

So where was Ana's spacey little brother?

5

LUZ

For as long as he was part of Milo and Milo was part of second grade, Luz was bound to the rules that govern the very young. He was forced to walk hand in hand with a buddy along the sunny path to the high school. Mrs. Stuart carefully counted them as they made their way to their seats in the dark auditorium.

Luz watched the play with vague disinterest. Penny watched him instead of the show, and her face was nothing shy of . . . well, Milo was terrible at comprehending facial expressions.

Milo's fingers tried thrashing.

All it had taken was one short greeting on the playground before school began.

Penny had approached Luz on stomping feet.

"You were awful on Halloween." She unmade her fists and made some slightly violent gesture. *"That's how awful you were."*

"Sorry."

"I'm still mad at you. You have to say sorry like you mean it. Sign it."

Unbidden, Milo's hands responded for him, repeating whatever sign they'd shown the Vasquez mother.

The Penny child took a step back. "Who are you?"

Luz trembled. "Milo, silly."

Penny narrowed her eyes, turned around, and sprinted away.

The seventh time Luz felt her eyes rake Milo in the auditorium, Luz hoisted Milo out of his seat, knocking first-grade knees as he made his way down the row to Mrs. Stuart.

"Milo, sit *down*."

"I need to use the toilet."

"You don't need your backpack for that." Mrs. Stuart took it from him and told him to wait for a buddy. He didn't.

In the hallway, Luz reassessed his options. He longed to walk outside, find a new elsewhere beyond this town. In Hank's body he could drive. In Ana's he could drive.

Milo's feet would not reach the pedals.

Then let's stay. Please, Luz, let's stay.

Luz knew only nebulousness around Eustace, desert and eventually ocean and bridges beyond, but the details were vague within the mind of this seven-year-old.

Please don't go anywhere.

"Be normal, Milo. We're in public," Luz chided. Carmella Spalding clipped past the auditorium. She spared them a friendly wave and a "Sorry, but I'm late for class!" before hurrying out of sight.

Luz forced Milo to put his outstretched fingers down.

"That's it." He took the body to the bottom of the stairs, gritting Milo's teeth against the pitter-patter of his voice:

Please, I don't want to go anywhere, Luz.

"We have to grow up. Think of all the bridges you'll see." Luz followed Carmella. Seeing her had reminded him of his days with Hank. There was a less conspicuous exit near the gymnasium, wasn't there? Or was this simply Milo's logic, now that Hank's mind was lost to Luz?

Once outside, maybe Luz could walk back to the canyon for the last hundred dollars and make do with that to start. Luz knew all sorts of things a seven-year-old didn't. Luz knew at least as much as a seventeen-year-old. People thought it was knowledge enough to send most young things out into the world with.

Please, Luz, I wanna say good-bye at least? Please?

"You think I don't want to?" Luz bit Milo's tongue; what was he saying?

It made no difference whether he ever saw the Vasquezes again.

I'm scared, Luz.

"We won't go anywhere *near* Gailsberg. And what else could you be afraid of?" Luz flicked Milo's ear to shush him. "You have many disadvantages, smallest Vasquez, but you aren't afraid of much."

"He's afraid of *you.*"

Tiny in the high-ceilinged hallway behind them stood the Penny child, all flush-faced. She held on tight to Milo's backpack.

"Hey, Penny." Luz mimed urgency, legs twisted together. "The high school is so big! I'm lost. Do you know where the bathroom is?"

She tossed the backpack at Milo's feet. "Take this and go. Go far away. Just leave Milo here."

Luz sensed there was no pretending with a child like this. Penny Dawson was whole. She saw the world for what it was. Where Milo had imagination, she had certainty.

Luz stood up straight. He took four strides toward her. "If you know so much, you must know that Milo *adores* me."

Penny didn't crumble. "I don't care. Get out."

"He *loves* me." What didn't she understand? "I matter to him."

"I don't care if he loves you. You made him scream so you need to go."

The scuttling in Luz's borrowed ears grew frantic. "You're so *smart*, Penny. So you know I could make him scream again."

Stop it luz STOP IT!

"Not if I scream first," Penny replied, and that's precisely what she did.

The horror-film wail, comparable to dozens in Ana's repertoire, did little to improve the rising rattling in borrowed ears. Luz scooped up the backpack and sprinted for the doors beside the gym, before any adult could be drawn to the racket—

First to appear wasn't an adult, but Carmella, who'd made it to her locker but not yet to class. "Milo? What—?"

She dropped her phone to reach for him but missed and Luz did not slow down—

A head poked out of the gymnasium. Luz growled. Did the Vasquezes have to know and love everyone? Did everyone have to know and love them, too?

Carmella had been too surprised to catch him, but Luz, forgetting that Milo lacked Hank's reflexes, barreled right into Orson Liu.

Orson grabbed Milo's forearm.

"Whoa, Milo, what's going on? Hey, calm down. Calm down!"

Luz felt something twist in his skull, and somehow in Milo's ribs—his loathing for these interlopers, these objects of Vasquez affection, was fueled by Milo's own affection for them. Something broke into pieces within the skull he inhabited.

The scuttling crescendoed and Luz split to bits and a broken fragment of him rattled right out of Milo's unblocked auricles, scurried down Milo's neck onto his shoulders with all the wayward speed of any insect.

The Vasquez family had pretended Luz was only termites. The piece of him that pitter-pattered out of Milo looked the part. Everything Luz was, he was because of the Vasquezes.

Luz realized growth could take place regardless of nebulous deserts—he realized there were bridges everywhere and perhaps they weren't dull.

Not only physical bridges, like Orson's arm linked to Milo's, the actual bridge that an insect-like organism could cross to get from one ear to another.

The lesson Luz had learned, during months of hibernation: It wasn't about being one organism. It was about belonging to a family.

The Vasquezes had extended their family of late.

Orson swatted at the scuttling white thing that was Luz, but the connection between Orson and the Vasquezes was all but magnetizing.

The termite of Luz crawled into Orson's open ear.

★ ★ ★

There were traces of confusion and fear in Orson's head, and for some reason Luz came upon a memory of old women in a humid park, brown poodles sitting at their feet.

I'll tell you what they were saying, Luz lied, to cow him.

In the same instant, Luz moved Milo toward the other two almost-Vasquezes. Bridges were astounding!

The next termite left Milo's ear and flew straight for Penny on translucent wings, ready to dart right up her flaring nostrils—

But Carmella was there. She smacked this piece of Luz to nothing but mist between her palms. Luz felt the loss, felt how Ana once felt slits in her skin—but it didn't stop him from trying again.

Carmella put herself between Penny and both of Luz's bodies and backed away as fast as her shoes would allow. Milo's legs were short but Luz worked them, taking three steps for every one of Carmella's—

"Run, Penny!" she cried, before another fluttering piece of Luz caught her chin and slipped into her mouth.

Luz took command just in time to stop her eyes from rolling back.

Elsewhere, both Orson's and Milo's bodies fell to the floor.

Carmella Spalding's head was filled with a thousand thoughts. She was more ambitious than the Vasquezes, and immediately tried to outwit him. He saw visions of Carmella prying him loose by way of pliers, cutting him out with a scalpel. Of course Luz wasn't corporeal once inside someone, but she thought and fought hard.

Carmella imagined flushing and fire and nasal syringes and pain, pain for Luz.

It took both Orson's and Milo's bodies slumping for Luz to get a grip on Carmella.

He found a weakness at the heart of her.

Carmella wanted to use her fantastic brain to study medicine and travel the world and set up a clinic for people with disabilities. All this before she was thirty. But Carmella suspected no one thought her capable. No one saw what Luz saw now.

You are more than a pretty face, Luz said in admiration, pushing her down.

The hallway had more than one adult in it now: Mrs. Moore from her classroom, Coach Huang from the gym. He couldn't keep building bridges.

Luz spun Milo around and sent him outside at last.

While Milo hurried across the parking lot, Luz took Orson and Carmella in tandem down the hallway, right past the place where Penny struggled against the arms of two uncomprehending teachers.

Carmella kept struggling. She had some very steady feet on her. Her quick thinking helped Luz decide what to do next, and her confident stance meant that no one disturbed them while they made for the auditorium.

★ ★ ★

Orson contained an excess of energy. His bridge was probably the quickest way back to Hank. Hank, who had shut Luz out so easily, who let him go as soon as Luz asked those hands to squeeze.

Luz would ask them to do even more this time.

Just stop it, please!

Really there was no reason to hold on to Milo now. Milo was very small and easy to hide, but they would be followed.

Luz did not release him. He walked Milo's body off campus, onto the long road leading out of Eustace, into the flood ditches and toward the canyon.

6

MARGARET

Maggie reached the McDonald's on the edge of Gailsberg before three songs had ended. From here, jammed between a Burger King and a Wendy's on the aptly nicknamed Hamburger Hill, she had a great view of Gailsberg's rusting heart-shaped water tower.

She knew he would be late. Maggie went in all the same, bought a vanilla latte, and took a seat within plain sight of both entrances.

The first thing she noticed was how tired he looked. He'd been balding even when they were together, used to joke about how his hair had migrated to live under his nose. In the three years since they separated, he seemed to have aged a dozen. He could say the same about her. It wouldn't be an insult.

Maggie smiled. *Oh, the imaginary mustaches I've seen.*

Maggie watched him order fries and a Coke as if he did this all the time. He seemed surprised to see her when at last he turned around.

Donovan sat down and pushed his tray toward her. "Fries?"

"No, thank you."

"Well, better change your mind quick." He smiled. The familiarity left her tender. "They won't be here long."

"We won't be, either. But I need to talk to you about our kids."

"Yeah, I figured. Did the last check bounce?" There was no cynicism there, no accusation. It was a genuine question, as frank as Milo's were.

"Nothing like that. Can I tell you what your kids don't know about you?"

"A whole lot, probably."

"When you told me you'd moved back to New Mexico last year, we agreed not to tell them. And I haven't."

Donovan nodded. "I don't see how it would do them any good. I really don't want to hurt them."

"That was the thinking, yes."

Donovan averted his eyes. "How are they doing?"

Margaret had been waiting for this. It was the most obvious question in the world right now, besides the Thanksgiving question. She considered what the past year had been to her children: screaming, cutting, laughing, crying, singing, dribbling, kissing, clawing, bleeding, adoring. The gravity of who they were now was too massive for an interloper to understand.

"I let them keep believing you're far away. I let them think you *can't* get to them, Don. That you went back to your first wife and daughters in Wisconsin and stayed there. I let them think whatever they wanted. We really don't talk about you much."

Donovan stopped chewing. "Margaret . . ."

"But if you think you can move into a house twenty minutes away from three of your kids and they'll never realize it, you have no idea how bright and capable they are, or how the universe works. Milo was at your house on Halloween."

Donovan froze. "He was what?"

"Dressed as a little skeleton boy. I'm not sure you'd recognize him even without the costume. But *he* recognized *you*. He's had three birthdays since you left and waited for you to show up for all of them."

"Oh, Mags. I'm sorry. Shit . . . is he okay?"

Maggie shook her head. "If you want to ask that, *you* have to ask them. Your children. Not me. I'm their mother, but I'm not them."

"I don't know what I'm doing here, Margaret."

"I'm not them, but I'm part of them. So are you, like it or not. But we can get by without you. Your kids are *amazing* people."

"I know that—"

"No, you don't. Not anymore. I'll give you one shot to find out. One shot to tell them where you are, where you've been, and why they aren't worth your time, before I tell them the truth as I see it, hand them your address, and leave the rest up to them."

He picked at the paper on his tray. "Hank still playing basketball?"

"He's taller than you. He'll be eighteen in December, and he's going to college."

"I know. I'll be paying for some of it, you know I will." Again, no accusation.

Maggie breathed in through her nostrils, because she knew he wouldn't ask. "Ana's finding her way, too. She's got a lead in the musical."

"Oh. Wow." There were shreds all over the table now.

"Tomorrow we're heading to the China Buffet for Thanksgiving. If you want to be more than another hole in their lives, come by the house at one."

"And what, Mags?"

"And we'll treat you to dinner." Maggie smiled. "You can have all the butterscotch pudding you want."

Donovan hesitated. "We're going to Angela's parents' house in Albuquerque. Leaving later tonight. Maybe we could try something later?"

"No. They needed you sooner, not later."

"It's like . . . it's been too long. I can't make it better now, you know?"

"Yeah, well. Sometimes things *don't* get better. And whenever things get . . . get *bad* for these kids, Donovan, I wonder what it'd be like to just leave. Drive away like you did. Take a plane to Prague or move back to the woods. I don't put it all on you, you know. I pulled you from those daughters. I don't pretend to be a good person.

"But I can't do what you've done. I can't do it and still call myself a mother. Even if that's screwed up. Even if I feel that way because women are *taught* to feel that way. The fact is, *staying* is part of what makes me feel like a goddamn human being."

A car alarm went off outside. At the counter, an employee called out for order number eighty-seven. Neither of the Vasquez parents sipped their beverages.

"I really did try to go back for the twins, Margaret."

She didn't want to hear this. The girl inside her wanted to, though.

"I went back to Spring Green and . . . and I met with Nina like I'm meeting with you. I told her about the nightmares and that I wanted to try again. She was angrier than you are, asked me to get the fuck off her doorstep. But then she said, 'Just wait outside for them to come home from school. Tell *them* about your nightmares.' Like she would forgive me for *them* but not for herself. I just couldn't get that." He shook his head. "I couldn't come back here and pull up in the driveway. I had to start over."

"Just one town over. You had to start over just one county away."

"I know it doesn't make sense."

He wasn't Ana. He wasn't Hank. He wasn't Milo. But he had aspects of all of them. Margaret couldn't hate him.

"Oh, *I* won't forgive you." She stood up from the table. "But those kids? They are better than me."

"You're a good mother to them, Margaret."

"You don't get to tell me what I am." She took three of his fries and left.

Maggie pulled her car out of the McDonald's lot and into the Wendy's lot next door. She breathed in and breathed out. The expressway whooshed and shook behind her.

Maggie licked salt off her fingertips and drove and drove. She managed to hear the entirety of *Kid A*. It ended with a song called "Motion Picture Soundtrack," but Maggie couldn't decide what kind of movie this was. It didn't really matter.

7

HANK

Orson was waiting for Hank outside the auditorium.

Hank had lagged behind the stagecraft kids, mulling over Brendan's words, and by the time he stepped outside the dark cave with a paint can in his grasp, the hallways were all but vacant.

Perhaps that was what made Orson's appearance on the steps so unexpected. Or maybe it was the way Orson's head whipped around and his face split open as he bounded up to meet Hank.

"Hank! *There you are!* I missed you!"

Hank started. "Oh. *Ha-ha.*"

Orson's hands went directly to Hank's elbows, pressed against rough skin. "Want me to carry that can for you, Hank? I can hold it if you want me to."

"No. It's cool."

"It really is, Hank. It's really cool." Orson's eyes were unfocused. His hands kept rubbing Hank's elbows.

"Are you . . . Orson, are you high or something?"

"Oh, *Hank*. I'm not high. I just want to be in you."

"Asshole. That's not funny." Hank pulled his arms free, looking for the laughter. "But wait. Are you saying . . . you want me to come back to practice?"

"Yes. Right now." Orson's smile was lopsided. A crack in his projector. "Just set that can down and we'll go. Don't you wanna touch me?"

Whiplash. That was what Hank was experiencing. "Orson . . . something's wrong with your face."

Orson's hands found Hank's elbows again. Slowly, certainly, grip unshifting, Orson edged Hank backward up the stairs, pressed him against the door and then through it, so that the two of them stood panting in the dark and then Orson pressed his teeth to Hank's, and he had bitten Hank's lip and—

Hank recoiled. "Orson—wait—"

The hands dropped from Hank's elbows.

"You are impossible, Hank. You want so many things but you never *take them*."

Something flipped over in Hank's head. He knew this *voice*. It wasn't Orson's. *And you think you're not smart!*

"Basketball and the boy. Art and the girl. You can take them all. They're right here. And those hands are big enough to hold everything." Orson's own hands hung slack at his sides. "Let me see them, please crush me with them. Practice, Hank."

"Okay, Orson. Yeah. One sec." Hank set the can on the floor. A little white light, glowing the same color as the buds that had speckled Nameless Canyon on June 7 now emanated from within Orson's skull, leaked out at ears and nostrils and eye sockets. Orson-o'-lantern.

"You're right," Hank said. Orson drew closer. "I really want the world."

"Start with me." Luz might not realize he was leaking from his host's skull. He didn't quite have the subtle grip on Orson Liu that he'd had on the Vasquezes. Maybe Orson was fighting back, bowling Luz over with terrible puns. Maybe Luz didn't realize that Hank could see pieces of him, radiant insects, creeping from Orson's orifices.

Luz didn't realize that no matter how long Hank lived, no matter how much he wanted to, he could never forget what Luz felt like.

Hank pulled Orson into an embrace that was really a choke hold and held it until Orson stopped squirming, until the white fluttering termite lights of Luz retreated into the safety of Orson's skull. When Hank let go, Orson slid all the way to the floor.

Hank didn't see Luz leave Orson, couldn't tell whether he had.

Hank vomited in the aisle. He wiped his mouth on his sleeve and pressed his eyes shut. Orson, supine. When would he wake up? Who would he be?

A rectangle of light from the doorway, and Carmella was beside them. "Is Orson—I just saw the thing go into him—Hank, are you . . . you?"

She asked this, Hank guessed, because he was staring at his hands.

"I don't know what to do. Luz never *felt* anything. He never *cared*." He turned to look at her. "Did you see what happened?"

Carmella nodded, eyelids fluttering. "Yeah. This *thing* just crawled into him."

"Where did it come from?"

". . ."

"Carmella!"

". . . I don't know." She covered her eyes. "Maybe from you? Did you touch him?"

Had he? Could he have been carrying Luz with him all this time, in his hands or in his smile? Hadn't he clapped Orson on the back at some point today? It seemed impossible. But here they all were, and this was what Carmella was telling him. And someone else had told him something similar, but Hank couldn't think straight.

"I don't know what to do. These fucking hands can't fix this." And the urge to tear something, to break something was stronger than ever, and Hank tore at his own clothes, digging through his own pockets for things to destroy—

"Hank!"

From his jacket he pulled a ragged piece of card stock. It had been tucked in there for months, was ripe for the tearing, this picture of mountains and—

Hank stopped. "Henry."

8

ANA

Ana was left without a ride. Once she wouldn't have cared, but she was ready to go home. She wanted to check on Milo, but Hank was missing in action and Brendan was intent on staying after to rehearse. "My vocals were off during the finale and god help me, everyone noticed!"

The way Ms. Yu jumped for joy, bumping against a mobile of planets that dangled over her desk, you'd think Ana was Rosalind Franklin.

"Hey, Ms. Yu. Anything I can do to help out today?"

"Ooh, Ana. Always. But don't you want to get home? It's Thanksgiving tomorrow."

"My ride's busy. Let me help out?"

Ms. Yu bit her lip. "Well. The work today is less than wonderful."

"Does it involve the cat corpses?"

Ms. Yu shook her head. "I'm afraid we've got something of a parasite problem."

"You . . . *what?*"

"I'll show you." She led Ana to the row of rat cages alongside the back counter. From the largest cage she plucked the largest rat, beige with brown patches. "Come on, Salvador, there's a good girl."

Ms. Yu set Salvador on the counter. The rat seemed bothered, but not terribly, squirming a little when Ms. Yu peeled back her ears. "Look there. Do you see them?"

Tiny black specks dotted pink flesh. "Ear mites. It's probably got to do with filthy bedding. Mites thrive in messy places. Even though I've been having a student help me out, changing the litter on top, underneath, the cedar chips were neglected. But I've got some drops for Salvador and the others."

Ana sat down on the stool, watching Salvador meander across the table.

"Hold her still for me, please?" Ms. Yu plucked a bottle of brown fluid from a drawer. Ana placed Salvador flat on the table and held her breath. Ms. Yu dribbled a drop from the applicator into each ear. When Ana let go, Salvador shook her head and pawed her ears.

"So the ear mites have to die."

"Well, of course mites aren't *intentionally* malicious. They nestled in Salvador's ears for warmth. But they're also biting her to bits, so they've got to go."

"Why? Why can't Salvador just . . . just live with them?"

"I'm glad you asked that, Ana." She really looked it, too. "I had to write a paper on this issue in grad school, and here's what I came to. Ready?"

"Very."

"And I quote myself: 'Any life—no matter how ambivalent—that exists *only* to the detriment of other life should be treated as *lesser* life.' Doesn't that *sound* cool anyhow? My professor was into it. Basically, if you can only live by harming others, your life becomes less valuable."

"That sounds like morality, not science." Ana hoisted Salvador into her palms, held her close to her chest.

"Oh, *totally*. But that professor was a total hippie. He loved it. Now, there *are* parasites with mysterious health benefits. For instance, there's a faction of people who claim that hookworms can cure you of pollen allergies and hay fe—"

"What about *people* who hurt themselves? Or hurt other people?" Ana let Salvador clamber onto her shoulder. "Human beings can be just as bad as parasites."

"Oh, sure. But *people*, unlike parasites, can learn to be better. In the end, I think the best thing to be is someone who does more good than bad. That's why I work with kids; I have to counteract my own damages somehow. And I'm clumsy, so the damage can be pretty literal at times—Ana, what's the matter?"

"Just . . . Salvador's a really pretty rat." Salvador's whiskers tickled her ear.

"She *is*, isn't she?"

Ana laughed.

There came a knock at the classroom door.

"Ah! Here's my usual help! Marissa, we're cleaning all the tanks today, and there's a Coke in it for you. Do you know Ana Vasquez?"

Marissa's hair was shorter than ever. She'd dyed it lavender and taken to combing it back like some of the silver-screen actors she and Ana used to watch in old horror movies: Vincent Price chic. She wore a suit vest, black pants, and no makeup.

"Nice to meet you, Ana." Marissa blinked but did not leave.

"Ana, Marissa wants to make movies about aliens one day. Marissa, Ana's in a *musical* about aliens. You guys might have a lot in common!"

"Yeah, I think you're probably right." Marissa joined them. She plucked Salvador from Ana's shoulder. "How's our pretty lady?"

The door came open again, this time with significantly more force. There was Brendan, still wearing stage makeup that made him hyperreal. He wasn't alone.

"Sorry, Ana. Found her in the auditorium. She ran back here after school let out, looking for you. She won't tell me what's wrong."

Penny looked ungodly pale. Something had sucked the air right out of her.

"What is it, Penny?"

"Luz took Milo!"

Ana felt the old itch in her eyes.

Penny relayed the story, stuttering between gasps. Brendan's eyes widened. Marissa didn't say a word. Ms. Yu seemed to think this was some bizarre in-joke. By the end Ana was halfway to the door with Penny.

"Who were the other people?" Ana asked. "The ones who 'caught the bug too,' like you said?"

"Um, the Chinese basketball boy." *Orson.* "And the girl with a name that sounds like candy." *Carmella?*

"I think Milo was going nowhere," Penny said, drying her eyes. "I think he was screaming inside. He kept signing 'help.'"

"Then we will."

"When something is this wrong, you *must* go to an adult." That was what Dr. Ruby once told Ana. "Not because we're adults. Because half of us were girls once, too."

"Mom?"

"Ana? Is that you?" The sound of chatter and music in the background.

"Where are you?"

"I'm just—no. I won't lie to you. I'm playing hooky. I'm at Gailsberg Mall, of all places. They have a trapeze in the food court now."

"Mom."

"How was the dress rehearsal? Do you need me to pick up anything before the show this weekend? I will *not* be back here on Black Friday, so speak now or forever—"

"You said to call you if anything bad happened."

All laughter left Mom's voice. "Tell me what's wrong, Ana."

Ana found speaking impossibly hard. "It's Milo. He's gone again."

A sharp intake of breath.

"Mom, I'm so sorry, I don't know what happened, Penny just told me he walked out of school, but Mom, *Luz* is back and I should have looked for Milo when I didn't see him at the show, but—"

"Ana. Shh. Breathe. I'll be in Eustace in twenty minutes. Okay?"

Ana choked. "I'm *so sorry.*" Not only for this, but for all the times she hadn't asked for help, all the times she thought Mom didn't want to hear that question.

"Ana. Stop. I'm glad that you called me. I love you."

"I love you, too. But Mom?"

"What is it?"

Ana steeled herself, shook all hesitance from her voice. "I'm going to fix this."

"Ana—what does that mean? Don't go anywh—"

Ana hung up the phone.

"Brendan. Could you possibly give me a ride to the desert?"

Brendan held the door open. "Not a question."

"I'm coming," Marissa said, joining her at the door.

"Marissa, this has nothing to do with you." There weren't words for this kindness.

"Are you kidding?" Marissa smirked. "This is the stuff of real cinema. Like we dreamed. And come on. Don't you remember?"

"Remember what?"

"*Don't you remember?*" And her smile focused like a lens. "We're the same person."

"I'm coming too!" Penny cried.

Ana shook her head. "Stay with Ms. Yu. Maybe Milo will come back here."

"I'm not stupid. You're just trying to get rid of me."

Brendan laughed at that. "Certainly true, Penny. But won't you stay anyway?"

Penny folded her arms. "Fine. Just in case Milo *does* come back here first."

"Well." Ms. Yu clung to what was familiar. "Penny! Do you know anything about ear mites?"

Penny uncrossed her arms. "I'm basically an ear expert. *Actually.*"

9

LUZ

It was much harder to control three bodies at once when two of the bodies were half-strangers.

Luz had taken up residence in the Vasquezes without knowing what he was doing, at a time when they were looking for a friend or a father and he was looking for shelter. And he'd left them brutally, raw, in a moment of panic, two-thirds cut loose, and the last third given in to retreat, burying himself in the only head that hadn't rejected him, hissing in those ears.

Though Luz had been quiet since, and though he was losing the feel of them, he remained colored by the thoughts of those three hole-filled children.

He'd seen Carmella as Hank used to, so Luz had suspected she'd be a challenge, but she was beyond reckoning. She counteracted his commands with images of him frying. She saw him as a severed hand that she set afire, causing Luz to stutter and stumble in her shoes.

If Luz had underestimated Carmella's powers of resistance, he had completely discounted Orson's. When Luz lived in Hank's hands, Orson and Hank were only teammates. Luz underestimated Orson in the same way that Hank might have before this school year brought them together.

Luz had not expected Orson to force him into submission as Hank squeezed the air from him, but that was exactly what Orson had done. Now Orson's body was incapacitated. Luz only knew where it was at all because the moment Orson's light went out, the light inside Carmella, now split only two ways, shone brighter.

When Orson awoke, Luz would wake with him, and constrict tighter.

Luz used Carmella's hands to open the trunk that Hank hoisted Orson into like a kidnapped thing. Luz used Carmella's silver tongue to lie about the origin of this new alien invasion, used Carmella's everything to drive Carmella's car while Hank directed.

Milo's body stumbled along the asphalt, headed toward home and Nameless Canyon, crisping in the late afternoon sun.

Why are you doing this?

"Don't be angry with me." Luz kicked a stone into the road, watched it strike a pothole and bounce. "I'm just living."

No you aren't. You're a coral snake, not a king snake!

That attempt at abstract thought again. "You're really growing up, kiddo."

Why are you hurting us, Luz?

Luz stopped Milo's feet on a rumble strip.

"You hurt me first," Luz hissed. "You're the only things that ever have."

Here was what existence had been, for Luz:

He became attached to a family, then quickly outgrew it.

Ana tried to cut him out. This was the first time Luz Vasquez felt pain that belonged solely to himself. It wasn't the pain of the blade on skin—without a physical body, how could Luz ever know that?

This was pain only something bodiless could feel. There was no filter between Ana and Luz. Self-hatred was nothing new to her, but it made cheese cloth of Luz when she loosed it on him.

What had started as something Luz considered inconsequential, natural curiosity—*how would it feel to kill a friend?*—had ended in a rejection so cutting and deep that had Luz lungs, he felt certain they would have collapsed. Not because Luz understood how Ana felt. He would never understand that.

Death was the thing these children had really failed to explain, in all the weeks he had lived with them. It baffled him. How could anything alive *not* fixate on death?

Ana had answered that. She showed him that living was painful enough. All Luz could think, with the blade and the hatred aimed at him, was that it must stop. He'd spun Hank's hands to Milo's throat. If Luz learned nothing else about death, he learned these children would die to save one another. They would kill Luz, to save one another.

When the Vasquez mother walked into her kitchen to see her son choking her other son and her daughter cutting her own face, the only real casualty in the room was Luz. The feeling was indescribable.

It was *feeling.*

When had that begun? When they named him? Maybe Luz became doomed the instant he pretended to be a father.

Had Luz felt pangs of loss during Milo's recollections of a ruined birthday party? Had Luz come to understand beauty only because Ana felt the lack of it? Had he lived in Hank's hands because those hands were made to hold things?

There was no telling. But *feeling* was insidious. By the time Luz had any understanding of what had happened to him, he couldn't stop the growth.

Emotions were the parasites that plagued him.

Where are we going, Luz?

"I'm still curious about something."

You won't hurt me. Luz caught himself crossing Milo's arms, stopped halfway.

"Why not? I've got other bodies."

You won't hurt me because you love me.

"I'm not your father, Milo. I don't love you."

You aren't Dad. But you *do love me!*

"Shut the *hell* up." Ana's curse words, Hank's denial. Milo's body.

For a jarring instant, Luz understood how Ana and Hank and Milo had felt, wanting Luz gone from their skulls. He felt this way about Milo as they reached the stop sign.

Simultaneously, Luz thought he could never let him go.

Both of these thoughts, there was no denying—*stung.*

Luz wiped sweat from Milo's neck and pulled him away from the road. He'd still be in plain sight if cars were to come by. None did.

Luz, we didn't mean to hurt you.

"And I didn't mean to hurt you. I meant nothing."

Now you mean to for sure.

"Milo, I'm not a good person. I'm not a person at all," Luz muttered, crossing the last road before the drop.

You're scared.

"Know-it-all," Luz muttered, leaning against the silver guardrail.

I want to know it all, but so do you! You're being a hippo-crit.

"Maybe that's why I'm still with you, in this useless little body." Luz paused and looked down over the railing. Here was the steepest drop, the closest thing to a plummet that Nameless Canyon offered. "We've got growing left to do."

There was no telling how Luz felt anything, being what he was. To have feelings but no body was an impossible plight. It was agony unlike the open air had been. Luz should have known that sharing bodies and minds might lead to sharing heart and soul, whatever that meant.

Abstract, Milo's brain supplied.

He hadn't known. He had only ever known what they knew.

"Milo." Luz raised one foot over the barrier. "What did Dad say when you threw the paper plane from the observation deck?"

And the real agony Luz felt now, had felt since: they had never known *him.*

Go on.

10

HANK

Henry Flowers and the battered RV he called home awaited Hank at the leaf-strewn parking lot of Moreno Park. It was a fixture of his mind, maybe of the actual lot.

Hank felt queasy about Orson being jostled around in Carmella's trunk along the bumpy road to the canyon's edge. The senseless appearance of Henry Flowers, with his flyaway puffs of hair and Hawaiian shirt and distorting bifocals, did not help.

Hank was feeling so much at this point. Every development felt as inconsequential as drops in a bucket long since overturned.

"Hank! Glad you called. I've been waiting. And watching, but that's a *creepy* thing to say, ain't it?" He eyeballed Hank's hands before crossing his arms and shaking both of Carmella's. "Nice to meet you. Henry Flowers, Extraterrestrial Expert."

Carmella's eyes flashed. Hank attributed this to surprise.

"Mr. Flowers! We've got one. In the trunk of Carmella's car, and you can have it, if you can get it out of my friend."

"Oh? Which friend?"

"Orson. He's on my basketball—"

"Mr. Liu! More than a friend, maybe. Well, we'll have to see how that unfolds."

"Can you help or not?"

"Don't wave those monster fists at me. Show some manners. Here're mine—come inside for a drink."

"But—"

"You locked that trunk, right? I speak from experience: he ain't going anywhere." Hank and Carmella let the elderly madman lead them into his elderly mad-Winnebago. The cracks at the doors and windows were blocked by cardboard. Virtually every surface wore a coat of tinfoil.

Henry sat them at a crinkly table and handed them "drinks": two packets of orange sugar, two plastic cups, and a bottled water.

"What is this?"

"Tang. You'll have to split that water. We're on tight rations aboard the *Alienator*."

Visiting Mr. Flowers began to feel like a poor choice. "Aren't you going to take a look at what's crawled into Orson—"

"Do you mean what, or *who*?"

"Sorry?"

"Didn't you and your siblings name your alien?"

"It doesn't matter what we called it!"

"Oh, it sure does. My daughter called him Alphonse, after her favorite Japanese whatsit—*Japanime* character. Said Alphonse was another boy with no body. And, funny thing, she decided he *was* a boy, just like you kids did."

"I'd love to hear all about this, Mr. Flowers, but right now we have to—"

Mr. Flowers slammed a fist on the table. "*Hank Vasquez!* After months of watching you, let me just say: you are not used to being honest with yourself, and right now you're making a real gorram mess of it. You want a favor from me?"

"*Please.*"

"Then let an old man talk."

"Hank." Carmella's stillness, the intensity of her gaze, knocked the words out of Hank.

"She's got the right idea. You want a favor, you're gonna have to learn to *listen* like your little brother. This thing, your *Luz*, my daughter's Alphonse—don't you wonder where he came from?"

"Space. He had to be from space."

"Why?" Mr. Flowers lifted his glasses. Underneath them, his eyes were cloudy with cataracts. "Did Luz tell you that?"

Hank thought hard. Beside him, Carmella watched in silence. "But . . . he *has* to be an alien."

"Maybe, maybe not. We can call him alien because it's life we don't understand, and we don't really understand the stars. But we don't understand the holes in the world, either. We don't know what springs up in the deep trenches of the ocean, in the unexplored caves of the Amazon. Nobody does.

"And Nameless Canyon's shallow, but it *is* a hole in the world." He stirred the packet of orange powder into gray coffee. "So was the gorge. And whatever we rafted into that day wasn't just water. It glowed too much. Like liquid moonlight, isn't it?"

It didn't seem relevant—Orson could be waking up, and he

needed to take that thing out of him and explain that no matter what he felt for Orson, god, he'd never hurt him or do anything he didn't want—

"Where are you from, Hank?"

"What?"

"It doesn't matter to me." Henry Flowers pulled his bifocals back into place. "But you can imagine how it would matter to this thing? This thing from nowhere? So where are you from, Hank Vasquez?"

"You already know."

"Just say it, boy."

"Eustace, New Mexico."

"And who makes up your family?"

"Um . . . my mom, my little brother, and my sister."

"Who else?"

After a pause: "Carmella. Orson. Brendan Nesbitt."

"Imagine having *no answer*. Imagine having, *being*, nothing. This thing might be a monster, but it's a damn pitiful one."

Carmella stood. There was something off about her eyes. "I need to breathe."

Then it was just the two of them. "Before Alphonse came along, my daughter was really into costuming. She'd go to these conventions dressed like superheroes and whatnot. Maybe that's why he liked her. He likes wearing people, doesn't he?"

Hank listened to the scraping drip of the sink faucet on tinfoil. "Why are you so certain this is the same person? I mean, not person—"

"*Yes*, person. We taught him enough to make him a person, don't you think?"

"What makes you think Luz and Alphonse are the same?"

"My daughter had your hands. After I chased him out of her. Spaghetti fingers." Henry shook his head. "She couldn't thread a needle anymore."

"You chased him out? But you said she was missing. Aliens abducted her. Or, I mean, Luz, I mean, *Alphonse*. You said he *took* her."

"It's not that he *took* her. It's that he's *still taking* her." Henry Flowers stood up. He placed his stained mug under the faucet. The dripping note became higher. "You get what I'm saying? He's taking her life *right now*."

"I don't—"

"My daughter ran away as a teenager and since then she's spent her whole adulthood *chasing* the person that abandoned her as a child. She's still playing dress up, too. You've seen her in a lab coat. Ridiculous."

Hank gaped. "*Dr. Ruby?*"

"Yep. She made her first name her last name. Now, am I a creepy old man? Yes. But am I here to spy on your family? Not really. I'm here to spy on mine. It's just that now we have one pain-in-the-ass alien relative in common."

Outside, a car engine growled.

By the time Hank's overgrown feet kicked the screen door and hit the pavement, Carmella was reversing.

He did his best to leap in front of the vehicle, but Carmella didn't hesitate to accelerate—*like she wanted to see what would happen*—

Hank rolled off the hood and slammed hard into asphalt.

"Shit," Hank gasped, trying to find his feet. "*Shit*. He was right there. He's in *Carmella*, too!" How little did Hank know his loved ones, that they could be someone else without him realizing?

That's what you've always been to your loved ones, too.

"You wanna keep punching the ground or you wanna go ahead and hunt the bastard?" Henry Flowers helped Hank up, clapped him on the shoulder. "Hurry!"

"We don't know where he's taking them," Hank gasped. He barreled into the RV so roughly that it shook, tripped up the steps, and fell against the mini-fridge.

"True, but first he'll have to get around this hole in the world!"

Seconds later, in the ancient RV, Henry dislodged a calico cat from the driver's seat and thrust it into Hank's arms. "Strap in. The *Alienator* is a crotchety old mistress, and she's been known to alienate bowels from their contents on rockier roads."

"The road shouldn't be that rocky here—"

"All roads are rocky when you're going a hundred miles per hour." True though this might have been, the Alienator went nowhere near fast enough to breathe the words "one hundred miles per hour." It didn't matter.

They could see the dust in Luz's wake, and they both knew their way around the canyon.

11

SISTER

Ana worried that she really had dreamed up this one.

But Dr. Ruby's camp on the edge of Perecheney remained almost exactly as they had seen it on Halloween, although by daylight it appeared much less sinister. Ragged, even—two sad tents, one drooping canopy.

When they made it to the camp, the squat man in the navy suit awaited them with a baseball bat in his grasp.

Ana was already halfway outside. Brendan snagged her arm.

"I'm not letting you face off against some—some *brute* on your own." Brendan opened the glove box and pulled out a Maglite. "I've seen these utilized as clubs in movies."

"You need to watch better movies," Marissa said. "Also, who says 'brute'?"

The squat man clearly wasn't used to being enticed out of his foldout chair in the desert or stepping outside his parasol's shade. He seemed rattled to see three teens headed his way. Without warning, he whistled. The whistle drew the tall woman from under the canopy. She wore a matching suit but held no baseball bat.

"I need to speak to Dr. Ruby," Ana told them.

They looked uncertainly at each other. Ana thought she might at last hear one of them speak, but then another voice reached them: "I'm here, Ana. I'm not hiding."

The voice emanated from another foldout chair, beside the unlit fire pit. In it, slumped almost in half, Ana found the woman who had pretended to help them for months, looking as though she could hardly help herself.

Dr. Ruby's hair was a tangle of greasy knots and her once-white coat was covered in stains. In her lap lay a bottle of Jack Daniel's, more than mostly empty.

"Ana! Welcome to my big reveal!"

"You're not a real doctor."

"Ta-da! And you're not a real patient." Dr. Ruby nodded at Ana's companions, eyeballing the ruddy cheeks and makeup-smeared features of Brendan, and the lavender hair of Marissa Ritter. Despite the scars, her incredulity was apparent. "But you've found therapy elsewhere. So no harm done."

"You're drunk."

"Not enough." She lifted the bottle; Ana took it from her and passed it to Brendan. He looked tempted to take a swig himself.

"Dr. Ruby." Ana spoke calmly. For once, being distant felt like an asset. "We need your help."

"Drop the 'Dr.' bit. You just told me I'm a fake. It's true. I don't have a high school diploma, Ana, let alone a degree. Your mom was just so desperate."

"Dr.—I mean, *Ruby*, why are you still here in Eustace?"

"I'm watching your damn family, of course. Why do you think I'm drinking?"

"Okay." Ana knelt down. Ana had never noticed before, with her eyes so groggy, but beneath the glasses Ruby wore, Ruby was young, maybe not even thirty. "But you were leaving town. Why didn't you?"

Ruby averted her eyes. "I don't have the energy to explain."

"Try. You're not a real doctor, but you sometimes made us feel better. Please. Tell me why you care so much about us."

Ruby met Ana's unbroken constellations, the eyes healed to new. Her own started welling. "You're the same as me. Because he left you, too."

"Luz?"

"Call him whatever you want. He was family."

Ana breathed deep, sat back on her haunches, and listened.

Ruby told them a sprawling fantasy, too bizarre and unfocused for any movie script. She spoke of a childhood on the road, of meeting a friend in the belly of a gorge, a friend made of light who became part of her and later hurt her, finally left her. But even after he was gone, Ruby felt the tug of him, a leash wrapped around one of her ribs that yanked her from one town to the next.

Surreally, impossibly, Ruby drove that white van around the country for years, two steps behind Luz, always arriving only days after he left some other human detritus in his wake. She mastered the act of allowing herself into the lives of strangers, employed the power of costuming. She met the squat man after Luz scarred his tongue, met the tall woman under similar circumstances.

Finally she found herself drawn to the Vasquez doorstep, having missed him by mere minutes.

Ana would have had a hard time believing all of this if Luz hadn't always been unbelievable. Or if Ana hadn't known all too well that the absence of a person *could* pull you, redirect your life and your thoughts, so why not your body as well?

All the mad, maddening details seemed less than important in the face of a single, striking truth:

Luz had wrecked others before he had wrecked the Vasquezes. Ruby wheezed. "I don't know why I can't let him go."

Ana tried not to scream, not to rush her. "You're the one who told me about emotional dependency."

A weak laugh. "I know. We're chasing ghosts, aren't we?"

"Ruby. Luz is still here. He's taken over Milo and he might have taken over—"

Ruby whooped. *"I knew it!"*

Brendan growled, "You're celebrating?"

"You have to help us get rid of him." Ana expected a protest, but Ruby nodded.

"Come on." She was steadier on her feet than Ana had anticipated, but stumbled once as she led them to the canopy and pulled the flap open. "I *knew*. I didn't feel the tug. I didn't feel any reason to leave Eustace."

The objects beneath the tarpaulin were revealed to be a generator and a row of blocky machines. This was almost the exact setup Ruby had installed in the Vasquez garage, but with one notable addition: a bank of screens along the back tarpaulin wall.

On those screens Ana saw her home, the auditorium, the cafeteria, and what might have been Orson's yard. Live feeds. Given the circumstances, the invasion hardly seemed to matter. Given the circumstances, it might help them find Milo.

"Milo could hear him all along. I wondered about that Roaring Nothing. But it's not important." The wildness returned to Ruby's face. "What's important is what we're going to do about it."

"I know it's crazy, but if what you've got is eardrops that poison him or something, I don't think I want that."

"Ana. We'll avoid hurting him at all costs. We're all a little fond of this monster. But we're going to have words with him. Understand?"

"A drunken imposter scientist in a ghost town just told me she still wants to be BFFs with the alien who's possessing my little brother. Who cares about understanding."

Ruby smiled. "Exactly. None of us get to decide, this far in, that we can no longer suspend our disbelief."

Marissa said, "Ana, did you get into LARPing? Is that what all this is?"

No one answered. Brendan patted her gently on the head.

"A real scientist wouldn't prescribe a termite tent and a hypnotist for PTSD."

"I was never really good at feigning professionalism. I'll tell you one thing, Ana, and I think you'll agree: you're never normal after something tears your head in two. Then again, a real professional wouldn't mind murdering a parasite. But I would."

Finally urgency entered Ana's voice. "I mind more what's going to happen to Milo."

"Well, of course we'll have to separate the two of them."

"How? I couldn't talk Luz into anything when he was part of me. Why the hell would he just crawl out of Milo when we're asking from the outside?"

"How did you make him leave you, Ana?"

"I . . . I threatened him."

"But you also made him feel unwanted. You and Hank both."

There was no doubt about that, but Ana had never put it so bluntly. She wondered, distantly, if they had somehow made Dad feel unwanted, too.

"Milo and the others have to reject him. We have to be there when they do."

"And then what?"

Ruby cleared her throat and diverted her attention to the screens.

"People don't walk far on feet that small. Iris?" The tall woman peered into the tent. "Keep an eye on the monitors. Holler when you find Milo. I'd check along the roads and by the canyon."

"Even if Milo rejects Luz, he isn't just going to vanish."

"No. He'll look for a new host immediately. And he'll find one." Dr. Ruby rested on her laurels, fingernails to her teeth. Suddenly she held her arms wide, much as she had on that haunted night. "I'm going to invite him to move back in."

No tumbleweeds rolled by.

"Welp, that's positively batshit," Brendan supplied.

Ana's stomach turned over. Brendan was right. But she also recognized the longing in Ruby's voice.

Ana had never told anyone but Ruby about the Dad dreams. No one but Ruby knew that sometimes, after the Chevy pulled away for good, Ana had stepped outside on purple evenings and sat in the driveway with her eyes wide open.

But even if he had come back, it wouldn't make him Dad again.

"You can't do that." Ana pressed her hands into her temples. Somewhere, Luz was walking Milo away, yet here she was, shooting down a possible solution. "He'll swallow you whole, and leave you again."

"Don't you wonder why Luz knew nothing when you met him?" Ruby murmured. "Not even what he was?"

Ana remembered the childish scrawl on the counters: *STaY plEAS?* Remembered endless questions about the brushing of teeth, about what toes were for. "He didn't know anything." Something clicked; looping film. "And he didn't remember *you*. We'd have known. But if he was still a child after being in all those bodies . . . Luz doesn't retain memories, does he?"

Ruby nodded. "Isn't it a nightmare? Luz's only desire is growth, but the moment he grows, it's clear he isn't human. He is monstrous, and he gets rejected every time. Luz reverts to mindless nothingness, an embryo of light. He can't actually grow up at all."

Ana's chest ached.

"That sounds awful." Marissa didn't know the context, but she was right.

"But Luz *is* capable of developing empathy, if he's occupying an empathetic mind." Ruby put a finger on one temple. "This time I know about his cruel streak. Maybe if I take him in, I can counter it. In so many ways, he's a child. If we don't teach him humanity, where's he going to learn it from?"

Ana chose not to blink, now for reasons unrelated to parasites, in a simple effort to take in this woman and her scars. Ruby wasn't the same without her glasses on. She wasn't the same without the lie. "It's not our job to teach him that. He was supposed to teach us, he was supposed to raise us and—"

Ana bit back the words that weren't about Luz.

Ruby set a hand on Ana's arm. "I don't know about you, but I'm just about fed up with neglectful parents. I refuse to be one."

"Maybe Milo *can't* make Luz feel unwanted." Ana wiped stinging eyes. "Maybe Luz is a better family to Milo than me and Hank ever were."

Ruby motioned with her hands. "Milo's been signing this a lot. By himself."

"What is it?"

"He's asking for help."

Something gave way in Ana's chest. She pushed past silent bodies to find open sky. Outside the tent she slumped in the dirt, sucking air.

Soon Brendan sat on one side, Marissa on the other.

"Ana. I have no idea what's going on, but I'm filming everything just in case."

"Marissa. I warned you not to come."

Marissa leaned closer. If her hair were longer, maybe lavender strands would have blended with Ana's brown. "I have no idea what's going on. But remember when we were making Lego stop-motion movies? Sometimes we did it at my house, and my demonic, heartless turd of a little brother—"

Ana snorted. "Felix wrecked our buildings."

"Yeah. And you helped me rebuild every tower even though it meant missing curfew and getting grounded. And so next time we filmed at your house. We went to the kitchen to make grilled cheeses and both realized Milo was missing, and we just *knew* where he'd be, because *little brothers are nightmare spawn*." Marissa's eyes crinkled around the edges. "But *your* little brother—we got up there and he was just like you, rebuilding the sets *we'd* broken, putting things back where they belonged."

". . . I don't see your point, Marissa."

"This would work better if I could write it down. I'm trying to say that Milo is a Vasquez. He's an annoying person who probably wants to put broken things back together. That's why he's so hung up on your dad in the first place, right? He's trying to put things where they belong."

Brendan nodded. "Oh, the incorrigible Vasquezes."

"Right? Vasquezes rebuild things. That's why you let me come with you today."

Ana stared, wondering how she'd gone a single day without missing Marissa.

"Kids, we've found him!" Ruby hailed, bursting from the tent.

Ana was on her feet with dizzying speed. "Where is he? Is he okay?"

"Better not to ask," Ruby replied, her mouth a line. "Just get in the van."

Brendan promptly pulled the keys away from her. "Are you kidding? I'm driving."

No one protested, least of all Ana, who saved her concerns for the dark of the van:

"And what if Milo's . . . gone?"

"Cross that bridge when we come to it," Marissa replied.

12

LUZ

While one part of Luz dangled Milo's feet on the edge of a precipice, two other parts sped along the freeway.

The Orson part awoke somewhere near the Huffton exit, and the sudden split of consciousness made the Carmella Luz's hands slip on the wheel—and, coral snake that she was, Carmella Spalding took advantage of Luz's lapse by trying to hijack herself:

GET OUT.

She didn't beg—it was a command that almost made Luz cower.

The car drifted onto the rumble strip and Carmella had to refocus on driving to bring the car back to center. She pulled the wheel and Luz pulled her back to heel.

When he felt he had a steady grasp on both bodies, he parked Carmella's car outside a rest area. He didn't bother checking for witnesses. Orson climbed out of the trunk and settled into the passenger seat. In another three minutes, the car was back on the road, driving away from the sunset.

"We're going to drive all night," the Carmella Luz said.

"You don't need to say anything aloud, dumbass," said the Orson Luz.

"And you didn't need to *answer* aloud, either." Luz used Carmella's most condescending trill. "So we're both dumbasses, aren't we?"

Minutes passed. Luz's bodies were sweating, though it was growing colder.

"It was better when we were cohabitating, not dominating."

"But that didn't work out."

Orson's head nodded. "I know you're right. But where are we even going?"

"It doesn't matter. We're just going."

"Okay. Fine. Just go."

For another ten minutes, they drove. Sweat beaded on two foreheads, under two sets of arms. Luz's vision blurred in two separate skulls.

On the edge of Nameless Canyon, the Milo Luz raised his arms over his shoulders. He prepared to jump.

"It's getting harder to fight the noise," said the Orson Luz. Within the shared skull, Luz was being reimagined into a ball of squirming larvae that Orson rolled into a basketball, and Orson was popping it, slamming it against asphalt. A vision of Hank helped him.

It was distracting. If Orson hadn't been in the passenger seat, all too capable of grabbing the wheel, Luz would have abandoned his body right then.

"Should have left you in the trunk," the Carmella Luz said. Carmella's mantra remained *GET OUT.* No matter that Luz rolled down the windows and turned up the radio—she only got louder.

"We're really far from home," the Orson Luz said.

"That wasn't home."

"Either way, I think we're lost."

"We're on the freeway."

"But we're lost."

"We're stuck with ourselves, no matter what," Luz echoed, as elsewhere, someone said those precise words to his other self.

It wasn't a conscious decision, the abandoning of Orson— Orson had mentally set fire to the termite ball and the screeching was horrendous, and it paralleled the screeching of Carmella's leg locking up on the brake, the car behind them honking like mad and zipping past as they rolled onto the shoulder, aimed directly at a speed limit sign . . .

"We're way over that speed limit," Orson Luz informed Carmella Luz.

The car slammed into the signpost.

Both air bags deployed. Clouds of white smacked into Carmella's golden face and Orson's tan one, an impact like no other that coincided with the popping of the termite ball in Orson's mind and a final *GET OUT* from Carmella's.

Luz dissipated before smoke started rising from Carmella's smashed Fiat engine, before determining if either Carmella or Orson had a pulse left to them, and was gone.

13

MOTHER

The responsible adults of the other five families who lived on the far side of Nameless Canyon were all at work.

Maggie's first sick day began with a McDonald's confrontation and ended with a Dairy Queen Blizzard dripping in her cup holder as she sped home, so she would never consider counting herself among any group thought of as responsible.

Responsibility found her soon enough.

Even before she hit the brakes at the intersection facing the canyon, she saw him.

There was nothing shocking about it. She'd come here to find him. And this was the same intersection where she'd stopped the car and he'd leaped out of it. Chasing roadkill, chasing the dead.

For the duration of Milo's short life, she'd watched this child do things some parents might have found shocking. Swallowing ants, cooking invisible dinners, birthday tantrums so severe they lost him for hours.

Milo sat so tranquil on the guardrail. Legs limp over the edge, arms spread wide on either side of him. The lightest tap on his back would topple him.

Blood rushed in Maggie's ears. She pulled onto the shoulder behind the stop sign.

"What else is new, Milo."

Maggie got out of the car.

When Milo was born, he was like many other babies. Seven pounds, nine ounces. He cried and laughed and played with things like all children do, plastic things and plush things. He perched on Hank's shoulders and was tickled by Ana's fingers. His first words were "ki-kat" though they had no cat, and "Mama" because he had one.

Maggie used to kiss his feet; sometimes he would kick her.

Maggie looked both ways before crossing the road. She noted how wide Milo's arm span had become, how it really was as wide as he was tall, how precarious his little fingers appeared in a breeze like this.

When Milo was three, he stopped speaking.

It happened without warning. When he stopped speaking he also stopped smiling, making eye contact. For a year, Milo said not a word. Doctors had much to say instead. Assessments were made, well-intentioned diagnoses granted. Ultimatums of Milo's oddment.

Maggie kissed Milo's feet; sometimes he would kick her.

The air that spun up from the base of Nameless Canyon couldn't help but whorl, couldn't help but lift and pull everything in all directions. Milo's wings tilted like a plane's in a high wind. Heavy turbulence.

Arms spread like that. Maggie wondered: Was this another sign for *everything*?

"Hey. What are you doing?"

"Something new," Milo said flatly.

"I can see that." She willed her voice not to tremble. "But didn't you want me to show you how to make coffee?"

"I'm not Milo." He tilted his head back, a little too far. He pointed one daggered eye at her. "I'm not your son."

"I didn't think you were," Maggie said. At last she was meeting the hallucination, the thing that knew them all.

This morning, in the kitchen—Milo had been *better*. But better wasn't Milo. What made Milo himself wasn't behaving how other kids did. It wasn't being calm in school or making sense or making breakfast for his mother.

"I never did fool you. The Vasquez mother."

"Milo can only ever be Milo." Maggie walked over gravel, into sparse grass. "That's one thing I do know."

"You have terrified me since I met you."

"Well. Ditto."

Maggie locked eyes with the thing behind Milo's gaze, the thing that wasn't him. "If I can have any body I want. If I can reach others, can grow bigger all the time, why am I holding on to this? These tiny useless hands."

Maggie quirked a smile. Maybe it was real. "Milo grows on people."

"He does." Milo's arms tilted up and down, back and forth. "Don't you ever want to get out? Just leave them and go?"

"Do you?" Maggie sat carefully beside him, with her back to the canyon. "Have *you* been able to leave my ridiculous kids alone?"

"They wouldn't be alone." There was bitterness in his voice. "They never are. Irritating things swarm around them. *Friends.* How can they be called friends? These things haven't even seen Vasquez bone marrow. I have seen it. I've lived in it."

Maggie cleared her throat. "I think I know how you feel. It's becoming pretty clear that they don't need me anymore, either."

"Yes." This close, she could see Milo's face twitching, fighting itself.

Maggie breathed in through her nostrils. She recalled her conversation with Donovan. And she set it aside, tucked herself into a compartment in her chest and lied, because Milo was here on the edge of a cliff. "Well, what are we waiting for, then? Let's get out of here."

Luz turned both eyes on her—the tilting threw Milo's body just off balance.

"Maybe you and me have just outgrown the Vasquezes, Luz."

Luz grinned at her, wider than his head. He lowered her son's arms, stopped her son's legs from kicking.

It took everything in Margaret not to grab him then.

Slowly, Luz lifted one leg back over the guardrail. Then the other. Finally he lowered both back to the earth.

"Well done, son." Luz's eyes widened, but Maggie knew what she was doing. When she wrapped this thing in her arms and held him close, she knew precisely what could happen.

She knew her son was buried in there, as he'd often been

buried in himself. She knew that any boy who kicked when his feet were kissed had spirit in abundance.

Milo could not be bested by the emptiness of the world if the emptiness had always been part of him.

As Luz appeared like a swarm of termites spewing from the ears of Milo while she embraced him, Maggie did not close her eyes, did not look away from all those buds of light leaving her son in dribbling lines, did not flinch when she felt their tiny needle-feet in her nose and mouth and ears and eyes.

Not for one second did she mistake this thing in her arms for anything but what it was. But she also knew how badly it wished she could. Luz wanted to be something else. She could understand that.

Margaret Vasquez had not traveled, but she had seen much of the world.

We'll travel now, Maggie, Luz said. *We can go anywhere.*

"Are you sure, Mags?" Donovan had kissed her head, put his hands over hers on her swollen belly. "There's probably a cheaper house closer to the school."

"Probably." Maggie extricated herself from his arms. "But I'm sure. They don't make houses like this back in Wisconsin."

"Nah. And they don't make families like ours anywhere."

Maggie walked to the lip of the canyon. "Not sure about that."

14

BROTHER

Hank had suspected it might all lead back to where it started. Nameless Canyon was the only part of Eustace with any depth, the only part vast enough to contain all that had happened to his family over the course of their lives.

Sometimes he imagined the reason Mom had chosen this house on the edge of the world was because the canyon was big enough to pour any amount of pain into.

In his imagination, pain looked like a nosebleed, red and wet.

In reality, pain looked like the scene he witnessed as Henry Flowers slammed his RV brakes before the sheer drop beyond an intersection.

Curled between the road and the cliff face as if napping in the dirt, the most horrifying roadkill: Hank would recognize Milo's sprawl anywhere.

"H-whoopsy daisy!" cried Henry Flowers. He'd taken the last turn too fast, way too fast, and the forces of momentum and gravity meant the right side of the vehicle lifted momentarily off its tires.

It should have been fine, except from the other direction, right then, another vehicle barreled, equally reckless, around the corner—

A flash of white—some kind of van?—and then two drivers slammed wailing brakes.

It was anyone's guess, whether the *Alienator* would tip—

And then it did.

Hank felt the pullback of his head on his spine, a violent snap as his teeth came together on his tongue and bit through it before he was thrown against the left side of the RV. In Hank's arms, the cat scratched his chest like Milo's fingers had. He cracked his head against the crinkled tinfoil walls.

The world stilled.

"Mr. Flowers?" Hank spat hot blood, but his speech remained slurred. "Sir?"

Mr. Flowers coughed. The seat belt had dug deep into his chest. He swung from his seat like an astronaut might. "See, that's why I told you to strap in."

Hank had, but his mouth was still a throbbing mess.

"Mr. Flowers, I'm gonna dry and"—spit—"climb oudda dop. I'll ged help, bud, my bruh-dur—"

"God, kid. Go. I'll hang in there . . ." His head fell limp.

We need to get out.

Escaping the RV seemed unfeasible. The only option was the driver's-side window above, suddenly part of a new ceiling.

Hank climbed, grabbing sun-bleached cup holders, wedging

his foot against the seat backs. He could only hope his fingers would be enough.

Pressed against the back of Henry's seat, Hank caught hold of the grab handle over the cracked driver's-side window. Suspended as he was by flagging hands, Hank couldn't roll down the window and hold on simultaneously.

The glass had to go.

Hank swung his right arm. One useless hand curled. The other strained to hold his weight.

You stupid fucking things.

His fist hit the crack at its nexus. Something that was not glass cracked and pain shot up his arm. But Hank swung again, and again. Just like shooting. Just like missing.

It took too many tries. Hank's knuckles were bleeding, and he knew it was futile but he couldn't seem to stop—

Just this once be what I pretend you are.

His fist found open air—glass hailed down.

Hank hoisted himself up, willing his shattered fingers to last just a little longer, willing them to remain fingers despite all the abuse he'd done them.

Finally he extricated himself, glass in his knuckles sparkling like glitter. He sprawled across the warm RV siding. He was panting, bloody all over. But he was out.

From this high up Hank could see the canyon gaping brown and gray and red under him, could see the van that they'd almost struck had spun out into a ditch but remained upright.

Milo's body lay precisely where it had been.

Hank wasn't thinking. He was only hopping down that ten-foot drop and twisting his ankle on the shitty landing in the dirt, worsening the twist by sprinting as fast as he could. As if he could stop an already fallen thing from falling.

He hardly registered the van door sliding open, revealing a pile of faces with Ana's at the fore, or the arrival of another car, a busted old station wagon.

Hank skidded to the earth beside Milo and scooped him up. He shook him, bled on him in the shaking, and as the sky bruised purple pressed his head against a chest altogether too soundless. Hank lifted eyelids without knowing what to look for, Hank was so *stupid*, and now Milo, *Milo was too quiet*—

He hadn't strangled him this time, but he might as well have. "Milo, what happened, what the hell happened, hey? What are you doing here?"

Milo seemed like nothing so much as a broken doll, joints poorly placed.

"Milo? Milo, hey, wake up, please, Milo—"

"Set him down, Hank!" Ana skidded to a halt beside them. "Hank, Luz might still have him!"

Hank had pulled Milo up to rest on his lap. Something about seeing him faceup in the fading light seemed to kill Ana's resolve, and suddenly she was kneeling, too. "Hank, hold him still. You're shaking and I can't tell whether he's got a pulse. Stop moving, you dumbass!"

The truth of the word stilled him. Ana pressed her ear to Milo's chest. Hank tried not to breathe, as if not doing so meant Milo would.

"He's alive, Hank. But we should step back, because Hank, *Luz*—"

"Forget Luz. I don't give a shit about Luz!" Hank pressed his head against his little brother's chest—there *was* a rise and fall there, though it stuttered like it shouldn't.

Ana took Hank's shoulders and held them steady. "Listen up. He might be possessing Milo *right now*—"

"Luz is in Carmella and he's in *Orson*—"

"And *maybe also in Milo*. We know he can split himself in three! So we need to back away and let Dr. Ruby deal with this, okay?" Ana craned her neck. "Brendan, where is she?"

Brendan Nesbitt was there between them and the amazing clown van. "I don't know—she got one look at that RV and just sprinted right for it. Marissa's gone after her, but honestly, I think we've aligned ourselves with a complete eccentric, Ana. I'm not sure she's going to be any help."

"Just find her, please!"

"I wonder how it got this bad. Again." Hank wiped his nose on his hand, forgetting that his knuckles were full of glass, forgetting that his face was full of blood. "After this summer. How did we end up hurting him again?"

Ana squeezed his arm. Their heads bumped together. When they were kids, this would have been cause for a squabble. Hank closed his eyes.

"You're dripping on me," Milo said. "And if that is blood, it will stain my clothes."

Neither Ana nor Hank had any rational thought in that moment, and this time their skulls hit harder in their collective struggle to wrap Milo up in their arms, tuck him away, and never let him go again.

"I need to breathe!" Milo protested.

Ana detached herself first. She pulled Hank back with her. "Wait."

"That's just Milo," Penny Dawson declared. Hank had no idea how long she'd been standing there, serious-faced, frizzy pigtails half-undone.

"I'm sorry," Ms. Yu gasped, huffing up in Penny's wake. "She demanded we head to your house, and when we saw—I mean, here we are. How can I—"

"Hush!" Penny said. She moved her hands together and apart, deliberate gestures in quick succession. Milo sat up straight, leaning on both Ana and Hank.

His mouth dropped open in some show of mock-horror.

He signed back. She giggled. Milo did, too. Hank wished it would echo forever.

"What did he say?"

"Doesn't matter. That's Milo. Luz doesn't know ASL." Penny smiled.

"Even if he did," Hank hazarded, "he's not very good with fingers."

For a moment Hank felt they had been lifted halfway to the stars.

The feeling was fleeting. In all the years Milo had been alive, all the sounds he'd made over those years, Hank had never heard a sob like the one that left him now. "Milo?"

"Milo." A breeze from the canyon lifted Ana's bangs. "Where did Luz go?"

Milo seemed lost for words. He put a hand to his chin, too ashamed to meet Hank's eyes.

"Mom," Penny translated.

Hank tilted Milo's face his way. "Hey. *Hey*. It's not your fault. But where did they go?"

Milo signed again.

Even Hank knew this one. He'd learned it years ago, when he was maybe only as big as Milo, in Cub Scouts alongside Tim Miller.

Home.

15

OTHER

Luz had never seen the Vasquez household through a mother's eyes before.

Maggie's footsteps made little sound as he pulled her past the basketball hoop and up the step. He couldn't help but notice the grass was underwatered. On the landing, he saw cobwebs in corners. Luz plucked a pair of tennis shoes and one of Hank's filthy duffel bags from the disorganized shoe rack.

What Maggie saw was something *less* than her children did; to them, this was home and always had been. Now the place looked like something struggling to be anything. Through Maggie, Luz saw shortcomings.

Here, in the bathroom, while he swept medicine and toiletries into the bag alongside the shoes, he saw the rusted stains where Ana used to leave bobby pins, the drain clogged with soap scum, flecks of debris on the cabinet mirrors. Here, in her bedroom, emptying a drawer into the bag: the unmade bed, dusty picture frames on the nightstand.

Luz, lopsided from the weight of Maggie's belongings, faltered during the walk down the hallway and to the kitchen. He noticed how the linoleum rippled and bubbled.

"You're too hard on yourself, Maggie," Luz whispered. "Really you are."

Luz thought he might have seen something of this trait in Ana, something curiously absent in the Vasquez boys. Luz had seen in Ana the obligation to perfect the imperfect, to condemn her own failings in a way that Milo and Hank did not think to. Had it been in the boys, too, in a different form? Who put it there?

Maggie's thoughts were quiet. "You don't have to worry about this place anymore," Luz assured her. "We don't have to worry about them, either. Whoever they are."

The time with Hank and Ana had been so long ago now, Luz couldn't remember what it felt like to be them, what *they* felt like being them. It seemed that upon Luz's leaving Milo only minutes ago, his memories of the children were fast fading.

Luz, standing in the kitchen entrance, was forgetting how Milo and Hank and Ana had felt about this room. He encountered a new thought. Perhaps he'd lived with a thousand families and left them, and when he left, forgot them all.

Even more chilling was the subsequent thought: he'd probably had this precise epiphany before, in endless kitchens.

This was exhausting. Above all else, Maggie was exhausted.

"You know," Luz told her, stepping her into the laundry room, "I think Milo wanted to be older. Or maybe it was Hank. Or . . . Ana."

He felt Maggie's heart swell for an instant—not at his words, but at their names. He leaned on the dryer to catch her breath. "They should rethink that. This hardly seems preferable."

He expected to feel her agreeing, confirmation that she would rather her children not grow up and face all the disappointments that colored her memories. Instead, Luz felt what he could only describe as a firm shake of Margaret's head within her head.

No.

"Suit yourself. Let them grow up. It won't be our problem." Luz flipped on the light switches beside the garage entrance.

Beyond the door, the walls were reflective. The table at the center of the foil-covered room was a lonely surface. Luz dragged Maggie's feet down the steps.

"Gosh, it's like your mother's mausoleum in Spring Green." He spread Maggie's body out on the table, let her feet dangle off the end. "Don't pretend you weren't thinking it. They were the living dead after Donovan left, weren't they? When you and I go, will they care?"

Maybe, Maggie replied. *Maybe not.*

"So forget them, Maggie. I mean, if *I* can, you can. We're going anywhere you want. You can die in a room with golden wallpaper in Rome after all. And I've got nothing to lose, quite literally."

Luz chortled; Maggie's tears transformed it into a gurgle. He sat her upright. The perfect ninety-degree angle made Maggie's spine crack. "Stop that. Stop crying."

They aren't my *tears, you sorry little thing.*

Luz saw Milo and Hank, fast asleep, a memory of Maggie waking them up.

He blinked and found his knees sticking to the plastic. "What was that for? Enough."

Luz put one hand on the table to pull the body back up, but down it went again.

Margaret followed up the last vision with one of her kids opening their eyes—all different ages at once, Margaret's sons and daughter.

"Honestly, those are hardly *good* memories at all. They do that every day."

Yes. They do.

Luz clutched Maggie's ribs. A flush bloomed under them. "Fine. You want to pretend your children are angels? Is that your parting gift?"

The garage made him think of it. He dragged the memory to the surface.

"I don't believe that. And neither do you."

What am I going to do with all this plastic cutlery?

That was Maggie's thought when, after forty minutes of pacing the driveway and swatting flies away from a birthday cake shaped like an anthill, she conceded that nobody was coming to Milo's seventh-birthday party.

Half of the Eustace Elementary first graders had been invited. Mostly boys, as that was expected. Milo claimed that Antonio wouldn't come if too many *girls* were there, because, Milo confessed, "I think Antonio may be *sexism*, too." Maggie wasn't sure whether to laugh or cry about that.

Which was how she felt now. It was rare to have them all

outside at the same time. Maggie had insisted. She hardly let Ana out of her sight these days, and hadn't since the hospitalization. Ana complied, with the concession that she be allowed to sit in a lawn chair and not be expected to pin tails on anything.

Hank was hanging the piñata from the basketball hoop. From the satisfied expression on his face, you'd think empty card tables and untouched cake were of no concern. Maggie didn't mind seeing him happy. She understood the cause. The piñata was a model of the Golden Gate Bridge, sculpted with care by Eustace's finest artist.

Speak of the devil. Brendan Nesbitt came out of the house with Saran Wrap for the punch bowl. Maggie didn't wonder what her kids saw in Brendan Nesbitt. There were times when, not without guilt, Maggie envied his parents. The day Hank had introduced her to him, she'd noticed immediately how real Hank became, breathless beside him, and wanted Brendan never to leave.

"Do you need help with anything else, Mrs. Vasquez?"

"Depends. Can you find a way to turn these one hundred sporks into an art project, Brendan?" She rattled the box at him. "You're our only hope."

"I think, Mrs. Vasquez, the question is not whether I could, but whether any man *should*."

"*Ms.* Vasquez, Brendan. It's *Ms.* So forget the sporks. Do you know anything about herding teachers?"

He shook his head. "Usually your species is trying to herd us instead, right?"

"Right."

Staff from Eustace Elementary had also been invited. Maggie was far from the oldest mother, but also far from the youngest.

Of course, it was hard to drag teachers anywhere in the summer.

Serves me right, I guess.

When was the last time Maggie had bothered attending any of their functions? Graduation parties, weddings, and baby showers had been neglected. Maggie often told herself she had enough on her plate.

The only things on her plate now were tortilla chips and guacamole.

"Milo, do you wanna go ahead and open some presents?"

Milo was quite the sight, statuesque as a gargoyle on a long two-by-four plank stretched across the base of the yard. He'd invented a game after Maggie had informed him that bobbing for apples was unsanitary. The rules were a little incomprehensible, but seemed to involve kids tightroping across the plank while Milo threw tiny doughnut holes at them, which they had to . . . catch in their mouths?

It was either genius or ridiculous or both. It was 10,000 percent Milo.

"Or maybe have some cake, Milo?"

"Sorry, Mom. I'm keeping an eye out."

"I can keep *two eyes* out while you eat." Hank always bent when he spoke to Milo to accommodate their vast height difference. "I'll report any suspicious activity directly to you, sir."

"Nuh-uh, Hank. This is my responsibility as the birthday boy. Bike lessons could start any minute!"

"Well. You're the captain." Hank hitched his smile up higher.

"Oh, come *on*. It's worse if we lie." Ana got out of her lawn chair. "Milo, are you a child? Hey, Milo? Are you a stupid little kid?"

"Ana!" Maggie hissed.

Milo stood on his bridge. "I have a high Lexile. I'm not stupid."

"Then I'm not going to pretend you are. Milo, your birthday party started more than an hour ago. No one's coming."

Milo turned his back on her. "They don't have to. I don't care if no one comes, so long as Dad gets here soon."

"Dad is *definitely* not coming. He doesn't care about us."

"Hey—" Hank started.

"Maybe he didn't care about *you*, Ana," Milo pondered.

The words weren't spoken with cruelty. Milo was just stating a fact, an actual possibility. From the way Ana cringed, clearly she thought so, too. From the way Hank closed his mouth tight shut, he couldn't deny it, either.

It was strange, really—seconds before, Margaret had been livid with her daughter. Now she found herself suddenly at the end of the yard, taking Milo by the back of his T-shirt, dragging him to the garage. Along the way his fingers caught on a plastic tablecloth and tore it free, spilling Cheetos and cake onto the blacktop.

"Sit down." Margaret shoved Milo into a seat at the picnic table in the shade. "Sit down and open your damn presents. Be *normal*, please. Just this once."

Ana vanished into the house. Hank looked completely disgusted with Maggie for half a second, before pasting on a smile. He spoke sweetly to Milo, pulling long legs over the bench. He tried to entice Milo with gifts, shaking them in search of Lego.

Brendan Nesbitt patted Maggie on the shoulder. "It's okay, Mrs. Vasquez."

"*Jesus.*" She spun on her heel. "*It's Ms.*"

Maggie slammed the door to the laundry room behind her and cried.

She felt as bad as her own mother, back in the Wisconsin woods. Her mother made amazing lebkuchen at Christmas and gave great advice about summer jobs and college applications, but also had a tack on the kitchen wall from which hung a flyswatter with a masking-tape label: *Child Rearer*.

Who the hell *was* Maggie? How was she allowed to keep these kids, when she couldn't keep herself?

That evening, Maggie couldn't keep Milo. She came outside to apologize, and found Brendan and Hank entangled in each other.

"Where's Milo?"

The rest was not her story.

"Tell me you didn't wish to be *anywhere else*, any*one* else, that day, and I'll tell you to sit down and open your damn presents." Luz smacked the switch on the wall. There came a screeching *crunch* as the garage door lifted, taking the foil with it.

Night had overtaken the cul-de-sac. "Tell me you aren't thrilled to leave them, and I'll call you a liar."

They approached her car. The stars reflected on the windshield looked more like Christmas lights, tiny blinking bulbs of artificial spirit. Another memory of Maggie waking them, this time declaring: "Look, everyone! Santa came!"

All moms are liars, Luz.

"You're completely impossible." Luz pulled the car keys from Maggie's pocket and reached for the door—

The keys hit the concrete. The duffel bag slipped from fingertips and plopped at Maggie's feet. The body froze in place.

"What?" Luz could move Maggie's mouth, but nothing else. It was inexplicable. "What are you doing, Maggie?"

Parenting, Luz.

This was nothing like occupying a young Vasquez. It wasn't even like fighting Carmella. There was no fight. Maggie simply took command of herself as if Luz had no more weight or power than cold cream, foundation: something she wore but could wipe away.

"... how?"

Maggie reclaimed her mouth, shoved Luz back from her tongue. "I've taught a thousand children how to tie their shoes, how to read, how to multiply, and how to *be kind.* I used to lift Hank; he was heavier than you. I used to argue with Ana; she's cleverer than you. And you can try to be alien all you want, but you've got nothing on Milo. This is easy, Luz."

Luz reverted to speaking within her skull; she gave him no choice. *You said we'd leave. We've outgrown them and we'd travel the world away from here. You said.*

"Again: moms are liars." She was walking them away from the car, toward the canyon. "Leaving isn't good enough, Luz. You nearly threw my son off a cliff."

Where are you taking us?

"You know, all this time I thought if I met you, I'd understand my kids. What they went through, what you did to them." Maggie threw one leg over the canyon barrier, and then the other, and set them down on the other side. "But I'm disappointed. You're not even an ounce of what Donovan was, and he's pretty small himself."

They began the descent. Perhaps it was traces of Milo's mind in Luz, fleeing down the pit, but the departure from the stars seemed vital.

You won't do this, Maggie.

Luz heard voices cry out as they sank below the horizon, but Maggie did not stop. Even when the scuffing of shoes and the clumsy, heavy pounding of feet grew louder, the cries of "Stop!" became shrieks, the plummet continued.

Ending your life won't end mine. It won't!

"You don't sound certain. And I know you're curious. Maybe I am, too."

Maggie didn't stop until they'd reached the observation deck. She pressed her body against the polished railing.

"Ana was right about the view," she murmured. "It's beautiful."

Beauty means nothing to me. Try as Luz might, Maggie's mind was unfathomable. There was no dissuading this. *It won't be my loss.*

Maggie ran a palm along the railing and received not a single splinter. She put a foot on the lowest rung of the railing. "You're wrong, Luz."

Luz heard panting behind them, but couldn't turn Maggie's head. He heard the boards creak as bodies put weight on the platform.

Funny how Luz could remember the rawness of hands and the perspiration on brows that didn't belong to him. He could just remember building this platform, and knew what it meant to Maggie.

But really Luz knew he'd had no part in it.

Maggie turned around. Luz wasn't at all shocked to see Hank, Ana, and Milo standing on the platform, wearing matching facial expressions. Luz wasn't at all shocked to see the company they'd brought, scattered up the slope behind them, pausing to listen. A handful of high schoolers, and some adults, and the little girl with pigtails.

None of the kids said a word. They moved closer, bloodstained and unified. Luz felt a twinge in Maggie's chest.

Stop that. I don't want to feel that.

"Get out of her," Hank growled.

"It's me, Hank. It's Mom."

She signed words to prove it. Milo's eyes blew up. He started crying. Another twinge; Luz shriveled in his nothingness. Maggie refused to let him retreat from it.

"Go back up to the house." Maggie's voice quivered. "I'm taking care of this."

"Mom," Ana said, "I know what you're thinking about doing. Don't. The heroic sacrifice is one of the *worst* movie tropes! Remember me in the hospital. Remember how it didn't make anything better."

"Ana, it isn't like that. I'm just . . . I'm trying to be a good mother."

"You *are* a good mother, Mom." Hank's bloodied fists were lowered, trembling. "You don't have to die to prove it. Just be here, like always. Okay?"

"*Mom,*" Milo sobbed. "Please stay."

Luz could feel Maggie's heart swelling. He wanted to carve it out, to make it go away. Feeling all that she felt now: this was pain incomprehensible.

Maggie staggered; Luz took her back.

"And what about me?" Luz asked. He tried smirking, but

found Margaret's face curiously limp. "Do you even realize it? How loving you is a nightmare? God. If you could feel what your mother does, you'd be worse than crying. You'd be jumping off this deck, too."

They didn't back away, but their posture changed. Cold, clear rejection. Milo wiped his eyes on his sleeve and took Ana's hand. Ana took Hank's.

"It's downright *sickening*, how much you're all loved. You're *spoiled* with it. Like that time Hank and Milo—you two, yes—ate all your Halloween candy in one sitting. Ruined your dinner. Do you remember?"

Luz's borrowed voice broke. "Because *I'm* forgetting."

As one, they came closer.

"I'm starting to forget it all." He stepped down to the deck. "Each of you is such a *mess* of memories, such a constellation of disasters. I can't keep you together. I can't keep you straight. You are chaotic. Who would choose you?"

"You did, Luz." How tall Hank had grown, inside and out. How big he was in the ways that mattered. "You chose us."

"Madness, isn't it? Next time I'll know better. 'Luz, if you must have bodies, do pick some that aren't fucking wrecks.' You ever heard your mother swear like this? She does all the time when you're not around. And oh, man. The secrets she keeps! I could tell you, if you want. Just let me stay?"

"Enough, Luz." How tall Ana stood, how firmly she held herself. The heart swelled again. Luz hissed; this was beyond untenable.

He shook Maggie's head. "You made me this thing that I am. You gave me this damn heart but did not teach me what it meant." He punched Margaret's chest. "Not this borrowed one. You gave me my own with no way to contain or comprehend it. How cruel are human beings?"

Milo stepped forward, alone. Margaret showed Luz what she saw—a boy, once mute, speaking clearly: "That's because we kind of loved you, Luz. But you have to go away. Okay?"

"You loved me?" Luz beamed wider than Margaret's head. He leaned back against the fence, eyes aimed skyward once more. He released a laugh that was his and no one else's. "You perfect, perfect pieces. Don't you realize? That means you love yourselves." Luz tipped Maggie's head farther back. "The pointlessness revolts me. So go ahead. Have it.

"I'll take the abyss. It is infinitely more real to me."

Before he became nothing, before he beaded through her pores and evaporated like glittering sweat and let her children catch her, Luz realized:

Darkness looked exactly the same through these eyes as it had through any others.

THANKSGIVING

The Vasquez family didn't own a dining room table. The Vasquez family home didn't have a dining room. There were four Vasquezes and their table had four sides.

There were more Vasquezes to account for this year.

After a night of heavy sleep, Ana pulled the silver table from the garage. Hank brought the picnic table from the lawn into the living room, and Brendan helped move the kitchen island alongside it. They pushed all of them together. Milo volunteered to set them as one, partly because it seemed like a grown-up thing to do but mostly because he just wanted to help.

The Vasquezes had hardly recuperated from the decimation of their plates and glasses. Ana, familiar with the pantry, ducked inside and emerged with her arms full.

All those untouched plastic cups and plates from Milo's party proved useful at last.

★ ★ ★

Maggie could smell turkey even before lifting her head from her pillow. It turned out that rendezvousing with an alien parasite for months left you irrevocably scarred, but rendezvousing with one for a single evening left you temporarily scabbed and immediately hungover.

"Milo, so help me." She salvaged stray ibuprofen from the bathroom cupboard and stumbled toward the kitchen. "You'd better not be cooking again."

The kitchen contained warm, familiar bodies.

Rahshad Dawson leaned over the stove with a turkey baster. Penny stood beside him, holding up a recipe book for perusal. At the counter, Milo clutched a potato peeler in one hand and a potato in the other.

It was the cruelest of dreams. For an instant Maggie felt the old urge to flee, familiar as her fingernails. Perhaps she would always feel that, but never act on it.

She felt so much else, too.

"Good morning."

Rahshad Dawson was surprised enough to squeeze juice from the turkey baster. "Ms. Vasquez! Good morning."

The details emerged in a flurry of embarrassed speech: Penny had absolutely demanded that her father bring Thanksgiving to the Vasquezes today, because the Vasquezes were a *real* mess and besides, there were so many people who usually gathered at Grandma Dawson's house that it was hard to get a word in edgewise, and someone always knocked over a candle and there was *never* enough turkey to go around, and what was the point of being a father-daughter household if you didn't get the perks of sneaking away to do actually cool stuff sometimes while everyone else complained about weddings and divorces, and did she mention that Milo and his mom were *a real mess because of aliens* and—

"I know I'm spoiling her rotten. To be honest, I'm more or less a terrible father." It was usually Maggie who spoke in turkey-baster bursts of embarrassment. "And though your children invited me in, I shouldn't have come into your home without invitation."

"You probably shouldn't have," Maggie agreed, "and I should probably be angry about it. But you know what? I'm more or less a terrible mother."

Less, Penny signed.

"There's no arguing with her," Rahshad said.

"Look, enough talk! We have a situation on our hands!" Milo looked betrayed, more than anything, eyeing a potato like it might explode. "Help, Mom?"

"Sure. They aren't going to peel themselves, are they?"

"They always do when I'm *pretending* to cook," he grumbled.

Maggie sat down next to him. She showed him how to hold the peeler, how best to angle it to tear away the skin in long, efficient pieces. Milo looked ready to take notes.

His soft hair tickled her chin. "Wanna tell me what happened on Halloween?"

"Maybe not right now."

"Should I make some coffee?" Rahshad asked.

Maggie looked at Milo. The tiniest crease had appeared between his eyes.

"Maybe not right now," she replied.

★　★　★

Ana refused to let Hank drive to the hospital, partly because he had bandaged hands but mostly because she didn't want him to go by himself. She didn't have a driver's license and the journey was alarming, to say the least. Making it to Gailsberg General felt like a victory, although Ana joked that she'd have to drop Hank at the ER because he basically had a panic attack when she almost T-boned a semi.

"Go on. I'll hold down the fort."

Hank nodded, wan and quiet, and turned around.

"Wait." She tucked in a tag at the back of his sweater. Ana was pretty tall herself.

"Thanks, BanAna."

She cuffed him. "Don't call me that."

Ana enjoyed the contrasting blandness of an empty waiting room for a few minutes, reading *Highlights* for nostalgia.

Ruby entered, looking like a stranger. She wore no lab coat, only jeans and a flannel shirt. Though she looked haggard, her hair and face were clean. When she saw Ana she nearly dropped her coffee. She collected herself and approached the counter.

"I'm here for my dad? Henry Flowers. Do you know if he can have visitors?"

The secretary referred to her screen and kindly advised her to take a seat. Ruby looked like she'd rather haunt the doorway.

"You can sit by me," Ana called, turning a page. "It's fine."

Ruby approached with caution. She sat, did not bump Ana's elbows.

"Your dad, huh?" In the aftermath of last night, the Vasquezes were almost devoured by fatigue. Still, the four had gathered in the kitchen and talked until they were empty. It took time; for too long the Vasquezes hadn't emptied into one another. They couldn't stop. "The extraterrestrial expert, right?"

"Ah. Right."

Ana turned a page. She wasn't reading.

"I just drove here from the impound lot," Ruby blurted. "That's where they put Dad's RV. They wanted me to pick up anything worth saving. I didn't know where to begin; I took the cat, some cassettes. But there was this map on the wall with pins and string in it, like you see in detective shows. All the pins were in places I'd stayed."

"You were following Luz," Ana said, "but your dad was following you?"

"Yeah." Ana caught a waft of coffee breath. "Mom died when I was four and after that we more or less lived in national parks. When your house has a motor and your dad chases chemtrails and weather balloons from coast to coast, you grow up weird."

"People grow up weird anyway, Ruby. An alien lived in my eyeballs."

Ruby laughed. "Fair enough. But I started early. My bat mitzvah was interrupted by a black bear. I had my first kiss in a petrified forest." She stopped laughing. "My dad had to push my face into coals to chase that alien out of me."

Ana stopped pretending to read.

"A decade of chasing a ghost who'd forgotten me. But when I saw that RV last night—that used to be my home, Ana. I didn't think. I just ran for it. On the trails, Dad used to always remind me to look back. It's the things that *follow* you in the woods that you have to worry about. Not whatever you're heading toward."

"Is your dad all right?"

Ruby wiped her eyes on her wrist. "He hasn't woken up yet."

Ana ran her fingers through her hair, tucked it back, and asked the question. "So, if Luz didn't . . . die. If he crops up again as part of some other family. Do you think we'll be drawn to him, too? Do you think the Vasquezes will feel the tug?"

"I don't know, Ana. Maybe. He leaves holes in people."

"Okay. That's fine. Even if we feel that way, we don't *have* to follow him. Holes are nothing new here."

Ruby just shook her head. "Ana. You're astounding."

Ana shrugged. "When they call your name, do you want me to go in with you?"

After a moment, Ruby nodded.

Hank had no clue what people brought to hospital bedsides in situations like this. Were Get Well Soon cards appropriate after an alien infestation? It didn't seem like enough, or it seemed like too much.

He thought all he really could say was a single, heavy word.

"Sorry." Even this was muffled by his swollen tongue.

Carmella, propped up in her hospital bed, didn't spare him a glance.

"Oh *please*. You don't apologize for something that happens *to* you, Hank."

"But if you hadn't tried to help us, Luz wouldn't've—"

"For the love of god." Carmella set down her phone. "It's painful to listen to you, and not because of the tongue. Is your name *Luz*?"

"But—"

"What, you think because you're a boy you can't also be a victim?"

"I wasn't."

"Of course you were. Get with the times." She wore her neck brace like an Elizabethan ruff. "But right now, *I'm* the one in the hospital and *I* don't want an apology. Let's let this one be about me."

It was hard to disagree with a queen clad all in white.

In the entrance to the room across the hall, Hank nearly collided with Grandma Liu. He did his best not to loom, but she grabbed his hand and held it. She didn't look at him, even after letting go.

"I think Grandma Liu and me just had a moment, Orson." Hank fell into his second squarish hospital chair of the day.

"Gross, man." Orson was a collage of purple-and-green bruises. Bandages seemed to be holding his nose to his face. "I don't wanna know."

Hank smiled. It proved disastrous.

Orson burst into laughter, soon chased by a short burst of swearwords, followed by a grand finale of gasping to catch his breath. When he finished dabbing his eyes with his sheet, he found air again. "*Holy shit, Tank*. You lost a front tooth?"

Hank smiled again in reply.

This time the laughter came softer. "Can I call you Jo Bob from now on?"

"Call me what you want. I'm not the one who looks like hamburger this time."

"Hamburgers are goddamn delicious, and you know it. Where's your patriotism?"

Hank stared at his purple hands. There were stitches in only three knuckles. "Orson, I'm sorry."

He waited for an interruption, a protest. But when Hank looked up, Orson had folded his hands behind his head.

"Go on."

"I'm sorry that the alien who infected my family infected you, too."

"That's not the apology I'm looking for." Orson waved a hand, Jedi-like, between them. "Try again, dumbass."

"I'm sorry you're in the hospital."

"Keep trying."

"I'm . . . confused."

Orson sighed. "That's because you are a certified dumbfuck, Hank the Tank."

"I'm sorry." Hank steeled himself. "Orson, I'm sorry the alien who infected my family made you kiss me in the auditorium. I know that wasn't you, and I'm sorry for how weird it's been at school lately, too, and I'm sorry I made you uncomfortable with my—my *gayness* because I know you're not interested in me like that, and I'm so *grateful to you* for—"

"HOKAY. Hold up, shitstain—*Jesus*, there's a reason you don't talk much, huh? And who the hell said I wasn't—that . . . shit. Who said I wasn't . . . interested?" It was hard to see through the bruising, but Orson's cheeks definitely reddened.

Hank gaped. "Um, what the hell? *You* did. You said that."

"*Um, what the hell?* I never said anything like that."

"Really?" Hank stood up, paced to the window and back. "Because I remember holding your plate while you ditched me on the stairs at the banquet, all 'ew, people think we're a couple.'"

Hank thought Orson might jump right out of bed.

"That's *so* not how that conversation went! And I quote, *Hank*: 'What, *us a couple?* You're totally paranoid, by *jove!* No way *we'd ever* be a couple, are you kidding, Orson, ew, gross?' End quote."

"I don't think that's totally accurate . . ."

But Hank could see how, from another perspective, a moment that so clearly meant one thing could have meant something else entirely. He shook his head at the wonder of that knowledge. A lesson he should have learned ages ago, something impossible and true.

"I started to . . . to *come out* to you, and yeah, I pretty much *sucked* at it." There was a stubborn gleam in Orson's black eyes. "But man, I feel like, okay, I do a lot of talking and a lot of it is stupid shit, but I thought you of all people would know when I'm being serious about something. I mean, I told you the *Taiwanese poodle ladies* story."

Hank just smiled.

"So yeah, maybe coming out to your crush at a MAN-BANQUET, a MANQUET, wasn't my best idea. But you!"— Orson pointed a reprimanding finger directly at Hank's heart—"you totally 'just friends forever'ed' me. All, 'but we can still hang out sometimes for basketball' and shit. It was fucking humiliating."

Again Hank just smiled.

"And now! Now you're—you're just sitting there smiling and creeping me the fuck out, *Hank Jo Bob*. Where's my damn apology, smartass? Did you leave it in your tractor, toothless fucking wonder?"

Hank settled back into the boxy chair and held up three fingers. "Orson, I'm sorry I 'just friends forever'ed' you. I didn't mean to. Scout's honor."

"Yeah, well. It's fine, I guess. Just . . . don't do it again."

"Okay. Anything else?"

"Hell *no*. Get out of here. Unless you wanna fondle me or something supergay like that."

Hank snorted. "Sure, maybe later."

"I'm pretty sure I'm a fucking horrendous influence on you, Jo Bob Hank Vasquez." Orson pulled a pillow in to his face. "Fucking humiliating."

Hank leaned in. "Pretty sure I'm okay with it."

"You know what, I'm gonna just go ahead and get in another car crash, okay?"

But after Hank pushed the pillow out of the way, Orson kissed him back.

Brendan was honor bound to spend his holiday with his chain-smoking parents, although he did drop a bottle of champagne off at the Vasquez home early in the afternoon. He didn't ask any questions, but managed to peck every single person in the house on the cheek before the wind ruffled his feathers and called him away.

Marissa Ritter snuck away from her poolside home shortly after Ana and Hank returned from the hospital. Ana thought having Marissa near might be awkward. After a few minutes, it wasn't. Things came and went, and people came and went. Sometimes you just had to exist in the same second that they did.

Marissa brought over two cameras for Ana's perusal.

"When we stopped talking and you quit volleyball, I realized I didn't even like volleyball. I was only ever playing it for you. Most of the things I liked, I liked because you were doing them, too."

"I know what you mean." Ana rolled a lens in her hand.

"Maybe that's why it hurt so much when you cut yourself. Ana—did you even think about that? If you kill yourself, you're killing pieces of me, too. You're cutting all the people who care about you. Please don't."

"So I'll call you next time? Punish you for being my friend. Whine at you for hours over the phone, bore you to death with my sadness?" Ana laughed.

Marissa didn't. "Seriously, that's all I want, Ana. Okay?"

Ana recalled Mom, silhouetted on the edge of the observation deck.

"... okay."

Mr. Dawson burned the turkey. It was about as flavorless as turkey ever was once Hank hacked to the center of it. The man and woman in navy suits, Reginald and Iris, were served first, because they were the closest things to strangers and therefore most guest-like. Hank served Ruby next, not because she was the next strangest at the table, but because she was being obnoxious, relaying conspiracy theories only Milo had any interest in.

"What do you mean, bar codes are evil?"

Milo was determined to soak up every possible piece of information about people who knew Luz. Watching them talk, he had a thought he'd never had, one that was maybe *abstract* or maybe not at all!

Milo thought since people had bridges in all directions, depending on how you traced them there were a million possible constellations! Even Luz had built bridges Milo would never know about.

That was potentially a really, really sad idea.

Milo wasn't sure, so he ate some more potatoes!

On the other side of the table, Maggie proved a better ASL student after two glasses of wine, and Mr. Dawson proved a worse teacher after the same number. Ms. Yu, scooping up green-bean casserole, managed to knock over a candlestick. Penny rolled her eyes, but failed to look condescending with so much mashed potato packed in her cheeks.

At about three p.m., Hank pulled a soothing Popsicle away from his tongue. He'd noticed a blank setting at the table.

"Who's that chair for?"

Maggie paused. "No one in particular."

"Want me to move it out of the way?"

Ana elbowed him. "Leave it. It's not hurting anyone."

Hank didn't argue with that. He and Ana soon argued about school instead.

The chair remained empty.

While the others were busy screaming their way through board games, Hank scrubbed the pots and pans. He probably shouldn't have, considering his hands, but he pulled plastic sandwich bags over them and set to work anyhow.

He heard the scraping of the footstool before he saw Milo clamber onto it, dish towel in hand.

"It's fine, Milo. I can take care of this."

"Your whistling is annoying. I'm going to help."

"Oh. Yeah. I mean, okay. If you want."

"I never read your letter," Milo whispered. "Luz wouldn't let me."

"That's okay, Milo. I think maybe we should just forget about it."

"Well, except! I read it today."

"I thought you just said—"

"*Never, until today*. I read it today."

"Oh. Okay?" Hank pulled turkey skin from prongs.

"You used 'of' instead of 'have.'"

Hank blinked. "I'm sorry."

"You should be." Milo looked sternly at his brother. "If you want, I can help you fix it later. After second dessert, though, because Marissa brought apple crumble! And that is very, very important to me."

It was very, very hard for Hank not to pick his little brother up right off his stool, pull him into piggyback position, and run laps around the house like they used to.

Hank held his hands under the sink water so that he wouldn't.

"Thanks, Milo. That'd be awesome."

It was long after dark by the time people started leaving.

Mr. Dawson packed Penny and a charred turkey thigh into his car, a process made more difficult by Maggie's hug. Hank had somehow convinced Milo to hold a basketball, and Milo did so as if he might break it, staring at the orange mass with such intense concentration that Marissa felt the need to record the moment. Ms. Yu was giving Ruby a ride to the hospital to visit Mr. Flowers.

Reginald and Iris had already vanished. People were leaving, but it remained lively outside the Vasquez home, with laughter and chatter and light.

Ana stood in the driveway and watched her family. She thought the next time she saw Mr. Chilton, her seventh-grade science teacher, she could tell him about a new biome shift she'd experienced: watching vegetation gradually re-form a lifeless desert into something green and alive that no one had ever thought could be in a place like this, but that perhaps had been living there all along.

But she probably wouldn't see Mr. Chilton again, and even if she did, she probably wouldn't say a thing. She could tell Ms. Yu instead.

"Ana," Mom called, present and whole, leaning on Mr. Dawson's car in the driveway, "should we go look at the stars?"

Ana thought she already was.

ACKNOWLEDGMENTS

This story began with Spielberg. Specifically, it began with the fridge horror realities lurking in Spielberg movies. (Forgive spoilers—the films are decades old!)

My roomie and I re-watched *Close Encounters* and spent an hour dissecting the twisted implications of the finale. Imagine you're the daughter or son of a man who decides to abandon your family and climb aboard a mothership. How would it feel to grow up with the knowledge that your father left you for extra-terrestrials? The knowledge that something alien and unknowable was preferable to raising you?

But the essence of this happens all the time. It has happened within my family tree, within the branches of almost every family tree. Sometimes adults leave their children for the unknowable. It's a hard reality, and exactly the kind of reality the lens of science fiction can help us come to terms with.

E.T. is hardly any better. If you're Elliott, you've *literally soul-bonded with an alien* and then been ditched by said alien.

Where do you go from there? How could you ever feel close to another human being? Would anyone ever "get" you? Again, there are traumas in our world that parallel this experience. I wanted to know Elliott would be okay one day. I wanted to write *that* story.

When Light Left Us would not exist without the support of my agent, my editor, and the entire Bloomsbury team, who did not flinch when I declared that I wanted to write a weird alien book at last. *When Light Left Us* would be a lesser book without the help of friends, family, fellow writers, and sensitivity readers who gave up their time to help me with the weird alien book. All remaining mistakes or misjudgments are mine and no one else's. I am just grateful to have been indulged on this one!

Finally, my fans and readers, few but mighty and hilarious— there will always be days when I wonder why I do this. Thanks to you, those days are fewer.

Two teens caught on either side
of a murder.

A truth that could change everything . . .

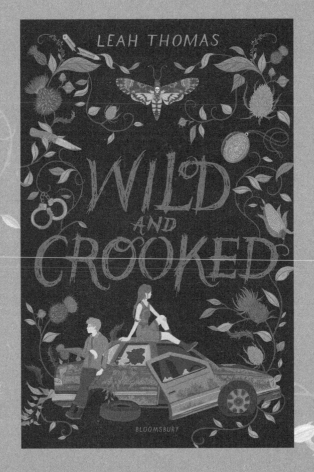

**READ ON FOR A SNEAK PEEK AT
LEAH THOMAS'S NEXT NOVEL!**

"Fiercely feminist and gorgeously inclusive."
—**Shannon M. Parker**, author of *The Girl Who Fell*
and *The Rattled Bones*

KALYN

Boy oh boy, is there nothing to see in Samsboro, Kentucky.

Nothing but corn and grass and grubby little houses and sun-baked faces, which combined is still basically the definition of nothing. It's almost the same kind of nothing we had in Alleghany, except here it's corn instead of cattle. There's a cereal mill in town, so the air smells a little better, but we're still stuck with dirt roads. Once we finally get ourselves to the van, it'll be a straight-and-narrow shot down M-12 to Jefferson High. It shouldn't take long.

But like Mom always says, "The straight and narrow's for bad drivers." It's never easy getting anywhere when you're a Spence.

Even the road to my conception was totally crooked and wide, and maybe that's why my parents were so eager to pop me into the world. They were troubled teenagers themselves, and the last thing they needed was a squalling poop-machine, but heck. Tell my parents "Stop!" and they slam down on the gas. Mom and Dad have basically driven circles all over the straight and narrow, spun out and done screeching doughnuts, too. I'm definitely their kid.

Maybe that's why I'm still standing in front of the bathroom mirror on my birthday, smearing basically inches of eyeliner under my eyes when we should've hit the road ten minutes ago.

Somehow the truancy officer found out about me. Mom blames the nosy neighboring of Ms. Pilson, the old lady who lives in the peeling house at the road-end. I blame plain old rotten luck. In any case, Officer Newton and his damp armpits appeared on Grandma's front step last Wednesday.

I thought Mom would fight him, tooth and bedazzled nail. I eavesdropped through Grandma's walls, waiting for her to claw him good.

Mom's *made* for the wide and crooked. She doesn't trust anyone in a uniform. She doesn't believe in turn signals. She's put so much peroxide on her hair across her lifetime that the smell's as good as coffee to her. I'm her pistol and she's a much bigger gun, maybe a Winchester Magnum, from a family of firearms. We've got gunpowder where most people have cartilage.

I thought Mom would stare Officer Newton down or pull the "it's a free country!" card, at least. Instead, Mom offered the man sweet tea before he left.

"Mom, *no*," I told her when she closed the screen behind him. The untouched glass of tea dribbled sweat onto the card table, and Grandma's mouth dribbled oatmeal down her bib. "It's bullshit!"

Mom lit her cigarette. "He says it's best for you. He ain't wrong."

I snorted. "Since when do people in this town want what's best for Spences?"

"Hopefully since now."

But it *is* bullshit. Even if Mom doesn't have a high school diploma, she teaches me more than all the teachers I ever had back in Arkansas *combined*. She taught me to drive, and to cook, and to use dumbasses against themselves, like the misogynistic creeps we could get to buy us dinner, and she taught me to read widely and often and teach *myself* words like "misogynistic." Getting certified in the Louise Spence education program means I'm *plenty* ready for Jefferson freakin' High today.

I slap a layer of glitter on the black eyeliner. It's my damn birthday.

"You gonna be ready before the cows come home?" Mom leans against the door frame, tapping ash from her cigarette into the pink porcelain sink.

Everything in Grandma's bathroom has a doily on it. The toothbrush holder is hemmed in lace, stained white with toothpaste buildup.

" . . . you *listenin'* to me, Kalyn-Rose?"

"Well, you're shouting right in my ear."

Mom takes a drag bigger than she is. "Don't let the assholes knock you down today."

Smoking's the last thing a five-foot-tall, thirty-six-year-old asthmatic should be doing, but I can't say jack about it, what with a pack of Pall Malls in my sock drawer that she doesn't know about. And if anyone told her to quit, you know what Mom would do? She'd light up two fresh ones and plug 'em into her nostrils to make her damn point.

"So what are you this year—eight? Twelve?"

"It's 2007, Mom."

Mom lets the cigarette fall into the clogged sink basin. "Fine. Ask me."

Other people break piñatas, but in the Spence household we've got an annual interrogation tradition.

"How'd you get pregnant?"

Like always, Mom replies, "Don't question miracles, sweetcakes."

I roll my eyes. It's not like I want the grossest details. I've got all kinds of theories about how the spunk that became *moi* made its way through the barbed wire, bars, and steel walls of Wilder Penitentiary, the largest high-security prison in the Bible Belt. Mom's never confirmed any of them.

Turkey basters, and forged medical reports, and maybe the sneaking of goods through a cake? Whatever it was, Mom started ballooning up like any other mom. Like Dad was any other dad, and not a convicted murderer sentenced to life.

I bite my tongue to keep from cussing. I'm trying to put my contacts in. Maybe that should have happened before the eyeliner.

For years I had this pair of old-man glasses that I downright refused to wear. My teachers in Alleghany kept throwin' fits, saying I couldn't see the board. I threw them right back because there was jack-all I wanted to see on that board anyhow.

Mom struck me a deal: if I helped her change some bedpans, I could use a cut of her earnings to save up for contacts.

Before we moved to Shitsboro to take care of Grandma, Mom took care of other old people. Checking their catheters, and making sure they took their meds, and giving them pep talks about how their lives were worth living regardless of whether their idiot kids bothered visiting.

It took me 137 bedpans to afford my fake eyes. Damn right I'll suffer for them.

I finally wedge the lens in and blink the pain away. After some nose blowing, I get a good gander at the mess I've made. Eyeliner has slipped down my cheeks in sparkling black trickles, but screw it.

I show the mirror my fangs. I might need them today.

Grandma's prefab's been egged five times since we moved in.

Dad's been in prison for two decades, but people don't forget. Killing a local golden boy has that effect.

I toss my braid over my shoulder. It's crazy long these days, this pumpkin whip that hangs past the small of my back. I step back to admire the mess of me. "I like it."

"You're your father's daughter," Mom announces, letting loose another coughle. "I'm gonna get off work early and pick up a cake mix so we can celebrate." Mom works at the Sunny Spot, a little gas station by the freeway. "Funfetti again?"

"Does the pope shit in the woods? Forever Funfetti."

We overhear Grandma hacking in the kitchen. If the walls were any thinner they'd be wax paper. Mom ducks away, saying, "Come help me get her settled."

I follow Mom to the kitchen. Grandma smiles at me as I wheel her into the living room where she can watch her soaps. I stare at her scalp through her silver feather petals of hair and wonder why it's so much paler than the rest of her when really it's the closest piece of her to the sun.

"You've got a head like a baby's, Grandma."

Grandma clears her throat best she can. "Uh . . . babies, no wavy time wig for."

I only met Grandma three times before her stroke: at Mom and Dad's wedding, and at two Christmas parties at the Alleghany Mobile Park. Both Christmases, Grandma got so drunk on peppermint schnapps that she couldn't speak English anymore, just rambled in Polish. I almost understood her then, like I almost understand her now.

Grandma always knows what she's *trying* to say, even if her mouth fumbles. Grandma not making a lot of sense makes sense to me, because I never make sense, either. Peas attached at the hip. That's exactly us.

Mom hates leaving Grandma home alone. She has a hard time swallowing, and sometimes we have to clear her throat for her, fingers like fishhooks scraping phlegm away. But Grandma's prefab sits in the center of the family salvage yard, resting on the same cinderblocks she uses as a doorstep. It's a painful process, lowering her down.

Grandma's hand lands on mine. Her eyes are rheumy and bloodshot, but her stare is clear as water. "Be good today."

Mom rolls her eyes. "If wishes were horses."

Sure, back in Alleghany I started shit with kids on the way to school, mostly because they thought it was *hysterical* that the bus was bigger than our house. There're only so many times a girl can call you "trailer trash" before you trash that girl's face.

Mostly, though, Mom's worried people here'll recognize me.

And that's why she pulls me aside toward the kitchen sink and says something awful. "*Listen*, Kalyn. Me and Officer Newton agreed it'd be a good idea to register you under a different last name."

It's shock more than anything that makes a sailor of me: "*You fucking what?*"

"You'll be Kalyn *Poplawski* this year."

"Poplaw—I can't even pronounce it!"

Grandma *tsks* one or both of us.

"Watch it. Poplawski's your grandma's maiden name!" She says the next part like she's banking on it: "She's been married since 1949, so prob'ly no one remembers."

"*I* want to forget, and you just told me!"

"*Kalyn-Rose Tulip Spence.*"

But Mom's request seems like a whole new blasphemy. She might as well be another mean girl on the bus. Might as well be calling us NASCAR-loving, cousin-marrying, Podunk garbage. I'm used to *other* people name-calling, but this?

"I can't believe you."

Mom squeezes her eyes shut. "This ain't a choice, Kalyn. You get it, right?"

Oh, I get it. This is the town that made Dad a murderer.

I glance out the kitchen window at the field of rusting cars under the cotton-candy-pink morning sky. Samsboro's treated my family like garbage for decades, dumping literal trash in our yard because they figure trash is the same as salvage (it's *not*, damn it, when your family makes a living selling auto parts).

"Kalyn, we've gotta try and make this work."

"For how long?"

"However long it takes."

I don't ask what "it" means. I can hear Grandma's wheezes over the blare of the TV. Grandma's not the only one in this room counting the breaths until she'll have none.

"You told me to be proud. You always said if people talk shit, take none of it."

"Guess I was talking shit, too. Sometimes you have to take it."

If anyone knows this, it's Mom. She's received a death threat a week ever since she married Dad. That's partly my fault; I just *had* to be the flower girl at the wedding.

Seeing me in a little white lace dress drove the media up the walls. Mom and Dad let me wear it anyway, because my pistol went off: I screamed for days straight (between meals) when Mom told me I couldn't come.

So she bought me an Easter dress from the clearance rack at Kohl's. Her dress was thrifted, faded red and slim fitting. She had to put a sweater on over it in the prison parking lot. They have very particular regulations in prisons about clothes. They wouldn't let Dad wear long sleeves, even though his arms are coated in burn scars.

The visitation room reminded me of my elementary school cafeteria. The fluorescents made my tummy rumble. I fidgeted through the half-hour service, eyeballing the vending machines until Grandma caved. She looked downright funny with her balding mullet, denim skirt, and blue eye shadow, but she knew Reese's Pieces were the way to a kid's heart.

In the photo that made national news, Mom and Dad stare lovingly into each other's eyes and I stand between them and beam at the camera, melted chocolate all over my face. The hateful moms of America had a lot to say about whether Mom should be a mother after that. I wonder if the hateful moms of America still want to adopt me now that I'm a juvenile delinquent and not a "baby angel cursed with evil parents."

"You're a coward," I tell Mom, and I close myself in the bathroom again.

No way in hell am I *nervous* about going to Jefferson High. I know I'm poor and angry. Changing my name won't change what I am. Even without my new tiger stripes, my old snaggletooth, the egg in my pocket, and my gunpowder marrow, people in Samsboro were never, ever gonna be pleased to have me here.

GUS

"I'd give my left arm not to go in today."

Dad's blue eyes twinkle through time and glass. He offers no consolation.

I lower my voice to a manly timbre: "But that's your *good* arm, Gus."

The imitation makes me cough. I slur the words, too. Dad wouldn't have. As far as I know, Dad didn't have a speech disorder.

Dad twinkles on, unbothered. Eternal smile, eternal indifference.

I have looked at my father's face every day since the day I was born, but I've never met him. Apart from the picture on my bookshelf, there's one on Mom's nightstand and a collage above the fireplace in the living room. A few summer camp photos are tacked to our refrigerator. The guest room contains dozens of pairs of his eternal eyes, trapped in the darkness of the shoeboxes that hold his personal effects.

There's a photo of Dad holding an enormous trout situated halfway up the staircase. This one is a real nuisance, because almost every time I trip on the steps, the frame rattles against the wall, slips off its nail, and clunks against the carpet. Every other day I am fumbling over that picture, trying to hang it back up before Mom can catch me.

One of these days the glass will crack, but it hasn't happened yet.

I can't complain about the stupid placement of the weird trout picture. If I do, Mom will want to talk about *why* it upsets me.

There are two ways that conversation can go:

1. Mom will assume I hate the picture because it's a picture of my dead dad, not because it's hanging in a stupid place. She'll explain to me, again, that even if Dad is gone, she wants him to be a comforting presence in our lives. She'll sit me down on the recliner and she'll sit on the settee and she'll ask me, again, *eternally*, how I feel about living with the ghost of my father.
2. Mom will realize the truth: the picture keeps falling because I keep tripping. The dead leg strikes again! So Mom'll sit me down on the recliner and she'll sit on the settee and ask me, again, why I don't consider moving into the downstairs bedroom.

"It's the guest room." If I stare at the bottom of my bifocals, I won't see her at all.

"We hardly ever have guests, and it'd be easier for you—"

When I lift my hands in exasperation, the right one won't lift all the way up; it never does. That will definitely catch her eye. "Mom. Let me keep my room."

Or maybe the words won't come out right. Maybe I'll say something like, "Mom. Let me hold, I mean, um, keep my . . . the . . . place?"

Because a conversation this uncomfortable might trigger my aphasia, and all the nouns in the world could abandon me. That'll convince Mom that I *must* move downstairs.

Mom *hates* seeing other people uncomfortable. She'd wet herself to let a stranger cut her in a restroom line. Unluckily for

Mom, discomfort is my default setting. I wonder if I feel like an itch she can't scratch. She'll never say so, and I'll never ask.

Today I make my way down the stairs and Dad doesn't fall. I wish some of his enthusiasm would infect me. I feel more like the trout in his arms, sucking empty air.

Mom stands when I enter the kitchen. I wish she wouldn't. "Perfect timing!"

I look at the stacks of fried batter cooling on the table and know it's not perfect timing at all. The chocolate syrup's sunken through two layers of cakes. Mom's ready for work but won't even eat until she knows I'm going to make it downstairs.

I maybe hate that about her. I hate myself for maybe hating her for anything.

The Dads on the fridge don't wink at me when I lower myself into the waiting chair. Mom makes sure I take a bite before digging a fork into her own soggy stack.

She rattles on about my class schedule, about sharing afternoon rides with Phil, about when I'll be seeing Alicia, my speech therapist ("It'll be Tuesdays and Fridays during lunch"). Mom makes me recite, between bites, the exact procedure I should go through in case of emergencies, followed by a memorized list of important phone numbers: hers, Tam's, Dr. Petani's, Mr. Wheeler's. If my cheeks weren't full of orange juice, this is one conversation I could have upside down with my eyes closed.

Without warning, Mom lifts up the left leg of my jeans. "Where's your new AFO? The starry one?"

I cough up pancake debris. Wearing a *cool*, cosmic-patterned orthotic boot is only actually "cool" in middle school, and I'm a junior now.

Mom never pities me, but she does treat me like I'm perpetually seven. She's only a decade wrong. In the grand scheme of the vast and unknowable universe, that shouldn't feel as awful as it does.

I tap the plastic on the black AFO encasing my foot. "This one matches better."

She can't argue. My jeans are black, and so is my long-sleeved shirt. You might think I'm trying to mimic my idols.

The Gaggle, I call them. They're this group of kids who've formed an artsy coven on Jefferson High's campus. You can't call them Goth, because they've evolved beyond that, and it's really hard to commit to corsets and Tripp pants in this sweltering patch of southern Kentucky. These kids shy away from the sun, but they aren't pretty enough to pass for vampires. But in this town of Wrangler jeans, the Gaggle is a local miracle.

Sure, they write poems about child funerals and sculpt inverted rib cages full of crows during art class. But they also fold colorful origami creatures and scatter them in the hallways. Their leader, a widow's-peaked wonder named Garth Holden, composes goofy songs to raise STD/STI awareness. Who can forget his classic hit from freshman year, "See Ya, Gonorrhea!" or the heartfelt ballad that rang from his sable ukulele last spring, "STI, ST-Me, ST-You"?

The Gagglers laugh through their piercings and pastel hair spikes. One of the members wears floor-length black gowns with hot pink rocking horse shoes and dozens of decora hair clips. It's like they fell right out of Harajuku.

The whole Gaggle might as well be there. I can't get near them. They have something I'll never have. It's *not* fashion sense.

© Jessica Hilt

leah thomas frequently loses battles of wits against her students and her stories. When she's not huddled in cafés, she's usually at home pricking her fingers in service of cosplay. Leah lives in San Diego, California, and is the author of *Wild and Crooked, When Light Left Us, Nowhere Near You,* and the William C. Morris YA Debut Award finalist *Because You'll Never Meet Me.*

instagram.com/fellowhermit

cutoothom.tumblr.com

Though **Ollie** and **Moritz** might never meet, their friendship is **boundless.**

Leah **Thomas**'s writing shines in these stories about unlikely friends finding their place in a world that might never understand them.

www.bloomsbury.com
Twitter: BloomsburyKids
Snapchat: BloomsburyYA